MOON DANCING

Anna Zogg

Moon Dancing

Published by Next Step Books, P.O. Box 70271, West Valley City, Utah 84170

www.nextstepbooks.org

Cover art by Rachel Dinda
Interior graphics by A.C.F.
Cover design by Nick Delliskave

Zogg, Anna
Moon Dancing

ISBN-13: 978-1-937671-12-9
ISBN-10: 1937671127

I love reading new talent and Anna Zogg is one to keep an eye on.

Lori Copeland
Bestselling Author of *Sisters of Mercy Flats*

In *Moon Dancing* Anna Zogg has created a fascinating blend of romance, mystery, fantasy and western adventure. Megan Gillespie returns to a Wyoming ranch she barely remembers, determined to leave again as soon as possible. But Shadow awaits . . . and the moon is full . . . .

Jim Cook
Author of *The Third Hand*
2013 Quarterfinalist, Amazon Breakthrough Novel Award

You've never read a novel like this before. Anna Zogg mixes western realism with fantasy suspense to create a romance murder mystery that has it all. Follow Megan Gillespie on a Hero's Journey to uncover her Native American roots and attempt to reverse the curse on her bloodline. Stuck on her uncle's ranch in Wyoming, she feels her only refuge is her horse, Shadow. Will she lose him like she has lost everything else she loves?

Marcia Hornok
Managing Editor of *CHERA Fellowship* magazine
Author of *Fruit of the Spirit: Inspiration for Women*
Writer for examiner.com, as well as numerous print publications

In *Moon Dancing,* Anna Zogg has the opportunity to share her incredible talent and skill with her readers. This page turner allows you to take a journey of imagination and intrigue without ever leaving the comfort of home.

Kimberly Malkogainnis
Author of *Promptings*

As a busy mom, I am picky about what I spend my time reading. "Moon Dancing" is a creative, wholesome, breezy read. I would put it down reluctantly and pick up with expectations of entertainment and fantasy that were always fulfilled! The characters are tied up in mystery, deception, and sacrificial love. Anna reigns in a blue-ribbon fairy tale.

Morgan Motsinger
Author of morganmotz.blogspot.com, musician, and voracious reader

A captivating story of intrigue and romance, artfully blended with a touch of fantasy – exactly the kind of book I love! Anna Zogg reaches into the depths of her Native American heritage to tell a tale that kept me enthralled from beginning to end.

Virginia Smith
Bestselling Author of *The Days of Noah*

For my parents
with love

Acknowledgments

A huge thank you to those who encouraged me during my ups and downs as a writer. Though I can't list you all here, know that you are greatly appreciated. To Marion who first ignited my writing passion ("Make good corn!"). To my faithful friend, Marilynn, who exhorted me to do better. To my sweet daughter, Morgan who always reminds me Who I write for. To the Utah Christian Writers Fellowship for their support and encouragement. To my beloved husband, John, for putting up with his sometimes insane wife. And to Virginia Smith who believed in me and gave me a chance. My humblest thanks.

Moonlight spills on shadowed land
Scorching through the darkness,
Devouring all no longer his
'til the night blinds him.

Helpless, he cries as winters fly
And fire consumes the shadows.
Blood in life, dawn in death, at last...
freed for moon dancing.

CHAPTER 1

A scream–long and agonizing–ripped the air. The hair on Megan Gillespie's neck stood on end while the scent of spring rain filled her senses. She peered through the pickup's windshield, seeing nothing beyond a mound of pinyon pine and withered grass. Shouts of men and the nervous snorting of horses battered her. *What is happening?* She flung open the door. As she sprinted up the dusty rise, she tripped on her long jeans skirt.

The scene below riveted her.

Like a pack of wolves, a group of men circled a black stallion. Head flailing, the horse fought uncountable ropes. He reared, hooves striking blindly.

Foam flecked his neck, teeth bared and mouth opened in a silent shriek. The setting sun painted his soaked hide in blood-colored lather. Dust boiled upwards, the air choked with pinpricks of glittering gold.

The horse fought in vain. His cry, one of rage and impotence, shuddered through Megan.

Pain! She doubled over, as though punched in the stomach. *Can't breathe.* Her eyes burned from the agony.

The stallion again reared, legs lashing out.

"Hold him. I said, hold him!" A tall man yanked a lariat from the hands of one of the men.

The next moment, the stallion lunged forward. Men scattered. Rope tore through the gloves of one cowhand, the sound like a zip-line at high speed. He howled.

The stallion's getting away! Megan's heart leaped with hope. *He's getting–*

Joy crumpled into terror. The horse charged directly at her.

CHAPTER 2

“Hey, ya hear me? I said, whatcha think of Silver Springs?”

The voice pierced the fog of her mind. Megan shook her head and blinked. A gentle breeze lifted a strand of hair and caressed her cheek. She turned to the speaker.

Miles, the driver of the van, scratched his ribcage as he grinned at her.

Where’s…?

A chill crawled through her. She could have sworn she’d just been standing…

“Cat got yer tongue?”

Miles spat a brown stream of unmentionable liquid into the dirt. She stepped back to avoid being splattered.

He smirked. "Better get used to it, Miz City Gal. Out here, don't need my spittin' cup."

She vaguely recalled the chipped mug and its foaming contents in the truck's console. Hadn't she just spent three hours coming from Cheyenne? She remembered thinking how hot the ride had been without air conditioning.

A door slammed. The other passenger opened the back of the van and grabbed his luggage, muttering under his breath.

"Hey, I can get those." Miles sprang forward to haul the man's belongings into the building.

A battered sign hung from the eaves of the self-proclaimed hotel, half the words blistered off. Weatherworn rocking chairs squeaked on the porch, propelled by invisible patrons.

As she stared at her grimy feet, Megan remembered stepping out of the van. *I distinctly recall worrying about my sandals.* Pedicured toenails had morphed from mauve to mud-colored. Dust streaked her skirt. Miles had asked if she were "rump sprung" as she'd gazed down the empty streets of Silver Springs. But after that...

The late afternoon sun beat down, warring with her lingering out-of-sync feeling.

She again glanced down the main street. Twenty or so sad buildings spread out on both sides of a potholed road. Peeling paint, grime and neglect stamped the worn wooden siding. At a distance stood a lonely corral and dilapidated barn. If not for three pickup trucks, Megan could swear she'd stepped back a hundred years into the old west.

I had these thoughts before. The sense of déjà vu rippled over her again. *What is going on?*

She remained alone by the van, staring down the vacant street and asking herself why she would voluntarily travel to the wilds of Wyoming. Was she crazy? Obviously, in light of the weird stuff that had happened since the moment of her arrival.

Three months. That's all I promised my uncle.

Megan took a deep breath and slowly exhaled. She could put up with almost anything for three months. Besides, she'd earned it. She'd worked multiple seventy-hour weeks to finish a major project so she could take the time off.

Down the street, a dust devil swirled hypnotically. The tan cyclone bobbed and gyrated, then lifted into the air, passing over her head as though parading out of town. For a moment, the sun blinded her with hazy orange. The cloud of dirt settled and split apart, spraying the horizon in gold and scarlet.

"Wow," she murmured, entranced by the beauty.

A white calf stood at the edge of town. *Is that a buffalo?* Nothing had been there a minute ago. Feet splayed, the ghost-colored animal calmly returned her gaze, oblivious to the dust storm. Animals didn't normally stare at people, but this one did. Wholly intent on her, the calf didn't move. Megan shivered.

The miniature storm continued to blow at the edge of town, then suddenly shifted, spraying dirt her direction. Dazzling sand particles danced around, without touching her. The storm raged for minutes. Then it unexpectedly died as though someone flipped a switch. She blinked and looked back to the edge of town.

The calf had vanished.

She straightened. *Where–?*

"Miz Gillespie?" A deep male voice sounded nearby.

Megan ignored the speaker. *The calf had been right there!*

"Did you–did you just...?" Unable to explain the event, she clamped her mouth shut, still staring.

"Did I what?"

Finally, she gazed at the newcomer.

I've seen him before.

The tall cowboy looked like he'd stepped out of a western movie. Sandy hair, blue-gray eyes, and deep tan made her gulp. Not only was he lean and square-jawed, but the huge silver belt buckle, shaped like a horseshoe, large hat and well-worn boots completed the picture.

He grinned. “Don’t tell me you’re overcome by our picturesque town.”

“Heya, Jack.” The voice of Miles boomed as he exited the hotel. “Thought that was you.”

The cowboy turned to the driver. “Where’ve you been? Stop to take pictures or something?” Annoyance roughened the words of the man named Jack. “I’ve been waiting over an hour.”

“I’m sure you found someone to keep ya occupied. Heard the new barmaid has her eye on you.”

“You could’ve called.” Jack poked the brim of his hat back with a thumb.

“Forgot my phone. ’Sides, I was busy talking to the purdiest gal I’ve seen in a while.” Miles winked at her. “This here’s Daniel’s niece.”

The cowboy stuck out his hand. “Jack Crawford. Foreman of the Double O.”

“Megan Gillespie.” As she shook his hand she hissed in a breath from his firm grip.

“Figured. You got his red hair.”

“That ain’t all of his this city gal’s got.” Miles guffawed.

What’s that mean? She pulled her hand away from Crawford’s.

“Course, she don’t have as many freckles. And good thing she don’t weigh near–”

“This your gear?” The foreman stepped to the back of the van.

Gear. She tucked away the interesting word as she shot him a grateful look. “Yes. Let me–”

“I got it.” He grabbed the three pieces of designer luggage, then stuffed one under his arm. “This all?”

“Let me get my purse and carry-on.” She hurried to the front seat to retrieve them.

“That’s one thing about Jack.” Miles dug into a can of tobacco, apparently oblivious to the fact they ignored him. “Always knows how to treat the ladies right.”

“I’m parked down the street.” Crawford indicated the trucks with a tilt of his head.

“So you could be closer to the bar?” Miles stuffed a

wad in his lip, then smirked.

The foreman glared. “We agreed to meet at the post office, remember? My pickup’s right out front.”

The driver spread his hands. “How’s I supposed to know we’d have an extra passenger? Jed Harper wanted me to drop him off at the hotel.”

Crawford straightened with a jerk. “Harper?”

“Harper Junior. Returning to the fold, so to speak.” Miles scratched his cheek without a break. “Staying in town overnight. Guess he wants to patch things up a’tween him and the old man.”

Megan raised her brows. The sullen man who’d shared her van ride didn’t seem the type who wanted to patch up anything.

“He tell you this?” Crawford’s mouth hardened. “Or you making it up?”

Miles looked taken aback. “Aw, you know me. Picked it up here and there.”

“And spreading it around.”

“Hey, ain’t still bad blood a’tween you and Harper, is there?”

The foreman’s jaw jutted as he glanced at Megan. “Let’s go.”

“You’re supposed t’forgive and forget, Jack.”

Without answering, Crawford stalked down the street.

She hurried to follow, wondering what Miles meant by bad blood. However, his parting shot distracted her. “Whatever you do, Miz Gillespie, don’t let Jack take the scenic route. He’d ruin your reputation, fo’sure.” His squawking laugh made her wince.

“Thanks again for stopping by.” An overly bleached blond popped out of a building and smiled brilliantly at Crawford. “Don’t forget you got that tab running.”

“You know I’m good for it.” He touched the brim of his hat.

Her smile faded as soon as she noticed Megan.

When he reached a blue Chevy, he tossed her luggage into the bed then climbed into the full-sized cab, leaving her to fend for herself. He could at least open her door, couldn’t he? She tucked her carry-on under an arm to free her hand. Crawford unexpectedly leaned over and opened the door from the inside.

"Thanks." Though she was grateful they'd gotten away from Miles, the foreman could be a little more helpful. And not toss her suitcases around like cattle prepared for branding.

He started the truck before she shut the door and began to back out. Megan fumbled to find the seat belt.

"You don't need 'em around here."

She glared at him. "I happen to value my life."

"Nobody uses 'em–trust me."

She ignored his comment and dug between the middle of the seat. The shoulder strap was missing, leaving her only with the lap belt. After locating the other half, she jammed the gritty ends together, and then struggled to tighten it. Clogged by dirt and disuse, the mechanism wouldn't budge. Crawford was already heading out of town, acknowledging the wave of another woman who walked along the street.

Megan hated to give up, but finally folded her hands to hide the fact that the belt lay slack. Without a word, Crawford reached over. With one hard tug, he tightened the strap.

"Ow! Enough." The material dug into her pelvis. She spent the next couple minutes trying to loosen it. "You didn't have to cut off circulation to my legs."

He remained silent, staring ahead at the narrow road.

After settling, she studied the landscape. Bare dirt, pinyon pine and spindly grass, all either brown or faded. Nothing else could be seen for miles and miles. What creatures could possibly survive here? Already she missed the lush green of Florida. Forbidding gray mountains dominated the horizon. Though she'd spent the first nine years of her life in Wyoming, nothing seemed familiar. Or inviting.

Megan threw a glance at the foreman. "How far to the ranch?"

"'Bout an hour."

"That far?" When he didn't volunteer anything else,

she tried again. “Is the road paved all the way?”

“Mostly.”

“Have you lived in this area long?”

“Some.”

“Like it?”

“Yep.”

She blew out a breath. “Definitely not big on conversation.”

He acted as though he hadn’t heard. Fingers choking the steering wheel, he stared ahead. Where was the charming, flirtatious man she’d first met? The moment Jed Harper’s name had been mentioned, Crawford had changed. Maybe there was still bad blood between them.

The subdued drone of tires on pavement began to grate on her nerves. Silence pressed on her, but instead of growing sleepy, she found herself tensing. She almost asked the foreman to turn on the radio. More than once, she unclenched her hands and forced her shoulders to relax. She sighed deeply several times, trying to get enough air.

The shrill ringing of a phone made her jump.

“Sup?” Crawford pressed the cell to his ear. After a pause, he said, “You’re kidding. When? Where? On my way.”

He stomped on the accelerator. When the pickup began to rock, Megan clutched at the door. She glanced at the speedometer. They were doing over seventy-five.

“What’s going on?” Her voice came out a little more sharply than she intended.

“Need to make a detour.”

“Where?” Miles’ warning about a scenic route flashed through her mind. “My uncle’s expecting me.”

“This won’t take long.” Gaze locked ahead, Crawford’s jaw stiffened.

The needle edged eighty. Eighty-five.

“Do you have to drive so fast?” She raised her voice over the whine of the engine. “I’m sure–”

“He doesn’t want me to miss this.” Crawford shot her a hard glance. “Believe me.”

She gulped, saying nothing more.

He slowed only slightly as they came to a dirt road and careened around the corner. The pickup skidded, spraying rocks into the air. They fishtailed. With casual expertise, he righted the vehicle, then sped up again. The truck bounced crazily over uneven ground. Megan banged her arm against the window then grabbed the seat back. Her carry-on leaped up, then crashed to the floor several times.

In the distance, men and horses crowded around something. Dread built in her. As the truck hurtled down a hill, she lost sight of them. Her stomach vaulted into her throat. Crawford slammed on the brakes, causing the truck to skid sideways. After shoving the gearshift lever into park, he flipped off the keys.

“Stay here. You’ll be safe.” He jumped out.

For several minutes, she heard only her panting breath. Her arm felt bruised where it had hit the window. Fighting to slow her pounding heart, she rubbed her neck. Megan pushed away the premonition of having been there before.

The sun dipped lower in the sky, the heat growing inside the truck until it became suffocating. She turned the key so she could roll down both windows a few inches. Outside, the blowing wind snatched at the nearby pinyon pine, rustling the twigs, the sound reminiscent of shuffling paper. The breeze moaned its way through the windows.

Help me. Someone, standing outside the cab of the truck, rasped the barely audible words.

“What?” Megan jerked around to look out her window. Imagining she saw a dark form, she shrank back.

No one was there.

“This is creepy.” She rubbed her arms.

The barrenness of the countryside and the utter stillness clawed at her mind.

I’ve been here before. I know it.

She shuddered. Where had Crawford gone? What was he doing? The cries of men and animals gradually welled up into awareness, as though someone slowly turned up the volume on a radio.

The scream of a stallion pierced the air. A shiver slithered down her spine. What were they doing to the horse? Déjà vu hit so hard, she clenched the door handle and dashboard to brace herself. The scent of spring rain enveloped her.

This can't be happening.

Megan peered through the dirty windshield, knowing she'd done that before. But when? How?

Her hand crept up her throat. The burn of something tightened around her neck. It pulled against her flesh, crushing her windpipe. The agony built and built until she could hardly breathe.

Out of the corner of her eye, a white blur streaked past the truck. Megan gasped in recognition as a buffalo calf ran up the knoll and disappeared.

The next moment, she bolted out of the cab and sprinted up the rise.

CHAPTER 3

Like a pack of wolves, a group of men circled a black stallion.

"Hold him. I said, hold him!" Jack Crawford yanked a lariat from the hands of one of the men. The horse plummeted, causing him to scramble out of the way.

Cowboys yelled, their mounts bawling in wild-eyed terror.

"Drag him this way." The foreman pointed. "Tighten those lines."

In a macabre dance, the stallion edged backwards on hind feet. His unexpected move threw riders and their mounts into a frenzy of activity. Crawford began spinning the lasso, shouting unintelligible directions to his men.

The next moment, the stallion lunged forward. Two unmounted men lost their footing while a horse with rider staggered. Men scattered. Rope tore through the gloves of one cowhand, the sound like a zip-line at high speed. He howled.

"He's getting away. I know he is." Megan spoke the certainty out loud as she stood on the crest of the hill. "I have to move. Now. Before it's too late."

But her feet wouldn't obey. Thundering hooves roared in her ears as the horse charged directly at her. Dust churned upward, curtaining her from everything and everyone but the stallion. He bore down on her. Black. Lethal.

"Run!" The distant shout sounded muted, distorted.

I am going to die.

It all made sense now. A strange calmness washed over her. She had several moments to contemplate the end of her life. The brown wall of dirt silhouetted the gleaming fluid body, moving in slow motion as he broke through the cloud. She saw nothing but the horse and her own hands, raised as though to embrace death.

Megan cried out as a human body collided with hers, knocking her to the ground. Together they rolled. Momentum carried them down the hill until they slid under the truck. The vehicle shuddered as the horse banged into it. Dull thumps sounded overhead, much too close.

Reality rushed into focus.

Men were shouting. Horses squealed. Pounding came from every side of the vehicle, making it rock. Dust billowed. She gagged as she inhaled the fine powder. On and on the battle raged. Finally, the storm ebbed. Men and horses moved away.

The man who'd knocked her down crawled out from under the truck. Hampered by her skirt, Megan followed. A hand grabbed her arm and yanked her upright. She came face to face with Crawford, his mouth a slash of irritation.

"Next time, stay in the truck like I told you." He shoved her away, then slapped at his jeans. Covered in dust, his eyes gleamed whitely against the brown of his face. He moved his jaw, then spat the filth from his mouth.

I'm alive.

Realization came slowly. She shook away grogginess and bewilderment. The dirt in her lungs made her cough. She noted her filthy skirt and blouse, the top button missing. A scratch across the back of her hand. The grit under her nails. A scraped elbow.

In the distance, the recaptured stallion cried his rage.

Crawford bent to retrieve something off the ground. After brushing off his hat, he shoved it on his head. "Your stupidity could've gotten us both killed." He strode away.

Still shaking, she crawled back into the cab. Her eyes burned as she slumped in the seat, seeing nothing. After a while, the foreman climbed into the vehicle and started the engine. Without a word, he yanked it into drive.

When they returned to the paved road, he pulled out his cell. "We got him." He paused. "Yessir, we're bringing him in now." He threw a glance in Megan's direction. "Yeah, she's here. See you soon."

Evening darkened, casting the sky in violet. As dusk blanketed the landscape, Crawford snapped on the headlights. The limited illumination revealed an endless ribbon of blacktop. Out of the corner of her eye, she saw animals. One or two disembodied spots reflected light before darting away. On and on they drove for what felt like hours. Megan's adrenaline rush faded, leaving only a dull ache.

Finally, they passed under a wooden archway. Beams flashed across the sign: Double O Ranch. Had it really been seventeen years since she'd lived there? It wouldn't be long now before she reached home.

No, not home. Not now. Not ever. The three months she'd promised to stay wouldn't be over quickly enough.

"Megan!" Daniel O'Connor reached toward her from the confines of his wheelchair, arms extended to engulf her.

In the illumination of the yard light, she examined his face which hadn't changed much. Though he'd visited her in Florida only a few years before, it felt like a lot longer. He was still a powerful man, proven by the strength of his hug. As she embraced him, she tried to swallow the tightness in her throat.

Her uncle pulled away, blinking rapidly. Two huge dogs barked relentlessly in the background, clearly thinking they were missing a party. A slightly plump woman and a wiry man stood a short distance from Daniel, their silhouettes outlined by the bright lights of the house. Further away, she noted a shapely girl, age masked by shadows.

Her uncle looked past Megan. "Somebody shut those dogs up." No one needed to. At the sound of his authoritative shout, they immediately stopped their yapping and slunk into the darkness.

"So good to see you, Megan," he said. "How was the trip?"

"A little rough. Long." She remained purposefully vague, aware that Crawford had stepped out of the truck. His footsteps moved in their direction.

Her uncle suddenly grabbed her wrist. "What in heaven's name happened?" He stared up at her blouse which she pulled together.

"She nearly got run down by the rogue." Crawford answered before she could. He set down her suitcases. "Nothing broken as far as I can tell."

She shot him a glance. *How would you know?*

"Sure you're all right?" Daniel's grip tightened.

"Yeah. I'm...fine."

"Anybody hurt?" He peered at his foreman.

"Nothing serious. Cuts and bruises is all. Mick may've sprained his arm. Stallion's fine."

Daniel mouth flattened. "Where'd you put him?"

"Back of the barn. For now. Till we decide what to do with him."

He frowned. "Maybe you should've shot the rogue instead of capturing him."

"No!" The word burst out of Megan.

Crawford and her uncle stared.

"He...he's too beautiful to destroy." She gulped. "And nobody was hurt."

Daniel glanced at his foreman, then back at her. "I'm glad you're okay. If anything had happened to you..." He left the sentence ominously incomplete.

"Perhaps your niece would like a hot bath." The plump woman moved forward, one hand extended. She spoke with a slight accent, not exactly rolling her r's, but more like she was slurring them. "And you are hungry? Yes? I have a meal ready. Come." She touched Megan's shoulder.

"Go on up to the house," Daniel said. "I'll be there soon."

As the woman drew her away, Megan glanced over her shoulder. Hand gripping his foreman's arm, Daniel spoke in such low tones she couldn't catch the words. Then he slapped Crawford's shoulder. In congratulations?

"I am Mrs. Danvers." The woman led her toward the house. They climbed several steps of the grand porch that ran the perimeter of the house. "You must be tired after your trip."

"It was exhausting."

"Did Miles pick you up in Cheyenne? That man chatters too much, does he not? I am sure he was most difficult."

"Actually Crawford's silence was worse." Megan bit her lip when she realized she'd said too much. But Mrs. Danvers had a way of putting her at ease.

She pursed her lips. "Jack? Silent? He must have had something on his mind. Usually he is a smooth-talker."

I believe that.

"Would you like to bathe first? Or perhaps to eat?"

Megan spread her hands over her dirty skirt. "I'd

prefer a shower, if you don't mind."

"Ah, yes. You want to look your best. And not give Daniel any incentive to shoot that horse." Inside the well-lighted foyer, Mrs. Danvers spoke over her shoulder. "Simone, bring Miss Gillespie's bags to her room."

Megan glanced behind her in time to see the sullen look in the girl's dark eyes. No, not a girl. She had a beautiful oval face, full bust and tiny waist, all too mature to belong to a child. Yet, Simone's exotic beauty made her age unguessable. She rolled her eyes, then swiveled on her heel as she flounced back outside.

"She is my daughter." Mrs. Danvers led the way up the large, wide staircase. "Simone helps around the house. When I can tear her away from the horses. She dotes on them."

"How long have you lived here?"

"Eight years as of last week." The woman reached the second level. She pointed down the hallway. "Your uncle's room is there. Your bedroom will be this way."

"Who else stays up here?"

"Just Randy, Daniel's personal helper. Simone's and my rooms are on the first floor."

"So, Mr. Crawford doesn't stay in the house?"

"No. He bunks with the other men, although he has his own quarters. You can see the building from the library upstairs."

Megan said nothing. Good, she wouldn't run into Crawford in the early morning. "This house is new since I lived here. Seems a lot bigger than my uncle led me to believe."

"Daniel planned for a houseful of people."

The statement left Megan feeling vaguely uncomfortable. Why build such a big place? Surely he didn't intend for her to fill it, did he?

"This is your room." Mrs. Danvers flipped on a light inside, then stepped back.

Megan smiled at the cozy interior. A queen-sized bed, framed in rugged logs, took up the middle of the room. End tables perched on both sides, draped with material that matched the quilt. Pale teal, taupe and peach were the dominant colors. A cattle skull perched on one wall, decorated with cactus and eucalyptus. Southwest decor? Interesting choice for Wyoming.

"You have a private bath." Mrs. Danvers walked briskly to a door and opened it. "And here, a walk-in closet." She turned on another light.

"*Excuse* me," Simone's sultry voice interrupted. Heedless of her mother's frown, she squeezed past Megan. She dropped the large suitcase by the bed, then left.

Mrs. Danvers smoothed the disapproval from her face and smiled at Megan. "I cannot get over how much you look like your mother. Except your eyes are much greener. Daniel has many, many photos of her in the study. Of both your parents."

"I'd love to look at them again sometime."

The housekeeper stepped closer, her gaze searching Megan. "I hope you feel at home. And soon. You might find life a little rough around here at times. But give everyone a chance."

Megan managed to smile. "I'll try." She could handle anything for three months.

Mrs. Danvers walked past her. "Take your time getting comfortable. The hired men already ate. Our dinner will be in an hour." She headed out of the room.

Her daughter entered immediately afterwards with Megan's smaller bags. Not once did she meet her gaze.

"Simone, isn't it?"

The young woman swept past her and tossed her things on the bed. Her mouth pulled to one side, eyes hooded. "Nothing wrong with your hearing."

Megan raised her chin. "Can't say the same thing about your attitude."

The young woman planted one hand on her hip. "That all you want, *Miz* Gillespie?"

"Yes. Except to know what's eating you."

Simone made a face, the sullenness marring her perfect beauty. "Nothing your leaving tomorrow won't fix." She slammed the door behind her.

Megan contemplated the closed panel. “Believe me, that thought has already crossed my mind.”

CHAPTER 4

Megan sighed as she stepped out of the shower and looked longingly at the jetted tub in one corner of the bathroom. "Next time. I promise." She toweled herself off, luxuriating in cleanness after having looked like a poster child for *The Grapes of Wrath.*

Once dressed, she studied herself in the full-length mirror on the back of the door. Her cheeks were flushed, emphasizing the freckles that danced across her nose and forehead. Too many. She sighed.

Gingerly touching a tender place on one cheek, she hoped a black eye wouldn't appear in the next couple days. She smoothed her cottony summer dress. Would the material be too light for the cool night air? Already she'd noticed how chilly it got when the sun went down. Nothing like the sultry nights of Jacksonville.

In the reflection, a long red scratch marred her left hand. The scrape on her elbow and knee made her look like she'd been in a barroom brawl. She chuckled.

Welcome to Wyoming.

She headed out of her room. At the bottom of the stairs she stopped, irresolute about which direction to take. The huge staircase split the foyer. Consequently, two hallways led away behind her, both rather dimly lit. Two rooms, with lights low, beckoned to her on either side as she stood on the bottom step. Dinner wasn't for another twenty minutes, according to the grandfather clock in the foyer. Plenty of time for a look at the photographs Mrs. Danvers had mentioned.

But which was the study? Megan headed toward one room. As she peered in, she realized her error. Native American artifacts stuffed the living room. Despite her plan to see the photos of her parents, she was drawn in. When had Uncle Daniel become a collector?

She stepped onto the woven carpet, then stopped to examine silver jewelry encased in the table's glass top. The work was intricate, beautifully ornate. A collection of arrowheads captured her attention next. Blankets, beads, wall hangings and pottery met her eyes wherever she looked.

However, the large painting of a warrior over the fireplace commanded her attention. Staring at the man poised on the half-rearing horse, Megan walked toward the portrait. The tip of an arrow pointed straight at her heart. His war bonnet was magnificent, as proud as the expression in his black-black eyes. Nostrils flared in a long straight nose while his sensual mouth flattened, almost in distain. Fingers of black hair caressed an invisible breeze, reaching toward the appaloosa's flowing mane. His biceps bunched as he pulled his bow taut. The strong grip of his legs kept him astride.

Her heart pounded against her throat. Air became scarce.

Megan's world narrowed to the warrior's eyes. They

called to her soul. Despite his proud visage, she sensed something hauntingly sad in their depths. In the dusky chasm of silence, she heard the echo of pounding hooves, the savage cry of a pursuer, the clash of bodies. The smell of blood and sweat pricked her senses. The scent of a horse made her suck in a quick breath as the mesmerizing painting enveloped her.

"When?" came a low, intense question.

She blinked, the trance broken. Was that Simone? Megan turned, studying the empty living room.

"When will you?" The question came again. "Tell me."

The sound had not come from inside the house, but somewhere else. From the porch? A fluttering curtain drew her eye.

A man answered softly, too softly for Megan to catch the words.

"That's what you said last time." A plaintive note resounded in Simone's voice.

Megan held her breath. She shouldn't be there. Shouldn't be hearing this.

"Please." The young woman's whisper cut through the evening. "I love you. Doesn't that count for something? Please say you love me. Please."

Again came a low reply, then the shuffling of clothing. *I have to get out of here.* She tiptoed across the bare wooden floor toward the stairs, silencing sandals before they clattered. A lampshade wobbled when she bumped it. After it settled, she continued on her way.

She'd nearly reached the hallway when heavy footsteps outside warned her that someone approached. Simone's lover? Megan sprinted up a couple steps and turned as the front door flew open. With studied nonchalance, she poised on the stairs, pretending to only now be descending.

Jack Crawford.

He looked up, the frown on his face deepening. Then he slowly shut the door. He strode to the bottom, his head tilted back. "Going up? Or down?"

She shrugged. "That depends on where the kitchen is." Heat crept across her cheeks. Did he guess she'd been eavesdropping?

"This way." He swept his arm toward the right half of the hallway as he partially bowed. "After you."

She stepped toward him, but stopped when he gripped the railing, blocking her from descending further.

His gray eyes bore into hers. "I hope you've recovered from that little incident with the horse."

Megan's heel hit the step as she backed up and almost lost her balance. "Oh, you mean when you tackled me? I'll survive."

He smirked. "You wouldn't have if I hadn't."

She clamped her lips together.

Crawford leaned toward her. "Didn't mean to hurt you. I hope you'll forgive me."

"No permanent damage." She managed to keep her tone light.

His gaze raked her. "I'm glad." However, no smile softened his features.

"Jack." Daniel shouted from another part of the house. "That you?"

"Yes, sir." He straightened, and then gestured that Megan should precede him through the dimly lit hallway.

She walked stiffly down the remaining steps, then in the direction he indicated. The tiled foyer gave way to wooden flooring as they passed under the staircase, then the passage widened. Megan's neck prickled from Crawford following too closely.

"Come on in," Daniel called, still out of sight.

She stepped through the doorway, then stopped.

The room was huge, a house within a house. Megan had seen "country kitchens" before, but none compared to what her uncle had built. A massive stone fireplace dominated one end the room, seconded by two immense tables which could easily seat twenty-four people. They were empty except for her uncle and the man she recognized from his Florida visit as Randy, his caregiver. At one end of the room was the cooking station, occupied by a smiling Mrs. Danvers who was clearly in her element. Three ranges and two huge commercial-sized refrigerators towered behind while an enormous work island spread out before her.

"I was just escorting your niece." Crawford eased by her. "Seems she got lost in this mansion."

Megan clenched her hands, forcing her mouth to remain shut. *I was not lost.*

Daniel waved for her to approach one long table. "We're all starving."

"Sorry to have kept you waiting." She sat across from her uncle at the place that was clearly reserved for her.

Randy sat by his employer. Crawford took a seat next to her.

"Where's Simone?" Daniel glanced around, then settled on his foreman.

He shrugged as he unfolded his napkin. "Haven't seen her." In the careless motions, Megan read contempt, not only in the lie about where Simone was, but in his absolute apathy toward her.

Liar! You were just outside with her. Making her beg.

"She will probably eat later." Mrs. Danvers set a huge bowl of mashed potatoes on the table. "Please do not let her absence keep you from your meal."

The aromas of roasting meat and buttered potatoes made Megan's mouth water. Crawford served himself, and then passed the bowl to her. The container was heavier than she thought. Megan's grip slipped, but Crawford's hand suddenly covered hers, supporting the weight.

For a second, their eyes met. She pulled the bowl away.

"You won't leave the table hungry." Her uncle helped himself to a slab of ham. "Celia's the best cook in five counties. I stopped counting after that."

Mrs. Danvers brought dish after dish as he spoke. Gravy, a platter of sliced beef, peas, a leafy salad, a gelatin salad, iced tea, milk. When would the parade end? Finally the housekeeper sat across from

Crawford. Megan took a little of each dish, but ended up cramming all the things together on the plate. She grasped the heavy pitcher of iced tea.

"Looks like Miss Gillespie's hungry." Crawford's dry tone was uncomfortably close. Had he moved his chair nearer?

"Oh, call her Megan." Daniel smiled in his direction. "We don't stand on ceremony around here."

"I will if she gives me permission." The foreman gazed expectantly at her.

Would pouring the iced tea into his lap constitute permission? When everyone stopped eating to look at her she managed a stiff smile. "Of course."

"Make sure you call me Jack." His eyes crinkled in the corners as he smiled.

"Absolutely." A gravy-laden chunk of beef poised on Daniel's fork. "The only people who call him Mr. Crawford are the hired hands."

"In Megan's case, that definitely wouldn't be appropriate." The foreman buttered a thick slice of bread, his gray-blue eyes flicking to her.

With an annoyed look at her uncle and his foreman, she poured herself some tea. Before she could set down the pitcher, Crawford held out his glass to her. "I'll take some."

She served him, hand trembling. Why did she get the impression they were ganging up on her? For what purpose?

"I like your hair down about your shoulders." Her uncle rested an elbow on the table as he contemplated her. "You remind me so much of your mother."

"I don't recall Mom's hair being this curly. I think I got that from Dad." She fingered the strands which came past her shoulders. Any longer and her hair became unruly. As it was, she was limited to styles. Straighteners only made her curls frizzy.

"From the photos I have seen, I believe hers was never that red," Mrs. Danvers added.

"Definitely not." Daniel again tackled his meal. "You and me, Megan. We are cursed with the pure Irish."

"I wouldn't say cursed, exactly." Crawford studied her. "Megan's hair is the color of wood that has burned down late into night. The glowing coals that remain for hours afterwards."

"Oh-ho." Her uncle slapped the table with one hand, then pointed at Megan. "You've made my foreman wax eloquent."

"I think I'll dye my hair." Megan took a sip of her tea.

A door slammed, drawing the attention away. Beside the fireplace, a lean man appeared out of the darkness. Megan stared at the odd scar that tugged the corner of his mouth, making him look like he permanently sneered. His eyes darted around the table, then settled on Daniel.

"What's up, Kit?"

"Sorry to disturb your meal, sir. I wanted to let you know we secured the stallion."

"No chance of him hurting anyone, is there?"

"No, sir. He's nice and cozy. We'll give him a few days to cool down before we start to work on him."

"Good. You have other work to catch up on first. The rogue isn't a priority."

"Yes, sir."

Daniel turned to Megan. "I think you'll like seeing Kit Gerard in action. He's the best horse breaker around. If he doesn't have that stallion taking sugar cubes out of your hand in a couple weeks, I'll eat my hat."

Though everyone laughed, she sensed the ominous tinge in the air. After the sound died down, she spoke. "What if the horse won't be tamed?"

Her uncle glanced at Gerard, then back to her. "Well, I wouldn't worry about that. Kit'll get the job done."

"But what if he doesn't?" Megan didn't understand why it was so important to know. When no one answered, she added, "Would you release the horse?"

"No. No, I couldn't do that." Daniel shook his head, jaw rigid. "You see, he's been a thorn in my side for almost a year now. Stole some of my best mares. Jack finally set the trap that caught him. He's been working at it for weeks. Finally paid off today."

She glanced at the foreman. But her question still hadn't been answered. "So, what will you do with the stallion if he won't be tamed?"

The answer finally came from Crawford. "If we have to, make him into dog food."

CHAPTER 5

I can't...get away!

Megan thrashed awake, fighting to free herself from the blanket and sheet. With a grunt, she flung them to the floor. The lighted digital next to the bed said three-twelve. What had awakened her? Then she shivered. Not from a dream, but the cold. The thin nightgown and open window had been unwise choices. Southern practices had been entirely wrong for an early May night in Wyoming.

From the end of the bed, she yanked the quilt up to her neck. *I'll warm up in a minute.* That hope died as arctic air continued to blast through the window. Megan vigorously rubbed her arms under the covering.

When that didn't work, she flung it back and hastened to the window. Her fingers poised on the sash when a distant scream made a different kind of chill reverberate down her spine.

The stallion.

He cried his anger, the loss of freedom evident in another drawn-out shriek. Megan shuddered once more before closing the window. She climbed back into bed, too wide-awake now. Staring into the darkness, she heard him cry again.

She squeezed her eyes shut. "Don't think about him. Don't think about what they might do."

Minutes ticked by, sleep eluding her. What was the use? She kicked off the quilt then fumbled for clothing in the walk-in closet.

After pulling on jeans, sweatshirt and tennis shoes, she quietly opened her bedroom door and listened. Nothing. She crept along the hallway, then down the stairs. Besides the muted squeak of her shoes, she made no sound. The house was too new and too well built to creak.

The front door swung open without noise, its unlocked state making everything all the easier. She walked out into the light of the half moon, then paused, scanning the numerous outbuildings. Two dark shapes bounded toward her. Alarm gripped Megan. The dogs! However, they merely nosed her, then whimpered as though begging to be included in an adventure.

"Good boys." She kept her voice low, allowing them to sniff her. After a moment, she patted their heads. The enraged squeal of the stallion made her straighten. A muted thump followed.

Dogs following with lolling tongues, she made her way down the gentle slope, away from the house. The barn dominated the landscape to the east. Multiple corrals surrounded the building, some quartering horses. Away from the barn stood a stock pen with cattle. The shaggy animals were standing or lying down, chewing their cud. The smell of dung burned her nose.

She skirted the large double panels on the front of the barn. When Megan reached a small door, she slipped inside, keeping the dogs out. Blackness enveloped her as she turned. How to keep from killing herself in the dark? After her eyes adjusted, the answer magically appeared in a sliver of illumination. Under a door? She cautiously made her way and opened it.

The main part of the barn spread out before her, a lone light bulb burning in the distance. When she glanced behind her, Megan realized that she'd been in a tack room. Polished leather, bridles and bits gleamed dully in the small chamber.

A horse nickered. She then saw that her uncle had built connecting stables, the addition coming off the barn at a right angle. In the darkness, a horse's eyes glittered. Further away, a foal whinnied a high-pitched cry to its mother who answered with a low rumble of comfort. Megan paused only a moment, knowing that the trainer hadn't put the stallion there. The rogue was too wild.

The very horsey smell and the greenness of hay struck her as scents of peace and happiness. She remembered being there before, though memories were a little hazy. The barn back then had seemed vast and horrific. Invisible creatures dwelt in the corners. Megan recalled running out of the barn when she was six, frightened by an imaginary monster.

She headed down the middle of the building, away from the stables, not certain where the stallion might be. Straw and hay were stacked all around, the once-used stalls attesting to their permanent change of utility. Dark shadows and misshapen structures crouched in corners, conjuring up frightening images.

A rasping shriek made her jump. She listened, then moved toward the corner stall. In the deepest recesses of the barn, the furthest from the stables, dwelt the stallion. She peered over the gate, afraid of getting too close in case the animal charged. After her eyes adjusted to the gloom, she gasped.

The horse lay in the center of the concrete floor,

his head immobilized by the ropes secured to the walls in opposite directions, eyes still blindfolded. Not only that, but his front legs had been hobbled to prevent him from rising.

So this was the "cozy" arrangement Gerard had bragged about?

Anger boiled up in her at the cruel treatment of this magnificent animal. He must have sensed her presence because he squealed in outrage and thrashed helplessly.

She opened the gate before realizing the foolishness of her actions. This was a wild horse, capable of killing her. Yet, she had to do something. A tear slipped down her cheek. The poor horse! No animal should be treated this way.

"It's all right, boy. Don't be afraid." She kept her voice low and soft.

Screaming, the horse thrashed futilely until he panted from exertion. Lather dripped from his mouth, splattering wetly on the bare floor. Then she saw blood. A long, slender wound across his haunches gleamed in the dull light.

"They hurt you." Her chest heaved.

The stallion didn't respond, his noisy intakes of air filling the night.

"If you only knew how much it pains me to see you. I wish I could help. I wish I dared. If I had my way, I'd let you run free. But they'd hunt you down and shoot you. I know they would."

The stallion remained immobile, either too exhausted to fight or saving strength to scream another protest. Megan gathered her courage and moved closer.

"Don't be afraid." She stretched out her hand as though he could see her. "Don't be afraid. I won't hurt you. I want to help." Another step closer, then she stopped, waiting for his reaction. When the stallion remained still, she crept closer still. "I care what happens to you. I don't want them to shoot you. You're too magnificent. I swear I'll do all I can to prevent that. I swear."

A low rumble in his throat sounded so much like the groan of a man.

"I'm so sorry." She sniffed, wiping away another tear. "How can they do this to you? How can they treat you this way?"

The stallion suddenly screamed and thrashed. Megan jumped back, but was never in any danger. Kit Gerard had done too good of a job making certain the horse was a threat to no one. She watched until it hurt to see his futile struggle. When he grew quiet again, she sighed.

"If only you would allow me to befriend you." She squatted, leaning against the wall.

A nearly noiseless sound above made her glance up in time to see an owl flap through the darkness.

"I remember being terribly afraid of this place when I was little." She paused. "I was only nine when my parents died in a car crash, along with my aunt. My uncle took me in for a while, but it didn't work out." She picked up a piece of straw and twiddled it between her fingers. Memories flew through her mind. "I lived here for another few months. But my uncle sent me away. To his wife's family. They aren't even related. Uncle Daniel's my only family. I always wondered..."

She squelched the rising bitterness. "I guess he thought it best. But I don't know. Looking back, I realize how lonely I was, even though they had kids about my age. They treated me like I was an outsider. Which I guess I was. You can't believe how glad I was when I finally moved out."

She stopped. What was that? When nothing more sounded, Megan rose, her legs tingling from being cramped. The stallion had to be in excruciating pain.

For many minutes, she remained in the stall, watching the tortured animal.

"Don't give up." Her voice cracked. "I promise I'll find a way to help you."

A low moan was the horse's only response.

Her uncle peered at her over a mound of scrambled eggs. “You look a bit tired this morning, Meggie.”

She smiled at the nickname. “I didn’t sleep well.” She yawned. “I can’t believe the memories that came back to me last night.”

“Not bad, I hope.” Daniel peppered his eggs, then waited, shaker in his hand.

“No. When I was out...” She stopped, realizing that she almost confessed that she’d spent almost two hours in the barn.

“What? You can tell me.”

“Well, what I was going to say was I’d forgotten how much I missed Wyoming.” Her throat tightened at the simple truth. Yet she also disliked the ranch. An enigma. “This place brings back so many memories. And yes, some good ones.”

Her uncle looked away. “How about more coffee, Celia?” He held up his cup for Mrs. Danvers to fill.

She glanced at the woman who hastened to obey. The housekeeper was rather pretty, in an older sort of way. A ribbon of silver streaked her dark hair at the crown. Megan didn’t miss the soft look that passed between her uncle and his employee. She smiled to herself. But of course...

The woman had lived there for eight years. A friendship, or something deeper, had to have developed.

“You always take such good care of me.” He smiled at Mrs. Danvers, who blushed.

“Not half so well as you deserve.”

“Bah. That I don’t believe.” Her uncle turned back to Megan. “When you’re done with breakfast, how about a tour?”

“After I put my dishes–”

“I will take care of them.” Mrs. Danvers planted a fist at her hip.

“Then a tour would be great.” She didn’t want to give Crawford another chance to announce that she’d gotten lost in the house. Especially during dinner that evening when her uncle introduced her to all the hired hands.

Megan finished her meal. After Daniel backed his wheelchair, he moved toward her. “Watch your toes. I can get pretty wild with this thing.”

She chuckled. “I believe it.”

He took her down a hallway that she’d not seen before. When they reached a plain-looking door, her uncle surprised her when he opened it to reveal an elevator. “Come on in. There’s room for two. We’ll begin on the second floor.”

They rode up, the motor purring softly. Now she understood the odd sound she’d heard late last night.

“We’ll start with the front of the house. My bedroom.” Daniel led the way to the spacious room which was equipped with hydraulic lifts, one in the bedroom and one in the bathroom. The unimpeded view out his low windows were magnificent. Mottled green and brown hills squatted before majestic blue and white mountains. Now she could see the ranch’s multiple buildings. What were they all for? Many appeared to have been recent additions.

They only glanced into Randy’s room that was next to Daniel’s. Upstairs, besides Megan’s bedroom, were two guest rooms, an exercise room, and a library, complete with a computer.

“Help yourself anytime.” Daniel indicated the room. “Maybe you could get a job through the web.”

She hid her surprise. What was he saying? That he planned for her to stay longer than three months?

True, her free-lance consulting allowed for greater flexibility than would a job, but she had no intention of staying longer than they’d discussed. This visit to Wyoming would be her first and last. For many years.

Daniel smiled. “Of course, you can always learn the ropes around here. We could use another good cowhand.”

“I doubt you’re talking about me.” Though she managed to keep her tone light, something tightened inside.

“Didn’t you take riding lessons in Florida? I hope they weren’t a waste of money.”

He turned and wheeled down the hallway. Megan

clenched her jaw. Trust him to bring up money. Daniel had paid for nearly everything in her life which included four years of college. Then, too, he had helped out financially during a brief, uncomfortable moment in recent history. She had promised to pay him back.

That'll happen in a couple months, after he signs over my trust fund.

As they headed downstairs, Megan caught a glimpse of the ramp at the back of the house. So, that's how her uncle got inside. The front porch steps didn't provide easy access for his wheelchair. Daniel shuffled the ramp, a symbol of his disability, to the back.

They passed through the kitchen and toward the three bedrooms on the first floor, two of which belonged to Simone and Mrs. Danvers. Megan only glanced in the study and at the numerous photos of her parents. Then they reached the living room.

"This is incredible." She indicated the artifacts.

"Like them?"

"Mm-hmm." She nodded as she looked around. "Where did you get all this?"

"Took me years to collect. I used to travel to various fairs and get-togethers so I developed quite a few contacts. However, I haven't bought anything for a long time."

"Looks like you have enough."

"Well, you know collectors. One more item couldn't possibly hurt." Daniel pointed to a case. "Now you see this blanket? This one is very special."

"And why's that?"

"It comes from our family."

She spread her hands. "What do you mean?"

He grinned. "You didn't realize that you have some 'Injun' in your blood?"

"How could I?" She fingered her hair. "My coloring isn't exactly right."

"Well, I suppose there'd've been no reason for you to be told. Your great-grandmother was Sioux–or Dakota. Western to be exact, from the Yankton tribe."

"Wow." She had no idea. "So why haven't I heard about this before now?"

"I discovered it only about a year ago. Did some digging around, so to speak, and found that since she wasn't full blood, she could pass herself off as white. She pretty much hid the fact. Your mother had this blanket buried in the bottom of a trunk, which she'd stored in a friend's attic. After Jean died, the friend forgot about the blanket until her daughter ran across it."

She glanced at the warrior painting. Was that why she felt such an affinity to him? "That's incredible. So, how much Native American does that make me?"

"A sixteenth." He shrugged. "Not much, but you're still authentic."

"After the blanket was returned, you started collecting?"

Daniel shrugged. "Before, actually. I was always interested, but this justified my fetish. Oh, and if you're interested, check out the library upstairs for books and documents. I wrote out our family tree."

Megan wandered about the room, touching various things. Finally, she stopped before the portrait that had so captivated her. "Tell me about this."

"Ah, yes." Her uncle spoke with a knowing grin. "I'd figured you'd like it, since you seem to prefer the strong, silent type."

She ignored the comment. "So, what's the story?"

"A few years back, a Wyoming artist put it up for sale at a gallery in Cheyenne. I snatched it up before someone else did. Paid quite a bit, but the painting's well worth it."

"Know anything about the subject?"

"Nope. I even tried to contact the artist, but couldn't find out anything."

Megan studied the portrait again. "He–it's very powerful."

"I agree." He paused for a moment. "You realize, of course, that when I'm gone, you'll get everything."

She turned slowly. "You're not hinting at something serious, are you?"

"No, no." Daniel waved a negligent hand. "I'm pleased you value my collection. Not only this, but the ranch. You are, after all, the only family I got."

She raised her brows. "But what about my cousins?"

"They're not blood relatives. You are."

"It doesn't seem right–"

"Meggie," he interrupted. "Your aunt and uncle received a generous compensation for the years they cared for you. But, I'll say it again. You're my only blood relative. And one thing you have to realize, we O'Connors stick together. I'm bequeathing everything to you."

She swallowed the tightness in her throat. Did he really care for her?

He patted her arm. "It's good to have you home, Meggie."

She shifted on her feet.

Of course. Was he saying he would bequeath everything to her *if* she changed her mind about how long she stayed? Was that it?

Turning so he wouldn't see her expression, she started. Jack Crawford was standing in the doorway.

How long had he been there? How much had he heard?

CHAPTER 6

"'Scuze me, Mr. O'Connor," Crawford drawled.

"What's up, Jack?"

"Sheba's ready to foal."

"Wonderful news." Daniel looked up at Megan. "Want to see a horse give birth?"

"I'd love to."

They headed for the stables, both Megan and Crawford going out the back where the ramps provided an exit for Daniel. A couple men were inside the stables when they arrived, including Kit Gerard. Something in her tightened when she saw him and his sneering mouth. Now that she knew how cruel he could be, she wondered why he was there. To start "cozy treatments" as soon as the foal arrived to prove he was boss?

Now didn't seem a good time to bring up the treatment of the stallion. Not after her uncle made it clear he expected her to make Wyoming her home. She didn't need to be beholden to him any more than she already was. And to plead for the stallion...

"Back here." Daniel indicated another room with a monitor. "Let's keep it down."

She stepped closer, realizing that they were going to remotely watch the birth. A beautiful roan, belly massive, paced in a straw-filled box. Off camera, Megan could hear the soft clearing of a throat. Was someone in the stall with the mare? Daniel indicated for her to take the only chair.

"Kinda late in the day for her to foal." Gerard spoke in low tones to her uncle.

"Sheba prefers late morning. Always has."

The mare continued to pace, stiff-legged. Time stood still as they waited. Megan leaned one elbow on the table and rested her chin. Silence settled in the room. The swish of the mare's hooves in the straw was the only sound.

"Must be a big foal." A tinge of anxiety rippled through Daniel's tone as he spoke to no one in particular.

After a while, Gerard coughed. "I called the vet. If all goes well, Sam'll check on Sheba and the foal in a couple days."

"Sounds good." Daniel didn't take his eyes off the monitor.

"Since Blade's with her, I got other work to do." He wandered out of the building.

Blade? Megan assumed that was the man she'd heard inside the stall with the horse. She glanced around, wondering what had happened to Crawford. He was leaning against the back wall. When their eyes met, he grinned and nodded. Megan's head snapped back toward the monitor, mortified that he caught her looking for him.

Another quarter of an hour ticked by. The mare finally pawed at the ground, then lay down. Daniel glanced at Megan, indicating the time had come.

The horse strained, pushing out a little hoof. It went back in as soon as she relaxed. The man named Blade whispered at the mare, perhaps words of encouragement. Finally, a low grunt, one of sheer willpower and pain, rumbled in her throat. The hoof gave way to an impossibly long leg. A lolling tongue and nostrils followed, then the other leg, bent back. A narrow muzzle, then ears made their appearance. Still in the birth canal, the foal shook its head. The mare strained.

"Come on, Sheba." Daniel leaned forward, gripping the table's edge. "Come on, old girl."

With a rush of amniotic fluid and a shriek from the mare, the foal slid out, still partially covered by a white sac. The baby snorted and puffed as it took its first full breaths. The mare scrambled to her feet.

"Looks like a filly." Relief rippled through Daniel's voice.

Megan was wholly consumed by the sight of the mare nickering softly as she licked the stunned-looking baby. The foal shook her head and blew fluid from her nostrils, appearing bewildered by the new world.

"Quite a sight, wouldn't you say?" Crawford's voice fell softly on her ear.

With a start, she realized that he'd come up behind her. His hand leaned against the top of her chair.

"Yeah, nice." She managed to answer coolly as she concentrated on the monitor. With him standing so closely, his warmth emanated toward her. The edge of the table pressed into her ribcage as she scooted away.

"I've seen countless births, but never tire of seeing another." Crawford seemed oblivious to her discomfort.

"I'll bet you'll have a dozen kids." Daniel glanced upward. "And watch all of them come into the world. That is, if you ever marry."

"I wouldn't say that was out of the realm of possibility." His gaze flickered to Megan.

She rolled her eyes and turned away.

The foal recaptured everyone's attention as she

tried to stand. Her too-long legs wouldn't cooperate, buckling at crucial moments.

"Oh." Megan couldn't help her soft cry when the foal fell on her face. The mare didn't help as she aggressively licked her baby.

"Want a closer look?" Daniel smiled at her.

"I'd love it." If it would get her away from Crawford's attentions, the trip would be worth it.

"Go on, Jack. Escort her down. I'll watch from here."

She stifled her sigh.

Crawford pulled her chair back as she rose. "This way."

Down a narrow corridor they went, past a few stalls until they reached the one where Sheba was. Megan leaned on the metal bars to get a better look. How many minutes passed, she couldn't have said as she stared in wonder. The now-standing foal had legs that were almost as long as her mother's. Their roan coats matched perfectly though the foal's was still wet. The baby moved stiff-legged toward the mare.

"How do they know?" Megan asked softly, awed by the foal's assurance that she was going in the right direction to nurse.

"Magic or..." Crawford's voice was soft, again too close. "To tell you the truth, Blade helps. He spends half the pregnancy instructing the unborn foal. Obviously, he taught her well, because she got it right."

"You teasing a city gal, Mr. Crawford?"

"No, it's a fact." The foreman's face appeared innocent.

The man inside the stall laughed as he patted the mare's neck. Megan blew out her breath in exasperation.

"Blade, this is Miz Gillespie. You didn't get a chance to meet her yet."

"How do." The man touched the air by his forehead as though saluting, or trying to tap the brim of a hat that wasn't there.

"You did a fine job with the mare, Mr. Blade."

"Just Blade, ma'am."

Crawford rested his boot on a lower rung. "He's had that nickname so long he doesn't remember his real name."

A look passed between the two men.

Blade spoke. "I hate to shoo you away, but mother and baby need some time alone now."

"Thanks for letting me in on the miracle." Megan smiled, even including Crawford in her look of thanks.

They headed back toward the monitor room. Daniel waited for them there.

"You haven't named the foal yet, Mr. O'Connor."

Daniel pursed his lips, then nodded toward Megan. "Why don't you name her?"

"Me?" She shook her head as she looked at the newborn on the monitor. "My mind's a blank."

"Come on. You can figure out something." Her uncle smiled encouragement.

Chewing her lower lip, she thought of and discarded a dozen names. They were either dumb or probably already taken by another horse. Spreading her hands, she again demurred. "I really can't think of anything right now."

"If she belonged to you, could you?"

She gaped. "You mean it? You'd give her to me?"

Daniel laughed. "Why not?"

"But...she has to be valuable. Even I can tell that both come from good bloodlines. I couldn't possibly–"

"Well, I won't insist on an answer now." Her uncle held up his hand. "Think about it. Tell me tomorrow. Or sometime in the next week."

Megan gripped the back of the chair. There was much more to this than was being said. If she accepted the gift, they'd expect her to stay around and help raise the foal. That meant she'd commit to two years. At least.

"Of course, I would offer my services when you set out to train her." Crawford tipped his hat back with his thumb. "That is, if you decide to accept the foal."

Oh, is that how it was?

"I'm sure the two of you together could handle it,

Meggie."

She glanced between the two men. Were they setting her up? She cooled her tone. "I'll have to weigh all my options."

"Can't ask for more'n that." Daniel pushed his wheelchair out of the building.

Megan followed with Crawford who fell into step beside her once they reach the open space. The sound of a muted whinny made her pause. She looked toward the barn. Was that the stallion?

The foreman cleared his throat. "I was wondering, Megan, if you'd consider taking a tour of the ranch with me."

She raised her brows. "In your truck or by horse?"

He grinned. "By horse. No other way to see the land."

Was he picking on her again? "You sure a city girl could handle it?"

His gray-blue eyes deepened as he studied her. "That remains to be seen."

Now what did that mean? Demurring seemed to be the best response. "It's been too many years for me to take an extensive ride–"

"Just a couple hours. We'll stop and take a break halfway." Crawford looked toward her uncle who was a few feet in front of them. "That is, if Mr. O'Connor can do without me tomorrow."

Tomorrow? He doesn't waste time.

"Oh, sure, sure." Daniel waved his acknowledgement. "I'd like Megan to see the land. You're obviously the one to show her around."

Great. He effectively wiped out any protest she could think up.

"Tomorrow, then. Eight o'clock?" Crawford tilted his head to look in her face as they continued to walk toward the house.

"I guess." Maybe a hurricane would hit before then and get her out of the commitment.

"Don't sound so overjoyed." His dry tone could blister skin.

"I'm not protesting the tour." She managed to

sweeten the lie. "Merely the early hour. I'm not a morning person."

"You might need to adjust some things in your life," Crawford said smoothly.

Megan narrowed her eyes. She was not going to play the flirting game. "How's the rogue coming along?"

The foreman frowned. "Fine. Why do you ask?"

"I heard him last night. Just wondering how the taming is progressing."

"According to Kit, as well as can be expected. No telling how long he ran wild."

"The horse or the man?"

Crawford grinned. They reached the porch.

"What do you mean by *ran* wild?" she asked. "Wasn't he born a mustang?"

Her uncle answered. "No, the stallion's not feral. We figure somewhere along the line, he escaped from somewhere. Before anyone branded him."

She stopped when her uncle swiveled his chair around to face her. "So, he doesn't belong to anyone?"

"Well, to me now," Daniel said. "If I decide to keep him, we'll brand him with the Double O."

"I see." The thought of a hot iron, searing the stallion's flesh, made her stomach clench. "Not feral. I wonder where he came from."

"Nowhere around here, that's for certain." Crawford leaned against the railing. "I've been checking up on him for months now, ever since we spotted him. No one's seen him before. It's like he came outta nowhere."

"But long enough to steal mares." Daniel's jaw stuck out. "My best blood."

Megan studied her uncle. How many? Enough to financially hurt the Double O? "What are the chances of recapturing the horses?"

"Slim." Crawford's arm swept the horizon. "This is a big country."

"I sometimes wonder, Jack, if someone used him like a Judas horse."

"What's that?" She had never before heard the term.

The foreman answered. "One trained to lure away horses."

"And then the thief took my mares and sold them."

Megan bit her lip at her uncle's hard tone.

"We've never seen any on the market." Crawford's voice soothed. "They're bound to show up."

Daniel threw him a sidelong glance that said it all. *Doubtful.* "Well maybe someday this stallion will sire me some beauts."

"If Kit can tame him." Crawford looked at Megan. "Otherwise, Blade'll do his job when the time comes."

Blade. The name suddenly struck her.

Megan looked at Crawford, her eyes widening. "Blade? You mean he's...?"

"That's right. Blade's our castrator."

"So, please give my niece your best Wyoming welcome." Daniel barely finished his speech before the room broke out in wild cheering.

Megan's cheeks grew warm as the prolonged whooping from twenty-odd men went on and on. "Thank you. Thank you." She stopped. No one could hear her over the din in the immense and crowded room.

Her uncle held up his hands. "And again, congratulations to all of you in capturing the rogue. Thanks to Jack for his well-thought and executed plan."

Another round of cheering echoed in the room while the foreman nodded modestly. The noise finally died down when dinner showed up. Mrs. Danvers, Randy and Simone served platters of food. The men dove into their meal, obviously ravenous from a busy day of work. And, as Megan had already discovered, the food was excellent.

She sat by her uncle, across from the foreman this time. Next to him was a Native American cowhand, introduced as "Trapper." No other name given. Several times, she noticed how he cast surreptitious glances her way. Crawford, however, blatantly stared.

Blade sat on the foreman's other side. "How'd you like your first day on the ranch, Miz Gillespie?"

"Actually, I spent part of my childhood here."

"Ah, I didn't know."

"She was here before me," her uncle inserted. "Her parents worked the ranch. I was the latecomer. Megan's mother was the brains of the outfit. She asked me to move here and help when the ranch began to grow. In work and profit. We had a nice operation going."

"So you know how to rope cattle and break horses?" Blade asked.

"Unfortunately no." Megan twirled her fork between her fingers. "Mom insisted I first get my 'book learning,' as she called it. I spent more time indoors than out."

Crawford grinned. "I could tell when I picked you up in town yesterday."

"Oh? And how's that, Mr. Crawford?" Megan didn't bother to hide her annoyance at his know-it-all tone.

"The way you were staring off into the distance. Like you'd never seen a small town before. Or dirt."

"I wasn't staring into the distance." Several sets of eyes fixed on her. She had to explain. Otherwise they'd believe Crawford and think she was an ignorant city girl. "I saw a calf. Standing in the middle of the road one minute. Then it was gone the next."

"A calf?" Blade's eyebrows rose.

Crawford made a sound of derision. "Probably someone's dog." He spoke under his breath.

"It was a calf. A buffalo calf." Megan glared at the men who looked like they were about to have a good laugh at the expense of the City Gal. "And it was white. Pure white." She raised her voice. "I swear I saw it. A white buffalo calf was standing at the edge of town one minute, then disappeared into that dust storm the next."

Around them, several of the men grew quiet.

Crawford tilted his head. "What dust storm?"

"The one that hit just before you came up to me.

You had to have seen it."

He made a face. "No. I walked up from the bar. Yesterday was sunny and calm."

She opened her mouth to object, and then closed it when her uncle patted her arm. "It was a little windy yesterday."

She was going to say more, then decided she should probably shut her mouth. Blade was busy attacking his food, barely hiding a grin. Crawford looked at her like she'd lost her mind. A couple of the other men wore amused smiles.

Megan clenched her napkin, knowing she'd make matters worse if she kept protesting. No one would believe her. Hand shaking, she grabbed her glass. As she swallowed the iced tea, she realized she was wrong. One person apparently believed her. Trapper, the Native American.

Meal forgotten, he stared, mouth half open. Then he lowered his gaze, face again impassive. For whatever reason, he didn't think she was crazy. Or a stupid city girl.

But why him and no one else?

CHAPTER 7

That night, Megan didn't bother to undress for bed. A few minutes after midnight, she headed out to the stallion. Her heart was hammering by the time she arrived at the barn. All evening, she'd been able to think of nothing but the horse. She'd not been able to put the thought of him out of her mind.

Blade. The castrator.

They couldn't do that. Not to the proud stallion.

He was in the same stall, abandoned in the corner. Forgotten. When she saw him, she sucked in a long, slow breath. The horse was standing, but hobbled so he couldn't move. Head hanging low, he still wore a blindfold.

She called softly to him. "Hey, boy."

He shrilled his anger, yet she could tell he'd grown weaker. His cry was nothing like the blood scream of the first evening. He jerked on the ropes, trying to toss his head, but that effort too was limited.

"It's me. Remember? Don't be afraid. I won't hurt you."

She moved a little closer, confident she was in no danger.

The horse attempted to paw the ground but was hampered by the hobbles. Megan stood watching awhile, wishing she could do something to befriend him. Then she realized there was no hay in the stall. She glanced around. No water either.

"They're letting you starve?" Disbelief battered her. "Those–those jerks! I can't believe they'd..." She wheeled. A dented dish lay discarded in a corner. Surely there was water around here somewhere. The process took some time, but she finally located a faucet. She filled the container, and then took it to the horse's stall.

Water leaked out, dripping onto her shirt and jeans. She maneuvered her fingers to block the small holes.

"There's a boy. I brought you something to drink. Easy, boy. Easy." She walked more slowly as she approached the stall, easing the gate open with one elbow. "Smell the water? Don't kill me or anything. I'm trying to help. Drink all you want. I won't tell that sadist."

The stallion's ear pricked forward as she moved cautiously. His nostrils flared, snuffing at the life-giving water. Megan inched closer.

"Easy, boy. I have what you need."

She got as close as she dared. The stallion didn't move. Megan scooted one foot forward, then the other, extending the dish.

"Come on, you've got to help too. Cut me a little slack."

The horse suddenly ducked his head toward the dish, making her jump. He sucked greedily at the water, taking long drinks until it was gone.

"Hang on." She edged away. "I'll get more."

She filled the dish and returned. Again, the stallion consumed all she offered. After the third trip, he drank more slowly, apparently satiated.

"Better?" She wished she could take the bandana off him. Unable to resist, she reached up carefully, her hand poised by his head. "You're so magnificent. I swear you're the most beautiful creature I've seen in my life."

She gingerly touched the soft cheek hairs. A tremor rippled through the stallion.

"That's a boy. We can be friends if you let me."

The water was gone, but the stallion remained immobile, allowing her to caress his cheek. She carefully stroked downward, getting lost in the sleekness of his neck. The hair was so soft. Muscles so warm.

"That's it." She kept her voice soothing. "Don't you feel better now? I promise I'll find you food next. I'll bring it every night. No one will know. We'll fool Gerard into thinking he's broken you."

The mention of the horse tamer seemed to enrage the stallion. He tossed his head suddenly, then sank his teeth into her upper arm. Pain shot through her body.

She cried out and staggered backwards, dropping the dish. The horse went berserk, screaming and thrashing. Someone was bound to investigate. She backed out, then spied the dish. *No.* It lay upside-down in the stall.

While the horse shrilled, she edged her foot toward the battered metal. The fourth try, she hooked a toe on the rim and drag the dish forward. Outside, footsteps thudded toward the barn. Arm still throbbing, Megan ducked into the tack room. She'd just shut the door when a bright light switched on in the main part of the barn.

"What in the...?" The irritated voice of one of the cowhands floated into the tack room where she crouched in the darkness.

"Sounds like he got bit by a blow fly," another said.

Blindly, Megan backed away and tripped. She landed on something hard, silently cursing. Whatever it was would probably leave a huge bruise on her thigh.

It'll match the one on my arm. Why had she trusted the stallion?

She shoved the dish under some heavy material, then rose. After feeling along the wall, she found her way out. Cracking open the door, she sighed. Soon she'd be home free.

"Stupid horse." Someone nearby spoke, making her freeze in her tracks. The heavy panel on the front of the barn slid along the tracks.

"Gerard should jes' shoot the bugger'n get it over with."

"He'd never do that. Got a reputation, after all."

"Huh."

From the sounds the two men made, Megan guessed they stood by the barn door. The light switched off, but the men seemed reluctant to head back to bed.

"Got a cigarette?"

"O'Connor doesn't like anyone smokin' in the barn."

"I'm not in the barn. Give me one, would ya."

Cellophane crackled, then the sound of a lighter being flicked. A long inhale followed.

"Hey, what do you think about his niece?"

A short barking laugh followed. "Too sassy for me."

"I didn't mean you and her, stupid. Didja see how Crawford looked at her? The guy's itching to get his paws on her."

"Ain't a woman in Silver Springs he hasn't been after."

He laughed.

Another cigarette was lit, making Megan grit her teeth in frustration. If she wasn't worried about someone discovering that she'd helped the stallion, she would've told those men to shut their mouths. That or marched past them and let them wonder how much she'd heard.

"Even Trapper seemed moonstruck or something by her."

"Are you kiddin'? That Injun ain't interested."

"I don't know. See the way he stared at her all evening? Freaked me out."

"Didn't you hear her talk about a buffalo calf? They're sacred to Indians."

One man made a sound of derision. "That's a buncha hocus-pocus. She probably made it up cuz O'Connor likes it. To get on his good side."

"He has a good side?"

They laughed.

Inside the barn the stallion settled down. The dogs came panting out of the darkness and nosed Megan. She tried to shoo them away, but they wouldn't leave. After she crossed her arms, they quit sticking their cool, wet noses against the palms of her hands and wandered off.

The men's voices came again.

"I heard Peterson's offering good wages."

"Yeah, I heard the same."

"Whatcha think?"

"You mean, cut outa here?"

"Yeah. While the cuttin's good."

"Come on, man. The Double O's been good to us. We can't up and leave."

"There're rumors. The ranch's in trouble."

"We're still gettin' a paycheck, ain't we? 'Sides, you think O'Connor would've brought his niece here if he was about to fold?"

"Yeah, but she's here for only a few months."

"I heard indefinitely."

What? Megan perked up her ears.

"I don't know. Maybe we should talk to Crawford."

The man snorted. "Are you kidding? He wouldn't tell us nothing. Anyhow, he's got his mind on other things."

His friend chuckled. "So true."

The one yawned noisily. "Come on. Let's hit the sack."

The two men moved away from the barn, but not

before Megan heard, "Crawford don't have his mind on other things. Jes' one."

"Then that makes two of us. Didja see her in them tight jeans? She's got a nice..." The words drifted away.

Megan smacked the doorframe with her palm. "All men are twelve-year-old boys!"

One thing was certain, she wasn't going to play into Jack Crawford's hands. If he touched her, just once, she'd give him a black eye. That wouldn't be all. He'd be limping for days, too. She'd not taken self-defense courses for nothing.

"They're not giving him food or water." Megan couldn't help raising her voice as she spoke to her uncle the next morning at breakfast. "That's beyond cruel."

"But if it's the only way to tame him, then it's gotta be done. I trust Kit, Megan. He's been the best–"

"It's not right." She hated being unable to control the sting in her eyes. "I know there's got to be other ways than his."

"I agree. However, I don't have the time or money to investigate other possibilities. Kit has worked for me for several years. He's always gotten the job done."

The bench upon which she sat scraped as she rose. Her half-finished breakfast felt as though it stuck in her throat, burning. Why was she so emotional? Perhaps it had to do with lack of sleep or the horrible nightmares that had plagued her when she had finally drifted off. All night, she'd heard the stallion's screams. She couldn't bear what they were doing to him.

Then her uncle had to bring up the topic of money. After what she'd heard last night, she felt torn in different directions.

Mrs. Danvers stood nearby, a worried frown on her face.

"Meggie, I'm sorry you're upset," Daniel finally said. "Ranch life is rough. That's all I can say. I'll try to insulate you from some of the brutal reality, but I can't promise anything."

She turned. "You don't need to. I'm just...it's just that I..." She stopped and shrugged. "I don't know why that stallion bothers me so much."

But even after she spoke, an inkling of understanding came to her.

She'd been trapped once. Ten months before, a job loss had forced her to ask her boyfriend for help. His solution? Move in with him, even though he knew she was adamantly opposed to that. When she'd steadfastly refused, he'd abandoned her. Megan had ended up going to her uncle for money.

The stallion personified that one very unhappy period in her life.

I'll never let that happen again. No man will control me. Ever.

She took a shaky breath as the outer door opened and Crawford stepped in. He glanced between the three of them, then looked more carefully at Megan.

She faced her uncle. "I need to go." She cleared her throat when the words came out raspy. "Ready Mr. Crawford?"

"Soon as I get our lunch from Celia."

Megan nodded to her uncle in farewell before exiting the house.

The foreman hurried after her, carrying bulging saddlebags. "Planning to go without me?"

Without responding, she slowed. Not until she could control her voice.

"Our horses are over there." With a tilt of his head, he indicated two that were tied at the corral. Both were saddled and bridled.

She pushed the unpleasantness of the morning from her mind. "Which one's mine?"

"You pick."

She glared at him, suspecting a prank. Crawford would've chosen a livelier mount for himself rather than the dud he'd probably saddled for her.

"I'm serious." He smiled without contrivance. "They're geldings, both great. Your choice."

She studied the horses which were nearly identical in size. "Come on. You obviously own your own saddle and would feel better using it."

He shrugged noncommittally.

Megan shook her head, then decided she'd figure out which was his. Both saddles were well kept, but one was obviously older. That one had to be Crawford's.

"I'll ride him." She pointed to the horse with the newer saddle.

"I'll help you mount."

"No, I got it." She squeezed between the two geldings, shoving her back against the one to give her more room.

She had an awkward moment when she tried to get her foot in the stirrup. The horse was taller than she'd anticipated. And her jeans a little too tight. She nearly fell over when she missed. The next time, she got her foot in the stirrup, but hopped awkwardly to keep her balance.

Crawford let out a noise that sounded suspiciously like stifled laughter. He slung the saddlebags over the other horse, then grabbed her stirrup and elbow. Megan was able to slide her foot in, then haul herself up by pulling on the saddle horn.

"There." His voice held a note of satisfaction. "Now if you give me a minute, I'll adjust the stirrups." He eyed the length. "I'd say up one notch. What'd'ya think?"

"Fine by me." Stirrup lengths weren't something she'd paid much attention to.

"Mind pulling out your foot?"

She obeyed while he raised the stirrup, then tucked the strap back under.

"There. Try that."

"Oh, *much* better." She spoke with mock relief after she slipped her foot into place.

He glanced up at her, his mouth pulling to one side. Then he headed to the other stirrup and adjusted it. Megan tested the length, rising a little in the seat. It was better.

Crawford remained by the horse, his hand resting on the saddle. "I filled us some canteens, but I'd caution you about gulping all the water too quickly."

"You implying you won't share?"

He grinned. "I didn't think you'd want to put your mouth anywhere mine'd been."

Heat scorched her cheeks. "Well, I'll make certain to ration my water."

"One more thing." He grabbed a hat that hung on the fence post.

"I don't need that. I put on sunscreen."

"It isn't enough to protect your head. I know this isn't great, but it'll do until you can get your own."

"Really, Mr. Crawford, I–"

"If you don't wear it, we're not going. Your uncle would kill me if I brought you home slung over the saddle, unconscious from heat stroke."

She glared at him. The last thing she wanted to do was put on that dusty piece of felt. However, she realized that a hired hand stood by a building, watching. She also became aware of Crawford's hand, still on the saddle. For all the worker knew, the foreman rested it on her leg.

Megan snatched the hat from him. "Now can we go?"

"Put it on."

She jammed it onto her head. "There."

"Good girl."

She would have liked to take the smirk off his face. Crawford undid the leads from the fence then handed her the reins.

"Which way?" She kept her question innocent. The minute he told her, she'd leave him in the dust. That'd teach him to quit treating her like she was in second grade.

"There. Gate's already open." He pointed to the fence, which led to a huge range. Before he mounted his horse, she steered hers to bump into his. Crawford lost his balance and stepped backward.

"Last one through the fence is a rotten egg." She kicked her horse, thundering out of the yard.

CHAPTER 8

"Hey! You don't have to wear out the horses to prove a point." The foreman finally caught up, holding his mount to a loping canter. They'd already been riding about a half hour by her watch.

"Worked, didn't it? You were treating me like a school girl who'd only seen horses in picture books."

"And you were acting like the boss' spoiled kid."

"Huh." She said it with as much derision as she could manage.

"I didn't know you could ride so well. Was that all put-on back there?"

"Not all." She lifted her chin, refusing to tell him which part. "Besides, you never asked."

"You did a good job putting me in my place."

She glanced at him. Was he mocking her?

His eyes glittered. "I wonder what other surprises you have in store for me."

Megan immediately sobered, recalling the conversation between the two men in the middle of the night.

"What was that look for?" he asked.

"Nothing."

"Didn't your mother ever teach you not to lie?"

"I wasn't raised by my mother."

"By age nine, you should already know better."

She stuck out her chin, looking straight ahead. How much more did Crawford know about her?

"Oh, I get it. As soon as a man gets friendly with you, you turn into an icicle."

"That's not it at all."

"There you go. Lying again."

"Mr. Crawford, if you continue to accuse me of prevaricating, I'll turn this horse around and head back."

"No you won't, because you don't know exactly which way's the ranch."

She glanced over her shoulder, realizing what he'd said was true. The buildings had disappeared behind one of many hills. She slowed her horse to a walk, Crawford following suit. *Fine, I'll call Uncle Daniel.* Megan took out her cell. Unfortunately, the phone showed no service. Again.

"That's more reasonable." His tone was maddeningly calm. "Now, explain to me why you turn into a class-A witch whenever I try to be friendly."

"Friendly? I'd say that word's a little weak."

"Okay. Very friendly. You frigid or something?"

She glared at him. "That's none of your business."

He leaned back in his saddle and poked his hat brim up with his thumb. "Got tired of those wimpy city boys? Came out west to find a real man."

"Maybe. But I'm still looking."

He burst into laughter, the first genuine one she'd heard. She kept her face serenely neutral as she stared straight ahead.

Crawford leaned toward her. "If you're really looking, and I mean really, you could give me a chance. I might surprise you."

She took some lip balm out of her pocket and spread it across her lips. "Is that the line you use with every woman? Well, it won't work with me." She snapped the cap on and shoved the tube back into her pocket.

Crawford grabbed her reins. "What will work, Megan?"

The question hung between them.

She spoke slowly. Deliberately. "Mr. Crawford, you may never know."

"May? Then there's a chance."

"Like snow in the Caribbean."

He surprised her by grinning. "Well, now that we got the air cleared, we can enjoy a nice day." With that, he released the reins and nudged his horse to a walk.

At a loss to figure the guy out, Megan followed. Then she understood. He'd not given up. He was merely biding his time. But for the moment, she'd enjoy the promised respite.

Crawford pointed out some interesting features of the landscape–like good hiding places for antelope and rattlers. Mustangs had been found up between those hills, a man had been mysteriously shot over there a couple years before, and once they'd chased off some squatters down that-away. Megan squinted at the places he pointed out, seeing little variation in the landscape. Everything looked nearly identical, the only difference being the altitude.

"How do you find your way around here?"

He shrugged. "How do you find your way around a big city?"

"Street signs. Obviously. There's no comparison."

"Sure there is. Dozens of signs are all over. You gotta know how to look for them."

She pressed her lips together, still not convinced.

"For example." He pointed upward. "The sun's position. The odd shape of that hill over there. The huge boulder at eleven o'clock. See?"

"I think I'll buy myself a compass."

He smirked.

"Well, if it was good enough for Gregory Peck in *The Big Country* it should be good enough for me."

"Oh. A movie."

"Yes, a movie."

He shook his head. "I suppose you're expecting a band of Indians to come over the hill at any moment. And I'll sling out my six-shooter and protect you."

"Well, first of all, they're called 'Native Americans' and second, the term is rifle or pistol."

He snorted. "White people call them that. They call themselves Indians."

"Whatever."

"How about my protecting you?"

"I can take care of myself."

He gave her the once-over. "I'll bet you can." Then he added quickly, "I only meant that as a compliment, in case you're wondering."

"I wasn't."

They rode in silence for a few minutes, and then she asked, "How far are we going?"

His blue-gray eyes grew speculative. "That's entirely up to you."

She didn't understand. "I mean, how far are we going to ride?"

"I knew what you meant. What did you think I was saying?"

"Nothing." She kicked her horse into a trot.

Crawford's mount matched her speed. "You get any more black marks on your soul from lying, your hair'll darken."

"Thanks for the warning." She wanted to say something about her hair wouldn't look like glowing coals any longer, but didn't. He'd only see it as an invitation to keep flirting.

They stopped a little while later for lunch, Megan's stomach already growling. She should've eaten more breakfast.

Crawford found a somewhat shady spot under a

scraggly, wind-blown tree. He dropped his horse's reins, and then pulled the saddlebags off while Megan got down stiffly from her mount. She straightened, surprised at the uncomfortable tingle in her backside and hips.

"Here's your rock." He pointed. "And there's mine."

She lowered herself to the hard surface. "What a great spot for a romantic picnic." As soon as she said it, she was sorry.

Crawford pushed back the flap of the saddlebag, and then looked at her, one eyebrow raised. "Didn't realize you were expecting 'romantic.' I'd've brought my truck."

She let out a hiss of irritation, both at him and herself. She'd walked right into that one.

He grinned. "Don't believe a truck can be romantic? Why do you think they call the back of it a bed?"

"You know," she said, turning to face him, "I don't know why men can't be satisfied with friendship. I am not interested in anything beyond that. So get it through your fat, egotistical head, will you?"

She swiveled away, propping her arms on her knees and staring down the slope to where the horses were grazing. Crawford didn't say anything for a moment, busy with taking their lunch from the saddlebags. Good. She'd shut him up for once.

"So, who was the guy in Florida who treated you like dirt?"

"I don't know what you're talking about." *Yeah, you do.* Megan's cell phone showed that Garrick had called. Five times already.

I'm never talking to him again.

"Let me guess." Crawford held up one finger as though thinking. "He lost his job. Or his old girlfriend showed up so he dumped you. Oh, I know. You poured your life into him but when the first crisis came, he wimped out."

The foreman was dangerously close to the truth.

"What did Mrs. Danvers send for lunch?" She pretended to study the things he unpacked.

He said nothing, but merely handed her a sandwich and an apple.

"Thanks." Megan slid the roast beef sandwich out of the plastic bag and bit into it.

They ate in silence for a while, until she began to glance around for something to drink.

"I'll get the canteens." Crawford guessed correctly what she was looking for. He brought both back.

Megan took a couple grateful gulps, and then remembered she needed to save enough water for the return ride. She bit into the apple, enjoying the sweet crunchiness.

"Want a few chips? They're a little crushed, but not bad."

"Sure." She took some.

He studied her face. "Bring more sunscreen? You look a little burned."

She pressed the back of her hand to one hot cheek. "That's inevitable. But no, I didn't."

"At least you'll get burned evenly. When we head back, the sun will get your other side."

She shrugged. "One of the hazards of having a redheaded complexion."

He crushed the empty bag in his hand, then shoved it into the saddlebag. "Listen, I didn't mean to be insensitive earlier."

"Just flirtatious."

"Yeah, well...I thought you enjoyed the banter."

She held her tongue. Banter sometimes contained a thread of truth.

"Tell you what." Crawford cleared his throat. "I'll quit the remarks if you do."

"What?" The word popped out of her mouth.

"You heard me. I'll quit flirting if you do."

"I've never–"

"Yes, you have. Like some of the suggestive comments you make. And the way you roll your eyes at me, and show off your camisole. It's hard on a man."

"You–! I–!" Megan rose. "I'm not leading you on, so get that straight right now."

"All right." Crawford spread his hands and rose. "I'll admit you may not be doing it consciously, but you are doing it."

"Oh, for Pete's sake."

"So, you'd better get it over with."

"What?"

"Slap me. The boys are expecting one of two things. Either I return with a grin, in which case they're going to figure we fooled around, or I have a hand print on my face."

She gaped. "You're out of your mind."

"Nope." He took his hat off. Leaning forward, he pointed to his cheek. "Right here. Pop me a good one."

"No."

"If you don't, your reputation'll be ruined. Mine, of course, will only be enhanced. Making out with the boss' niece after only three days. It'll be good."

"You...you jerk!"

He shrugged. "I'm only trying to protect you."

"I don't go around slapping men."

Crawford grinned. "You should. Startin' with that last boyfriend of yours."

Megan made a sound of irritation.

"C'mon. Do it. I guarantee it'll keep you outa trouble in the future."

"I don't get myself into trouble." She crossed her arms. "I'm not going to do it."

He looked away for a moment, and then tossed his hat aside. "Okay. Remember, you asked for this."

With one step, he covered the distance between them and grabbed her. His lips barely grazed hers when she twisted in his hold. Before she could think, her knuckles made contact with his mouth. He yelped and abruptly released her.

She almost apologized, but then clamped her teeth together. He deserved it. However, she felt a twinge of mortification that she'd punched him. He'd asked for a slap but had gotten a whole lot more.

Crawford sucked on his already-swelling lip.

She again crossed her arms. "Can we go now?"

Without a word, he bent and swooped his hat off

the ground.

Not until they'd nearly reached the ranch did he speak. "Guess we both got a smack on the kisser. 'Cept mine was a little different than I'd anticipated."

"If *the boys* wonder what happened, I'm sure you'll make up a good story." Megan kicked her mount into a canter. Crawford's laugh floated behind her.

CHAPTER 9

That night, Megan smuggled out sugar cubes. She went through the same procedure as before, speaking softly until the stallion grew calm. His legs were still hobbled and he remained blindfolded. Kit Gerard had a deeper malicious streak than she'd first imagined.

She leaned on the gate. "I forgive you for biting me. Though I have a lovely bruise to remember that by. Wasn't very nice of you. But to show you that I don't hold a grudge, I brought a couple presents."

The stallion nickered as though in apology.

She gave him water. "I don't know why I don't feel silly talking to you. I haven't told anyone half the stuff I've shared with you already."

The horse seemed friendlier. Since her arrival, he

had not screamed once. Megan found a few cupfuls of oats, which he gobbled down.

"Good thing I finished up my project when I did. So I could come to Wyoming." She shuddered to think what would have happened to the stallion if she'd not been there. "I got laid off about ten months ago, so I've been doing some free-lance consulting to hold me over until I get my trust fund. It won't be a million dollars, but enough for me to pay for school. Best part is I won't ever have to beg my uncle for money again. Or ask a scummy boyfriend either."

She made a sound of disgust. "Hard to believe I once thought I loved him. Goes to show, men are always after something." Megan drew closer. "Ready for your gift? You have to take it out of my hand. And if you bite me, I won't give you any more. Understand?"

She took a deep breath then held out one sugar cube on her palm.

The stallion snuffed it from a distance, drawing back when she drew closer.

"Come on. You must've had sugar before. It's sweet. Generally liked." Inching forward, she extended her arm. Fingers tight, Megan flattened her hand.

The stallion finally grabbed the sugar, crunching it between strong teeth. She waited until he finished. "Good? Want another?"

This time, he seemed more willing to let her approach him. He gobbled down the second, then third. As he ate, she touched him again.

"Don't be afraid." She kept her caress feather-light. "I won't hurt you." She avoided the bandana over his eyes and gently stroked his cheek. "See?" She spoke in her softest voice. "That doesn't hurt, does it?"

Flesh quivering, the stallion stood stiffly immobile, allowing Megan's caresses. She carefully reached to his neck, enthralled by the sleek skin. A low rumble in his chest warned her that he grew nervous.

She stepped back.

"There. That's enough for you to think about until tomorrow night."

She slowly edged away then stepped through the gate. The stallion's nicker made her smile. They were definitely making progress.

Megan dreamed she was running across the hills. Her hair blew as she moved effortlessly over the stubble of brush. As the ground flew under her feet, the wind whipped around her body, cooling her. She laughed at the sheer joy.

Then she realized something odd. She had four legs instead of two. *I'm a horse.* The euphoria of movement quickly outweighed the oddity. She heard herself laughing…a very human laugh. Her hooves ate up the ground.

I'm not alone.

A horse materialized out of the tall mountains, sleek and black. Her stallion. A living shadow against the billowing whiteness of the dream landscape. He thundered toward her, then ran by her side. At first Megan stumbled, finding it difficult to keep up, but the stallion adjusted his stride to match hers.

She stopped when the stallion rushed into her path.

"I have to go," she said to him. "Let me by."

He didn't speak, blocking her when she tried to pass.

"Please. Please, let me go. I have to leave."

Looking down, Megan realized she was again human.

The horse had disappeared. She was alone.

She sat up in bed, crying. Out of control emotions gripped her, feelings she didn't understand. Still gasping from the tears, she arose, fumbling for the box of tissue on the end table. Perched once more on the bed, she sobbed into the delicate paper.

I've not felt such pain since…

Her mind skittered away from the thought. No, she couldn't bear to think about it. Not now.

Bright light streamed into her room. Almost ten already? A cool shower eradicated all evidence of tears. Then she took her time dressing and applying cosmetics.

When she reached the kitchen, no one was around. She helped herself to some toast, homemade jam and strong black coffee that she doused with cream. When she took her meal to the table, she gasped at the silent figure seated there. Simone.

"Finally up." The girl smirked. "I thought you'd stay in bed all day."

Megan sat down. "I've never stayed in bed all day, even when sick."

"Congratulations."

Why so hostile? She glanced at the young woman. "Why aren't you in school? Or something?"

Simone's eyes narrowed. "Trying to get rid of me?"

"No. Merely wondering why a girl your age is wasting your life on a ranch."

"I could ask you the same thing."

She took a sip of her coffee. "I finished school, landed a couple jobs and now do some free-lance consulting. What's your excuse?"

"I like it here. Don't see any reason to change anything."

Made sense. She had seen the way the young woman smiled and flirted with all the cowhands. Perhaps she felt threatened now that Megan was there?

"Have no fear, I don't plan to change anything either."

Simone's eyes narrowed. "What's that mean?"

"It means that in a couple months you'll have this place back to yourself again."

"Couple...?"

"Yeah. When I go home. To Florida."

Her mouth tightened. "That's not what I heard."

"Oh?" Megan raised her brows and merely waited.

"Aren't you here to stay?"

Why did people think that? First that one man by the barn and now Simone. Who was spreading rumors? And what did they know that she didn't?

Before answering, she spread more jam on her toast. "I have plans. They don't include spending my life in the middle of nowhere in Wyoming."

Simone made a face. "Oh. So this place isn't good enough for you."

"I didn't say that."

"Yeah, but you meant it." The young woman abruptly rose. "You come here, disrupt everyone's life then, when you get tired of this place, you'll clear out."

She opened her mouth to protest, but shut it. Whatever she said seemed to be used against her.

"That's what I thought." The girl whirled away, her dark hair flying. A door slammed in the distance. Silence returned to the house.

She sighed. Why was Simone acting the way she did? Jealousy? Megan wasn't interested in Jack Crawford or anyone else on the ranch. But the young woman might not believe her. Not after what had happened yesterday. More than once, Megan had caught her wary look at Crawford's swollen lip. Wasn't that proof enough?

After Megan finished her meal, she wandered out to the stables to look at the foal. She'd still not come up with a name, not even certain she should accept a gift with so many strings attached. Blade was inside the stall, checking over the pair.

"Oh, I'm sorry." She held up her hand in apology. "I'll come back later."

"No need. I'm almost finished here."

"Mind if I watch?"

He shook his head.

He wasn't as good-looking as Crawford, but almost as tall with an openness of face that she found appealing. His brown eyes were widely spaced, giving him the appearance of boyishness. His hair was light brown, jaw long and lean. And his shoulders were incredibly broad, almost too broad for his height.

"How is she doing?" Megan pointed to the foal.

"Great. Gaining weight. Getting friskier. The vet will check her out this afternoon to make sure, but I'm betting Sam'll give this little girl a clean bill o'health."

As he spoke, the foal whinnied and tried to wriggle from his hold. The mare nickered calmly.

"Is she as valuable as I think?"

Blade nodded. "Your uncle paid dearly for the mare, and I'm guessing as dearly again for the stud service. This filly is the beginning of winners."

"Race horses?"

"No. Cow ponies. The kind that is intelligent, loyal, quick. The type we need around here."

"I see." Megan leaned on the top rung.

"You can come in if you want."

"Really? The mare won't freak out?"

"No. She's smart. Move slowly so you don't frighten the foal."

How well she already knew about quick movements. Megan opened the gate and stepped through.

"Watch the pile." Blade pointed at her feet.

She smiled and stepped over the manure.

He held onto the filly though she tried to pull away. "Go ahead, pet her. The more she's handled, the better. That's it. Over her body, down her legs. If you breathe in her nostrils, she'll never forget you."

Megan felt silly blowing air at the foal, but did as he directed. The baby calmed down after a moment, not as anxious to get away.

"See? It's working already."

She caressed the fuzzy hair for a few minutes longer. "Blade, can I ask you something? If this method works on foals, why doesn't it work on older horses?"

"Oh, it can. Just takes patience. That's the biggest factor. There're other methods out there, too."

"So it'd work, right?"

He nodded.

"What if I asked my uncle about your working with the stallion?"

"Whoa, now. Hold it. First off, that's not my job

and second–"

"I know it's not your job. But what if it *could* be yours?"

He looked like he thought about it, but then shook his head. "Kit'd be madder than...well, he wouldn't like it. Probably figured I was buttin' in on his territory. He's pretty temperamental."

She let out a frustrated breath. "So, you're saying no?"

"O'Connor's not stupid. And he won't insult Kit. I'm betting your uncle wouldn't agree."

The foal had grown tired of the attention, whinnying to her mother. Blade released her and she promptly went to nurse.

Megan chuckled. "She's developed quite a hunger."

"All foals do. And calves."

A clanging in the distance caught their attention.

"Speaking of hungry..." Blade said. "Lunch bell. We'd better go if we want any."

"I just ate breakfast. If you don't mind, I'll stay here a while."

"Okay by me." He slipped out of the gate, and then raised his hand in salute as he exited.

Megan turned back to the mare and foal, mind churning.

It was worth the ask, despite her conversation with Blade. Her uncle might say no. But she had to try. Megan couldn't let the situation with the stallion go on too much longer. Someone was bound to notice that he wasn't weakening. Gerard would probably figure it out. Then she'd be forced to admit that she'd been interfering.

Best to take the offensive.

CHAPTER 10

"Absolutely not." Daniel hadn't even given her a chance to explain. He cut her off before she told him her idea.

Megan thought she'd chosen a good time. It was midafternoon. No one was about. Her uncle had been working in his study.

"Wouldn't you at least–?"

"No. Megan we've been through this already."

"Not this exactly."

He let out an impatient breath. "Kit's methods are good enough. Now that he's started, I don't want to switch."

"But–"

"I'd appreciate your dropping this matter." Daniel's

red brows collided above his nose.

"Why are you treating me like I'm eight or something? I'm not a kid."

"If you're acting like one, then I should."

"Why won't you listen...?" Megan fought with herself about saying more. If her uncle intended to send her back to Florida early, he was doing a good job of it.

Should she threaten him with that? No. She'd agreed to three months. But once that was up...

I am so out of here. And once my promise is fulfilled, I'm never coming back. She wheeled and left the study.

Simone was leaning against the wall opposite the room. When she saw Megan, she slowly straightened, a satisfied smirk on her face.

"I have to get out of here." Megan clenched her teeth as she stared out the kitchen window. "If I don't, I'll claw somebody's eyes out."

Everyone was against her. Everyone had an agenda. She could neither confide in nor trust anyone. Blade and a woman walked across the yard, heading for a white pickup.

In a flash, Megan made up her mind. She ran upstairs and grabbed some cash and a credit card out of her wallet, then her cell phone, even though she couldn't count on the intermittent service. She ran back down.

The woman was still in the yard, packing some things into the back of the truck. Blade had gone.

"Hi." Megan drew close.

She straightened. Her jaw-length blond hair had a wide streak of white in it. And her eyes had deep crow's feet, pale next to a tanned face. Not as young as Megan had first imagined.

The woman nodded. "Hello."

"You waiting for the vet?"

A slow smile creased her face. "I am the vet."

"Oh, sorry." Megan crammed her hands in her

pockets. "I thought they said the vet's name was Sam."

"M'name is Sam. Short for Samantha."

"That explains it." Megan laughed. "You heading into Silver Springs by chance?"

"Eventually. After one quick stop."

"Mind giving me a ride?"

The vet raised her brows as she glanced at the house, then back at her. "Nope. Hop in."

"Thanks." Megan climbed into the cab and waited.

The vet soon got in and started the truck. They drove out of the yard in a billow of dust. As far as Megan knew, no one had seen her leave. *Good. If they're going to treat me like a child, then I might as well act like one.*

"By the way, I'm Megan Gillespie."

"I could tell you were related to Daniel." She smiled, and then extended a well-worked hand. "Sam Farrell."

Megan shook her hand. "You mean Doctor, don't you?"

"Yeah, but I don't stand on ceremony. Not out here. I prefer names."

"Are you from the Silver Springs area?"

"Montana. But close enough." She slid her fingers around the curve of the steering wheel. "So, tell me. What ticked you off enough to make you run away from the Double O?"

Megan didn't answer, staring out the windshield.

"Hey, it's not my never-mind, but I was only wondering how far you're going to run."

"Just to town for now."

"Oh." Sam spoke knowingly. Her thin lips pulled to one side.

She was pretty in a homey sort of way, made rugged by the hard job and tough weather. But her face was open and exuded caring. Like a mother.

"How long've you been the vet around here?"

"Five years. Still a newcomer."

"Then I'd never fit in."

"My take? Unless you're raised here, you're not part of this country. But give folks time. Eventually, they'll accept you for who you are. As long as you put away big-city airs."

"I don't have any airs."

Sam shot her a grin. "Didn't say you did. Just givin' some friendly advice."

"Well, I appreciate the advice. And ride."

"No trouble a-t'all. And if you need one back, let me know." She fished in the ashtray, keeping her eye on the road. "I've got a card around here somewhere. Don't need them much anymore, but I've never taken them out of the truck. Ah, here." She handed Megan a dog-eared business card. "Shows you how green I was when I first arrived. Had these cards made up. Waste of money. Word of mouth is better'n anything printed."

Megan stared at the fancy card. Printed above a phone number and address was *Doctor of Veterinarian Medicine.* She fingered the gold-embossed seal and heavy paper. "Impressive. Must've cost you a bundle." She tucked the card into her shirt pocket.

"Like I said, total waste. I should frame one. Remind me of my vanity."

"So, have you practiced other places?"

"Couple cities. Got a hankering for the country again. When it gets in your blood, nowhere else'll do."

Megan ran her hands across her knees to smooth her jeans. Had she ever longed for Wyoming in the years she'd been away? She wrestled with the answer.

Do you really prefer the traffic, muggy heat, endless rushing? An unnamed something tugged at her. What was it? A need for family? A need to belong? Independence, which had consumed her twenty-six years, fought to retain its place in her soul.

But the argument with her uncle cemented her resolve to remain detached. Her life and future were back in Florida.

"Where'd you grow up?" Sam asked.

"Jacksonville, Florida area. I was sent there when I was nine. Parents died. My uncle's sister-in-law and her husband raised me with their three kids."

Sam threw her a sympathetic look. "Bet that was difficult."

"Yeah. It was." Why did that still hurt so much?

The vet was silent a moment. "Then?"

"I went to school. Got a degree in finance. Landed a couple jobs at a few banks. When I got laid off last year, I started doing some consulting work on my own. Moved here. End of story."

"Moved here? Not visiting?"

She bit her lip at the blunder. "That's what I meant."

Sam threw her a quizzical glance. "Here's my turnoff. Shouldn't take long. A prized dog is having trouble whelping."

"Mind if I sit in the truck?"

"Yeah, I do mind. Besides, these folks will think you're putting on city airs if you don't stop in and say hello."

Megan grinned. "'K. Give me a sec. I'll be right in." Her cell vibrated in her pocket. Her uncle's number. She wasn't quite ready to talk to him. Before she turned off the phone, she texted, "I'm fine."

The stopover took longer than Sam indicated. However, Megan enjoyed herself more than she imagined. The pet was inside the kitchen, panting in one corner while the owners hovered. She had to smile at the huge man, face creased with worry and hands clenching.

After checking the birth canal, Sam gave the dog a shot. The first puppy arrived dead, its huge body the obvious reason why the dog couldn't whelp. She worked to resuscitate the newborn. After several moments, the pup snuffed, then grunted his displeasure at being away from his mother. Megan blew out a breath of relief. When both owners and Sam echoed her sigh, she had to chuckle. Who knew they all had been holding their breaths? While they waited, puppies began to appear at regular intervals, the owners visibly relaxing each time their Bessie pushed out another mewling pup.

Sam stayed until all of them were born. They drank cups of coffee and chatted about a rodeo they'd seen a few weeks back. After a couple hours, Megan and the vet were on their way, waving to the couple, both wearing smiles.

"That was a satisfying job." A huge grin split Sam's face. "The kind I like. Now, we can get to town."

They chatted about different parts of the country, then cities and weather. It wasn't long till the time flew by and they were driving down the main road of Silver Springs. The sun had set, casting the buildings in a more flattering light than Megan remembered from her first day.

"Sure you don't want to join me for supper?" Sam pulled over to the side of the road. "Wouldn't be any trouble."

"Maybe next time." Megan opened the door.

"Well, you have my card. My place is above the barber shop."

"Thanks again." She shut the door, and then waved as Sam drove away.

Where to? She walked down one side of the street, then up the other, peering into the small shops and stores as she went. Most of them were closed because of the hour, but they boasted of being able to fulfill all the needs of those in the area. A general store, barber shop, tack and feed store, a doctor's and dentist's office...she lost track of the rest of them.

Her stomach grumbled, reminding her that she'd not eaten since breakfast. The gallon or two of coffee made her feel hungrier. Where could she get a meal? Megan looked up and down the street. The hotel was down quite a ways at the edge of town. A bar was directly across the street. Maybe they'd have food. And entertainment?

The place was dark. Typical. Megan scanned the room, counting five patrons. A television clung precariously to the ceiling in one corner, showing old reruns. Booths lined three walls, the rectangular-shaped counter squatting in the middle. The bartender, a burly man, wiped the wooden countertop. He didn't even glance in her direction when she entered.

She sat on a stool, noticing the parquet dance floor

in one corner. There was no stage for a band. And no juke box.

"Hey." The bartender's gaze raked her, probably gathering all the information he needed.

"Hello. Could I get some supper?"

"All we have is sandwiches. Ham or beef with chips."

"Ham'd be great."

"Hey, Dolly," he bellowed over his shoulder. "Get me one ham plate."

A woman's face appeared in a square frame against the back wall. "You got it."

"Want a beer?" The bartender had already grabbed a glass and was prepared to pull one for her.

"No, thanks. Ice tea?"

His eyebrows rose. "Okay."

He slid the frosted glass and bottled tea toward her.

"What'll I owe you?"

He shook his head. "This's on the house."

"Thanks." Her cheeks grew warm. Obviously he knew she was new to the town. He also probably guessed she was related to Daniel O'Connor.

The bite of the icy brew slid its way to her stomach. Megan smacked her lips, the chilled taste reminding her of a hole-in-the-wall cafe in Jacksonville. She glanced at the label that boasted of being the strongest tea in the west. She sipped it, growing to like the tang more with each swallow.

"Here'ya are darlin." A faded middle-aged woman set a plate in front of her. "Enjoy."

"Thanks. This looks great."

A huge sandwich on thick slices of bread took up most of the plate. Nudged out by the bread, several potato chips floated to the counter. Megan took a bite of the slab of ham, her mouth going wild with the mustard, onions and salad peppers. Her eyes watered as the heat hit. She finished her tea, then got another.

The food settled comfortably in her stomach. She pushed the plate away, the sandwich mostly gone. The television blared the local news. A few more patrons had wandered into the bar, but no one had said more than a hello or given her a polite tip of their hat.

I need one of those. Megan liked the look. It dressed up the most weather-beaten face, adding grace to the wearer. She couldn't get over how many different styles and colors there were, the decorative band around some of them adding more variety. No two were alike. And the way a person handled one made him unique.

More than once, she'd seen a man take his off and run fingers along the brim, as though to reshape the hat before putting it back on. Crawford liked to tilt his back with a thumb. Blade took his off and slapped it against his thigh as though he couldn't tolerate a speck of dust. There was only one man she'd not seen wear one, the Native American who worked on her uncle's ranch. Trapper was the only exception.

The bartender wandered over, bringing another tea. They'd begun to chat when the bar door banged open. A young man stood on the threshold and whooped loud and long until he got the attention of everyone in the room.

"Wake up, everybody." He flung out his arms. "It's Friday night!"

CHAPTER 11

"What is this, Roy?" He bounded into the room. "A funeral parlor? Crank up the music. Get some life into this place."

From behind him, four men poured into the room.

The tawny-haired man slapped his hands on the countertop. "I'm drier'n a hollow rock on Mars. Hurry up, Roy."

"Hold your horses, I'm getting you a drink." The bartender slid a glass his way.

The newcomer grabbed the beer and drained it in a few gulps. When he slammed down the empty glass, his eyes lit on Megan. "Well, well, well, what have we here? You been holding out on me, Roy. How come you didn't tell me the prettiest gal in three states was in your bar tonight?” He sidled over, his gaze never leaving her.

Megan smiled at him as he slid onto the bar stool next to her.

“Be polite, Ben,” the bartender warned. “This is Daniel O’Connor’s niece.”

“I won’t hold it against her.” An impish light flashed in his eyes. “If she’ll let me have the first dance.”

Without waiting for her response, he grabbed Megan’s arm and hauled her toward the parquet floor. He started dancing, one hand holding hers, the other loosely around her waist.

The other patrons tittered, probably because no music was playing.

She laughed. “You’ve got a great sense of timing.”

“Hey, I’m fantastic. Everyone knows it. They even asked me to join *Dancing With the Stars*.” Then he yelled past her ear. “How ‘bout some music, Roy? You’re embarrassin’ me in front of the lady.”

A country tune skipped on, then off, and then back on again. Ben didn’t miss a beat, adjusting his timing to the music. He really was good. But when he started humming off key, Megan couldn’t resist her chuckle.

He pulled his head back to look in her eyes. “Don’t you like Garth Brooks?”

“Yes but, you sound nothing like him.”

“Well, shoot. Know anyone that gives voice lessons?”

“Sorry.” She shrugged. “I’m new to the area.”

“No kiddin’. Let me be the first to welcome you.”

“I’ve been here for almost a week already.”

“Really?” His eyebrows rose. “Then Crawford’s been hogging you all to himself.”

“Crawford’s been doing nothing with me.” She couldn’t keep the hard edge out of her voice.

Ben grinned. “Good.”

He finished one dance, and then continued with the second without pausing although the music stopped for nearly thirty-seconds. “How long’re you staying?”

"In the bar? Or at my uncle's ranch?"

"In Wyoming."

If the issue with the stallion wasn't resolved soon, she could be leaving Monday morning. "Don't know for sure."

"Then I'll have to give you a few reasons to hang around longer." He leaned a little closer. "Man, you smell good."

Megan giggled. A delicious sense of abandon crept over her. She was having more fun than she'd had in months.

Ben stiffened, glaring at the cowboy who interrupted them.

"My turn." A man tapped Ben's shoulder again. "If you don't mind."

"Yeah, I do. But I'll share." He graciously handed her off. This man wasn't interested in talk. Just dancing. By the time a fourth tune blared over the speakers, another man claimed his chance to be her partner.

The floor started to fill up and the room grew progressively smokier. Megan was aware of little besides the building heat on the dance floor and her partners, pulling her around like they were wrestling cattle. She loved the strong smells of horse and sweat and their ease, no matter what kind of dancer they were. Most of them didn't want to talk, merely dance.

She ended up with Ben again. Finally, she pulled away, claiming she had to visit the ladies' room. He gallantly escorted her and was waiting when she exited.

"How 'bout a beer?" He had to yell over the music and voices of the packed bar.

"Water for me."

They pushed their way to the counter. A seat opened up, and Ben steered her to the spot while he stood behind her, his belt buckle brushing her elbow. Water found its way into her hand. She noticed that he too had ordered the same.

"So, how'd a nice girl like you," Ben drawled in her ear, "end up related to O'Connor?"

"Lucky, I guess."

"Heard you were coming, but if you don't mind my saying, you're a lot prettier than him."

"Glad to hear it. Otherwise, I'd've called him to take my place."

"Oh, don't do that. Please." He leaned his hand against the bar.

"So, Ben, what do you do for a living?"

"Cow punch, what else? I'm foreman at the Lazy Z."

"I see." That would explain the mild hostility toward Crawford. "I always imagined foremen were older."

"I'm actually seventy-eight. But don't tell." He said it with a grin.

"Uh-huh. Wyoming sure is nice to people.'

"So am I." Ben smiled slowly, his gaze straying to her lips, then back to her eyes. "Why don't you give me a chance to show you how nice I can be? How about dinner and dancing? I'm tied up next Friday, but I'm free the week after."

"I'd like that."

"Six okay? I'll call if I'm gonna be late."

She set the half-empty glass on the bar. "Sounds great."

"Ready to dance?"

After she nodded, he took her arm as they wended their way through the crowd. As they danced, they were continually jostled. He didn't seem to mind. Talk was impossible, but she didn't care.

The song was coming to an end when he pulled back. "Not again." Someone was cutting in.

Megan laughed at the expression on his face. It died abruptly when she found herself looking into the hard face of Jack Crawford. He said nothing but glared at Ben, eyes unreadable in the dim light. The grim slash of his mouth and the line between his brows were neon signs of brooding anger.

Without saying a word to her dance partner, he grabbed her arm. "We're leaving."

"I'm not..." Her protest was drowned in the sudden

blare of the next song. He relentlessly pulled her through the room, then out the door. Several men sprang out of the way when they barreled their way through. She heard the surprised comments.

"What gives you the right–?"

"Shut up. Don't say anything at all."

She struggled to escape his grasp, but he was too strong.

He pulled her to his truck, then opened the driver side and shoved her in first. Before she could scoot all the way over, he'd started the truck and backed out with a squeal of tires. She banged her elbow against the back window as he slammed on the brakes, then whipped the vehicle into drive. They flew out of town.

"What do you think you're doing?" She clicked on her seatbelt.

"Protecting you from your own stupidity."

"Who asked you? You're not my bodyguard."

"Yes, I am. You were dancing with one of the biggest studs in this area."

"So?"

He glared at her. "I suppose you thought he'd give you a free ride home? What're you? Naive?"

"I was going to ride with the vet, Sam Farrell."

"She wasn't there."

"I know. I was going to call her when I was ready to go." Megan fumbled in her shirt pocket for the business card. Then her jeans. Where had it disappeared to?

Crawford frowned.

"I'm not lying. She offered me a ride."

"I doubt your *date* would've let you excuse yourself when you were ready to go. How many beers did you have? Three? Four?"

She blew out her breath in frustration, refusing to answer. "Did my uncle send you?"

"I spent the entire afternoon trying to track you down."

She rolled her eyes. "I texted my uncle."

"Yeah, I know. 'I'm fine'?"

So Daniel *did* send him. She crossed her arms.

"That still doesn't give you the right to treat me like a hired hand."

"Like it or not, Miss Gillespie, you have your uncle's reputation to uphold. Hanging on the foreman of the Lazy Z while he's groping you isn't the way to do it."

"And the way you pulled me out of the bar won't cause gossip?"

Jaw flexing, he refused to answer.

"I don't think *reputation* has anything to do with this, but *possessiveness*. You've staked your claim and are irritated that I was having fun with someone else."

"Is that what you think?"

"Yes. And I'm right."

He glanced at her, eyes murderous. "And do you know what I think? I think you're a spoiled child who hates not getting her own way. When Daniel told you 'no' about the stallion, you pouted. Your running off has interrupted everyone's day. You wanted it though. You wanted everyone to search for you and beg you to come home."

She'd die before admitting he might be right. "Who told you about the stallion?" The answer was obviously Simone. Or had her uncle told Crawford?

"I know it's probably impossible for you to imagine, but not everyone thinks a temper tantrum is cute."

She did owe the foreman an apology, but not after the way he'd treated her. "I just needed to be alone."

"Alone? Yeah, I'll bet Gossner had that on his mind too. Get you drunk. Then get you alone."

A new wave of annoyance washed over her, pushing her beyond caution. "Would you quit harping on him? You're carrying on like you have a right to be jealous."

"You'd like that, wouldn't you?"

"Yeah, whatever." She inserted as much sarcasm as she could.

When Crawford slammed on the brakes and pulled to the side of the road, she knew she'd pushed him too far. Her heart started pounding in trepidation. What was he going to do?

"We're going to prove something, once and for all." He jammed the gear into park.

Megan instinctively reached for the truck's handle, her seatbelt undone in a flash. Whatever he planned, she wasn't going to stick around to find out. Crawford swiped at her as she escaped his hold and slid out of the truck. Before she could sprint away, he vaulted himself at her and grabbed her.

Without thinking, she kicked the side of his knee, instinctively knowing that stomping his booted foot with her gym shoe would have little effect.

He grunted, bending a little, but managed to secure his hold. His fingers dug into the flesh of her upper arms, bruising. With one jerk, she snapped up her elbow, catching his jaw. Howling, Jack let her go. He backed a couple steps, holding his mouth. Had he bitten his tongue?

Panting and with raised fists, she stood prepared to do more damage. Or run. However, he'd apparently had enough. Palm pressed to his mouth, he merely looked at her. In the dim light, she could see his widening eyes. Good. Maybe he was ready to listen.

"Like I said, Mr. Crawford. I planned to get a ride from Sam Farrell." She kept her ready stance. "Now do I call her or are you going to be civil and drive me home?"

His hand dropped away from his face. It took a few moments, but he finally answered. "I'll take you." He slid through the passenger side. Gripping the steering wheel, he stared ahead without speaking or looking at her.

Megan hesitated a second longer before getting back into the pickup. With satisfaction, she noticed he waited to put the truck into drive until she shut the door and buckled herself. Neither of them said a word all the way to the ranch.

She didn't need to. She'd made her point. For the first time since Megan had arrived in Wyoming, she felt like she'd gained the tiniest bit of respect.

Now that she had some, she wasn't going to let any go.

CHAPTER 12

Help me.

In the depths of the nightmare, Megan groaned. The whisper came again.

Help me. Please.

She fought the illusionary spider webs, unable to free herself. Suffocating heat crushed her until she panted, trying to escape the dual torment of pain and impotence.

"I can't." She struggled to find the speaker in the black-shrouded bindings tormenting her. *"I'm sorry. I don't know where you are."*

Her cry finally awakened her. Sunlight streaming into the room stabbed her eyes.

She moaned softly. "Oh, my head." Pressing her

fingers to her temples, she stumbled into the bathroom to get some ibuprofen. After swallowing several, she again lay down and pulled the covers over her face.

Shadow. The name came to her, the name she'd given the stallion. With all that had happened the night before, she'd forgotten all about him.

"Oh, no! Why didn't I...?"

She flung back the covers and sprang out of bed. He had probably waited for her, counting on her to give him water and food. How could she have been so wrapped up in herself?

She threw on clothes, yanked her hair into an elastic band and vaulted down the stairs.

Mrs. Danvers met her in the kitchen. "Megan, your uncle–"

"Back in a minute." She ran outside, shading her eyes against the bright sunlight. She wasn't certain how she could approach the stallion without anyone knowing.

I can't think of that right now. Her pounding head and the sharpness of the dream precluded rational thought.

The barn doors were open, but even before she reached them, she heard Shadow's low cry. Heart hammering, she slowed. What was happening?

"Hold him. I said hold him!" Kit Gerard's voice grated against the pain in her head.

Megan stepped inside, squinting in the gloom. Several men were grouped at the corner of the barn, blocking her view. Gerard swore as several solid kicks landed on the walls. Then he cried out as one apparently connected with him.

"Grab him." A scuffle ensued. "Get him away from Kit."

One of the men slipped through the gate into the box. No one noticed her as she came up behind the spectators.

The trainer was gripping his thigh as he staggered away from the plunging horse. Three men hung on to the ropes that bound Shadow. Thrashing with his front legs, the stallion screamed and fought the men and the ropes that bound him.

Guilt clutched at her. If only she'd gone to Shadow last night. *He must think I abandoned him.*

The men subdued the stallion, immobilizing him between the ropes. Gerard straightened, face twisted with fury. The scar by his mouth pulsed red. "I'll teach you..." He grabbed a quirt then limped toward the stallion.

He's going to beat Shadow!

"Don't!" She shoved past the men who were still in the way. When they jostled her, she pushed harder.

Ignoring her, Gerard savagely hit the stallion. Then again. The rogue screamed, twisting to avoid the whip. Megan fought her way to the gate and squeezed through as one of the men tried to block her. A drop of moisture flecked her cheek. Was that...blood? Her stomach roiled.

"Stop it, do you hear me?" She threw herself at the trainer, clawing his arm.

The stallion tried to rear, the movement throwing Gerard backward. He tripped and fell, knocking her down as well.

She scrambled to her feet as Gerard kicked her. On purpose? After wrestling the quirt from him, she struck his chest with it. "There! How do you like that?" She raised it to strike him again when someone grabbed her from behind.

Megan shrieked and twisted while the trainer leaped up and yanked the whip out of her hand.

"Let me go!" She pounded at the imprisoning arm. Behind her, the stallion continued to scream his rage.

"Everyone, outa here," came an authoritative voice.

Jack Crawford.

She fought all the harder to free herself, knocking his hat off. He responded by picking her up and dragging her out of the stall. Men boiled out ahead of them, leaving the ropes. Shadow charged. Gerard barely managed to slam the gate shut.

After hauling her unceremoniously out of the barn, Crawford dropped her in the yard. Megan immediately bolted back, but he grabbed her around the waist and lifted her off her feet. She kicked him in the shin.

“Get control of yourself,” he said low in her ear.

“Let me go!” She shrieked, kicking him again.

“The men are watching,” he rasped.

Her T-shirt had ridden up. And they had an audience.

She squirmed, but he wouldn’t release her. Under her breath she ground out the words. “Okay. You win.”

He freed her then. Still panting, Megan yanked down her shirt. She and Crawford were glaring at each other when her uncle demanded, “What’s going on?”

Her vision cleared. She became aware of six men, including Kit Gerard, standing in a semicircle around her and the foreman. Behind her uncle, Simone and her mother watched.

Gerard stepped forward. “Your niece interfered while I was working with the rogue. She struck me with a whip.”

She swiveled to face her uncle. “He was beating the stallion!”

“I’m only doing my job.”

“Liar! You were punishing him because he kicked you. That’s not training. That’s revenge!”

“How I operate is none of your bus–”

“All right! Enough!” bellowed her uncle. “You men, get back to work. Kit, Jack and Megan, come with me.”

“What about the stallion?” She planted a fist at her hip. “He’s hurt. He needs–”

“Now!” Her uncle was already turning his wheelchair around.

Megan crossed her arms, refusing to go. Not until—

Crawford nudged her forward. Would he pick her up and haul her to the house? Not worth the risk. She threw him a murderous look before slowly following her uncle.

They went into his study. After Daniel nodded, Crawford shut the doors.

Megan stood in the center of the room, trembling as she clenched and unclenched her hands. Her uncle took his place behind his desk, and then looked at each of them intently before settling on Crawford. "Tell me what happened."

"He doesn't know," Megan said before he could answer. "He wasn't there."

"I'll get to *you* in a minute." Daniel's hard voice silenced her.

The foreman ran his hand through his hair. "I was working in the back corral when I heard Megan scream. By the time I reached the barn, she was wrestling with Kit for the quirt. The rogue was going nuts, so I pulled her out of there."

"Wrestling?" Gerard inserted. "She hit me with it."

Her uncle turned a narrowed gaze on her. "What have you to say, Megan?"

She calmed herself with a deep breath. Nothing could be gained by shouting. She took a moment to tuck her T-shirt into her jeans, but she couldn't control the quavering in her voice. "The stallion kicked Gerard so he started beating him. I stopped him." She pressed her lips together, hating the anger that burned her eyes when she thought of what the horse had suffered already. Starvation and now boundless cruelty.

"That true, Kit?"

"I was only doing my job, Mr. O'Connor." He shot her a hateful look.

She glared at him. "Your job doesn't include abusing animals."

Her uncle hit the air with his hands. "Megan–"

"It isn't right." She stepped closer to him. "An animal will never be tamed by cruelty. You'd have nothing but a broken horse. You might as well shoot him. That would be more merciful."

"Such a cry baby." Gerard got his comment in. "You don't know nothing about working horses."

She wheeled. "How would you know? I helped my friend train dogs. Kindness always worked better than cruelty."

"Dogs." Gerard snorted.

"Enough." Daniel slammed his palm on the desk. "I

am sick to death of hearing about this."

"Give me the horse." Megan pressed her hands to the desk's surface. "You offered me the foal, but I'd rather have the stallion. You haven't paid any money for him, so you'd lose nothing. If that isn't acceptable, I'll buy him from you."

Gerard scoffed. "You're out of your mind."

Megan ignored him as she gained, then held eye contact with her uncle. She pressed on, even when his face hardened. "Name the price. I'll pay it. Right now. I've got some money–"

"You don't know what you're asking."

"Let me train him. Let me at least try."

"That horse'd kill you if you got within three feet of him."

"Not after I worked with him."

Gerard let out a hiss of scorn behind her.

"Please. Give me a chance."

"You'd be the laughingstock of the country if you let her have that horse." The trainer slapped his hand against his knee.

Daniel's eyes narrowed. He looked beyond her. "I'll speak to you later about this matter, Kit. You can go now."

"Not until we discuss her hitting me with a whip."

Crawford stepped forward. "After we discuss you deliberately kicking her."

That silenced him. The foreman jerked his head in the direction of the door. Gerard slunk out.

Her uncle leaned back in his wheelchair. "Megan, you can't possibly understand the foolishness of your request."

She set her jaw. "I understand one thing perfectly. I can't bear how Gerard is treating that stallion. If this is the only way to stop him, I'm willing to take that risk."

The foreman stepped closer. "She might have a point, Mr. O'Connor."

Megan stared at him. Was she hearing things or did Crawford just take her side?

"Kit isn't succeeding with the stallion. And this'd

give your niece something to do while she's here."

Daniel's eyebrows shot up at his foreman's speech.

A tremor of gratefulness toward Crawford swept through her. But she didn't allow herself to think she'd won the argument. More than once, she had learned the hard way that her uncle never gave ground. Not if he thought he had the upper hand.

Daniel shook his head.

She saw no other way than to play her final card. A trump, she hoped. "If you allow Gerard to break the stallion, then I understand that my opinion–and feelings–mean nothing to you. In that case, come Monday morning, I'm leaving."

Her uncle's brows clashed over his nose. *Bluffing*, his expression said.

"I mean what I say." She hardened her voice. "You may not sell me the stallion, but I will not stay and see him ruin the spirit of that horse. If this is what ranch life is all about, then I'm gone."

She turned on her heel and swept out of the room.

But not before she saw the gleam of admiration in Jack Crawford's eyes.

I am leaving. They can't stop me.

The thought, once planted, continued to grow as she prepared for bed that night. Who cared what anyone said? She'd had enough of this ranch. *And* her uncle. All men were alike. If they didn't get what they wanted, they became tyrants.

After she flicked off the bedside lamp, she settled in bed. Determination hardened her resolve. Leaving the day after tomorrow was her only option.

She sighed as sleep claimed her. Immediately she fell into the middle of a dream.

Megan looked down at her feet, feeling as though she'd leaped from a great height. Darkness shrouded her. She could see nothing. Nothing but the endless void.

"He's gone. Where is he? I can't find him!"

She heard the cry. Her own voice? It echoed in the blackness, anguish rising in the tone. A form shimmered into focus. A woman? Megan shivered as she realized who it was.

That's me.

She saw herself, standing before the open barn doors, barefoot, wearing only pajamas. Shoulders bent, the form bowed with sorrow. A crushing weight pressed upon Megan until she too began to weep. Almost as if she was a spectator to herself, she approached the figure that shook with grief. She peered over her own shoulder into the open barn.

Shadow was gone, the stall empty. Ropes lay on the floor. Still tied, the bandana lay crumpled on the concrete. Where was he?

The phantom-Megan turned, face streaked with tears. *"Hurry. You must find him. Hurry. Before it's too late."*

She gasped awake, then shivered as she stared at the ceiling. Wave after wave of icy cold rocked her body. In the corner of the room, movement caught her eye. A ghostly buffalo calf shook his shaggy head. For countless minutes, she lay paralyzed by the sight. Was she still asleep? The calf made no sound as it stared at her, and then leaped through the window.

Megan bolted upright in bed, panting in terror. Was she really awake this time? Chills ran through her body. Uncontrollably. Different than before. *Real.*

Shimmering moonlight spilled into her room. The dream continued to haunt her, filling her with anxiety. "I need to go." She spoke aloud to give herself courage. "I need to go...*now*."

Megan slipped out of the house, not bothering to change from silk shorts and T-shirt. When she stepped out of the shadows of the house, still barefoot, she quivered as she looked at the full moon. An eerie ring of mist wrapped around it, drenching the landscape in silver and ice. The light seemed to stifle the sounds of the ranch. Gone was the occasional snort of a horse, the muted grunts of the cattle, the far-off cry of a coyote. Even the dogs were nowhere in sight.

Shadow, her heart cried, urging her forward. When she reached the barn, she paused, gasping for breath as though she'd run a race. The similarities to her dream made a shudder run through her. Everything felt unreal. *Am I dreaming? Sleepwalking?*

What if he really was gone? What if someone had taken him?

A whisper of sound scraped against her senses. Who was there? She turned and stared into the darkness, fully expecting to see her ghostly self emerge from the shadows and walk toward the barn. Like in her nightmare.

Heart hammering, she pressed against the rough wood of the building. Something wasn't right.

I need to get out of here.

She pushed away from the building, ready to sprint across the yard. A sixth sense made her stop. The hair on the back of her neck prickled.

A dark form leaped at her from the deep shadows of the barn.

CHAPTER 13

Megan whirled, but not quickly enough. A hand grabbed her throat while a body propelled her against the wall. She clawed at the relentless grip. Bright color exploded in her vision, snapping and flashing in quick succession. Unconsciousness barreled down.

Her arm shot up between them. She twisted and loosened the imprisoning hold. Letting her weight work for her, she ducked and swiveled, slipping free.

In two steps she reached the moonlit yard. She grabbed a lungful of air to scream, but her attacker was too quick. His body slammed into her. She hit the ground with a *whoosh.* The effort torturous, she gasped for air. In a second he was on her, straddling her waist. She had no strength and no breath to fight when he flipped her over.

Poised to strike, the man raised his hand. He froze as he looked down at her.

She stared up, straining to get breath into anguished lungs. And again. Still he did nothing.

The light of the full moon splashed over his features. *An Indian.* Long black hair hung to his bare chest, loose and flowing. His eyes were dark pools in a chiseled face. Shadows molded the muscles of his neck and chest. All he wore was a rough loincloth.

She sucked in a breath to scream when he clamped a hand over her mouth, and then pulled her up. He hauled her backward. Her back crashed into the unyielding wall of the barn. She could not move. His grip tightened.

"You will not speak," he said in a clipped tone.

She whimpered in his painful hold, head grinding against the rough wall.

As though responding to her soft protest, his hand over her mouth loosened. However, his body still pinned her. "Do not be afraid. I will not hurt you."

He paused as though waiting for her reaction.

"Do not be afraid." He slowly moved his hand from her lips.

Megan shuddered. Hard. "Who are you?"

He didn't answer, his piercing gaze confining her as effectively as his body.

She tried again. "What do you want?" Then a thought struck her. "Where did you come from?"

His eyes narrowed. "You ask too many questions." He stepped away.

Megan remained where she was. What would he do if she tried to escape? But now, strangely, she didn't want to. An odd sense of recognition began to build inside her. But how? Did he work for her uncle? No. She'd never seen this Native American before.

Why do I think I know him?

He sighed, his body suddenly losing its taut readiness. His shoulders slumped as though it cost too great a price to keep them thrown back.

"Are you hurt?"

He didn't answer as he limped away, staying in the shadows of the barn.

"You *are* hurt." Megan followed, compelled to do nothing less. "Please, let me help you."

He lowered himself to the ground, and then leaned against the wall.

"I'll get my uncle. He can–"

"No." The word cut through the air. "You will not."

She shivered at the savage tone. Was she out of her mind not to run? Escape while escaping was good?

I can't.

The man propped his arms on bent legs, head falling forward. His silent pain cried out to her. She sensed that he'd reached the end of his strength. Not only that but helplessness, and hopelessness, imprisoned him. Yet, how could she know this?

"Tell me what I can do for you." She tentatively touched his arm.

As though unaware of her, he didn't respond.

Megan sucked in a deep breath at how his skin felt. Warm, supple, yet the muscles underneath were molded power. Mesmerized, she allowed her fingers to linger. He slowly raised his head, nothing of his pupils visible except two sparks of reflected light. She withdrew her hand, mortified that she'd so boldly caressed him.

"Food. Water." The words rasped from his throat.

She nodded. "Stay here. I'll be right back."

Megan ran for the house. As quickly and quietly as her shaking fingers would allow, she grabbed fried chicken and two apples from the refrigerator. Then she got some bread out of the pantry and wrapped everything in paper towels.

What could she use for water? Something larger than a glass. She filled a quart-sized jar. Halfway across the yard, she slowed. How foolish to return to danger. Or the man would be gone by now. He'd only tasked her so that he could escape.

He needs me. She felt it so strongly that she couldn't resist the emotion that impelled her forward. His agony sprang from more than mere physical repletion. She knew it.

Megan crept toward the barn and peered around the corner. Head still back, he remained as she'd left him. He didn't seem to be aware of her, not even when she set the items down. Was he unconscious?

She knelt beside him. "I'm here." When he didn't respond, she slipped her hand behind his head and held the water to his lips.

He jerked upright, then grabbed the jar with both hands and drank. Megan shuddered at the painful beauty of his need. His hands captured hers while they both held the jar. Her palm on the back of his head registered a different sensation. His hair was soft, as fine as silk. A sweet scent, one of rain-drenched prairie grass filled her senses. Her breath came in uneven gasps, which had nothing to do with her hurried pace across the yard.

Who are you? Her heart pounded the question.

The man pushed the jar away.

"These are for you." Megan handed him the bundle. The grease of the fried chicken had soaked through the paper. She wiped her fingers on her silk shorts.

He tore into the food, devouring everything while she sat on her heels and watched. After he finished the chicken, he tossed the bones aside. He consumed all she'd brought, even the apple cores. Then sighing deeply, he rested his head against the wall.

Again, she swiped her fingers, this time on a scrap of paper towel. "Did you get enough to eat?"

Megan wasn't surprised when he didn't answer. She sat back. What else could she do for him? He obviously needed clothing and a bed. Probably a job. "Would you reconsider seeing my uncle? He would give you some place to sleep tonight and help you find–"

"No." The man didn't even raise his head.

She stayed where she was for a moment longer before rising.

He grabbed her wrist. "Where are you going?"

"To bed. Since you don't need anything else."

"You will stay." His grip tightened.

She raised her eyebrows, hackles rising at the demanding tone. *Now that he feels better, he thinks he can boss me around?*

"Stay." He spoke in a softer tone, his hold loosening. "I ask it."

Still she hesitated.

His fingers slowly slid from her wrist. "Please." His voice soothed, inviting, mesmerizing.

She lowered herself beside him, her acquiescence surprising even herself. For many minutes, they said nothing. He studied her in the darkness, and then asked, "Why did you come here?"

She debated how to answer. What did he want to know? "I am visiting my uncle for a few months."

The man's eyes narrowed. "I mean tonight. Why did you come tonight?"

She sat back again, knowing instinctively what he really asked. And confounded again at the sheer oddity of her answer. "I–I had a dream. My stallion was missing."

"*Your* stallion?"

She bit her lip, considering the depth of the lie. "Yes, mine. Or he will be. I am going to buy him from my uncle."

"How can you buy what cannot be owned?"

"Around here, a rogue is up for grabs." When the man didn't answer, she added, "It's the law of this land."

"But not the law of the one you call God."

Baffled by his reply, she remained silent.

"If you buy this horse," the man said slowly, "what will you do?"

The way he asked filled her with a prickly sense of unreality. "I would take care of him. I wouldn't confine him to the dark corner of the barn. Certainly not with ropes tying him up. Then I would train him, not using the cruel methods that Kit Gerard uses. But gentler ways."

"For what purpose?"

"To ride him. To own him. Prove to my uncle and every man on this ranch that cruelty and greater strength don't make one right." She stopped, feeling foolish at her outpouring of passion and idealism.

When the man beside her said nothing, she went on. "I'll admit that my uncle may not sell me the stallion. In which case I'll free him. I'll sneak out in the middle of the night and release him."

She stared at the man, wondering why she admitted such things. Something deeply sympathetic responded to him. But why?

He turned, staring into her face. "Do you swear this? By your life?"

Her heart hammered at the intensity of his tone. *By my life?* Would he kill her if he thought she was lying?

"Do you?" The words struck her like a whip.

"Yes." She panted the words. "Yes, I swear."

In one fluid motion, the Indian rose, moving so fast that Megan scrambled to her feet with a small cry.

In the waning shadow of the barn, she could see how powerfully built he was. Though he wasn't tall, mere inches more than she, he seemed to tower over her. Sculpted muscles shaped his body, making her mouth grow dry. Had she really touched this man? And treated him like a sick child?

"Step into the light." His imploring tone impelled her.

She didn't consider the oddity of his request, only heard the quiet pleading from his soul. Moving slowly, she stopped when the moonlight spilled down on her.

Gaze devouring, he moved closer. Then he reached toward her, hand brushing her hair. His touch sent a strange shiver through her, one that quaked to the depths of her being. Her breath came in uneven intervals, as though she fought pain. No, not pain. Sweet intoxication that had nothing to do with alcohol.

"Fire and moon–dancing together." The Indian's voice wove a spell about her.

Though shadows masked his face, familiarity tugged at her. As he studied her, she said nothing, the silence too precious to break. Around her, moonlight splintered, small fragments of magic shimmering down from the heavens. In the gentle vortex, she felt trapped, captivated by not only the light from the moon, but the dark man before her.

Again, he reached out of the shadows, but his hand paused. One minute she trembled, dying for his touch, the next he faded noiselessly into the shadows.

The sound of booted feet, crunching in the dirt, shattered the enchantment.

CHAPTER 14

"Megan."

The deep voice rent the stillness of the night.

Blinking, she glanced around. Where had the Indian gone? She fought to focus on the tall figure that moved toward her. He appeared to be walking at an angle. *Crawford!* Megan shuddered.

"What in the...what are you doing out here?"

She felt as though a filmy veil had been pulled from her mind. Glancing down, she realized that she was still in her pajamas. Nothing but silk boxers and T-shirt. How could she explain what had happened to her? That she'd spent an hour or more with an Indian? Someone who was no longer there?

Was he only a phantom from my dreams?

"Megan." Crawford spoke more insistently as he drew closer and peered into her face.

"I was–I..." She stammered to a halt.

"You sleepwalking?" He took her arm. "Let's get you back to the house."

She let him lead her across the yard, her mind speeding ahead. What if he went back to the barn afterwards? What if he saw the man?

Other worries crowded into her mind. What if he woke her uncle? Daniel might not believe she'd been sleepwalking.

They reached the kitchen door. Megan turned, grabbing his shirt. "Jack."

Expression visible in the moonlight, he gazed down at her. He looked surprised at her use of his given name. "What is it?"

"I'm..." She couldn't get the words out, slowly loosening her grip. What had she wanted to say? She no longer knew.

His hands slipped up her arms. "Are you awake now?"

"Yes. I am." She nodded for emphasis.

He blew out a slow breath. "You scared the tar outa me, standing there like you were in a trance. I swear you stared at me for five full minutes. I called you a couple of times."

"You did? But...how did you know I was out here?"

He let go of her. "I didn't. The dogs howling in the chicken coop woke me."

"How'd they get in there?"

"I don't know. When I started walking around, checking the place out, I saw you." He stared hard at her. "Did you lock up the dogs?"

She gazed up at him, no longer certain what was real or unreal. "I don't think so."

He let out a soft chuckle. "I'd heard sleepwalking was genetic, but didn't believe it."

"You mean, my uncle did too?" Because of his disability, he obviously could no longer.

"Yes. When he was under stress. I guess you're under quite a bit too."

Megan folded her arms, suddenly feeling very peculiar about being outside in the middle of the night, wearing her pajamas. She stepped back when she sensed he was about to embrace her. "I appreciate your sticking up for me. This afternoon."

"I did it 'cause I believe in you."

"You do?" She looked up into his face.

He grinned. "Anyone with as much determination as you can do anything."

The praise made her uncomfortable for some reason. She fumbled for the doorknob. "Thank you, Jack."

"My pleasure." He captured her other hand, tugging on it.

Megan resisted. "I'd better go."

He frowned, but didn't release her. "Do you want me to take you to your room?"

"No," she said a little too sharply. "No, that won't be necessary."

"Guess that's not a good idea." He loosened his hold.

Backing away, she hurried through the kitchen door without bothering to shut it. She didn't tiptoe through the house, but ran on the balls of her feet.

Not until she reached the stairs did she slow, her heart banging wildly in her chest. She paused to catch her breath, thinking she heard the sound of a creaking door. Was he following her? She waited, but heard nothing more as she stared into the dark hallway. Then she crept noiselessly up the stairs. Once she reached her bedroom, she locked the door.

For a long time, she stared at the ceiling, imagining she heard someone prowling in the hall.

Megan started awake when she heard a car start. Rolling over, she saw that it was a little after nine. She stretched, then staggered out of bed.

What a night! What a nightmare!

Of her encounter with Jack Crawford, she had no

doubts. But what had preceded their meeting had to have been a dream. While she lived with her aunt and uncle as a child, she recalled being a sleepwalker. Did that inclination follow her into adulthood? Must have. The fantasy she'd experienced was quite out of this world.

She filled the tub, and then stripped off her clothes. Heat soothed her aching body. After turning on the jets, she let the water pound against her skin. While she lathered herself, she noted the deep bruise on the inside of her upper arm where the stallion had bit her a few days before.

The stallion.

She clutched the soap as she remembered her nightmare. Shadow had disappeared. Or had that been her imagination? She struggled to recall details. Was the barn empty? She'd never checked. Was he gone as she'd imagined?

If he's there, then last night was all a dream. The whole night. Right up to when Crawford found me.

Hurrying now, she finished her bath and left her nightclothes on the tile floor.

Mrs. Danvers was in the kitchen when she flew through the room. "Megan, would you–"

"Back in a sec." She ran out the door.

Blade was standing by the barn, boot propped against the door. A half-consumed cigarette bobbed in his mouth as he ran his knife over a sharpening stone. He straightened when she approached, holding up his hand. "Whoa. Where do you think you're going?"

"I wanted to see...to find out how the stallion's doing."

Blade crushed the cigarette in the dirt, shaking his head. "Can't let you."

"But–what if he's–he's dead or something?"

He smiled, the gesture lopsided. "I've got orders from Mr. O'Connor. No one passes."

"I only wanted to look–"

"No can do. Sorry." He went back to sharpening his knife.

Megan remained confounded with how to proceed.

"Well…how does he look to you this morning?"

"Fine."

"You mean you've seen him?"

Blade's eyes narrowed. "How could I tell you he's fine if I hadn't?"

"Be serious, would you? You *did* see him, right?"

He spread his hands. "Yeah."

"In his stall?"

He made a face. "Where else would he be?"

She exhaled a breath of frustration.

"You weren't expecting him to have run off in the middle of the night, were you?"

"I don't know. I had this dream he was gone. And I wanted to make sure he was all right this morning."

He grinned as he swiped the blade's edge over the sharpening stone. "He's same as usual. Ornerier than a cuss and twice as mean."

She forced a smile at his words. "Thanks just the same."

"My pleasure." Knife in hand, he saluted her.

Megan headed back to the kitchen, relieved yet more confused than ever. Last night had seemed so real. Yet, the disappearance of the stallion had been the beginning of unreality until Jack showed up and escorted her back to the house. Since the stallion was in the barn, she clearly had been dreaming. All of it. Disappointment rocked her. She rubbed her forehead, suddenly very tired.

"How would you like pancakes this morning?" Mrs. Danvers asked when she reentered the cool kitchen. "I have sausage ready too. Still warm."

"That'd be great, thanks."

She got out a plate and flatware. "Your uncle asked to see you as soon as you are done with breakfast."

Megan nodded, slumping as she leaned her elbows on the counter.

Mrs. Danvers tested the heat of the skillet by putting a drop of water on it. The bead sizzled and danced across the surface. She expertly poured some batter, and then grabbed some sausages out of the warmer. "Syrup and butter are on the table."

"All right."

After the housekeeper flipped the pancakes, she held up a pot of coffee. "Care for some?"

"Yes. But I need some cream."

When everything was ready, Mrs. Danvers carried the breakfast to the table. "Anything else I can get for you?"

"No. Thanks. This all looks wonderful."

The woman sat across from her as she poured syrup on her pancakes.

"I hope you do not mind my prying, Megan. Can we talk about yesterday?"

She glanced up, steeling herself for an impending lecture. "Sure."

The housekeeper glanced around, and then lowered her voice. "I am not going to try to change your mind about what transpired between you and your uncle."

"Okay." Megan answered slowly, not really believing her. In light of her dream of the night before, she felt more strongly than ever about protecting the stallion. Clearly her subconscious was warning her to remain strong and unyielding. Then something struck her. "How do you know what happened in the study?"

Mrs. Danvers blushed. "I overheard. Impossible not to. But also Daniel, your uncle, confided in me."

"Oh." Megan studied her, again wondering what relationship existed between them. "He told you what I plan to do?"

"Yes. I am not saying I agree with your methods, but I admire you for standing up for what you believe."

Sugar before poison? Her aunt had used the same tactics numerous times when she wanted to coerce her into something.

"I wanted to tell you..." Mrs. Danvers smoothed her fingertips along the edge of the table. "I wanted to let you know that things have not been easy around here." Again, she stopped. "No matter what happens when you talk to your uncle, please believe that he loves you. He wants things to work out."

For himself. The thought crashed into her mind.

"Megan." The way the woman said her name held a tremendous amount of pleading. "Whether you go or stay, you will always have a special place in Daniel's heart."

She rose, pushing back her plate, half of the food untouched. "Thanks for breakfast." But instead of going to her uncle's study, she headed outside. She wasn't going to let that woman soften her up. Her plans were set. No matter what, she was going to stick to them.

As she exited the house, Simone and Jack came out of the chicken coop, laughing together. The way the young woman hung on his arm made something tighten in Megan's stomach. She'd wanted to talk to Jack. To have him bolster her courage and convictions like he had the night before. Now, he seemed the wrong person. She no longer trusted him either.

He has an agenda too.

She walked to the blind side of the house, away from everyone who might see her, and slumped against the building. Where could she go? The land sloped away with no trees, no tall grass, no lake. Only barren land. For the first time since she'd arrived, she found herself hating the country. She would leave with no regrets.

Sighing, she headed toward the front door. Might as well get the talk with her uncle over with. She stepped onto the porch and walked slowly along one length.

Megan reached the living room windows, but stopped as her gaze landed on the portrait of the Indian warrior. She sucked in a deep breath as his dark eyes bore into hers. A tremor of recognition ran through her.

He's the one I saw last night!

CHAPTER 15

It can't be. Megan mentally shook her head. Lately, her imagination had gone into overdrive. The man she'd seen last night couldn't be the same as the portrait.

She pushed the thought from her mind as she stood in her uncle's study, fist raised to knock. *Inquisition time.*

"I want Jack here, too," Daniel spoke in a business-like tone to Mrs. Danvers once Megan was inside the room.

"I will get him."

"Blade as well."

Feeling as though she were on trial, she stood straight and tall. Her uncle wore a tight frown, his mouth rigid. Inflexible. She'd seen that look before.

On my own face.

He'd bully her. To get his own way. This time she wouldn't capitulate. No matter what he said, she would not change her mind. Tomorrow, she was leaving.

Unless a miracle happens and he sells me the stallion.

"Come in, gentlemen." Daniel directed all of them to sit, including Megan. "I want your honest opinion about my niece's desire to own and train the rogue."

Her heart began to pound in her chest.

Jack glanced at her, saying nothing while Blade swiveled his hat brim through his fingers. He shot a furtive glance at Megan, then down at the hat whispering through his hands.

Daniel tapped his desk with two fingers. "You first, Blade, since you seem to have a lot on your mind."

"Honestly, sir?"

"Yes. Honestly."

He threw an apologetic look in her direction. "It's a fool idea. She could be killed."

"Your opinion is duly noted. Jack? And don't repeat that high and mighty speech you gave yesterday. I know you want to impress my niece, but now's the time for gut-level truth."

Jack sat up straighter. "I think she can do it."

"Why do you say that?"

"Because she has the same hard-nosed determination as you." He glanced at her. "And she'd risk it all to prove her point. Exactly like you."

Daniel sat back, his face tightening. "Keep me out of this."

"Blood is thicker, as the saying goes. If you don't let her try, she'll kill herself doing it behind your back."

Megan caught her breath. Had he guessed of her secret visits to the stallion?

"No, she won't. She'll skip out on us. Tomorrow."

The foreman looked at her. "Megan's no quitter."

She glared at him. If she stayed to prove she wasn't

a quitter, it would be akin to capitulating to her uncle's wishes. But if she left like she'd threatened, she would look like a quitter. A lose-lose situation.

"From the look on her face," her uncle said, "I don't think she agrees."

His gaze remained fixed on her. "Perhaps not now, but after reflecting she would."

Daniel tapped his fingers on the desk again, as though making up his mind. "Thank you, gentlemen. You're dismissed."

After they exited and closed the door, Megan rose. "And I get to say nothing?"

Her uncle looked at her. "I think you said enough yesterday."

"So you're going to pass sentence. Just like that." *Just like when he sent me away to Florida. And when he refused to bring me back even though I'd cried and begged.*

"No. We still have some bargaining to do."

"Bargaining? Don't you mean compromising?" He'd already made up his mind. Now he was just figuring out some way to coerce her.

"Cool down, Megan." Daniel hit the air with his hands. "You need to hear my end of the deal."

Deal? She kept her guard up. Her uncle didn't bargain unless he planned to win all.

What is he after?

She remained standing. "What kind of deal?"

A grim smile played across his lips. "Let me show you something." He reached into his desk drawer and pulled out a sheet of paper. "Take a look."

She glanced over the figures jotted down in neat rows. Debits. Credits. Balances. The minuses exceeded the pluses. It didn't take a degree in finance to figure that out.

"Is this a statement about the ranch?"

"Yes. A short list, of course."

She slid it slowly back to him. Why was he showing it to her? So she could feel sorry for him? Then give in?

Daniel eyed her. "Don't you want to know how this happened?"

She shrugged. "It's really none of my business." That sounded too cold, so she added, "How much time do you have before you go bankrupt?"

"A year. I might even hold out for eighteen months."

She spread her hands. "Then why invite me here, protesting when I threatened to leave, when everything's going to fall apart?"

His mouth flattened. "I hoped your coming would turn things around."

"How?"

He glanced away, a deep frown gathering on his brow. "You may think the worst of me, but I wondered if you would delve into your trust to bail out the ranch."

She let a breath of incredulity. "You planned to use me? And my money?"

"No." He thumped the desk with his knuckles. "That is an ugly thing to accuse me of. Though I grant, it may look that way." He sucked on his lower lip. "I wanted you to fall in love with the ranch. To invest your future in it."

"You mean my fortune, not future."

"It'd be the same thing."

"This is despicable." She turned to leave.

"Sit down. We're not done talking."

She growled. "Oh, yes we are. And I suppose you'll now threaten me with the stallion. What did you plan to do? Sell him to me for the entire amount of my trust?"

His hazel eyes burned. "That thought had occurred to me."

"A hundred thousand? That's a hefty sum for one horse, and a rogue at that."

"Would you be willing to buy him for a hundred K?"

"Ransoming my future?" She couldn't buy the stallion *and* pay for school. It would have to be one or the other.

"Investing, Megan. *Investing.*"

She pressed her lips together.

Her uncle leaned back. He spoke with studied nonchalance. "It was just a thought."

He still hopes I'll agree. Daniel's silence confirmed her suspicions. Eyes narrowed, he watched for her reaction.

This was his way. Throw out an idea. See how she reacted. Throw out another.

I'm not going to play by his rules.

Letting her shoulders relax, she spoke coolly. "Then why tell me?"

Got him. Daniel fingered the paper, and then slowly put it away. "I wanted you to know. But there's something else. Something you are not aware of."

"And that is?"

His gaze met hers steadily. "This ranch is half yours."

She felt as though she were a balloon that suddenly deflated. "The ranch…?"

"Is half yours."

Of all the things he could have said, she hadn't expected that. "How? When?"

"Your grandmother deeded it to both your mother and me. At first, neither of us wanted the ranch. It was run down and needed a ton of work. But after a short time, we fell in love with this place. However, your parents wanted you to get a good education. Have options when you grew up. So we all agreed I would run the show. As a matter of fact, the paperwork had been finalized when my wife and your parents drove up from Laramie. I couldn't go for some reason…" He left the rest of the story unfinished.

Megan already knew. A freak car accident on an icy highway killed all three passengers, making an orphan out of her and a widower out of her uncle.

"Oh." The word came out as a half-sigh, half-groan. Her knees gave way, causing her to sink into the chair. She hadn't known the details of that day. Only the awful sorrow. Her throat burned.

Daniel wheeled himself around to the other side of the desk. "I'm sorry, Meggie. I didn't mean to tell you in such a manner."

She stared across the room, seeing nothing, not knowing what she could say as her uncle patted her limp hand. It took a few moments to rally her thoughts. "If the ranch goes bankrupt, can that jeopardize my trust?"

His tightening mouth told her he'd hoped for a different response. "I haven't investigated all the legal ramifications."

She sat up straighter. "What if I deeded the whole thing to you?"

"Throw a rope to a horse in quicksand?"

He was right. How would that help?

Megan chewed her fingernail, jiggled her leg, and then ended by twirling one strand of hair around her finger. A childhood habit that returned with vengeance. "Are things all that black? Do you really think you'll go bankrupt?"

"If things continue the way they've been going. I've had a rotten streak of luck for the past several years. Some of my best mares disappeared, thanks to that stallion out there in the barn. None of them have been recovered." He shook his head. "Of course, I keep wondering if I could have managed better. That's the hardest part."

She clenched her hands together. "I had no idea how bad it's been for you."

"You mean, for us."

She nodded, still cautious. They hadn't yet decided the fate of the stallion. Though glad Daniel had shared the information, she sensed it was a distraction. "So, now what?"

He slapped his knee. "Let's do nothing about it now. Not until we've had time to think things over. I'll call the attorney this afternoon."

"All right. But let me remind you, I can't touch my trust until I'm twenty-seven. That's still six weeks away."

"I know. Your mom was a shrewd businesswoman."

She stretched out her legs in front of her. *Get it said.* "There's one thing we need to decide upon now."

"And that is?"

"The fate of the stallion in your barn." Then she amended, "Our barn."

He nodded. "Technically speaking, the stallion may be ours as well."

Her heart began to hammer.

"I don't like that gleam in your eyes." Daniel shifted in his wheelchair. "If your mother looked like that when we were kids, it meant trouble."

"Glad you have such a good memory, because it means the same thing with me."

"Probably worse." He made the words sound like a lament. Then he sobered. "Are you still going to run off tomorrow?"

"Maybe." She clamped her mouth shut. And waited.

He rubbed his forehead, mussing his bushy eyebrows. "What should I do, Meggie?"

Her chest tightened every time he used his pet name for her. But isn't that what he wanted? She remembered times when she, as a child, used to sit on his lap. Together, they'd rock on the old porch swing while he sang her funny songs, making her laugh. He'd called her "Meggie, my favorite eggie."

"That rogue is extremely dangerous. Unpredictable. If he hurt you..." Daniel made a gesture toward his wheelchair.

Understanding flooded over her. Of course. His disability had been the result of a horse accident. Was it twelve years ago now?

But that has nothing to do with me. Megan knew she could handle the horse. *I have to tell him what I want. And I can't back down.*

"Give me a chance with the stallion, Uncle Daniel."

"How can I? Your life is too precious to..." He trailed off, face growing red.

More contrivance? She struggled to overcome the skepticism.

Megan smoothed her jeans over her knees, realizing the risks of a confession, but seeing no other way to convince her uncle. "I've already worked with him. Believe it or not, I've actually touched him." She rolled up her sleeve. "Here's my bruise to prove it. I knew the danger, but I have made progress."

He stared at her, mouth gaping. "And when have you been doing this?"

She picked at a loose thread along one seam in her shirt. "In the middle of the night."

Minutes felt like they crawled by, Daniel saying nothing.

Finally, he let out a breath. "Mind proving what you've boasted?"

She lifted her chin. "You mean...go out to the barn? You and me?"

"Yes. Right now. This instant."

A strange knot settled in her stomach as she nodded. Would the stallion really be there? Regardless of what Blade had said, she'd not established that fact.

Closing her eyes, Megan reached out with her senses. *"Are you really there? Will you let me touch you?"*

In the stillness of her mind, she swore she heard a whispered, *"Come."*

"You backing out?" Her uncle's sharp voice made her jump.

"No." She shot to her feet.

She walked ahead of her uncle, and then slowed so that he could catch up. Randy joined them, helping Daniel over the uneven terrain of the yard. Her accelerated pulse throbbed through her whole body, reminding her of movies where the sound pounded like a heartbeat.

Blade was back on duty at the barn.

Daniel waved a hand. "Open the door."

"Yessir."

Megan became aware of other men working around the yard. Too many. They were waiting to see the result of her and Daniel's showdown.

"We must be very quiet and not frighten him."

"I'll stay here by the barn door." He pursed his lips and squinted up at her. "How about if you bring me the bandana around his eyes?"

If her heart had been beating too hard before, it now felt as though it stopped.

"You can change your mind," her uncle said.

"No. No, I'll go." She sounded breathless.

She stepped inside, allowing her eyes to adjust to the gloom after the bright sunlight. Staring hard at the corner, she walked unsteadily down the middle. A sharp snort made her stop and tremble.

The stallion was there! She could see his darker shadow in the stall. Disappointment gripped her.

Last night had *been a dream. All of it.*

"There's a boy. Don't be afraid. Remember me?" She spoke softly, hoping he would respond the way she needed him to.

Megan glanced at her uncle. The harsh light behind him masked his face, expression unreadable. His wheelchair sat just inside the barn, the large form crouched in it. Waiting.

She turned back, softly crooning to the stallion as she approached. "Please, oh please cooperate." She moved closer. "This is our chance to prove how friendly you can be."

After opening the gate, she stepped inside. So far the stallion hadn't moved. His ears pricked forward as though he stood at attention. Megan felt as though he were waiting, either calmly because he sensed she was a friend or because he was getting ready to attack. He couldn't seriously hurt her. Ropes bound his neck, securing him to the walls. But when she got close enough, he could probably knock her down or even bite her.

"Don't be afraid." She reached toward him. "I won't hurt you. I'm only going to take that blindfold off your eyes."

She jumped when the stallion nickered. Her breath coming in short gasps, Megan fought to breathe normally. Her hand trembled as she touched him.

"That's it. Don't be afraid." She rubbed his cheek, and then moved higher to undo the bandana's knot. It gave her trouble, so she worked slowly, careful not to frighten him. When it loosened, she let the material slip down by itself, but it caught in the ropes.

The stallion tossed his head then blinked at the light.

"There. Is that better?" She tentatively rubbed his neck, and then pulled the bandana away. "We'll work on the ropes next. In a little while."

The horse gazed steadily at her, his dark eyes knowing. Megan gave him one final pat, and then backed slowly out of the stall.

"I'll return. Soon. I promise. Please be patient."

She shut the gate, moving carefully, and then edged away from him.

Only when she turned did she notice that her uncle was no longer alone. Several men had joined him, their silhouettes lined up along the open space of the barn's door. One man spoke. "I'll be a son of a skunk."

Megan thought her knees would buckle as she held out the bandana to her uncle. It waved like a flag while her arm trembled uncontrollably.

"Well, Miss Gillespie," Daniel said. "You just bought yourself a horse."

CHAPTER 16

“You’ve got to be kidding.” Megan looked at the bill of sale her uncle had written. “Twenty dollars?”

“I think that’s fair.”

“But...but twenty is ridiculous. I could get a manicure for that.”

“You changing your mind?”

“No.” Owning a horse would complicate things, but wouldn’t alter her plans. Once she had her trust fund, she could still get her master’s. And afford a place in Florida that could accommodate a horse.

“Then sign here. Celia!”

The housekeeper joined them in the study.

“Get Jack for me. Then come back.”

She left.

"And Meggie," he said when they were again alone, "would you keep the financial matters we talked about to yourself? I don't want any of the hired hands to know our business."

"Of course."

"Morale has already been low. I had a man walk off the job yesterday. Trapper. He's not the first."

"Oh, no." Megan regretted she'd not had a chance to talk to him like she'd planned. She had wanted to ask him about the white buffalo calf.

"Well, you know the old saying. It never just rains..."

A solid footstep behind them interrupted. "Y'wanted to see me?" Jack tilted his hat back with his thumb.

"Would you please witness this sale?"

The foreman strode in, flashing Megan a smile before picking up the paper. He whistled, and then glanced at her. "You drive a hard bargain."

She lifted her chin. "That's right. And don't forget it."

"Sign here." Her uncle held out a pen to his foreman.

"Yes, sir." Jack wrote with a flourish.

"And Celia?" Daniel indicated his housekeeper. "I want this legal."

"I'll be right back." Megan ran upstairs and got the money from her purse. She wanted no slip-ups. When she returned, she flattened the twenty on the desk. "There you are, Mr. O'Connor."

He slid the bill of sale across the desk to her. "It was a pleasure doing business."

"The pleasure's all *mine*." She firmly shook his hand. "Now that the sale is complete, we need to discuss how much it'll cost to stable and feed my horse. I, of course, plan to take care of him, but we need to work out a fair arrangement for boarding."

Her uncle wore a huge grin. "I would say, Megan, that you'll make a great rancher."

Is that what he's after? She pushed the thought away, determined to revisit it at a later date. Instead, she made a sound of skepticism. "We'll have to see about that."

"What do you think, Jack?" Daniel asked him.

The tall man studied Megan, taking so long to answer that heat rose to her cheeks.

"We'll have to convince your niece to hang around long enough to find out what kind of rancher she'd make."

Megan spent the rest of the day with the stallion whom she now openly referred to as Shadow. Her uncle advised she not completely untie him. To give the horse a chance to get used to the new arrangement.

She saw the wisdom in his advice, taking her time loosening the lassoes and letting them slip from Shadow. The rogue was remarkably well behaved, but she wasn't taking chances. All the while, she talked to him in a soothing voice.

Finally, the ropes were off except two that tied him to the stall. She debated removing them, but decided to leave them until she'd worked with him longer. Sliding her hand along his neck to his withers, she marveled at the texture. His mane was matted and some of his spring coat not quite completely gone.

"There." She caressed his shoulder. "You may not believe it, but one of these days you're going to let me ride you. Then we'll take long trips out to the range. But first we have to get to know each other better."

Chattering about his beauty, she continued to touch him. The stallion seemed to understand and accept her worship. He stood proudly, ears pricked forward, eyes calm. His intelligence and confidence amazed her. Something in her spirit called to him. Why did she feel as though her entire life had come into focus?

She got him some hay and figured out how to turn on the automatic watering system. "Sometime soon, I'll clean out this messy stall." Her heart nearly burst seeing him calmly eat, yanking hay out of the bin and thoughtfully chewing it.

The lone bulb came on automatically as the barn grew darker. She ignored her own grumbling stomach until she was certain Shadow was comfortable. She was leaning on the gate, watching him when his head suddenly shot up and his ears laid back.

"Megan?" Jack's voice came from the barn door.

"Yes. I'm here."

"It's getting late." He approached, but stopped when the stallion whickered in a threatening tone.

She moved toward the foreman, not wanting him to undo all her hard work. "I'm ready to go."

Shadow shrilled, the sound reminding her of how wild he still was. Megan turned for one last look as he snorted and grumbled his displeasure.

"Ya hungry?" Jack's hand touched the small of her back.

"Yes."

The rogue continued to shrill. Was he upset that Jack was there? Or did he dislike the attention this man was giving her?

"Supper's long over with," the foreman said once they reached the yard.

"I'm sure Mrs. Danvers will have plenty of leftovers."

"She's gone. It's her night off."

Something unspoken hung in the air between them as they made their way toward the house.

He cleared his throat. "I was wondering if you want to grab a bite to eat somewhere."

The lack of places in town flashed through Megan's mind. Did he mean the bar?

They reached the steps, the porch light detailing his face. "The Silver Tap's good, or we could run over to a steak place I think you'd really like. It's a bit of a drive, but the food's worth it."

Then what would follow? Megan cheeks grew warm as her imagination filled in details. *What is he hoping will happen?*

"So, what'd'ya think?"

She glanced away, unable to escape her vivid thoughts. “Oh, um, thanks, but I–I’m pretty tired. I didn’t rest much last night, you know. I’d probably fall asleep...” She stopped, biting her lip.

His mouth pulled to one side in amusement. “Fall asleep...with me?”

“That’s not what I meant.”

He rubbed a finger along the corner of his mouth. “I was about to jump at the offer.”

Her face felt on fire. “Please, just drop it.” She reached for the door, but he leaned a hand on the panel.

“You know, Megan, when I invited you out to dinner, I wasn’t suggesting anything else.”

“Um-hmm.” She kept her head ducked, refusing to look at him.

“You don’t believe me.”

“Frankly, I have no reason to. Not after what happened in town.”

“Yeah, let’s talk about that.” He leaned down, his face drawing closer to hers.

She instinctively stepped back.

“You were drinking–”

“I was not. Nothing alcoholic, anyway.”

“All right.” He shrugged. “You think I tried to take advantage of the situation?”

“Didn’t you?” She stared up into his face.

He ran his tongue over his lower lip. “Okay, I admit I got a little crazy when I saw Ben Gossner acting like a stud around you.”

“And that excuses your behavior?”

He face tightened, but he said quietly, “Are you excusing his?”

“He wasn’t doing anything wrong.” Megan turned and walked away from him.

“Gossner’s nothing but trouble.” Jack followed her as she marched toward the front door. “I want you to stay away from him.”

She exhaled a breath of exasperation. “I am not one of the hired hands. I don’t take orders from you.”

“I’ll telling you for your own good.”

She looked up at him. “Are you two competing? Let’s see. Both of you are foremen. Both of you have reputations, especially with women. What else?”

He opened his mouth to say something more, but then snapped it shut.

She crossed her arms. “I am not going to be part of your rivalry. I’ll go out with whomever I wish. If you don’t like it, tough. Or I may stay home every night and never go anywhere. But it’s my decision. Mine.”

Still he said nothing.

“Right now, I’m tired. I’m going upstairs. To sleep. So if you’ll excuse me...”

He stepped out of her way, but she caught his grin. “Stay home every night? Huh.”

Instead of shutting the door, she slammed it. On her way up the stairs, she passed Simone heading down. The young woman shot her a look of hate. Had she overheard their conversation?

Jack is toying with us both.

Megan reached her room and locked her door. “Ooh.” She thumped the mattress with two fists. Why did everything have to be so complicated? Things had started out so calmly when she’d first arrived.

No, they hadn’t. Her arrival had started an avalanche of opposition. However, the thing that worried her most was Daniel’s agenda. What was he planning? Megan sensed it involved Jack, but the matter was complicated now that she knew he and Simone had a relationship.

“And I thought the politics at work were bad.”

Forget food. Megan searched through the drawers for her favorite nightclothes. Weren’t they still on the bathroom floor? She changed into a cotton nightgown. After washing her face, she looked at herself in the mirror. Her eyes seemed greener than usual, betraying the turmoil in her life.

“Quiet country living? What a joke.”

She bent down to pick up her pj’s when something caught her eye. A discolored blotch on her shorts. What was that? A chilling answer came to her, one that made her catch her breath and stare at her pinched face in the mirror. Grease from fried chicken?

Last night was not a dream!

CHAPTER 17

Megan awoke, as if on cue, in the middle of the night. After wrestling with herself, she got up and dressed, then headed out to the barn. She found the jar on the backside of the barn, gleaming dully in the limited light.

I wasn't sleepwalking. Or dreaming.

She held her breath, waiting for the Indian to materialize out of the darkness. Nothing happened. Everything sounded, and felt, like a normal night.

Ears pricked forward, Shadow stood looking at her from the stall. She ran her hands along his ribs. With care, she touched his cheek, allowing her fingers to linger over the small crescent spot on his forehead, his only marking.

Where had the Indian come from? Who was he? Now that she'd had time to ponder the events, she'd dismissed the crazy idea that he looked like the portrait in her uncle's living room.

But other questions galloped through her mind. Did Shadow belong to him? Perhaps he couldn't care for the horse himself. She shook her head, dismissing all attempts at explanation. If the stallion truly belonged to him, he would be back. No doubt.

Megan found a couple brushes in the tack room, not certain in which order they should be used. The stallion wasn't frightened after she showed them to him. She worked slowly, letting him get used to the feel. Who knew how long ago or if he'd ever been brushed?

Dust flew from under his coat, stirring the oils to bring out the shine. Shadow didn't move, standing at attention the whole time. He only kicked when she pulled at the matted clumps of hair from his belly.

She chuckled. "That tickles, doesn't it?" She continued to speak to him, telling him of her childhood, hopes, sorrows. He seemed to listen. *At least Shadow doesn't have an agenda.* Not like everyone else.

"And someday, I'll get my master's in finance. It'll give me a ton of options I don't have at the moment. I'll be able to live where I want, do what I want. Then Uncle Daniel can't..."

She straightened, wondering what she was going to say. *Can't guilt me into doing anything I don't want to do?* Megan slowly continued to work.

The pieces of her future were falling into place. Obligatory stay in Wyoming, check. Access trust fund as soon as she turned twenty-seven, check. Pay for master's degree, check. Get a well-paying job anywhere she wished...that would soon follow.

She hummed, running her palm over Shadow. How much time passed, she didn't know. Megan became totally engrossed in slicking the brush along his coat. His sleekness made her hand tingle, the controlled power of his bunched muscles filling her with awe.

The night rushed toward morning when she finally stopped. She yawned, wondering how late it was. When she stepped out of the barn, the graying morning surprised her. The dogs whimpered as they rushed to her, nosing her before scampering off. One smelled like it had gotten too close to a skunk.

In the distance, roosters crowed, heralding a new day. She paused to gaze at the beauty of the shimmering sky. The gray slowly transformed into a pale violet, the color intensifying by the second. A fresh breeze blew toward her, wild grasses rustling. The elusive scent of flowers promised to release their fragrance in the full heat of the day.

For the first time since her arrival, she felt at home.

A door slammed. From the bunkhouse? No, she was mistaken. A man strode from the back of the house then disappeared.

Jack? She couldn't be certain, but it looked like him.

Had he spent the night with Simone?

"I say again, that's not your concern." Daniel's raised voice floated upstairs to Megan.

She quickly finished dressing, then opened her bedroom door to listen. Who was arguing with her uncle? Across the hall, movement caught her attention. Randy? Apparently she wasn't the only one eavesdropping. As soon as she opened her door, he'd closed his.

"You hired me to do a job, but if you won't let me then why'm I here?" The unmistakable voice of Kit Gerard cut through the quiet.

"As I've already explained, that horse is out of your hands." Her uncle's voice had lowered, but she could still hear every word.

They're discussing Shadow. She leaned over the railing.

"It ain't right. That rogue was mine to break."

"He belongs to my niece now."

"That don't change anything."

A paused followed. "We're done discussing this, Kit. I want you to stay away from the horse as well as Megan. And I don't want to hear about this again. Understand?"

A pause followed. "No problem. You won't have to worry anymore." The study's panel banged open. Heavy boots thumped through the foyer. A moment later, the front door slammed.

She glanced out the window in time to see Gerard stalk across the yard.

The vet was standing beside her truck. She called to the trainer, but he apparently ignored her as he tromped toward the bunkhouse. From the second story window, Megan could see her puzzled frown as she stared after him.

By the time she walked down the stairs, her uncle was no longer in the study, so she headed out to the yard. "How's it going?" Megan approached the back of the truck.

The vet smiled a greeting. "Good. I was just packing up my gear." She threw a mischievous look. "Don't tell me you need a ride to town again."

She laughed. "Nope. Someone else is mad at my uncle this time. Not me."

"Ah. Why does Kit have a bee in his bonnet?"

Though no one was nearby, she lowered her voice. "He doesn't like the fact that I bought the stallion from my uncle."

Sam nodded, face speculative.

A car roared from behind the bunkhouse. A few moments later, it flew past them, dust churning. As Gerard drove by, he threw Megan a look of pure hatred.

The vet watched after him. "Bettin' you won't see him here again."

"You really think he quit?"

"No doubt." She shut the back of her truck and walked around to the driver's side. "He's been squawking about the rogue to a few folks in town. I'm not surprised this happened."

First Trapper, now Gerard. Gone. What would her uncle say?

"Don't look so worried." Sam climbed into her truck and leaned an elbow out the open window. "I hear the Bakers are looking for a trainer. They're the next ranch over from here."

Maybe she should call them up and warn them. Megan shoved away the unkind thought.

"Got a busy schedule today, so I can't stay and visit." The vet started her vehicle. "But Megan..."

Seeing the woman's tight face, she stepped closer.

Sam briefly touched her arm. "You be careful." She pursed her lips, looking out the windshield as she apparently debated saying more, then back at Megan. "Kit can be vindictive. I hate to say it, but...well, just watch your back."

CHAPTER 18

Megan.

She sat up in bed, listening. Did someone call her name? After a few moments, she relaxed against her pillow, ears alert. Every nerve in her body seemed to be intent...on what? She rolled over in bed, trying to get comfortable. When she glanced at the clock, she noted with surprise that she'd lain awake for twenty-four minutes. Useless to try to sleep now.

After slipping on a robe, she headed to the kitchen to make a cup of tea. Megan searched the pantry until she found an herbal. She heated water on the stove, avoiding the microwave which would be quicker, but noisier. Mug in hand, she went out the kitchen door and found a seat on the porch.

In the distance, the yard lamp hummed and snapped. Its glow streamed to the ground and painted the barn, stable and chicken coop in pale yellow. With the new moon, the light kept the night from being too dark.

As she cradled the hot tea, she pondered the progress she was making with Shadow. After almost three weeks, everyone was amazed at how much she'd accomplished. She'd not yet been able to convince the stallion that a saddle was good, but she wouldn't give up. Already she'd ridden him bareback a few times in the corral. But each time Shadow moved into a trot, she felt like she'd fall off. Very soon she hoped to take him out on the range. It was time.

While she sipped the steaming tea, movement across the yard drew her attention. Megan sat up. The hot liquid, sloshing over the rim, burned her finger. A tingle of premonition crept across her neck. *That isn't one of the hired hands. Or Jack.*

The figure moved as though not touching the ground, body gliding as he walked. As he drew closer, she could see that he stared in her direction. He knew she sat on the porch.

Was it Kit Gerard? She rose, knees shaking. As she stared, she realized her error.

The stranger stepped closer, but stayed out of the circle of the glowing light. He wore a pair of pants but his chest and feet were bare. His hair, dark and shiny, hung down over his shoulders.

The Indian.

He came back. She set the cup down on the bench. What did he want? More importantly, what should she do?

He waited, staring at her across the distance.

Megan.

She gasped. Who...? Looking around, she saw no one that could have whispered her name. No one but the man who stood in the yard a distance away. He hadn't yelled. Her name had been spoken softly, carried on the breeze that lifted her hair and tickled her cheek. The dark night pressed around her, compelling her to go to the man who waited so solemnly.

"Am I out of my mind?" She whispered aloud to dispel a curtain of haziness that had begun to wrap around her.

Or am I dreaming? Her finger, still throbbing from the hot tea, denied that possibility.

Without considering what might happen, she stepped from the porch and walked slowly toward him. He mirrored her movements, skirting the edge of the light. Reason collided with desire. *I have to see him. Have to talk to him. Find out how real he is.*

She stopped, still many feet from him. He, too, stopped. The light of the yard glowed behind him. For many moments, he said nothing.

"Why did you come?" The question burst from her.

"I called to you." His peculiar accent sent a chill through her. The feeling wasn't unpleasant, merely unsettling.

"You...called to me?"

"And you came."

She shivered as she remembered why she'd awakened. "What...what do you want?"

"To see you with my own eyes."

What could that possibly mean?

Before she could ask, he held out something. "And to give you this."

Megan hesitated a moment, then stepped forward for a better look. He held a beaded bracelet, made with strips of leather and polished, white stones.

"Thank you." She merely stared at his gift.

He startled her by suddenly stepping closer. "It goes here." He grasped her arm with warm fingers, and then wrapped the double strands around her wrist.

Her pulse throbbed where he touched her. Megan studied his bent head as he slowly fastened the bracelet. *Who are you?* The question burned anew in her heart.

When he finished, he didn't immediately release her wrist. Instead, he lightly caressed the inside where the skin was most sensitive. Her racing pulse battered even harder. He looked up, eyes glittering like black gems. "I give you my most precious possession. Wear it. To remember me."

"I–I will." Megan's lower lip began to quiver. No matter how hard she clamped her teeth together, she couldn't stop the tremor.

A movement in the heavens distracted her. She gasped as a billion stars plunged toward the earth. A meteor shower? Not possible. The entire sky was aflame with falling pinpricks of light, streaking downward. In seconds, it was over.

Megan looked at the man before her, but his gaze was fixed on her, not the sky.

What just happened? Did he see that?

She became aware again of his fingers wrapped about her wrist. A fire originated where he touched her, spreading up her arm and igniting her heart.

When he released her, she immediately cooled.

"Are you...?" Megan cleared her throat when the words rasped. "Are you okay now? Your ankle better?"

"Yes."

"Do you have somewhere to live? Food? Shelter?"

He nodded.

"Do you need a job? I'm sure my uncle could find you something."

She caught the faintest tightening of his lips, so very fleeting, as though smiling was something he did rarely.

"I have no needs."

"Oh." She couldn't keep the disappointment out of her tone. She'd wanted to meet him in the light of day. To see him and get to know him.

What masked sadness presses on his soul?

"Perhaps some time, you could come and meet my uncle."

"Perhaps."

"Great." Now that that was settled, she could relax. He wouldn't disappear from her life. And now that she'd had time to study him, she realized that he couldn't be the warrior in her uncle's painting, despite the similarities.

He stepped closer. “Tell me…why did you help the wild horse?”

She opened her mouth to answer, and then closed it. Why had she? “I guess, I could not bear to see him in pain. Tied up. No longer…free.” Megan fingered the bracelet. “Everything he knew and loved was taken from him.” For some reason, her voice shook. She ducked her head.

The man was silent for many moments. “You have a heart of compassion. Some think that makes you weak, but they do not know you.” He lifted her chin. “You have fire. Together these give you great strength.”

What a spell he wove with his words. No one had ever talked to her that way before.

Megan stepped back. Finally, she felt she could breathe. She cast about for something to say. Anything. “Have you see Shadow? The stallion? You know Kit Gerard is gone. He won’t hurt the horse ever again.”

The man’s head tilted a little. “Yes, I know. Many things.” He leaned closer. “But until now, my life was empty.”

Was empty? Megan pushed back a strand of hair that blew into her face. For the thousandth time, she felt out of her depth. “Is he…is the horse yours?”

“He belongs to you now.”

“I was afraid…” She stopped.

“Afraid I would take him away?”

“Yes.” She saw no harm admitting that.

“He will stay with you as long as you wish.”

She nodded. “I’m glad.”

He looked away, toward the barn, then the sky. “I must go.”

“Wait.” Megan held a hand out toward him. “Will I see you again?”

“Yes.”

“When?”

“Soon.”

She couldn’t squelch her sigh of relief. “May I have your name?”

He again turned his head, staring off into the

distance.

Was he a wanted man? Was that why he wouldn't tell her?

"My name," he said softly, "is hidden in the earth, written in the snow of the winters to come."

What did that mean? She released her breath. "What can I call you?"

His black gaze returned to her before he answered slowly. "You may call me 'Dwells In Shadow.'"

"Dwells In Shadows." An apt name. In the times she'd seen him, he'd avoided light. "A beautiful name."

He nodded, then turned and moved toward the back of the barn. Megan watched until she could see him no more, the darkness swallowing him.

Now that she knew he was real, she needed to find out who he was. How had he ended up wounded and on her uncle's ranch? Her uncle knew practically everyone in the area. She promised herself that she'd start asking questions.

CHAPTER 19

The next day, Megan didn't get to see her uncle. He'd left early in the morning and hadn't returned before Ben Gossner picked her up for dinner. After two postponements he finally was able to keep this date. A little after six, he pulled into the yard, dust flying as he skidded to a stop.

She was acutely conscious of the stares of the hired hands as she walked out to meet him. Even more so when he whistled appreciatively.

"You look prettier each time I see you."

"Thank you."

When she drew closer, she blinked at his strong aftershave. His tawny hair was still wet from a shower, slicked back and curling at the neck. But Ben's face was clean-shaven and his clothes spotless. Even his boots were polished.

He opened the passenger door, and then climbed in on the driver's side. As soon as he started the pickup, a country song blared on the radio. He turned the volume down only a little. Megan waved to Mrs. Danvers who stood at the kitchen window. When they reached the main road, Ben turned the opposite direction of Silver Springs.

"Where are we heading?"

"I promised you dinner and dancing. Though Silver Springs is great, I'm taking you somewhere special."

The truck engine whined as he pressed harder on the accelerator. Megan glanced at the speedometer, gulping when she saw the needle climbing past eighty.

"How was your day?" He yelled over the radio.

"Long. But I did get a saddle on my horse."

"Good for you. Maybe someday you can bring him to the Lazy Z and show him off."

"Might be weeks from now."

He flashed a grin in her direction. "You'll be around for a while, won't you? At least, that's the impression I'm getting from the gossip."

"Let me guess, Miles?"

"You got it." Ben laughed. "So is it true?"

"Wyoming is beginning to grow on me." She avoided the whole truth. In less than two months she planned to leave. She had her future to think of, after all. But why spoil the evening?

Their conversation turned to other things, Ben asking some questions about the east coast. That soon changed with him talking about his life and work. Megan smiled at her initial worry that they'd run out of things to say. No problem with Ben. He didn't brag, but shared easily and naturally, as though they'd been friends for a long time. And, as he'd already proven, his sanguine personality wouldn't allow for lapses of silence.

When they drew closer to the bright spot she saw on the horizon, she realized over an hour had elapsed since they'd left the ranch. But before they reached the main drag of the city, Ben turned onto a side road.

He shot her a grin. “I know this great place, but it’s out a ways.”

“Okay.”

“Didn’t want you to get nervous or nothing.”

Truth to tell, she had begun to wonder.

He drove his Ford into the packed parking lot, cruising up and down the cramped rows. Finally, they found an open space.

Megan studied the jammed parking lot. “I think we’re going to have a long wait.”

“I got reservations.” His hand rested in the small of her back as he steered her through the packed foyer. Then he glanced at his watch. “Phew! Made it. If you’re more’n five minutes late, they give away your spot.”

The hostess immediately led them to a table. In the background she heard the muted boom of drums and bass guitar, but couldn’t see where the sound was coming from.

“Anything you order’ll be great,” Ben said. “Their prime rib is good, if you like that. Otherwise get a steak.”

Megan squinted at the menu in the dim light. When the waitress came, she chose a filet mignon. Ben ordered the biggest New York strip they had, joking about how the steak had been misnamed.

“Everyone knows the best beef’s in Wyoming.” He spoke in a loud voice as though challenging those around him to disagree.

She caught amused grins.

“And make it rare,” he told the waitress. “I want it still bellering.”

After she left, he leaned forward and tapped Megan’s arm. “We’ll go dancing after dinner. There’s a band next door. The buildings are connected to make it easy.”

“Sounds great.”

He propped his elbows on the table, grinning at her. “Having fun?”

“I am.” She smiled sincerely. “I appreciate your taking me out on my first date here.”

"Really? I mean, this is really your first date? In Wyoming?"

"Yes. That unusual?"

"I figured Crawford would've taken you out several times already."

She made a face. "Because of his reputation? Or mine?"

Ben grinned. "Your reputation's spotless. It's his I'm talking about." He took a sip of water as though to wash the bad taste out of his mouth.

Megan chewed her lip. Should she coax more information out of him? She didn't need to.

"I don't want to say nothing against him, 'cause that reflects on your uncle. Well, to be honest, I don't have a great opinion of him or Crawford. But now that I've gotten to know you, I might reevaluate my opinion of O'Connor."

"Exactly how do you view my uncle?"

"Kinda hardnosed. You have to be to make a go of ranching. To a degree. But there comes a time when that won't do. He has never struck me as the kind of person who'd give an inch. Ever. O'course, I've mainly dealt with him through Crawford."

Megan nodded, absorbing the information. "Some days I feel like my uncle's a stranger. I've lived most of my life apart from him. Never had much time to really get to know him."

"Then here's your chance to be a good influence on him."

The waitress brought salads. After she left they got to talking about horses and training methods, Megan listening raptly. Ben had quite a few good ideas. Steaks arrived, causing only a minor lapse in conversation as they both delved into the tasty meat.

They both turned down dessert, and then headed toward the sound of the band. A connecting hall led past the restrooms and into the bar.

She raised her voice over the boom of the band. "I'd like to put my purse in the truck."

"I'll walk out with you."

They were on their way back into the building

when a blue Chevy, parked along the street, caught her eye. It looked familiar. Too familiar.

It can't be...

As Ben ushered her back into the crowded bar, she couldn't leave the suspicion alone.

"Hey, I'm going to hit the restroom before we dance." She spoke nonchalantly.

"Sure. I'll wait for you here. Want anything to drink?"

"Maybe later."

She pushed her way back through the crowd. After she exited the restroom, she glanced toward the bar. She couldn't see Ben. Good. He was still buried in the crowd. Megan made her way toward the restaurant, and then stood in the breezeway, looking over the patrons. Her suspicions were soon confirmed.

Blade and Jack sat at the counter, eating dinner.

CHAPTER 20

They didn't see her. Clenching her teeth, she turned back to the bar. Had they followed her there? The thought made her blood boil.

"What's up?" Ben asked her when she reached him.

"Oh, nothing. Just a couple jerks." She didn't want any trouble between the three men.

Ben rose up from the barstool. "Where?"

She grabbed his arm, amazed at the hardness of his flexed muscle. "It's okay. They left."

"I'll follow them out to the parking lot and give 'em a piece of my mind." His clenched fist proved he'd do more than talk.

"Please, just let it go."

He looked down at her. “If they show up again, I won’t.”

She pulled on his sleeve. “Come on. Let’s dance.”

After the second song, Megan lost count. Ben was a great dancer, as he’d proven the night she’d met him. They drank sodas, reassuring her that this date was different than their first meeting.

He still had that wild streak, proven when he’d sometimes whoop as he swung her around the dance floor. As the bar filled though, they were frequently jostled as they danced. Finally, Ben leaned closer.

“Let’s go somewhere else. This place is too crowded.”

“All right.” A quick glance at her watch told her it was only nine-thirty.

He steered her through the crush, then out to the much cooler parking lot. They paused on the front steps, Megan shivering in the differing temperatures.

“I didn’t realize how hot it was in there,” Ben said. “Guess the word is out about this place.”

“We’ll have to find another nice spot.”

He smiled down at her. “I’d like that.”

A patrol car cruised by them in the parking lot, its searchlight scanning the rows of cars.

“Looks like there’s trouble.” Megan rubbed her bare upper arms.

“Yeah. Let’s stay here for a moment.” He pulled her away from the bar door as three men barreled out. Ben put a casual arm around her shoulders.

“I’ve had a really nice time tonight,” she said. “In case I forget to tell you later on.”

“I enjoyed this evening myself. But it ain’t over yet.”

She smiled up at him.

He looked down at her, but the traffic in and out of the bar door distracted him. “Come on. Let’s go.”

The police car was no longer in sight. Ben was fumbling for his keys when two shadows moved out of the darkness. When Megan let out a little cry of alarm he jerked around, pushing her behind him.

A bright light shone in their faces.

“This your truck, sir?” Behind the blinding beam,

Megan saw a uniform.

"Who wants to know?" Ben apparently was not yet aware that he spoke to an official.

"Highway patrol. Is this your truck?"

Ben's head snapped back. "Yeah."

"May I see your registration and license?"

"Sure." He reached for his wallet. "The registration's in the truck."

"I'll get it," Megan said. The more cooperative they were, the sooner they could be on their way.

"In the glove box." Ben handed her the keys.

Fingers shaking, she opened the passenger side door and searched for the document. What was this all about? By the time she was back at the group of men, a curious crowd had gathered at the steps of the bar.

"What brings you to town?" one officer asked Ben. The other was back at the patrol car, sitting inside the lighted interior as he read something.

"Just out on a date." Ben's voice rippled with annoyance.

"Do you have I.D.?" the officer now asked Megan.

"Yes. I'll get it." She rushed back to the truck for her purse. The strap snagged on something as she pulled it out from under the seat. For a moment, she played tug-of-war with the leather. By the time she returned to Ben, an officer had bent him over the hood of the patrol car.

"What's going on?" The nightmare continued to get worse and worse.

"I'm under arrest," he said with a grin. "Heckova way to end a date, huh?"

"For what?"

"Seems I have a couple outstanding tickets."

That didn't seem out of the realm of possibilities. "So, what's going to happen?"

The officer pulled Ben up by the arm.

"I'm going to be a guest of Uncle Sam's tonight."

"You're kidding. For speeding tickets?"

"Would you hang on a moment? Please?" Ben asked the officer who began to escort him to the back seat of the patrol car.

The man graciously complied.

Ben spoke to Megan. “How about you taking my truck home? I’ll get it later.”

“I’m sorry,” the officer broke in, “but your vehicle is going to be impounded.”

Impounded? That seemed way out of proportion for a couple speeding tickets.

“Then how’s my date supposed to get home?”

“That’s not our problem, sir.” The man spoke in a cool, professional tone. “Is there someone you could call, ma’am?”

“Yes. Yes, don’t worry,” she said to Ben.

He shook his head. “I’m really sorry, Megan.”

The other officer came up to her. “Identification?”

She got out her Florida license while Ben was put into the back of the patrol car.

“Is there something I can do for you?” she asked him through the open door while the officer checked her I.D., then handed it back.

“I’ll be okay.”

One officer shut the door while the other radioed headquarters.

She felt sorry for him, sitting in the back with a sad grin on his face as he looked at her.

“Sorry,” she mouthed, smiling to encourage him.

His grin broadened, then suddenly fell. His eyes narrowed to slits. Megan glanced over her shoulder.

“What’s seems to be the problem?” Jack asked.

She felt like dying. “Just a little mix-up.”

His eyebrows crept up. “Looks like more’n that.”

They stood silently for a few minutes while the highway patrol finished up and a tow truck arrived. Ben continued to glare at Jack, his face twisted with something more than irritation.

Then Megan realized that the foreman had moved closer.

“How’re you getting home?” Jack asked.

She shook her head. “Hadn’t thought that far. Yet.”

“Let me take you. Blade’s with me.”

“Yeah, explain how that happened exactly.” She turned to him.

Jack shrugged. "Coincidence. Remember my telling you about a great steak place? This is it."

"You're kidding."

"No. Ask Blade." He indicated his friend who stood a few feet away.

Blade shrugged, spreading his hands. "You're no more surprised than us."

His testimony soothed her suspicions.

"There he goes," Jack said as the patrol car moved slowly away.

Megan raised her hand in farewell, still feeling bad about the incident. Ben, too, would have unpleasant memories of their date. She stared after him. Brake lights came on, and then the patrol car pulled into the street.

"We'd better get you home." Jack indicated his truck across the parking lot.

"You sure I'm not keeping your from anything?" She headed toward his vehicle.

"Blade and I just came out for a steak." He smiled easily. Then his eyebrows rose. "Actually, I wanted to stop at this store. Mind a little detour?"

"I guess not." After all, they were doing *her* a favor. Did she have a right to dictate the terms?

"And while we're there, why don't we pick you up a hat?"

She shrugged. "I'm not doing anything else."

"That okay with you?" Jack looked past her to his friend.

"Fine by me. If you don't mind my tagging along."

"This isn't a date." She managed to keep her tone sweet.

"Yeah," Jack chimed in. "Megan's date had to unexpectedly leave."

A glance passed between the two men, one that left her wondering. She turned back in time to see the satisfied grin on Jack's face.

CHAPTER 21

Megan stayed out later, and spent more, than she planned. She not only got a hat, but a pair of boots. Jack insisted on buying her a belt buckle to go with the outfit. When she demurred, Blade split the cost with him, a “welcome to Wyoming” gift. So she also bought a belt to go with the buckle. A couple western shirts, suggested by Jack, completed her purchases.

By the time they started for home, it was after eleven. Megan rode between the two men on the bench seat of Jack’s pickup. Conversation didn’t lapse, not with them chatting about the ranch. As she listened, she grew sleepy.

She didn’t know how it happened, but she leaned her head back for a minute. The next thing she realized, the truck was stopped though the engine purred quietly. And she was snuggled up to Jack. Blade was gone.

"I'm sorry." Still groggy, she struggled to sit up.

"No worries." One of Jack's arms was draped over the steering wheel, the other across the top of the seat. "You looked so comfortable, I hated to wake you."

"Had to happen sometime." She rolled her head to one side, then the other to remove the kinks. Now she could see that they were parked behind her uncle's house. It was very dark out.

The dashboard indicator lights gleamed, illuminating his face. His expression made her stomach clench. "I'd better go."

Jack turned off the truck. "Can you wait a minute longer?" His voice was soft.

She hesitated before answering lightly. "Sure."

He bowed his head as though pondering how best to say what was on his mind. "I hope you don't take this wrong, but I was really worried about you tonight."

She pressed her lips together, not wanting to invite further confessions.

He chuckled, the sound apologetic. "I can't say how relieved I was that we were there tonight. And that we could come to your rescue."

She plucked at the button of her skirt. "I really appreciate your giving me a ride home."

"Can you imagine my trying to explain to your uncle any other course of action?"

"No, I guess that would be awkward."

He paused. "Listen, I don't want to further spoil your evening, but..." He tapped his palm on the steering wheel.

She shifted in her seat.

"I won't go into specifics...but Gossner makes me nervous. And when I think about you being out with him, alone...well, it's an uncomfortable feeling." He hit the steering wheel again. "I guess I feel responsible for you. And I hope that doesn't offend you."

She took her time answering. "No. It doesn't."

"It goes deeper than that." His evident unease somehow endeared. "But, well, I'll leave it at that."

Abruptly, he opened the truck door, and then held out a hand to help her. Megan grabbed her purse and scooted out.

"Let me get your things." He reached behind the seat and pulled out her two bags.

"I can take them."

"It's no trouble." He led the way to the house. When they reached the kitchen door, he shoved one bag under his arm then let her in. "I'll set them here." He put her things on the table. The room was almost pitch black.

She'd figured he would offer to take them up to her room. His different choice momentarily confounded her. Where was the aggressive man she'd grown used to expecting? Jack had transformed somehow, making her uncomfortable with the new person he'd become.

"Well, goodnight." His quiet voice came out of the darkness.

Megan shifted from one foot to the other, trying to figure out how to gracefully escape. "Thanks again for your help. And for the gift."

"No problem." He moved toward the back door, and then was gone.

She stood in the darkness, trying to figure him out. And she couldn't help but admit to herself that she liked him better this way.

"You sure you're ready?" Daniel asked Megan in the morning.

"I've got to try him out some time."

"Take a hired hand with you. Or Blade or Jack."

"I'd rather not. Shadow will do better without anyone around. And I won't go far."

His bushy brows collided over his nose. "Then keep the ranch in your sights. It's easy to get turned around out here."

"I'll stay by the road."

She hurried through breakfast, and then went outside, wearing the things she'd purchased the night before.

Blade's path crossed hers as she walked toward the barn. He stopped and let out a low whistle. "Look at that cowgirl," he called in a teasing tone.

"How-do." She squeezed the brim of her hat.

Grinning, he watched her.

Megan pushed her hat back when she entered the barn. One day soon, she hoped to move the horse to the regular stables. But right now, she didn't want him to get spooked, either by the new place or the unfamiliar men he'd encounter.

Shadow nickered in welcome as she approached.

"Good morning to you, too." She led him out of the barn and tied him to a fence post. Taking her time, she bridled and saddled him.

"Today's the day." She settled her hat more firmly on her head. "We're going for a run."

His ears pricked in her direction, eyes gleaming as though he understood her every word. When he was ready, she unhitched him, and then pulled herself into the saddle. Shadow moved fluidly forward, his smooth gate amazing her. Though he pranced in eagerness, she held him to a walk as they passed through the yard. When they got far enough away from the house, she let him move into a trot, then a loping canter.

He stretched out. Megan held on, adjusting to the comfortable pace. When they reached the main road, Shadow turned one way without her directing him. She let him choose the direction, unconcerned about where they went as long as she could find her way back. His gate lulled her.

The warmth of the day surrounded them, the smell of wild flowers filling the air. In the distance, the mountains looked violet-gray, their jagged peaks cutting the pale blue sky. Against them crouched brown bluffs. Wispy streaks of clouds stretched across the expanse, giving an appearance of endlessness. A hawk soared motionlessly, his faint cry lost in the vast eternity.

The road wound before her, disappearing behind shimmering waves of heat. Every direction she looked, wavy lines blurred the horizon. Time melded into the landscape while she and Shadow went on and on. He seemed to have some destination in mind, ears turned forward, and pace steady. She went along, curious to see where he would take her.

Perspiration pricked her forehead by the time he turned down a dirt road. He finally slowed to a walk, neck wet with sweat. They went a distance, still without seeing anyone, and then Shadow moved off the path.

"Whoa." Megan pulled on the reins. "I don't have a clue where you're going."

He stubbornly strained forward, ignoring her wishes. When she tried again to stop him, he fought her, tossing his head. Without warning, he broke into a trot. Megan steadily pulled back on the reins, but there was no stopping him. Shadow was too strong.

Arms aching, she finally gave up. Wherever he was taking her, she hoped she could find her way back. He again slipped into a canter as though to make certain she wouldn't try to direct him.

Trust me. The thought hit her so strongly that she shook her head to dispel her imagination. Trust...Shadow?

Glancing around, she tried to memorize landmarks. They headed toward a row of hills and passed between two of them. The landscape changed into a ravine, Shadow slowing to skid down the rocky slope. So far it was a straight shot when she wanted to turn back. The further they went, though, the more she began to wonder where the horse was taking her.

A nagging suspicion came to her that he was heading home. To Dwells in Shadows? Despite his adamant statement that no one owned the stallion, she suspected that of all possibilities, the horse belonged to him.

On and on they went, Megan becoming more nervous the further they got from the ranch. A river gouged its way through the ravine. Thirsty for water, trees dotted the landscape, growing denser the further they traveled. Finally, Shadow splashed into the river until water brushed his belly. He stepped gingerly across submerged rocks, walking up the middle of the growing torrent. Trees completely shaded them now, the water mottled with shadows and dancing jewels of light.

She again pulled at the reins. “Come on, boy. I don’t have a clue where you’re going.”

He whinnied softly as though reassuring her that all would be well.

“No way. We’ve got to go back.” She tugged more insistently. The water roared around them, filling her with unease.

He lowered his head and trudged on. One minute it was all battle, with Megan losing. The next, he climbed onto a bank and shook the water from himself.

She stared at the little grove, somehow knowing this had been his destination. But why here? Shadow didn’t move, waiting for her to do something. She slid from the saddle, hanging on to the reins to keep him from taking off. He followed willingly.

A huge tree had fallen across the river, providing additional seclusion for the grove. Other saplings bent toward the water, eroded dirt threatening to give way. But that’s not what caught her eye. Together, she and Shadow moved toward a space under the fallen tree. It was large enough for a man to crawl into. She stopped.

“Hello?” She hoped that if anyone were there, it would be Dwells in Shadows.

No answer.

Megan wrapped the reins around a branch, and then ducked into the space.

The opening, she could see as she squinted, sloped downward a little, then broadened. She remained where she was, afraid that a snake would have made a home in the small cave. Or some varmint. Her eyes adjusted to the gloom as she took another crouched step inside.

A couple rolls of material lay bundled neatly against the wall. A film of dust on them attested to the fact that they hadn't been moved for a while. A couple weeks? Months? Was this where Dwells in Shadows lived?

She backed out, feeling like a trespasser. The stallion stood calmly, gaze fastened on her.

"Well." She patted his neck. "You certainly have taken me on an adventure."

She glanced around, noting a place further on where a campfire had obviously been made. Despite it and the bedrolls, this didn't seem like a very comfortable home. The Indian either greatly exaggerated about his needs being met, or he was a man of very simple wants.

Had he been forced to live away from society?

She stayed a little longer, allowing Shadow to drink at the river and graze. She too took a taste of the chilled water, marveling at the sweet freshness. The sound of the muted roar filled the grove, drowning out everything around her. No wonder Dwells in Shadows would choose such a place. Here, she felt an incredible sense of peace.

Megan touched her wrist, wishing now that she'd worn the bracelet he'd given her. For many minutes, she stared into nothingness, merely recalling how she felt when she was with him. He seemed so different from other men she knew or had known.

She couldn't help chiding herself. "What do you mean, you know him?"

And yet...

With reluctance, she climbed on Shadow and urged him back into the water to head downstream. He seemed to understand what she wanted, giving her no trouble now.

"Stubborn mule." He'd had his way almost the entire day. A glance at her watch confirmed that it was afternoon. They'd been gone for hours.

When they reached the main road, a truck approached. Was that the vet? The vehicle slowed. Megan took a tighter hold of the reins, uncertain how Shadow would respond.

"Hello!" Sam's arm waved out the window. "Am I

glad I found you!"

CHAPTER 22

“What’s the matter?” Megan asked, immediately worried.

“Nothing you’re appearance hasn’t fixed.” Sam put the truck into park. “I was just at the ranch and your uncle’s fit to be tied.”

“Because I’m not back?”

“He’s convinced you’re...well, it doesn’t matter. Obviously, you’re okay.”

She hadn’t meant to break her promise to leave the main road. It had just happened. “I’d better hurry home.”

“I’ll call Daniel and alert him.”

“I’d appreciate that.” She nodded. “My phone service is spotty.”

Sam studied her horse. "This the rogue I've been hearing about?"

"I wouldn't know exactly what you've heard. But this was a rogue."

The vet's gaze swept him. "He's a beaut. Looks like you've done fantastic work with him."

"I'd like to take the credit, but can't. He's remarkable. Incredibly intelligent." She glanced down the road. "But I'd better get going before my uncle sends out the posse."

Sam laughed. "Yeah, I heard about the last time."

Megan's cheeks grew hot as she thought of Jack hauling her out of the bar. Was that what the vet referred to? "You sure seem to hear a lot."

"Sorry. But gossip or sharing or whatever you want to call it, gets around."

Megan was about to nudge her horse down the road, but asked, "You ever hear anything about a Native American in the area?"

"Lots of them. Anyone in particular?"

"I've seen a man a couple times. He's not dangerous, or anything. Seems to be a loner."

"Around town?"

"More in this general area."

Sam frowned as she pondered it. "Quite a few drifters come and go, especially in the summer. He may have come to hire himself out."

Megan was certain that wasn't the case, but she said nothing.

"I'll ask around, if you'd like."

"It's no big deal. I was only wondering. He looked like he could use a little kindness."

"I see." Her friend's face cleared as though she accepted the reason for the interest. "Take care. I'll make that call."

"Thanks." She nudged Shadow forward.

"I'm sorry I worried you," Megan said to her uncle when she reached the house. She'd left Shadow tied at the hitching post so that she could go immediately to Daniel. She hugged his neck. “I’m so sorry.”

His sputter of indignation suddenly ceased. “Where’d you go?”

She decided to keep the destination secret for now. “Oh, down the road. I went a lot further than I planned, but it was really wonderful. Shadow’s the one who led me home.”

“Glad to hear the horse has some sense.”

“And a wonderful sense of direction.” On impulse, she leaned over and hugged her uncle again. “Thanks so much for giving him to me.”

“I didn’t.” His voice sounded gruff. “I sold him to you, and don’t you forget it.”

“I know.” She straightened, suddenly embarrassed by her emotional display. “Well, I’d better see to Shadow. Be back in time for supper.”

Megan spent a long time brushing her stallion down. He stood motionless as she smoothed the brushes and combs over him, as though knowing he deserved the attention.

“You are so magnificent.” She ran her hand along the path the brush made across his silky coat. His powerful body awed her, especially since she’d tapped into his strength that day. Though they’d traveled for miles, he’d not seemed to grow tired at the sustained canter. How would it feel to gallop, the wind whipping through her hair?

When she led him into the barn, the sound of a shovel scraping on the concrete startled her. Blade was in Shadow’s stall.

“What are you doing?”

He didn’t stop. “Taking care of this little matter.”

“You didn’t have to.”

“I know.” He kept working. “That’s the way of things around here. You see a need, you take care of it.”

“Still...” She let the unfinished thought drift off.

“There.” He straightened, viewing the result of this work. “Spread a little straw and it’ll be all ready.”

“Thanks so much.”

Shadow walked calmly past him as she led the horse into the stall. Blade stayed longer to help her get oats and a bale of straw, chatting with her comfortably all the while. When the dinner bell rang, he touched the brim of his hat.

"Thanks again, Blade."

"You coming to dinner?"

"I'll be there in a bit."

She leaned on the gate, watching Shadow finish his oats and thinking about the wonderful day. A sound from the other end of the barn made her glance in that direction. Was Blade back?

No. It was Simone.

Megan straightened, immediately on guard. What new poison would the young woman shoot her direction now?

"Seems you had an interesting day." Her seemingly innocent comment contained an element of sarcasm.

"It was nice," she replied warily. "Well, I'm hungry. You heading to the house?"

"You want my company?"

"Merely trying to be friendly."

The girl fell into step beside her. "Is that what you call it?"

"What?"

"Being friendly? From what I hear, you're being friendly with an awful lot of people."

"I've found it's generally more pleasant than sarcasm or rudeness." Megan kept a tight rein on her tone.

"I suppose. The men sure like it."

She stopped and faced Simone. "What's that supposed to mean?"

"I think you already know."

Megan didn't answer, sorry now that she'd asked.

"Let's see." The young woman counted on her fingers. "There's Jack, Ben, several men at the Silver Tap, and now Blade. Did I leave anyone out? Maybe one or two of the other hired hands?"

Hating what wasn't being said, she stalked away.

"Can't be content with one man, can you?" Simone

hurried to catch up.

She walked on, counting the steps to the back porch.

"Word has gotten around about you, Miss Priss." The girl's tone grew malicious. "I wouldn't be surprised if more men become *friendly.*"

Megan wheeled. "Do you know what I think? I think your vicious little temperament turns off men. When they get to know you, they discover what you're really like. And the only way you can keep a man is to have him crawling to you in the middle of the night."

Simone blanched.

Before she responded, Megan rushed up the steps and into the kitchen.

"Another Native American?"

Megan and her uncle were alone in his study after dinner.

"Possibly full blood." As far as she could tell, he looked it.

Daniel scratched his chin. "Can't say I do. Only ones I personally know are Trapper and Mick."

"Oh. I was merely curious."

"Why?"

Megan was ready for the question. "Since I found out that Sioux blood runs in my veins, I wanted to know more."

Daniel grinned and nodded. "You, too? I find myself drawn to my books some evenings, and read and read. That would probably be your best place to start. Mick is part Crow. Not sure about Trapper. Possibly Lakota. More'n likely, this other man you've seen is as well."

"Thanks." She left the study, no further ahead than when she'd entered it. Instead of heading upstairs, she went to the living room to look over her uncle's artifacts. Again, though, she was drawn to the portrait of the warrior. His eyes mesmerized her, pulling her toward him as though drawing her with an invisible lasso.

Megan stared at him, unblinking, the world around her blurring as she saw nothing but him.

His beauty awed her. His black eyes gazed steadily into her soul, wholly consuming her. The tip of his arrow pointed straight at her heart, promising not death, but something more. Something elusive that made the breath catch in her throat the longer she studied him. Not death, but bound to his side for life?

Again, she saw the sadness in his eyes, as though he were pained by a deeper reality than was evident. A local artist had painted him, according to her uncle, an unreadable scrawl on the corner of the portrait. Who? Megan had an overwhelming need to find the person so she could ask about the warrior.

Her eyes swept the half-rearing stallion, his mouth opened in a silent scream. She imagined the horse looked a little like Shadow. The faint crescent shape on his forehead furthered the illusion that he looked like her horse.

Odd that the artist had placed the marking there.

Something caught her eye, making her lean forward and stare. Nape hairs prickled the longer she looked. *No. Can't be!* Even so, she broke away from the painting and hurried up the stairs to her bedroom. She yanked open a dresser drawer then searched under some clothes to discover the truth.

In a moment, she'd found the bracelet Dwells in Shadows had given her. Not trusting her memory, she ran back down the stairs. She held the beaded bracelet up to the portrait and stared hard at the warrior's arm.

They were identical.

CHAPTER 23

Dwells in Shadows came to her that night in her dreams. Wherever she looked, he appeared out of the recesses of her imagination, stepping forward to gaze steadily at her with his dark eyes. The truth of his identity wouldn't let her escape. Dwells in Shadows was the man in the portrait. Megan awoke, staring at her dark ceiling, heart pounding in certainty.

"I have to find the artist." The more she knew, the more she needed to know. The mystery surrounding him drew her. No, it was more than the mystery. His pain? His hidden sadness? Megan ached with wanting to know.

He said he'd come back.

That thought calmed, though she told herself she

was crazy for wanting to see him. What if he were a criminal? What if he was hiding up the ravine because he was dodging the law? Even as she came to conclusions, something told her they were wrong.

She lay awake a long time, her mind going over the facts again, trying to understand, but getting no closer to an explanation. Finally, she promised herself that she'd go back to his hideaway the next day. That settled, she was able to sleep.

Her uncle spoiled her plans when he announced that the lawyer was coming to speak to them both. Since he was driving up from Laramie, she waited. After getting the gallery's name from her uncle, she headed upstairs to the library to contact them in private. Online, she found the information, then called.

The woman who answered the phone couldn't give Megan any details because she was a relatively new employee. Daniel had purchased the portrait seven years before. The only person who could answer her questions was the owner. He, unfortunately, wouldn't be back for several days.

Sighing, Megan hung up. She rocked back on two chair legs. Then on a whim, she looked up white buffaloes. The information about them was sparse, but she discovered they were extremely rare in nature. One in ten million? The last two times she'd seen one had clearly been figments of her imagination, but the one at the edge of town? Unlikely that it was real either.

White bison were considered sacred or spiritually significant to Native Americans. So why had she see one? Because she was a descendent of the Dakota? But what did that mean?

Her eyes lighted on books in her uncle's library. She scanned some of them, intrigued by Daniel's handwritten notes. Apparently, he'd done some research about their heritage. With interest, she followed the ancestry until she saw Native American names listed in the genealogy.

"Not just his ancestry," she reminded herself aloud. "Mine too."

Megan smiled at some of the names, wondering if they had any significance. One in particular caught her attention: *Scares At His Shadow*. She hoped that didn't mean he was a coward, afraid of his own silhouette, but that others found him so fierce that even his shadow would cause them to flee.

A car driving into the yard tore her away from her studies.

Downstairs, Megan tried to listen politely to the small talk of Paul Halleck and her uncle, but her mind kept wandering. After what felt like an interminable lapse, they got to the details of her trust. The attorney cleared up the matter of creditors and protecting her inheritance should the ranch go bankrupt.

"But I understand things are going better for you," Halleck said to Daniel.

"Yes. We have several foals that have promising futures. And I have a buyer for one that's still unborn."

"What about your mares disappearing?"

"We believe that problem's solved." Daniel smiled at Megan.

"Glad to hear it." Halleck nodded. "Nice to know things will start to look up for you."

"I hope so. We've got my niece's future to think about."

The attorney looked at her. "You'll have access to your trust soon. On your twenty-seventh birthday."

"Only a couple weeks away now."

"Any plans for what you'll do with it?"

"Actually, yes. I've already enrolled in a master's program at the University of Florida." Out of the corner of her eye, she saw her uncle's startled expression.

"For this fall?" the attorney asked.

"Yes. Will there be a delay in getting the money?"

"Shouldn't be. Since Daniel is the trustee, all he has to do is sign off on the paperwork." He consulted his notes. "I'll call you in a few weeks to set up the disbursement of funds."

"Thank you."

They moved on to other business, and then headed to the kitchen for a late lunch. Mrs. Danvers had prepared a special meal of chicken Caesar salad with homemade bread. Megan listened to the three of them chat like old friends. Finally, she was able to excuse herself and head upstairs to change.

Soon she rode down a familiar path, as eager as Shadow. They splashed their way up the river, the grove looking no different than the day before.

This time, however, she was ready.

“Hello?” When no answer came, she added, “It’s Megan.”

Still no answer. Satisfied he wasn’t around, or convinced he wasn’t going to come out of hiding if he was, she returned to the saddlebags she’d brought. Inside, she’d placed a few items she hoped would help make his dwelling more comfortable. First, she took out a flashlight and let the beam sweep the cave before crawling in. No critters hid in the small space that she could see. She found a long stick and poked at the bundles, reassured that nothing hid behind them.

She pulled them out of the cave, and untied them. Ah, they were furs, not bedrolls. When she shook them, dust flew. Megan draped them over a small log and beat them with a stick until she’d purged most of the dirt. One bundle contained some clothes. A wad of money fell out.

Nervous about being seen, she glanced around. She counted the money, amazed that she held over three hundred dollars. So much for imagining Dwells in Shadows was destitute. She rolled the bills back into a wad, and then shoved it into the pants pocket. The last bundle of fur contained some leather straps, a beautifully carved bowie knife, matches, toothbrush, and comb.

She shook her head over the supplies, the mystery growing in her mind.

Shadow tugged at the reins and nickered, as though he wanted to go. Megan ignored him and packed everything away, adding a few other items she’d brought: a small sewing kit, antibiotic ointment, bandages, a bar of soap, a note she'd written. *Thank you again for the gift of your bracelet. If there is anything I can do for you, please let me know. I remain your faithful friend.*

She left the note unsigned.

"What do you think, Shadow? Will he appreciate what I brought him?" The fifty-dollar bill in her pocket would go home with her. She wished she could think of something else he might need.

A razor? No, this man didn't need to shave from what she could remember. His bloodline was too pure.

Shadow tossed his head and snorted.

"All right, all right, we'll go." She undid the reins. However, he resisted heading back to the stream. Recognizing that she'd never be able to overpower him, she quit fighting him.

Her horse followed the bank upstream. More explorations? She gave him his head, allowing him to take her where he was intent on going. The stallion found another log that had fallen, and then pawed at the soft ground near the upturned roots.

"Another mystery?" She stared at where his hoof dug at the ground.

Both afraid and intrigued, Megan dismounted. Shadow stepped back, clearly waiting for her to do something.

She hesitated a moment, then bent to the spot he'd pawed. Her pulse quickened as she began to scoop at the sand. It came away easily.

The stallion snorted when she paused for a moment.

"There's nothing here."

He pawed at the ground, urging her to continue.

Uncertain about how deeply she should go, she kept digging. What was buried here? A body? When her fingers scraped against something hard, she scooped the sand from around it. A flat, metal surface met her touch. She continued to dig and pulled out a container which looked like it could hold canceled checks. Before opening the box, she glanced around. The day had already fled, shadows creeping up the ravine. She took a quick breath, and then lifted the lid.

Several items lay inside, protected by clear plastic bags. She pulled out a book, some old-looking bills, and silver jewelry. Two leather scrolls lay bound by string, which she didn't open. Megan pulled the book from the plastic, then ran her hand over the worn binding. The leather warmed under her fingertips.

Take them with you.

She heard the words so clearly that she straightened and looked around. But only Shadow was with her. With shaking fingers, she put the items in her saddlebags. She shoved the empty box back into the hole and reburied it.

"I hope he understands." She mounted Shadow. "You'll put in a good word for me, won't you? I'm only going to borrow...no, that's not the right word. I'll hold them for him until I see him again. They'll be safer with me."

She turned her horse toward home. This time, he willingly went as though satisfied that nothing else awaited them at the grove.

Late that night, she finally had a chance to look at the items she'd brought home. Heart pounding, Megan locked her door, and then pulled the saddlebags out from under her bed. She sat on the floor, spreading out the things.

The money...wow! She looked at the ancient U.S. currency, a small fortune of perfectly preserved bills. Carefully, she put them back into the protective plastic, debating about getting a deposit box where the money would be safer.

Next she scrutinized the odd artifacts. Arrowheads that looked very much like the ones her uncle owned. Some feathers, beads, pretty things. The silver jewelry was beautifully crafted.

She paged through the book, fascinated by the foreign scrawl which gradually changed to English. Was this a record of the Indian's travels? Wanting to take more time later studying it, she put it away.

Lastly, she unrolled the two leather scrolls. One was more of the unreadable words. As she opened the other, she caught her breath and stared.

The painting was a duplicate of the portrait in her uncle's living room.

CHAPTER 24

"You've been busy." Jack cornered Megan a few days later while she was in the tack room. "What's going on?"

"Oh, I've been exploring this land of yours." She smoothed oil over the leather of the saddle. She bent her head to study the work in the light. "Fascinating country. It's really grown on me."

"I'm glad." Then he seemed to scrutinize her more closely. "Why are you smiling so much lately?"

She searched for an explanation that would satisfy him. "I'm happy here. Things are going well."

"Even if Gossner hasn't called?"

She caught her breath. Trust Jack to know. Ben had been released from jail the day after his arrest, but he hadn't let her know how he was doing. And Jack was right. Ben hadn't called though she'd left him a couple messages. Not only that, but she learned he was dating someone else now. It sounded pretty serious.

She managed to shrug. "Guess he learned all he wanted to know about me."

"Hmm." Jack narrowed his eyes. "And that doesn't hurt your feelings?"

"*Weeeelll.*" She dragged out the word. "Maybe a little. At first. But I hear he's seeing someone else."

"From whom?"

She saw no harm in relating who'd told her. "Sam Farrell. I ran into her yesterday in my travels."

"And she volunteered the information?"

"I think you ask too many questions, Mr. Crawford." She concentrated on getting the oil into the seams.

He didn't say anything for a moment. "If you need someone to talk to, I'm available."

"Thanks." More than likely, she'd talk to Shadow. He didn't offer any biting comments. Nor did he have an agenda. With Jack she could never be sure.

"I mean it," he said quietly. "I care about how you feel, Megan."

That required a more serious answer. She stopped working to look at him. "I appreciate it."

He smiled softly.

Again, she was struck by how different he'd seemed from the first days. Gone was the arrogant egotist. The man before her was sensitive, gentle, respectful. Yet, she couldn't forget he was involved with Simone. The young woman subtly continued to remind Megan that she disliked her. Understandable. Jack treated Simone like a stranger when they were together, as though nothing existed between them. That had to drive the young woman insane, especially when he always managed to sit by Megan at meal times and chat with her almost exclusively.

Why were they so secretive about their relationship?

"Ready to head to the house?" Jack interrupted her musings. "I'll walk with you."

"Go on ahead. I'll be awhile yet."

He nodded. "Don't stay out too late."

She turned back to her work as he walked away, keeping busy until he shut the door.

With the saddle well saturated, she put the oil away. The ploy had fooled him so he wouldn't linger. Leaving on the light, she headed toward the stables where Shadow now was. She'd moved him there a few days ago and he appeared content with the new arrangement. Daniel didn't trust him out in the open pasture, though he allowed the stallion out during the day.

"Hey, Shadow."

He nickered a greeting as she opened the gate and went inside. Smoothing her hand along his withers and back, she then patted his neck. Never did she tire of touching him. The more time they spent together, the more she needed to be with him every day.

After a while, she settled herself in the corner and turned on a small lamp she'd installed. A soft bed of straw awaited her, the loose stuff her seat, with a couple bales to lean on. After pulling out the diary, Megan picked up where she'd left off.

She read of Dwells in Shadows as he traveled through the southern part of South Dakota. Writing mostly of the terrain, he told little about the people he met or the jobs he must have had to survive. It had been that way since she'd begun reading his accounts. Nevertheless, his journal was fascinating. He had beautiful, poetic language to describe everything.

Some of the things she found amusing. He described the first time he'd been in the back of a pickup, as though the experience had been unusual. He found the ride exhilarating. Standing in the bed, he held out his arms as he rode a "metal horse of the wind."

He was innocent in so many ways, yet mature beyond his lifespan. He occasionally waxed philosophical as he lamented about how his people had lost their vision in the last two hundred years, yet were also altered by the events in history that irrevocably changed them. His recounting of the death of his nation made tears come to her eyes. He wrote as if he'd watched the destruction of his people.

My people too.

His tribe was fiercely proud and highly emotional. She understood that determination in the painted eyes of the man she'd met in the shadows.

One of the most interesting entries was a reference to a 'spirit of fire' that would someday break a curse. The brief statement didn't seem to fit anything else recorded. Megan scanned ahead, but saw no other reference.

As she read, yawns consumed her. She blinked and sighed deeply, the air heavy and intoxicating. Foggy-brained, she gazed at Shadow who stared at her with a puzzling look of comprehension.

Finally, the book slipped from her fingers to the straw. The light from the full moon danced through a nearby window. In the stables, dust swirled like sparks of light. Megan tried to fight the overpowering undertow. A soothing vertigo dragged her under.

Warm hands smoothed over her face, yet she couldn't open her eyes in the darkness. Gentle fingers made concentric circles on her forehead, temples then cheeks, the touch so feather-light that the sensations drugged her. She felt the hands in her hair, the gentle strokes sending tingles through her body.

She felt no alarm.

This isn't real. I know I am dreaming.

When the touch disappeared, she sighed in disappointment. The fingers reappeared and lingered on her hand, as though enjoying the skin's softness. Slowly they tested the tendons, then each finger. Again, the contact faded away.

A warm breath brushed her face, then smooth, cool skin. A man's cheek. Megan held her breath, fighting to open her eyes. But they wouldn't obey and reveal who was with her. The phantom touched her other cheek with his.

She heard her own breath, yet she couldn't awaken from the dream that wasn't a dream. She gasped when warm moisture lingered on one eyelid, then the other. His soft lips touched her cheeks.

He is kissing my face.

Her heart beat so hard that she feared it would burst in her chest.

"Woman of fire." A whisper cut through the night. "Sleep again and dream of me."

The gentle reverie enveloped her.

CHAPTER 25

"Don't go!"

The shriek that came out of her own mouth startled Megan into wakefulness. She sat up, confused, devastated, alone...and began to cry.

Gray light filtered through the window, heralding a new day and swallowing a night that had passed without her being able to stop it. The stallion stopped eating to watch her as she let her face fall into her hands.

Why was she crying? Why couldn't she stop? She felt as though she'd missed something terribly important. Snatches of memories and vague emotions tugged at her.

Shadow nudged her shoulder, nickering softly. She

rose, then flung her arms around his neck and buried her face against his soft coat. Sobs wracked her body, tearing at her soul. Gradually, she grew calm. The horse hadn't moved, neither had he grown impatient while she clung to him.

"I don't know what's the matter with me." Yet, the answer came to her as soon as she spoke. "How can I love someone I don't even know? Except through a book about him? How many times have we met?"

She sighed, pressing her nose against Shadow's soft coat.

"Yet, I know I love him. I long to be with him, to learn about him. His beautiful words speak in my mind. When I read them, I can hear him. I swear he's speaking to me. But to not be with him..." She took a shuddering breath. "Every cell in my body cries out for him."

Shadow shifted his weight. Megan trailed her hand across his shoulders, and then leaned against his ribcage, letting her arms rest across his back.

"You love me, don't you Shadow? Don't ever stop loving me. Even though my heart feels like its breaking."

He rubbed his head against her side as though promising. She smiled, tears ebbing as she stroked him, immersing herself in his scent, one that not only smelled horsey, but something else. Something otherworldly.

A hired hand came into the stable, oblivious of her presence. She glanced out, knowing he was there to muck out the stables. He would avoid Shadow's stall. No one could enter it but her. Or Blade.

Megan collected the diary, planning to quietly leave while the man worked. Before she slipped out of the stall, she glanced back where she'd slept, hoping to see...what? Everything appeared as it had the night before.

Memories tugged at her mind, begging to be recalled in vivid detail.

She departed without the worker seeing her. After she was in her room and had tucked the diary away in a safe place under her bed, she realized what had appeared strange. The light had been on when she'd fallen asleep reading.

Someone had turned it off.

"Megan Gillespie?" the voice at the other end of the line asked in a cool, polite tone.

"This is she."

"I understand that you called several days ago about a painting?"

"Yes!"

The gallery owner. She couldn't keep the excitement out of her voice. "Thanks so much for getting back to me."

"I'm sorry it's taken me so long, but I've been out of town. Just got in last night."

"No problem." They chatted for a moment, then Megan went on to describe her uncle and the portrait that he'd bought seven years before. After a minute, the owner of the gallery finally recalled the artwork.

"Do you know about the artist?" She fabricated a reason to find him. "I am fascinated by his work and am interested in buying more paintings."

The man on the other end of the line hummed in thought. "I don't think that's possible. Jay Rush actually did very few portraits. He was more of a sculptor."

"Do you happen to have any of his art at your gallery?"

"I think perhaps one sculpture. It's a small piece. You're welcome to come look at it."

"I was also wondering if you knew the location of Mr. Rush."

The gallery owner paused. "I would have to do some research on that, Ms. Gillespie. Would you mind my calling you back?"

"Not at all. Perhaps I could drive down to Cheyenne in a few days."

"That would be great. I might be able to give you an

answer by then. But I need to warn you, I lost track of Mr. Rush several years back."

"I'd appreciate anything you could find out."

After she hung up, Megan went upstairs to the library and got online. She did find a little blurb about Jay Rush, but the information was brief, neither describing his individual works nor telling where he resided.

Other sites weren't helpful either. After another hour, she gave up.

When she headed downstairs, the men were assembling for lunch. Glad of the distraction, she pitched in and helped. Mrs. Danvers had made corned beef hash, which the workers consumed in great quantities, along with several loaves of homemade bread.

After lunch, Megan helped clean up. "I don't know how you do it. You don't spend the entire day in the kitchen, so how do you manage to have all this food prepared every meal?"

"A magic wand." The woman laughed. "Honestly, Simone is a great help. And since I have been doing this a long time, it is second nature now."

As Megan loaded one of the dishwashers she shook her head, part in admiration and part in disbelief. Simone help? She had rarely seen the young woman around. The young woman preferred being out with the boys, getting dusty in the corrals. Or riding away in someone's truck.

"Seems to me you're wasting your talents working here, Mrs. Danvers. Restaurants would pay you big bucks for what you do. I never imagined ranch food would include stuffed pork chops, clam chowder and homemade bread."

The housekeeper smiled with serene modesty.

"You sure you wouldn't consider a job as a chef?"

"I already have one, and I am perfectly content." She wrapped up a half loaf of bread and put it away. "Besides, there is more to life than a paycheck. I am happy here. I cannot say I would be someplace else."

Because she and Daniel had an understanding?

More than once, Megan had seen the look of affection between them. Apparently, they'd allowed their relationship to progress no further, content to love from afar. Or was there more going on than she suspected? Something that kept them apart?

They finished loading all the dishes, then Mrs. Danvers said, "I forgot to tell you, but you received a letter from Florida."

"Oh?" Megan rinsed and dried her hands as the woman retrieved the mail.

Her heart sank when she saw the return address. Garrick. *Trust him to track me down.* Megan had quit using the email address he knew about. She refused to answer his calls or listen to his messages on her cell phone. Should she read this letter? A glance at Mrs. Danvers confirmed she was consulting the menu on her bulletin board. Megan sat at the table and tore open the envelope.

"World falling apart" and "desperate" leaped off the one-page letter, ending with "can't live without you." She reread the letter, feeling like he tossed a lariat around her neck in an attempt to pull her in.

"Bad news?" Mrs. Danvers asked.

She looked up with a start, having forgotten she wasn't alone. Face lined with concern, the housekeeper stood a few paces away. Megan debated with herself, then handed her the letter.

Mrs. Danvers read it, and then slowly folded the sheet. "You have much to think about."

Megan expelled a pent-up breath. "I doubt I'll rush off to Jacksonville because of this, if that's what you mean." She was beginning to wonder if she should return to Florida at all.

But I planned to start school. All my stuff is there in storage in preparation for my move to Gainesville.

"Does this Garrick wish to marry you?"

She shrugged. "Maybe, but as usual, he's vague." *He always was. Until our one showdown.*

Mrs. Danvers tapped the letter with her index finger. "He sounds certain about what you mean to him."

Megan held her tongue.

The woman sat across from her. "I appreciate your sharing. And I will not pry any further. But if you want to talk, I am willing to listen."

She gnawed her lower lip, fighting the urge to confide. Old habits were hard to break. Finally, she blurted, "Once I would've jumped at the offer of marriage. But somehow he never got around to proposing. Just hinting."

"Like in this letter."

"Exactly."

Mrs. Danvers opened the sheet again. "He sounds eager for your return."

"It's not the first time. And nothing changed when we did get back together."

"What is that phrase...? His way or the highway?"

Megan nodded. That's exactly what had happened when she'd been laid off last year. Garrick's only solution was for her move in with him. When she'd refused, sparking an argument, he'd abandoned her. Like he was punishing her for not doing things his way.

"Can I give my opinion, Megan? It is by no means an attempt to make up your mind."

"Please do."

"Anyone who clings this tightly to someone to the exclusion of their own self-respect does not have a healthy love for the person they are pursuing. Or a very stable view of himself."

Megan stared across the kitchen, seeing nothing but the past. "I'd have to agree."

Garrick had only wanted his way. Her feelings, her convictions, had no bearing on his thinking. When she wouldn't give in to him, he'd walked away.

Should I answer the letter? Even if she told him to quit contacting her, Garrick would see it as an invitation to continue hounding her. But remain silent and he might show up someday on her doorstep.

A risk she'd have to take.

She tore the letter in half twice, and then threw it in the trashcan. Time to move on with life.

"I guess you have made up your mind," Mrs. Danvers said.

"Definitely." Not only that, but Megan decided she needed to go to Cheyenne. She'd borrow her uncle's car and leave tomorrow if possible.

CHAPTER 26

“I’m sorry, but we’re not allowed to give out information about our clients.” The young receptionist at the retirement center smiled apologetically and shrugged. She stood behind a massive counter, her stance akin to guarding a fortress.

“I’m not looking for information about him, I just want to know if I can see him.” Megan raised her hands, pleading.

“You’re a family member?”

She debated lying. “No. I wanted to see Jay Rush because of his artwork.” When the woman’s expression didn’t soften, she added, “Listen. Yesterday, I drove four hours to Cheyenne to find out where he lives. They sent me here, another five-hour drive. I spent last night in a terrible hotel so that I could be here first thing this morning." She took a deep breath. "All I want is to talk to Mr. Rush for a few minutes. Surely that's not against anyone's rules."

Frustration edged into her voice, though she tried to filter it. Countless hours in the car, nominal food at a diner, a restless night...all were taking their toll on her. Add her inability to see the attorney in Laramie yesterday as she'd wanted. He'd been tied up all day, unable to see her for even fifteen minutes.

My fault. I should have planned better before setting out. But she'd been too anxious for answers.

"Please." Megan sought to soften her voice. "Is there anyone you can get permission from? Or even ask Mr. Rush yourself? I promise I only want a few minutes of his time. Aren't unannounced visitors allowed?"

The receptionist's fingers twitched. She bit her lip. Megan waited.

"Well, okay. I admit that I don't know everything. I've only been working here a couple weeks. Give me a sec."

"I'll wait in the lobby." She watched the girl head down a hallway.

Megan paced in the small space, squelching her rising agitation. Nothing but roadblocks since she'd set out to find Jay Rush early yesterday. First the Cheyenne gallery owner had unexpectedly left town, so she hadn't a chance to talk to him. Then this additional drive to find a retirement center across Wyoming in...Evanston? The moaning wind, blowing all night, had awakened her numerous times at the rustic hotel where she'd stayed. In the sound, she swore she'd heard her name being called. Over and over.

Am I out of my mind? What was so important about finding out about the painting? Why had she bothered?

I have to know. I have to settle this.

"Miss?"

Megan turned. An older man, clearly an

administrative type in an out-of-style suit, approached.

"I understand you're seeking information about Jay Rush?"

"I just wanted to talk to him for a few minutes." When the man frowned, Megan quickly added, "I'm a great fan of his artwork. I planned to ask him about one of his paintings."

A regretful expression passed over the man's face. "I'm so sorry. But Jay Rush passed away four months ago."

In the parking lot, Megan slumped against the car and released a long, pent-up sigh.

Now what?

She passed a weary hand over her forehead. This had to be the most frustrating series of events she'd faced in recent history. Dead ends everywhere. Again she asked herself, *Now what?*

Might as well head back to the ranch. A long drive awaited. Her fingers fumbled for the door handle.

Wait.

Megan turned, swearing she heard someone speak. No one was in the nearly empty parking lot of the retirement center. The moaning wind swept a blast of dry heat her direction, drawing her gaze to rolling grass-blown hills. In the distance, a herd of horses grazed. She caught her breath as one horse in particular seemed familiar.

A lone black stood out in the middle of the pack. But what made a shiver run down her back was that his head was up. He was looking at her.

He looks just like...

"Excuse me."

Megan took a second to focus on a young woman who called to her.

"Excuse me. Are you the lady who was looking for Jay Rush?"

Megan dragged her attention away from the horses.

"Yes. Yes, I am."

The young woman tilted her head. "I couldn't help but overhear your conversation. I knew Mr. Rush before he passed. Really nice gentleman. He and my grandmother used to visit a lot. They played checkers."

Megan smiled politely, not sure where this was going.

The girl adjusted her glasses. "I know his daughter wouldn't mind your visiting. She doesn't live far from here. It took me a second, but I found her address. Glad I caught you before you drove off."

Megan stared at the paper she held out. It took a moment to find her tongue. "Thank you! I appreciate this more than I can say."

"Ellie Rush?" Megan held her breath, afraid to hope.

The woman in the doorway had to be more than sixty, hair pulled neatly into a bun. A silver filigree cross hung around her neck.

"Yes?" Her response was cautious, face tight.

"My name's Megan Gillespie. I'm sorry to bother you, but could I have a few moments of your time? I have some questions about a painting your father did." She chewed her lip, debating how much more to say. "I've driven nine hours to talk to him. But just found out about his recent passing. I was so sorry to hear." She stopped when Ellie's brow wrinkled. Had she said too much?

The woman glanced at her watch, then back at her. "I have an appointment in about an hour, so don't have much time. Won't you come in?"

A flood of relief swept over Megan as she entered the modest house.

"Sorry, I thought you were a bill collector at first." Ellie walked down a hallway. "Unfortunately, Dad didn't handle money very well. And he gave away so much all the time. Things and money. To whomever..."

Her nose tickled at the odd smells in the house.

"Oh, you're a painter too?"

"I dabble a little. But Dad was a great artist." Ellie indicated a worn chair in her cramped living room.

The place was packed with frames, rolls of canvas, silk flowers and crafts of every kind. From the numerous paintings, Ellie apparently preferred roses and orchids to the rugged western art of her father's.

The older woman smoothed the skirt over her knee. "So what painting did you want to know about?"

Megan briefly described the portrait in her uncle's living room. Now she wished she'd brought the small one painted on canvas. When the artist's daughter frowned, she added details, hoping to jog the woman's memory. A growing sense of frustration sprang up in her, warning that yet again she'd hit a dead end.

"I think I know the one you're talking about." Ellie bobbed one finger in the air, her brow smoothing. "Just a moment while I look something up." She hurried from the room. Footsteps thumped up the stairs.

As minutes ticked by without the woman returning, Megan got up and paced. She glanced out the sliding glass door at the neighbor's overgrown backyard, then sighed. A cuckoo clock chirped, reminding her of the disappearing time.

After almost fifteen minutes, the artist's daughter returned, carrying a large volume that was about the size of a scrapbook. The edges were worn and stuffed with paper. "Sorry, it took me awhile to find this. Buried in a closet." She thumped it on the coffee table. As she looked through the pages, Megan bent over her shoulder.

"Dad was more of a sculptor than painter. But I remembered that he had this sketchbook." She turned ivory-colored pages, which were filled with pencil and charcoal drawings.

Megan held her breath, her gaze searching the art. So far nothing looked like the portrait. Jay Rush had done quite a few horses, coyotes and cattle, but no humans.

"Ah, here." Ellie smiled triumphantly. "I thought I

remembered this...”

Megan sank on the couch beside her, letting out a breath of relief. “Yes. That’s him.” Jay Rush had sketched several aspects of the Native American warrior: his hands, nose, eyes, head.

The woman turned a page, revealing more drawings.

Any lingering doubts ebbed. The man in these drawings, as well as her uncle’s painting, were the same. Jay had perfectly captured the proud visage, the firm set of his jaw, the noble brow, the strong hands. Yet, again, she couldn’t help but see an element of sadness. Despair?

The artist had done six pages of sketches. Ellie turned back when she reached the last drawing.

“I remember Dad talking about this man...years ago. Oh, my. I’d forgotten.” She sat back, lips pursed. “Seems to me I recall him saying he discovered this destitute Indian hanging around one winter. He saw him only occasionally. But finally, Dad convinced him to come inside one particularly cold night. He did that a lot. Inviting strangers in.” Ellie’s cheek twitched at the memory. “I recall Dad giving him money too. Even though he refused it at the time.”

That might explain the stashed bills Megan had discovered if this was indeed Dwells in Shadows.

“I guess he thought the Indian would make a good subject for a painting, although like I said, Dad was more of a sculptor. Did you want to know anything more?”

Megan thought a moment. “Do you recall his name?” She had to be sure that her imagination wasn’t conjuring up a likeness. After all, she’d never seen Dwells in Shadows during the day.

“Hmm.” The woman’s chin pressed on her chest as she leaned against the back of the couch. “I know I know it. The name’s on the tip of my tongue...” The clock in the kitchen cuckooed eleven times. Her head shot up. “Oh, dear. I have to go. I really can’t miss my dentist appointment again. They’d shoot me for sure.” She rose.

Megan stood as well. “Could I leave my number in case you do remember?” She fumbled in her purse for a piece of paper and pen while Ellie flew about the room, getting ready to leave. She followed the artist’s daughter out the front.

The woman locked the door as Megan located a receipt to write on.

“Wait. I remember.” Ellie’s gaze fixed on her, the flurry of activity abruptly pausing. “Moon Dancing. That was his name. It seemed unusual, but made sense since Dad said he saw him only at night.”

Megan’s thrill of discovery was dampened by the name. Moon Dancing? Not Dwells in Shadows? Had she been wrong in thinking the man she’d met was the subject of the portrait?

“Now I must go.” She held out her hand. “It was nice chatting with you, Megan. I hope I answered all your questions.”

“Thank you again for your time.”

Ellie was about to turn away when she said, “You’ve come an awful long way for a name.”

“I suppose.” Nine plus hours in a car was a little long. Especially since the names didn’t match. She manufactured another reason as Ellie continued to scrutinize her. “I guess I’m hoping to find Moon Dancing someday.”

The woman’s brows shot up. “That might be quite a challenge. Or impossible.”

“Why?”

Ellie shook her head. “He’s probably dead by now.”

“Why would you think that?”

The artist’s daughter again pursed her lips. “That portrait of Moon Dancing was done over sixty years ago.”

CHAPTER 27

Sixty years ago. The number pounded in Megan's head as she drove back to the ranch. Sixty. Then Dwells in Shadows couldn't be the subject of the portrait. Was the warrior his father then? Or grandfather?

Though reasonable explanations, something still nagged. But equally foolish was the only other explanation. Moon Dancing, alias Dwells in Shadows, had discovered the fountain of youth. He had to be in his eighties. Or nineties.

Maybe it isn't him.

It has to be.

But I've not seen him in full light.

"I just have to convince him to meet me during the

day." As soon as she spoke that aloud, Megan grew calm...and in a hurry to get back to the ranch. Maybe he'd come while she'd been away and she'd missed him. She pressed harder on the accelerator, hoping highway patrol wasn't in a ticketing mood.

The day was late when she finally drove into the yard. She hauled her suitcase inside, then found out from Mrs. Danvers that her uncle napped, having come down with a cold. Without bothering to unpack, Megan headed straight for her horse. He was in the back corral.

"Shadow!" She climbed over the fence and jumped to the ground.

He whinnied, the sound high and shrill. Then he rushed up to her, hooves thundering. She didn't flinch as he stopped at the last second in front of her. Leaning against him, she patted his neck.

"It's good to see you too." She rubbed him vigorously, loving the calm beauty of his steady gaze.

The horse nudged her, a low sound rumbling in his chest.

"I see I'm not the only one who's glad you're home," Jack said from behind her.

Megan raised her head while Shadow snorted his disapproval and swished his tail.

The foreman stepped on the lowest rung of the fence and leaned his elbows on the top one. "I was beginning to think you weren't coming back."

"I was only gone a couple days." Her hand rested on Shadow's quivering shoulder.

"Felt like forever." His blue-gray eyes wouldn't leave her. "And you didn't even say goodbye."

"I'm sorry. I didn't see you. And I left so early."

He smiled softly. "Well, anyway. You're back. Good to have you home."

"Thanks." She looped her arm under Shadow's neck, tangling her fingers in his mane.

"He's looking mighty possessive these days." Jack indicated her horse.

Megan laughed. "That's because he knows he's won my heart. Completely."

"Rather you've won his heart." He tilted his hat back with a thumb. "If he were a man, I'd be downright jealous."

She laughed again. "It's good to be home."

Jack smiled, gaze softening. "It's great to hear you say that." Then his face clouded. "Promise me you won't run off again without saying goodbye?"

Seemed a simple enough thing to promise. Especially if it would end this uncomfortable scene.

"All right." She cast her gaze down to the dust under her feet. *Please, just go.*

Shadow jerked as he kicked at a pesky fly with his back leg.

"I'd better get back to work." Jack jumped down from the fence. "I should warn you. There's something special going on at the house tomorrow night."

"Oh, no," Megan lamented. "Did my uncle plan a birthday party for me?"

He spread his hands. "If you tell him I said anything, I'll deny it."

"Oh, bother!" She sighed noisily. "Thanks for the warning."

He nodded, then sauntered away.

She pressed her face into her horse's neck. "Oh, Shadow. I wish you were a man. That would keep Jack away."

Her horse made a sound that she was sure meant agreement.

"Megan Gillespie? This is Paul Halleck, the attorney."

"Oh, yes." She pressed the phone to her ear and turned to see who might overhear. No one was in the foyer at the moment. Mrs. Danvers was in the kitchen preparing dinner.

"I'm sorry I wasn't able to see you when you stopped by Laramie a couple days ago."

"My fault. I should've called and warned you I was coming."

"Anything I can help you with over the phone?"

"Yes. I was just wondering why I hadn't heard from you about my trust fund."

The silence at the other end of the phone seemed to go on too long. The attorney finally cleared his throat. "I had hoped Daniel would have talked to you by now."

"Is there a problem?"

Again, awkward silence. "He has not yet signed the papers releasing your trust fund. Until he does, the monies cannot be dispersed. Your parents' will is very specific."

What? Megan clenched the phone.

"Miss Gillespie?"

"Yes, I'm still here." She blew out a breath of shock. "Isn't there anything I can do? I mean, it's *my* money..."

"You could contest the will. That would take time and expense. Or you could wait until your thirtieth birthday. At that point, Daniel's signature would no longer be needed."

"But that's three years away."

"I'm sorry, Miss Gillespie. Besides contesting the will, the only thing you can do is convince Daniel to sign the papers. Our hands are tied until then."

After she hung up, Megan clenched her teeth. *I don't believe this...!*

She knew why her uncle hadn't signed the trust fund over yet. He wanted to keep her in Wyoming. She'd seen his expression when she'd foolishly mentioned her desire to pursue a master's degree. Daniel was deliberately holding back the money.

Unless I want to go into debt up to my eyeballs.

The dinner bell clanged in the distance.

I can't face my uncle now. I'll say something really rude in front of the hired men.

Megan made up her mind in an instant. She headed upstairs, intending to stay in her room until dinner was over. Afterwards though...

On her way up, she met her uncle's caregiver heading down.

"Not coming to dinner?" Randy asked.

"I'm not hungry."

That's the most he'd spoken to her. Ever. Most of the time, he hung in the background, merely doing his job without much fraternization with the others.

Once she reached her room, Megan flopped on the bed. Thinking. Fuming.

"So, what's this all about?" Daniel had waited until she shut the door of his study.

Megan turned, hands clasped. She kept a tight rein on her emotions, having rehearsed her speech. "Can you tell me the reason for your delay in signing my trust fund papers?"

Her uncle's smile slowly faded. He fidgeted and had the grace to appear embarrassed. "I meant to talk to you about that..."

"Well, here I am. Seems as a good time as any."

Daniel scratched his neck. "I was wondering if you could extend your visit a little longer here. At the ranch."

"Impossible. I've already enrolled in school."

"I know it's a lot to ask, but–"

"I agreed to three months. Any more than that is unreasonable."

Daniel made a small sound of indecision, but he remained silent.

She clenched her teeth. "So, in essence, you're blackmailing me to stay longer."

Her uncle's head shot up, brow clashing over his nose. "That's not it at all."

"Yes, it is. And you know it." She kept her voice low, controlled. Megan waited, giving him a chance to explain.

Say something! Tell me I'm wrong.

When he didn't answer, she went on, keeping her gaze locked on his face. "As soon as arrangements can be made, I'm taking Shadow and leaving."

And never coming back.

She resisted speaking the last thought aloud. But from the stubborn look on her uncle's face, she knew he guessed what she thought.

The next day, she purposely stayed out of the house while birthday preparations were underway. She delayed making arrangements for her return to Florida, not wanting to spoil all of Mrs. Danvers' plans. Just because she was upset at her uncle didn't mean she should hurt the housekeeper's feelings. They'd begun to form a friendship.

However, after tomorrow...

As she rode Shadow, she mulled over what had transpired in the last few weeks. Her uncle's actions kept hammering her.

He planned this all along.

She clearly saw how he'd manipulated everything and everyone so he could get his own way. Her imagination galloped through scenarios. Her uncle wanted to use her money and use her. Marry her off to Jack Crawford, his beloved foreman, and secure the future of the ranch. Who cared what she felt or wanted?

"Well, I'm not going to be party to his despicable plans." She spoke aloud, cementing her determination to leave Wyoming as soon as she could.

Reining in Shadow, she stared down the dusty road. Despite her turmoil, the quiet of her travels seeped into her soul. Dry grass rustled while a distant bird chirped happily. Her skin tingled where the sun warmed. She breathed deeply the fresh air.

It'll be hard to go.

Her horse snorted as he patiently waited.

How can I leave Dwells in Shadows?

Her mind roamed over their two meetings. Or more? She had a vague sense of carrying him around in her heart all the time. Perhaps his diary, which she read every night, had something to do with it. From the book, she'd learned of his thoughts and feelings, things rarely discussed with another person until after years of building trust. He had become so real to her that she expected him to show up one day and take her away.

"I can't think of this now. I can't think of *him* right now." Megan spoke aloud, wondering at her conflicting emotions. The man wasn't a friend. Already he seemed beyond that. The "why" and "how" confounded her.

"We'd better turn back." She nudged the stallion into a trot, then into gallop along the long, straight stretch of road. Shadow flew over the ground, his speed making her crouch in the saddle. All she could do was hang on. She jammed her hat harder onto her head when she felt the wind grab at it, teasing her with the possibility of snatching it away. Her eyes blurred, the tears creeping out and trailing along her temples. The road beneath the horse's hooves raced by.

She was scarcely conscious of turning toward the ranch. As they drew nearer to the house, Shadow slowed, bunching his back legs to decrease speed. Megan chuckled at the surprised look on some of the men's faces as they stopped working to watch her.

"Hi-ho, Silver." She wished she knew how to make Shadow rear as the Lone Ranger did his horse.

Her audience grinned, and then returned to their work while Megan walked her stallion to cool him. Her earlier irritation had ebbed, contentment returning. For now.

She spent extra time brushing him, but kept her eye on the clock. Supper was in twenty minutes, she calculated as she got Shadow some oats.

"You haven't been eating much." She viewed the hay still in his feeder box. "Pining away for me?"

She pulled out some of the older hay, preparing to get him some fresh feed when something stabbed her palm.

"Ouch." Megan withdrew her hand and stared at the pinpricks of blood that oozed through her skin. She stooped to examine the hay. "I don't believe this." Gingerly, she pulled a four-inch piece of rusty barbwire from the depths.

"How did that...?" She glanced around, trying to figure out where it had come from. Above the box and along one side of the stall was some that looked like what she'd found. Had someone deliberately pulled the wire out of the wood? Then dropped it in the box?

Megan gritted her teeth. Who would do such a thing? She checked inside again, careful to keep from getting stabbed should there be any more wire. Her search revealed another two-inch piece.

"Who could be so careless...?"

Blade? He was the one who'd cared for Shadow while she'd been gone. As soon as possible, she'd have a word with him.

CHAPTER 28

“Megan, you shouldn’t accuse someone unless you know for certain.” Her uncle glared at her. “You don’t know how that wire got in the feed box.”

She glanced around to the semi-angry faces at the dining table. “I’m not accusing anyone. I only want to know how it got in there. Seems to me that the choices are limited.”

“If you’re accusing Blade–”

“I’m not,” she said firmly. “I didn’t say it was him.”

“I don’t know anything about this.” Blade shrugged. “I noticed your horse was off his hay, but I thought he was moping for you.”

Megan managed a half-smile.

“It would’ve cut up his mouth pretty badly,”

another man said.

"Who would do such a thing?" Mrs. Danvers said.

Megan shot a look at Simone, but she appeared as shocked as everyone else. Besides, she loved horses. Everyone knew that.

"The wire obviously fell off the fence." Daniel thumped the table with his palm. "The explanation is simple."

Several men nodded, quietly discussing the incident amongst themselves.

"Actually, there may be a person who'd want to harm Megan's horse." Jack waited until he had everyone's attention. "We all know someone who has a mean enough streak to seek revenge."

Megan glanced around, noting the acknowledgement in their faces. Kit Gerard. He's the one who could have done it.

"Of course, we don't have proof." Jack fingered his glass of milk. "Wouldn't be wise to spread rumors. But we'll all be on the alert."

A couple men nodded.

Mrs. Danvers tapped a ceramic mug with a dinner knife. "This seems a good time to change the subject. After all, we have a birthday to celebrate."

She nodded to several men who leaped up on cue. One man brought out a commercial-sized bucket of ice cream, another a banner that said, "Happy Birthday Megan." Mrs. Danvers rolled out a massive two-tiered cake, which had been meticulously decorated.

"Simone did the frosting and decorations," the woman explained.

"They're beautiful." Megan smiled stiffly in the girl's direction, trying hard not to imagine the icing flowers having thorns. Daniel banged the table with a spoon after Mrs. Danvers got all twenty-seven candles lit, then led the men in a rousing version of "Happy Birthday."

Megan rose, taking a huge breath to blow out the candles. She didn't quite get them all. After she blew the last one three times, the flame popped back. Realizing she'd fallen for the trick candle that couldn't be extinguished, she laughed. Jack finally pinched out the flame.

Mrs. Danvers gave pointers about how to cut the cake. While the housekeeper served ice cream, Megan carved huge chunks for the men.

Daniel again banged the table with his spoon to get everyone's attention. "In celebration, not only for my niece's birthday, but her arrival, you all have a half-day off tomorrow."

A few of the men cheered.

"That's not all." Jack nodded to a man by the back door. "But a gift for us all."

He rolled in a keg of beer, which elicited greater cheers. Soon, everyone got dessert while he oversaw the drinks.

"A toast." Jack raised a frothy glass. "To the best reason to have a party...because of a special lady who's not only sweet, but a looker as well."

"Here, here." A couple men stood, raising their glasses higher.

"My turn." Daniel waited for everyone's attention. "To the best niece a man could ask for. A woman who's the spitting image of her pretty mother."

Again, drinks were gulped.

"Keep toasting me," Megan said, "and you won't finish the keg until tomorrow afternoon."

Several of the hired hands laughed.

"There is plenty more cake." Mrs. Danvers held up a slice. Men lined up for another.

Megan was glad the barbed-wire incident had been forgotten for now. The party was in full swing with everyone appearing to enjoy themselves. Even Simone lost her perpetual disgruntled look as she hung on Blade's arm, a beer in her hand. Mrs. Danvers was the only person besides Megan who cautiously sipped one drink.

Finally, Daniel said, "I almost forgot your present." He signaled to his personal helper, Randy who disappeared from the room.

He came back a few minutes later, carrying a shiny black saddle. Randy set it down on a spot that was hastily cleared. Megan gaped as she studied the hand-tooled leather and shiny studs. She leaned over to smell the newness of it.

"This is...is very beautiful." She ran her hands over the stiff leather. "Thank you."

"There's a matching bridle that goes with it."

She smiled in appreciation, but couldn't help but think his generosity always seemed to have a price. "I can't wait to try it out."

"I got you something too." Mrs. Danvers handed her a large box.

Megan unwrapped bath salts and soaps, a delicate lavender scent filling the air.

"This will help when you are with a group of smelly men." The housekeeper looked pointedly around the room. Her comment elicited several hoots and chuckles.

"And I got you something as well." Jack pulled a small box out of his pocket.

Megan gulped, her fingers trembling a little as she accepted the gift. The tape gave her trouble. Inside, a tiny horse dangled on a silver necklace. "Oh, it's lovely." She fumbled to put it on.

Jack stepped forward. "Let me–"

"No, I got it." She slipped the jewelry on, not wishing for his help. Already, his gift must seem quite personal.

The horse danced on the end of the chain. "Thank you." Before he could respond, she turned to the men. "And thanks to all of you for making this day special."

The party lasted a couple hours, the hired hands working hard to finish the keg. Knowing her limit, Megan stopped at a couple sips. Daniel chatted with Jack about some plans for a wind generator to provide an endless supply of electricity. With it, her uncle boasted, they could revolutionize the ranch.

A couple men turned in for the night, again wishing her a happy birthday as they exited. Playing hostess, Megan stood at the door to see them out, some solemnly shaking her hand as they bid her goodnight. A few men had obviously gone past their limit in beer, evidenced by their slurred speech and unsteady gate. However, they were all good-natured as they staggered into the night.

"G'night, Meggie." Her uncle nodded in her direction. "I hope you were pleased by your party."

"I had a wonderful time."

Daniel disappeared with Randy, leaving Mrs. Danvers, Jack and Blade, who yawned and mumbled something about being a morning person. He waved goodnight as he went out.

Mrs. Danvers had been cleaning up, but she clearly wasn't finished by the time Jack rose. Megan was aware of the woman, quietly working, as she and the foreman stood at the open back door.

"Been a pleasure, Miss Gillespie." He shook her hand.

"Likewise." She kept her tone light, hand consumed by his large paw. She gently, but firmly, removed it. "But I'm not sure I believe you, Mr. Crawford."

"How so?"

"You don't sound like you've had a good time. Or look it."

"Are you expecting me to reel out of here like a couple of the fellows?"

"Well, perhaps just a little."

"I had enough to make me content." He grinned with a bemused look. "Any more and somehow there's trouble. Not started by me, of course."

Megan chuckled. "I'm sure."

"Sounds like you don't believe me."

"Let's just say, I've been around Wyoming long enough to know that trouble follows some people."

"Hmm." He stood for a moment, gazing down at her, and then glanced at Mrs. Danvers as she passed him. "Do you need any help, Celia? I'd be glad to lend a hand."

"No, thank you," the housekeeper said. "You heard Daniel. Take a half-day off tomorrow. Most of the men will need the extra sleep."

He shifted from one foot to the other. Was he trying

to outstay Mrs. Danvers? Then get Megan alone?

"Well, I'm beat." She yawned.

"Then go upstairs." Mrs. Danvers busily wiped off one table. "I will take care of the rest."

"Thanks." She smiled at Jack. "And thanks again for the nice necklace."

"My pleasure." His eyes grew speculative as she stood before him.

"See you tomorrow." She moved away from him. "Goodnight, Mrs. Danvers."

Megan headed up the stairs without glancing back. After she dressed for bed, she paused at the window, wishing she could go for a late night stroll. The cool air and mysterious sounds beckoned. As she gazed out, she realized the moon was waning. Megan leaned against the windowsill. Perhaps Dwells in Shadows would come.

She sighed as she thought of him. Longed to be with him. The breeze brushed her cheek, making her sigh again.

Movement outside caught her eye. One of the men at the bunkhouse was walking along the front of the building. When he passed the lighted windows, she could see him, but he again disappeared into the shadows, in between the windows.

He stopped, his silhouette framed by the light behind him.

Jack.

She imagined he was staring up at her window. He must be able to see her.

Heart hammering, Megan pulled back and flattened against the wall. Did he think she was looking for him? She railed at herself for being so careless. Despite the fact that he'd changed since her arrival, Jack wasn't the one she wanted. No, she wasn't interested in him. She thought only of the one who dwelled in the shadows of her mind.

She turned on the small bedside lamp, and then shut off the overhead light. After she climbed into bed, she pulled out the diary to read. Instead of going to her place in the middle, the book opened to one of the last entries.

"I saw my angel of fire," he'd written. "Her name is Megan."

CHAPTER 29

She read the entry again, seeing the words, but unable to comprehend them. Angel of fire? Her?

This can't be about me.

Megan read on. "Her hair is the color of the sky after a raid. As she sleeps, silky fire spills over golden straw. Light dances through the curls. I am bewitched. I cannot stop myself from touching her. She is like a newborn foal. She trembles as though in fear. Yet she knows I will not harm her. Her soft cries pierce me, like a twisting knife in the heart. I bleed, yet gladly spill my life for her."

Quivering at the cadence, she placed her hand over the words. She felt like a voyeur who'd stumbled upon the secrets of a man's soul. She shouldn't be reading this.

After putting the book inside a suitcase, she shoved them under her bed. Shaking, she climbed back under the covers, but could not sleep.

Why was she so drawn to this man? She didn't even know him. Nor he her. How could he write such things about her? Despite appeals to logic, something of him called to her from the pages of that book. They were attracted to each other, the powerful pull as irresistible as the moon rising over the mountains.

On impulse, she got up and retrieved the small portrait of him. As she sat on the floor, Megan adjusted the light of her bedside lamp to study the square of leather more closely.

There was no doubt in her mind. This man, who was also called Moon Dancing, was Dwells in Shadows. She was positive. But how was that possible? How could this portrait, a duplicate of the one that had been painted sixty plus years ago, be the same person? She didn't understand, but knew it must be so.

Megan scrutinized the painting which was not as clean or well-kept as the portrait in her uncle's living room. She noticed some differences. The horse was a dark gray with a crescent moon on his forehead. This Moon Dancing didn't hold a bow and arrow, but held on to the horse's mane with one hand, carelessly as though he had no fear of falling from the half-rearing steed. The bracelet, the one he'd given her, dangled from one strong wrist as he rested his hand on his thigh.

"Moon Dancing." She wondered where he was and what he was doing. When would he come to her again? She had no doubt that when the time came, she would know. Somehow.

As she leaned against the bed, staring at the portrait, she felt as though she softly slipped into its dream world. Reality–the hard frame of the bed upon which she leaned, dresser, end table, lamp–faded. She stepped into the darkened half-world of the Indian warrior.

The sharp tang of sweat stung her nose, of both

horse and man. Something else, something much more subtle, invaded her senses. Warmed body oil? She stood at the feet of the horse, waiting for Moon Dancing to snatch her up into his arms. The sound of stamping hooves pounded against her.

She rested her hand on his horse's shoulder. *"Take me with you."*

His dark eyes fastened on hers, pulling her more deeply into the dream.

She reached toward him, fingers brushing his warm arm. After drawing back her hand, she pressed her fingers to her nostrils and inhaled his scent. Fire, danger, aching sadness filled her.

"Please. Please take me with you." Her plea hung between them as she stared into his black eyes.

You must first free me from the shadows. He spoke without his lips moving, arms poised in readiness. The corded muscles flexed in preparation, waiting...waiting for her.

"I will. I swear. Tell me how."

Something hit the screen, jarring Megan from the dream. A moth fluttered at the window. She glanced around. The bedside lamp edged out the endless dark space of the painted canvas. After rolling up the portrait, she rose.

She knew exactly what she must do.

After telling Mrs. Danvers that she wouldn't be back for dinner, she left in the afternoon. To make the housekeeper happy, Megan let her pack a meal for the journey. Deliberately, she kept the time she'd be away vague.

"Before nightfall," she assured the concerned woman.

Then Megan rode off.

She and Shadow spent hours in the grove, waiting for Moon Dancing. She fingered the beaded bracelet, hoping that touching it would somehow summon him. When he didn't come, she packed her things and returned to the ranch. The next afternoon, she followed the same pattern. As well as the next. And the next.

She didn't grow discouraged. He would come. She had no doubt.

Her uncle cornered her after lunch one day. "I was wondering...have you reconsidered leaving?"

She had an answer prepared. "I'm delaying my departure. For now."

His expression melted in relief. "I'm glad."

In a hurry to get to the grove, Megan didn't prolong the conversation. But she couldn't help the verbal jab. "I promised a three-month stay and I'll keep my word. I guess I can put up with this place for a few more weeks."

Her uncle actually looked sheepish, but he didn't reply. Apparently he hadn't relented about her trust fund. *Fine.* She hadn't changed her mind about leaving either. But the departure was going to be on her terms. Not his.

Megan rode out shortly afterwards. A few more weeks and her promise would be fulfilled. Then what? She had to have answers to the questions that plagued her night and day.

When she and Shadow reached the grove, anticipation stretched her nerves, playing her like an instrument. She pressed her hands to feverish cheeks. What insanity gripped her? Though Moon Dancing had not yet come to the grove, the place still soothed the burning that threatened to consume her. This is where she must be.

Many feet from the river, she spread out a blanket on the packed dirt and sat down. Shadow, unbridled and unsaddled, wandered along the bank, nibbling at the tender grass. He'd proven many times that he wouldn't leave her no matter how long they remained in the thicket.

Megan unpacked some of the food she'd brought, not really interested in eating. The task gave her something to do. The afternoon wended its way toward evening, and still Moon Dancing didn't come. Lulled by the gentle roar of the river, she leaned back and stared at the mottled sky through the lacy leaves of the trees. Tired from many restless nights, she closed her eyes.

Megan awakened later, shrouded by darkness. Disoriented, she sat up. Expectation clutched at her. And a sense of unreality. She saw little in the moonless night. A coyote yipped in the distance, the nearby roaring river muting the sound. Above her, the sky was brighter, but the tree-laden grove cut off all light.

A branch snapped, and then she heard the soft *brush-brush* of footsteps in the sand. She sat very still. Was her wait over?

Someone stopped not far from her. Twigs crackled, and then whispered together. Something scraped softly. A flame burst into existence in the blackness. The spot of light moved downward, and then disappeared. Another tongue of brightness appeared, multiplying, gaining life, licking at dry twigs and leaves. The blaze consumed a portion of the dark. In the brightness, she could see the profile of the one who transformed the night into day.

Moon Dancing.

He wore the buckskin clothing from the cave, tasseled ends moving in a hypnotic way as the fire's light danced across his body. He crouched before the flames, dark eyes fixed on the crackling twigs. His hair hung to his shoulders, shiny, inviting.

She could clearly see his features, light chiseling his high cheekbones and square jaw. His straight proud nose and high brow spoke of danger, yet deep passion. But his forehead...*his forehead!*

The mark of a small crescent moon marred his bronzed skin. She gulped.

He looked in her direction. Then he rose and moved noiselessly toward her.

I am in the dream.

This felt just like many other reveries she'd

experienced.

The scent of spring rain and wild grasses filled her senses. Moon Dancing stepped closer, stopping before her, his form and face blanketed in shadows.

"Come." He spoke in a deep, preternatural voice. The light banked against his outstretched hand.

Still a dream? Megan placed her fingers against his smooth, warm palm. He pulled her to her feet. Her shoe catching on the blanket, she stumbled, but he held her steady.

"You are cold." His soft voice wrapped around her as he led her to the fire.

Reality and unreality blended, lines blurring.

He still held her hand, and then raised it to stare at the bracelet she wore. His eyes glittered with pleasure as he released her fingers and stepped away to crouch before the warmth.

She hesitated to speak, afraid her voice would shatter the dream. "You came." She stretched her palms toward the fire. Heat skipped across her skin.

"I was always here."

She blinked at the blazing fire, her sense of time and place still teetering. If she were dreaming, then it didn't matter what she said. "Why did you write those things about me?"

He studied her, light flickering across his face. "Because they are true."

Megan returned his perusal. The portrait, as fine as it had been executed, fell short of the person before her. He *was* the one Jay Rush had painted. She didn't know how, but could not deny the truth.

"Why did you go away?" he surprised her by asking.

"To find out about you...Moon Dancing."

He didn't react beyond his eyes gleaming more brightly. "You know who I am."

She wanted to make that claim, but couldn't. "No. I only know your name. I still don't know who you are."

He stood. "My name isn't important. Who I am, is."

Her heart started to hammer. "You left your diary for me to find."

"Yes."

"To tell me about yourself. Why?"

He drew closer, and then touched her arm. "For you to learn of me more quickly than time allows."

She couldn't ask why, that question unable to escape the recesses of her heart. The sense of unreality pressed on her harder.

"What do you want of me?"

His grip on her arm tightened. "Only what you have given already." He drew her gently to him.

"I've given you nothing." She was powerless to resist his gentle, but persistent pull.

"Yes, you have. And now you will do so again, while I am in my own flesh. The same, only different. Human to human."

He tugged her closer, slowly. Megan kept her eyes open, watching the dream unfold.

"I did not kiss your lips as you slept in the stables, though I was tempted." He spoke softly. "I wanted you awake, fully, to share in this delight."

Mesmerized, she watched as he bent his head.

At the first touch of his lips, she shuddered. His mouth softened as it moved over hers, testing, delighting, savoring. Full of promise, the kiss tantalized her beyond the enchantment of sleep.

This isn't a dream. It can't be.

Under the soft tunic, she felt the very real ridges of chest muscles. The smell of the leather and the heat of the fire were too real. The sound of the spitting wood as flames consumed it was too real.

Warm, gentle hands slid up her arms, pulling her more tightly against himself. Megan sensed the raw masculinity that sought to bend her to his will. His heartbeat pounded, drumming through her, demanding that her pulse match his accelerating rate.

Megan pressed her hands against him, arching away. "This, no…you go too fast."

"You are afraid." Though his words were soft, his hold was relentless. "Do not be. I will not harm you. Do not be afraid."

She gaped, comprehension suddenly flooding

through her. "That is what I told Shadow. Several times. The first time we met at the ranch, you said that as well. You used my exact words. How did you know?"

"You spoke them to me."

"To Shadow."

"To me."

"No, I spoke them to my..." Her gaze again strayed to the crescent moon on his forehead. The white marking looked just like...

A chill gripped her, rending the powerful illusion that had wrapped her in warmth. Megan struggled to pull away.

His hold tightened. "You spoke them to me. Many times. When my eyes were blindfolded, ropes choking me, you said them. Your gentle voice called to me in the darkness of pain. I did not believe them at first. Until you touched me. I trembled at that first caress, my savage spirit soothed by the touch of a human. Of you."

She struggled more. "You're not...you can't be..." She left the sentence unfinished, unwilling to voice the folly.

"I told you who I am by the name I gave you. And still you do not believe."

"Dwells in Shadows."

"Not Shadows, but *Shadow*. Dwells in Shadow."

No. This cannot be.

The man released her. Megan felt as though the night held its breath while she stood trembling before Moon Dancing.

"Now you know the truth," he said. "I *am* Shadow."

CHAPTER 30

Megan stepped backwards toward the fire. Heat scorched her back.

I am with a madman.

She glanced around. “Where’s my horse? What did you do with him?”

He stepped closer. “I told you. I am he.”

“No.” She shook her head. “That’s not possible.”

He spread his hands. “I have given you all that is mine so that you will know the truth. And still you will not accept this?”

She stared at him, his face fully illuminated by the light. He didn’t look crazy. Yet what he spoke was out of the realm of reality. She refused to delve into that insanity.

I need to run. To escape. Now.

He seemed to know what she thought because he crouched again by the fire. Carelessly, he tossed in a twig. "If you will not believe, then I have no hope."

The simple cry wrenched her heart. She couldn't escape. What folly to think so. Something deep inside responded to his pain, keeping her more of a prisoner than if he'd bound her hand and foot.

He glanced in her direction before staring again into the fire. "It was on such a night, many, many winters ago, I gave up hope of truly living again. I chose to act and survive as a rogue. I hated the men who set out to capture me and bend me to their will. By my wits, I eluded them. For many moons. Then one called Crawford set a trap for me. I could not escape.

"His men stole my freedom, then my sight. I could not run fast enough. My strength failed me. I could not free myself. Ropes burned my skin. They tore me in many directions at the same time. They jeered at me, crushing my spirit. Then they starved me."

He paused, and then looked slowly up at her. "Until a woman called to me out of the darkness. I fought giving in to her sweet voice. She brought me food and water, and tamed the savagery that consumed me. They did not know she helped me. She came at the darkest hours, when despair ate at me. Yet, I believed she was only an illusion.

"The full moon came, a promise of freedom, but my strength left me. I vowed to kill the next human I met. To show these men that they failed to break me. As I escaped my prison I heard someone. I gathered my strength and waited. A woman passed. I did not care. Hatred strengthened my sinews. I sprang. My hand closed around her throat. Then I saw her hair."

He stopped, his jaw clenching and unclenching.

Hypnotized by his story, Megan squatted across from him. "What happened?"

He took so long answering that she thought he wasn't going to. "I stopped myself from killing her. Yet when I did, my spirit withered. I prayed to die."

"Why?"

"I remembered the legend. A legend from countless winters ago. A spirit of fire–one you call angel–would one day set me free."

Megan remembered the journal entry and gulped. "How?"

"At first I thought she would free me from this body of flesh. I was wrong."

"Then how can you be freed?"

He shook his head. "I do not know."

She scooted back a little as the fire singed. "What do you want from me?"

"I told you. What you have already given."

"Given? I've given you..." She stopped, rubbing her palm over her forehead.

"Food. Water." He waited until she again gazed at him. "Love."

Megan folded her arms, both cold and hot at the same time.

"Each time you touch the one you call Shadow, you touch me. I know the gentleness of your caress, the passion of your embrace and kiss. Your tears. Many times, I called and you came. I know your heart. Your strength. Your fire."

Her teeth began to chatter.

"The last time I became human, during the full moon, you lay in the straw beside me. I touched your hair and your face. But you slept. I vowed next time you would be awake. I knew that you thought of me because you came here, every day, waiting for the new moon."

Megan scrambled to her feet. "You were hiding somewhere around here. That's how you know I came."

"Always I was with you. Did I not bring you here the first time? Did I not show you were to find my book? The writings of my life?"

She shook her head. "Coincidence. Shadow used to belong to you. That's why he knew where your things were."

Moon Dancing studied her, and then shook his head. "Why do you not believe what your heart tells you?" When she crossed her arms, refusing to answer, his face hardened. "Go. There is nothing here to hold you."

He sat down, his dismissal complete.

Megan studied the chiseled features of his face. A door had shut, closing her off from him. She felt as though an arctic breeze swept through the grove. Gone was the warmth of the fire though she stood mere feet away. Emptiness echoed in her, the vacuum frightening.

"I–I c-can't go." She wrapped her arms about herself. "I have no way to get home."

He didn't look at her as he spoke. "Wait until morning. Then you will have a way."

What was she supposed to do in the meantime? Stand there all night?

Teeth chattering, Megan retrieved the blanket and pulled it around herself. Then she sat away from the fire. Any closer would be an intrusion on the man who stoically ignored her.

He stared into the flames, oblivious to her distress as the night grew darker. By the time midnight came, her eyes burned. Exhausted to the point of tears, she rested her head on drawn-up knees. She grew more chilled, miserable in her half-asleep state.

Sometime later, between dream and wakefulness, she felt herself lifted and carried. Warmth flooded over her. Her body floated down. Megan stretched, and then snuggled onto the soft place that smelled of moist soil and green grass. She sighed deeply as sleep pulled her under.

Glowing embers were the first things she saw when she awakened. Megan sat up, flinging away the covering.

Her horse, Shadow, stood calmly watching her, the saddle and bridle where she'd left them nearby.

She gulped, and then glanced around.

A dying fire crackled softly before her. Under her

was a blanket, yet on top was a heavy fur that had come from the cave. She knew that she'd not gotten it and pulled it over herself. Just as she'd not made the fire.

"This is impossible."

The sky reddened with the promise of morning, reminding her that she'd spent the entire night outdoors. She flung together her things, then saddled and bridled Shadow. The last thing she did before she left the grove was roll up the furs and put them away.

Right now, she would not think of Moon Dancing...or Shadow.

Her horse took his time as they plowed through the river, then out of the ravine. When Megan tried to kick him into a faster pace, he refused to obey.

"Come on, you stubborn...stubborn..." She broke off when she realized what she almost said.

Stubborn man?

They passed between the hills, plodding toward the dirt path which would lead them to the main road. Shadow trudged on, uncaring that she seethed with frustration and impatience.

"Can't you move any faster?" She kicked his sides again.

His hooves seemed to drag.

Something collapsed inside her. "It is impossible for a man to be a horse. Impossible. Do you hear? Things like that don't happen. You can tell your master, whatever name he goes by, that I don't believe him. I'll never believe him. I don't care what he says."

Shadow stopped.

Growling, Megan kicked his sides. Then she slapped his neck. Hard. He turned his head and nipped her leg.

She shrieked, and then leaped off. For several moments, she stared at him. His large dark eyes calmly met hers. "I don't care who–*what*–you are, you have no right to do that to me."

Face expressionless, Shadow merely looked at her.

Megan shut her eyes, trying to figure out what to do. "You aren't human. You can't be."

He hadn't moved, but she didn't have the courage to climb back onto the saddle.

"I know," she said in a sweet tone. "Moon Dancing has trained you so that whenever someone speaks to you in a cross voice, you become aggressive. I'll talk to you nicely while calling you a stubborn mule and you'll never know the difference."

She kept her smile in place as she approached him. "There's a good boy. Now, let me climb on your flea-bitten hide and we'll be on our way."

He bit her again, this time catching her forearm.

"Ouch!" She slapped at his nose, but missed. "You mangy, worm-infested mule." She swiped at the reins, but he swung away, taking a kick at her. Megan chased after him, but he kept out of her reach. For more than twenty minutes, she tried to recapture him. Finally she stopped, gasping air as she gripped her knees.

Shadow whinnied victoriously, then bucked a few times as though trying to rid himself of the saddle. The last thing she saw was him disappearing around a bend of the road.

She was stranded.

Megan shrieked her frustration. If she'd know she was going to walk, she would have headed out the night before. For over an hour, she followed the direction he'd gone, her anger slowly dissipating.

"A horse that isn't a horse. Why, oh why did I buy him?"

As she trudged down the road, her certainty grew with each step. Shadow wasn't just a horse. She could refuse to believe the evidence all she wanted, but she couldn't escape the truth.

"He really is a man."

After she voiced the thought aloud, conviction washed over her. Now she understood the intelligence in his eyes, the way he anticipated her moves, his gentle affection. The extraordinarily easy time she'd had "taming" him was no credit to her.

She also understood his temper. And pride. Not because he was an animal gone wild, but a man gone wild.

"It can't be true." She sat down on the ground. "I'm in love with my horse."

She was still sitting beside the dirt road when a whistle pierced the air.

CHAPTER 31

Three men thundered down the hill toward her. As she rose to meet them, Jack pulled up his horse. He flung himself from his mount and grabbed her into his arms.

"Are you all right?" His gaze searched her face, and then raked over the rest of her. "We've been out of our minds with worry."

"Yes, fine." Megan glanced at the two men who sat on their horses nearby. She tried to push away from him.

He wouldn't release her. "What happened? Where's your horse?"

"Took off. Stranded me." The statement seemed

enough explanation for why she'd been gone all night.

Jack took off his hat and reshaped it before putting it back on. "If he shows up again, I'll shoot him myself."

"No!" Megan clutched his shirt, afraid he was serious.

He looked down at her, the corners of his eyes crinkled from weariness. "I didn't mean it. Betting we'll never see him again."

Frightened of the very real possibility she caught her breath. "I'm sorry for giving you all such a scare." She included the two men with Jack. "And thanks for searching for me."

"We've pretty much been on the trail since last evening."

She blew out her breath. "I'm so sorry."

"Don't be. It wasn't your fault. You haven't been walking all night, have you?"

"No."

"Musta been a cold one for you."

Megan chewed her lip, debating how much to admit. "Let's just say, I've had more comfortable."

Jack flashed a grin. "I'll bet. We need to let O'Connor know." He pulled a cell phone out of his saddlebags. Megan listened wryly as he told her uncle that they'd found her and the reason she'd been out all night.

He listened for a minute at the voice on the other end of the line before hanging up. Jack turned to her. "You won't believe this, but your horse just showed up at the ranch. Seems he reconsidered the good deal he's got."

"Meggie, I was so worried." Her uncle reached for her from his wheelchair. He'd been waiting in the yard when she arrived with Jack and the men. "I thought..." He didn't finish his sentence.

Hesitating only a moment, she went to him. His embrace tightened for a second.

Though humbled by his show of affection, Megan couldn't forget that he still blackmailed her with her trust fund. She fought against the softening of her heart. His red-rimmed eyes and tight mouth, spotlighted in the brilliance of the morning sun, would not wipe out that truth.

"There now, enough of that." Daniel's gruff voice pushed her away. "Glad you're okay."

She stood awkwardly before him, aware of their growing audience. "I should probably go take care of Shadow."

"Blade already did." Jack moved closer.

"Thanks again for rescuing my niece." Daniel stuck out his hand to his foreman.

"My great pleasure, sir."

Megan didn't miss the way her uncle's other hand clasped Jack's arm or his grateful expression.

"I'm going to head upstairs and sleep, if you don't mind." She hurried into the house without waiting for a response. A glance over her shoulder confirmed that her uncle and his foreman appeared deep in conversation. They were making it sound like he'd rescued her from an armed assailant.

As she stood in the shower, she braced her hand against the wall. Water pounded on her body as one thought pounded her mind.

"Moon Dancing," she murmured, closing her eyes. Despite the sound of the shower, she swore she could hear Shadow's whinny. And later, though she pulled the blankets over her head to sleep, she heard his whispered call, even in her dreams.

When she later awoke, she stared at the dancing shadows and light on her ceiling, her thoughts still full of him. How had he become a horse? If she'd not been so close-minded, she might have found that out. What did he mean by her being his last hope? How? One thing was certain...she had to help him. But in order to do that, she had to know more.

What does he want from me?

Her heart started to hammer as she remembered his voice.

"What you've already given. Food, water, love." Apparently, he didn't want or need anything more from her. He was content with how things were.

Why? One possible answer touched the fringes of her heart, daring her to examine it.

Last night, she'd sat in the cold darkness, shivering in misery. He'd carried her to the fire and covered her with his furs. Megan squeezed her eyes tightly shut, remembering his kiss. And then in the barn...he'd touched and caressed her, like she touched and caressed Shadow.

He loves me. He gave, wanting, but not expecting, anything in return.

A whinny made her bolt upright in bed, then rush to the window. Shadow ran in the pasture, galloping back and forth along the fence, mane and tail flying as his hooves ate up the ground under him. His coat gleamed under the afternoon sun. Leaning on the windowsill, she watched, captivated by his beauty.

"Shadow," she whispered.

He stopped as if he'd heard her, pawing the ground and whinnying again. Calling to her.

Before she could think, she ran barefoot down the steps and outside. As she drew nearer, she slowed. Panting, Megan stopped several feet from the fence.

He tossed his head, encouraging her to come to him. Her heart was so full that she felt like weeping. She extended her hand as she stepped forward. He didn't move as she touched his soft nose, sliding her fingers up until she touched the pale crescent on his forehead.

The truth overwhelmed her again. "Moon Dancing. You are Moon Dancing."

He nickered softly, nuzzling her shoulder.

She flung her arms around his neck.

"I found shards of glass in his oats." Heartsick, Megan showed her uncle the coffee can with the evidence. It had been four days since the incident of her being out all night. Apparently the maliciousness concerning Shadow was back.

She set the glass-laced oats on his desk. "This is no harmless prank. Nor is it just a coincidence. Someone has deliberately set out to hurt Shadow."

Daniel stared at the can, his face pinched. "Have any of the other horses been given this?"

"I don't think so."

"Have you told anyone about it?"

"No. Not yet."

"Then let me handle this."

She took a breath, and then pressed her hand against her mouth, unable to hold back her tears.

"Ah, Meggie." Her uncle moved around the desk. He took her hand, rubbing it comfortingly. "I'll do all I can to find out who's responsible, then whale on 'em. They can't get away with this, and I won't let them. I'll talk to Jack and Blade. They'll keep a lookout."

She stifled her tears, relieved to know that her uncle was going to do something this time. That he didn't brush it off like the incident with the barbed wire. She trembled to think what would have happened if Shadow–Moon Dancing–had eaten the oats.

She wiped her cheeks with the back of her hand. "Think it might have been Kit Gerard? I heard he got fired from the Bakers."

"I don't know, Meggie."

"Sam said no one knows where he went."

"I'll check that out. I promise." Daniel patted her arm. "Go get some supper. You'll feel better after eating."

She nodded. At the door she turned. "I'm going to sleep in the stable tonight. I'd feel better about watching over Shadow myself."

He nodded. "Good idea."

Instead of going to the kitchen though, she headed outside. With the men assembling for dinner, no one would be at the stables. If Gerard were responsible, he'd know this was their mealtime. It would be now, or sometime at night that he'd do his dirty work.

She went to the stables, passing through the tack room to grab a hoof pick. As she shut the door, the inner one opened, having been improperly latched. After searching the shelves, she found the tool. Voices from inside the barn made her pause.

"So will you?" begged the voice of Simone.

A low, man's voice responded. Jack's?

The sound of their embrace came to her before the two moved out of the building. She had an urge to rush into the barn, to let Jack see that she knew about him and Simone, but what would be the point? When Shadow whinnied, she thought only of him.

Megan ran her hand over his neck. "What are we to do? Who wants to hurt you?"

The discovery of the altered oats hadn't been because of her, but him. Shadow had refused to eat them after they'd gotten back from their ride. Upon examining them, she'd seen what he already knew was there.

She stopped petting his neck as something occurred to her. "Do you know who's responsible? Did you see who put the glass in your oats?" Then she realized that he couldn't tell her, could say nothing until the next full moon. Full and new, those were the only times Moon Dancing shed his animal covering and transformed into a man. In less than two weeks now.

She resumed her caress. "You and I have much to talk about next time."

Shadow tossed his head and pawed the ground, she hoped in agreement.

CHAPTER 32

"How-do, Miss Gillespie."

"Hello." She nodded at Miles, the man who'd driven her from Cheyenne.

"In town to do a little shopping?" He stood squarely in her way on the sidewalk.

Megan smiled at his obvious prying. "Merely picking up some things for the ranch." She stepped past him, moving towards the general store.

He stopped her by saying, "I see Jack Crawford came too."

"What'd'ya know. I guess that is his truck."

Miles grinned broadly. "You sure do make a handsome couple, if you don't mind my saying."

She tilted her head. "Thanks, but we don't make a couple at all." She walked away before he could say anything else.

While she was checking things off a list, Jack joined her a little later. "Finished at the feed store?" She consulted the pile of things before her on the counter.

"Yes, but take your time. I'm in no hurry."

"Good." She shook her head over the many things that Mrs. Danvers had included on the list. "I got a few more things to pick up."

"You know, it's awful nice of you to do this for Celia." Jack crossed his arms and leaned against the counter. "With Simone leaving and all."

"I won't believe it until I see her walking out the door with her suitcases." Megan still had trouble comprehending the young woman's sudden announcement that she wanted to go to school. More surprising was that she was moving to Denver in the middle of the summer to get a job ahead of time.

"What can't you believe? That you're the only one capable of uprooting their life and starting over somewhere else?"

"No. It's just that..." She pressed her lips together, realizing she'd said too much.

"That what?"

"I heard her crying the other night. Didn't sound like someone eager to move away."

Jack shrugged, and then glanced at the door as the jangling bell announced another patron. When he frowned, Megan looked over. Jed Harper, the man who'd ridden up with her to Silver Springs, entered the store.

"Must be my lucky day," she muttered under her breath. "First Miles, then him."

Jack grinned. "You know, now that we're here, I think I'll pick up some things for myself." He moved away while she went back to her list.

Aspirin, matches, non-iodized salt, pencils, black thread...among other things. She read through the list, comparing it with what was waiting to be rung up. Some of the items looked like things Simone would take with her.

Again she was struck by the young woman's decision. Why now? And why so far away? Then to hear Simone secretly sob her heart out? It didn't make sense.

Megan realized that she'd forgotten rubbing alcohol and wide gauze bandages. She headed to the back of the store. Bending, she found the alcohol, but didn't immediately see the other.

The murmur of quiet voices didn't strike her at first, until she realized one of them was Jack's. She found the bandages, and then rose in time to see him escort Jed Harper to the door. The foreman had his hand on his shoulder and was speaking to him in a low voice.

"This everything, Miz Gillespie?" The storeowner magically appeared from the back.

"I hope so."

"Mrs. Danvers sick? She's the one who usually does this shopping."

"I gave her a day off." Megan was hanged if she was going to tell the town's busybodies more than they needed to know. She wasn't going to fertilize the gossip vine that grew so prolifically.

As she paid, Jack showed up at her side, and then took five of the seven bags. "This isn't bad when you consider how much food everyone on the ranch consumes."

"Well, about half are groceries, half are other things."

They put the bags in the back of the truck.

"I almost forgot. I need to get the mail." Megan headed down the street.

"Hold on. I'll go with you."

She slowed, even though she disliked their public togetherness. Out of the corner of her eye, she caught sight of their reflection in the windows of the stores they passed. Faces peered out, some of them smiling, others smirking.

When they reached the post office, she mentally groaned when she saw that Miles had ensconced himself in the small cubicle and was gabbing at the postmistress.

"And here they are now." He grinned broadly.

"Hello, again." She managed to speak with scant politeness. "I need our mail," she said to the woman whose nameplate indicated she was Dorcas.

"You know Daniel O'Connor's niece, don'cha?" Miles said.

"Sure do." The woman beamed at her. "And I knew her mother. We went to high school together. If you don't mind my saying, Miss Gillespie, you're a spitting image. I always did envy your mom's red hair."

Megan smiled. "Mail?"

Dorcas nodded. "I'll be right back."

"An' how're you doing, Jack?" Miles slyly winked a couple times.

"Fine. Something wrong with your eye?"

"Nah." He rubbed it, barely suppressing a grin.

"I'm sure the doc could look at it. If nothing else, Megan bought some rubbing alcohol. She'd be glad to pour some in your eye to wash it out."

Miles slapped his leg and squawked while Dorcas called from the other room. "What are you saying? You don't put rubbing alcohol in folks' eyes."

Megan pressed her lips together to keep from smiling.

"Well, here it is. Quite a stack for the Double O." The woman set the sizable pile on the counter. Then she tapped the top letter. "This one looks mighty important. And it's addressed to you, Miss Gillespie."

"I see. Thank you." Megan picked up the stack, merely glancing at the letter. A letter from the university? However, she knew better than to open it with three witnesses.

Miles was craning his neck. "Sure looks official. You ain't in trouble with the law, are you Miz Gillespie?"

"Does appear like they caught up with me." She turned to Jack, smoothing on a solemn look. "Maybe we'd better head directly to the sheriff."

Miles hooted, but her teasing accomplished what she'd hoped. The man momentarily forgot about the letter.

"If she turns herself in, she'll be lonely, y'know," the busybody said, turning to more embarrassing play. "You'll have to visit her in jail."

"Yessir. I'll make it a point to be here every morning." Jack's gaze fixed on her.

"And stay all day, I'll warrant," Dorcas threw in.

"Daniel'll have to find himself another foreman." Miles chuckled again, and then sobered. "Hey. Speaking of foreman, did you hear about the upcoming marriage?"

"Now, Miles." Dorcas pushed his shoulder. "You shouldn't be embarrassing these young folks."

Megan felt as though someone had lit a match to her face. Jack's expression was unreadable as he shifted from one foot to the other.

"I'm not talking about them, Dorcas. Leastways, not right now." Miles glanced at them and smirked.

Megan edged toward the door.

"Now hold on, Miz Gillespie. I ain't told you my news." He paused, lifting a chipped fingernail in the air. "Ben Gossner's getting hitched."

Megan raised her brows. So, what Sam had told her was true. Not surprising. Ever since the bad ending to their date and then his refusal to return calls, she'd figured any relationship was over. Before it had begun.

"Ben's getting hitched?" Dorcas said in mock disbelief. "Who's the girl?"

"Candy, his high school sweetheart. Guess they patched things up a'tween 'em. Hey, Jack, didn't you date her too?"

His gaze shot to Megan than back to the gossip. "Don't remember."

Miles hooted. "Not if you got a better girl here, right?"

"Well, thanks for the visit." Megan grabbed the doorknob. "But we really have to be going."

"Catch you later." Jack tilted his hat in the direction of the two older people.

Before the door closed behind them, she heard the

woman say, "Wasn't Miss Gillespie dating Ben once upon a time? Wonder what happened."

Her spine ramrod straight, Megan stalked to the truck and yanked the door open. In her haste to escape from town, and anyone else who wanted to corner her, she bumped her arm. Several of the letters flew onto the dusty street.

"Let me." Jack bent to retrieve the mail.

After she awkwardly gathered the letters, she tossed them onto the truck seat. Jack climbed in, but not before she saw him stuff something into his back pocket.

"It's mine," he said easily before putting the other things on the stack.

She noticed that her letter was on the top. In order not to draw any more attention to it, she left the envelope there, determined not to touch it until they were at the ranch.

They pulled out of town before he spoke again. "I'm sorry for the embarrassment at the post office."

"Wasn't your fault."

He shot her a grin. "Miles has too much time on his hands."

"That's the understatement of the year."

They rode in silence for a while. Finally, Jack cleared his throat. "I'd heard about Gossner. And was going to tell you. Miles beat me to the punch."

"Is that what Jed Harper was telling you?"

He looked startled for a minute. Then he nodded. "Yeah. Among other things."

"I'm glad to see you two getting along now." She recalled her first day in Silver Springs and Jack's blatant hostility toward the man.

Again he nodded, and then apparently made up his mind about something. "Jed had some trouble with the law a few years back. Folks don't talk about it, since the incident greatly embarrassed his father. I, uh, happened to be friends with Jed. Before the trouble. He implicated me in the crime. Though I was subsequently cleared, it caused a breech in our friendship."

"I should say so."

He pulled at his ear. "So...you okay about Gossner getting married?"

She shrugged. "He can do whatever he wants with his life." Then she scrutinized him. "But turnabout's fair play."

"What's that supposed to mean?"

"You asked me about Ben, so I get to ask you about someone."

Jack spoke slowly. "All right. Who?"

"Simone. How do you feel about her leaving?"

He shrugged. "She can do whatever she wants with her life."

"That's not fair. You're using my words."

"What exactly do you want to know then?"

"Well..." Megan dragged out the word, not wishing to admit having eavesdropped. Even accidentally. "Sometimes it seemed like she preferred your company."

"Ah-ha," he said in a knowing tone. "And because of that, you think I might pine away for her?"

"I'm only asking."

His jaw jutted, then relaxed. "You hear something on the grapevine?"

"I couldn't divulge my sources."

"Well, I won't deny that there once was something between Simone and me–"

"Or you and Candy."

"Or me and Candy. At one time. But they're in my past. A long time ago. That is something you can rest assured." He took his gaze off the road longer than was safe.

Megan managed a stiff smile before looking out the window. Rest assured? And a long time ago? Perhaps with Candy, but not the young woman back on the ranch.

A thought suddenly struck her. What would happen once Simone left? Would Jack turn his full attention on her?

CHAPTER 33

The hot sun beat down on Megan's head as she walked Shadow alongside the road. A perfect, lazy-summer day. She glanced to the horizon, an odd lump settling in her stomach at the thought of leaving.

I like it here now. I'd hate to go.

Her mind skipped back to the letter she'd received from the university. The long-awaited acceptance letter to the master's program. Her dream shot.

Empty now. She had no way to pay for school without her trust fund. If she moved back to Florida, she would have to get a job. Her free-lance consulting work wouldn't support herself and a place suitable for Shadow.

But could she really leave Wyoming? Would Moon Dancing go with her?

What if he refuses?

The next thought rapidly followed.

If he won't go, I can't.

Still wrestling with herself, she wasn't immediately aware of a vehicle that came up behind her on the road. When a horn sounded, Shadow shied.

"I'm sorry." Sam called out the window. "I thought you heard me coming."

"My fault. I was daydreaming."

"A dangerous thing to do on that much horseflesh."

She pulled Shadow to the side of the road. "What brings you out here?"

"Investigating some sheep deaths at the Alberton ranch. Then I was heading over to your uncle's to find out how his mare's doing. He's nervous about her foaling. As usual."

Megan smiled. So that's what had preoccupied her uncle. "Well, I'm heading that way, so I'll catch a cup of coffee with you in a few."

"Sounds great." She got a furrow of worry between her brows. "Before I get to Daniel's though..." She paused and pursed her lips.

"What is it?"

"I was wondering. Have you heard anything about pranks on animals or anything?"

A chill gripped Megan, especially at the way her friend looked up at her.

The vet continued. "I don't want to alarm you, but some weird stuff has been going on in the last few weeks in this area. But not on your ranch? I wasn't going to bring it up to Daniel unless necessary."

"Actually..." Megan licked her dry lips, wondering how much to tell. "A couple incidents have happened."

"Could be coincidences, but I'm going to start keeping a log." Sam revved the engine a little. "Hey, wanna race?"

Megan tossed her head back and laughed. "All right. But be prepared to lose."

Her friend revved the engine again, and then squealed tires as she shot down the road. Shadow was ready, taking off the second the truck moved. For a few minutes, they gave some competition, but couldn't hope to keep up. The last Megan saw of the vet was an arm waving out the window.

She let the stallion keep up the pace for as long as he wanted, enjoying the nearly non-vertical movement of his body as he galloped all out. Down the road, she saw where the pavement had washed away, creating a tiny chasm. Because Shadow had jumped it before, she leaned forward in preparation. He slowed ever so slightly.

Body bunching, he soared over the spot. She laughed aloud at the joy of flying through the air. Then the ground came at them, Megan tightening her hold as they hit. Another second to recover...

Something seemed to snap somewhere. One minute, she was on Shadow, the next she was hurtling toward the ground.

She screamed. Or perhaps Shadow. Then she knew no more.

Megan. Megan. Megan.

She moaned, feeling as though her head would fly apart if she moved.

"She's coming around."

The voice pierced her eardrums, the growing ache reverberating inside her head. She heard herself whimper.

"Megan." Worry consumed Sam's tone. "Wake up, Honey."

Someone patted her hand. Megan couldn't move her other arm. She fought to slip back to the realm of no pain, but those nearby wouldn't allow it. A cool wetness touched her forehead, jarring her from that nether world.

Far off and away, she heard a shrilling.

"Moon–Moon..." She struggled to call to him, knowing he cried for her.

"Moon...what?" Sam's voice turned away. "I don't know what she's asking for."

Megan blinked open her eyes, knowing she must reassure him. *Something happened to me.* She had to go to him. “My…my horse.” She gingerly ran her tongue over her swollen lower lip.

“He’s fine.” Sam touched her shoulder. “He’s fine, Megan.”

She looked around the room without moving her head. Her uncle patted her hand. Mrs. Danvers stood to one side, holding a wet cloth. Sam knelt beside the couch. Jack stood a short distance away, face ashen.

“Sha–Shadow.” She fought to make herself heard, wanting to go to him.

“He is unhurt, Megan.” Mrs. Danvers drew closer and touched the wet cloth to her head. “He helped rescue you.”

She squeezed her eyes shut, frustrated that they didn’t understand what she wanted. More frustrating that she couldn’t tell them.

A rustle of plastic scraped her hearing.

“Let me repack the ice bag,” Mrs. Danvers said.

“Good idea.” Daniel cleared his throat. “And Jack, go see what you can do about that horse. If you can’t handle him, send Blade.”

“Yessir.” Jack’s heavy footsteps strode away.

When the room became quiet, Sam said, “I think you should have the doc look at Megan. She has a nasty sprain and may have a concussion. No broken bones though.”

Megan’s uncle made a sound of relief.

“I don’t want to downplay this though, Daniel. She could have been more seriously injured. Or even–”

“It was an accident. That’s all.”

“Accident? With a tampered cinch strap?”

“Keep it down.” Daniel growled. “Listen, I’ll handle this, okay?”

“You have to get the sheriff involved, Daniel. You can’t let this go.”

“I’ll handle it my own way.”

“Like you handled that other incident?”

He made a low sound in his throat. “You promised not to bring that up again.”

"I'm bringing it up because I'm your friend."

"Drop it."

"Only if..." Sam broke off as footsteps came toward the room.

"Here is the fresh bag, Daniel," said Mrs. Danvers.

"Great." His enthusiasm sounded forced. "Put it around Megan's wrist, would you please? I want to escort Ms. Farrell to her truck."

Megan moaned as Mrs. Danvers wrapped the ice around her wrist and secured it. Then she forced her eyes open. Shadow was still screaming outside.

"What is it, Megan?" Mrs. Danvers softly stroked her arm.

"I have to see my horse."

"No. Not with that nasty bump on your head. You must rest."

"I can't. Not yet." She groaned as she struggled upward.

Mrs. Danvers put her hand behind Megan and helped. Head swimming, she sat up.

At that moment, Jack came back through the door. "What are you doing?"

"Help us, Jack. Megan needs to see her horse."

With Mrs. Danvers on one side and Jack on the other, she managed to rise. He cradled her right hand, still wrapped in ice. Together, they progressed slowly across the room.

"Open the door." The housekeeper's hold tightened.

He flung it wide, and then helped Megan through.

The bright light stabbed her eyes, making her wince.

"He's running back and forth in the pasture." Jack gripped her waist. "Not even Blade can settle him down. Call to him."

"Shadow!" she called weakly.

He stopped immediately, as though paralyzed by a lightning bolt. Blade, who'd been running toward him, paused to look back at the front porch.

Shadow whinnied, long and clear.

"It's okay, boy. I'll be all right." The effort of trying to raise her voice drained Megan. She slumped.

The stallion cried again, except this time the sound betrayed anger. She knew what was wrong...Jack touching her. But there was nothing she could do about it.

The foreman lifted her and carried her upstairs. Outside, Shadow sounded his disapproval. Her world spun and plunged into pain.

CHAPTER 34

“I’d say she is definitely on the mend.” The doctor put away his things as he spoke to Daniel. Then he turned to Megan. “Give yourself a couple weeks before you resume cattle wrestling. And call me if you have any questions.”

She smoothed the hem of the covers. “Thank you.”

The man nodded, then he turned again to Daniel. “I’ll let myself out. Take care, you two.”

Footsteps retreated down the hall as Megan glanced toward the window. An awkward silence fell on the room.

Shadow, her heart whispered. Too many hours had passed since she’d been with him. Through her open window she heard his clarion call from the nearby pasture. He waited for her. She longed to see him.

The movement of Daniel's wheelchair distracted her. "Glad to hear you've almost completely recovered."

"Me, too." She kept her response brief, wanting to keep the visit short.

"If I'd have known a conk on the head would get you to stay longer, I'd have done it sooner."

Megan smiled stiffly at his attempt to joke.

"Speaking of that..." Daniel fingered the blanket at the end of the bed, clearing debating how to continue.

She waited, not helping. Despite her uncle's kindness, she'd resolved not to allow her heart to soften toward him.

"I've been thinking a few things over recently." His hazel eyes wouldn't meet hers. "Especially in light of your injury. And having reconsidered...reconsidered my position..." He paused, his mouth working.

What's he trying to say?

His fingers tightened on the coverlet. "I just wanted you to know that I signed the papers and sent them to the attorney."

She sucked in her breath at his admission.

Her uncle still stubbornly refused to look her direction. "It might take a couple weeks for everything to get finalized..." He glanced at her, then back at the footboard. "But I just wanted you to know."

Stiff-necked and red-faced, he turned his chair to leave.

"Uncle Daniel."

He stopped, finally meeting her gaze.

"Thank you." She gulped, not sure of how much more she should say. Part of her believed him, but part held back. What if this was a ploy?

Can't be. One thing about her uncle...he might be strong-willed and manipulative, but he was no liar.

His head wagged a little as he seemed to struggle with saying more. "I still don't want you to go. But I'm not going to force you to stay."

"I appreciate having a choice." She spoke quietly, still confounded by his change of heart. And this new side of him she'd never before seen. For some reason, her eyes teared.

Does he really care for me?

He studied her, the red of his face deepening.

They were silent for many moments. Megan's heart pounded with hope. And...love?

Daniel finally spoke. Gruffly. "You don't know how lucky you are. I've never given others time off to lie around in bed. And pay them a hundred grand to do it, either. Usually I dock their wages."

She grinned, genuine joy cascading within her. "You'd better not dock my pay," she managed to say in a teasing tone.

"I considered that." Though his words fit the humor, he glanced away, his mouth moving in a way that she recognized meant he was having trouble keeping his emotions in check.

He really does love me.

"Someone handing out money?" Jack's voice came from outside her room. His face peered around the door jam. "I'm up for some."

"You always are." Daniel turned to her, appearing grateful for the interruption. "Jack continually claims how little he gets, but I don't see what he does with the money I give him."

"The money I *earn.*" The foreman folded his arms.

"He probably squirrels it all away, and then whines that I don't pay him enough."

Jack spread his hands. "Standard practice for a boss and employee."

"So, did you come here to argue with me in front of my niece?"

"No." He looked at her, swiping off his hat. "I came to see how Megan is doing."

Daniel turned his wheelchair. "Then I'll go so you can do just that."

Before she could voice a protest, he wheeled himself out.

Jack shuffled his feet as he ran his hat brim through his fingers. Then he indicated a nearby chair. "May I?"

"Sure." She pulled the blanket a little higher.

He grinned. "Must be a little awkward for you. I

don't suppose you ever thought you'd entertain me while you're in bed."

Her cheeks burned, but she managed to say, "You're the one who's supposed to entertain. *I'm* the injured one."

His face clouded. "I haven't been able to forget that. Not for one moment since that black devil came home without you. Two times in the last couple weeks are enough to unsettle any man."

Megan plucked at the covers. "Would you mind filling in what happened? It's kind of a blur."

He shrugged. "Not much to tell. Sam arrived, saying you'd be home soon. Your stallion came without you, making such a racket in the yard that we all ran out to see what was going on. He's pretty amazing. I've never seen such dedication. He led us right to where you were. And hasn't been the same since." Jack looked at her with a peculiar expression. "You seem to have a way of making deep impressions. On beast and man."

She flexed her still-sore wrist, and then settled her hands.

"Bothering you?" Jack indicated her arm.

"A little. I'm glad I hold the reins in my left hand."

"So you're ready to ride again?"

"As soon as possible." She glanced out the window, then back at him. "Tell me, did someone tamper with my saddle?"

"Nah." Jack pulled at his ear. "Just a misunderstanding. It's getting fixed and will soon be as right as rain."

"But yesterday–"

"I'm sorry about that. I made some hasty judgments, then opened my big mouth with Sam. I was wrong, though. Just faulty stitching."

"Okay." Megan smiled, not believing him. But why would he lie? She indicated the roses on her nightstand. "Thanks for the flowers. They're beautiful."

"Seemed the right thing to do."

Her gaze strayed toward the window. Before Jack said something more personal and embarrassing, she said, “Well, I really need a shower. If you wouldn’t mind....” She left the sentence hanging.

“Hang on a sec.” He scooted his chair closer. “Megan, I know now’s probably not the best time to say something. Or maybe it is because you’ve been so much on my mind, but I nearly went crazy with worry about you.”

“I appreciate–”

“I know we didn’t start out the best.” He dropped his hat to the floor, and then rested his elbows on his knees. “I thought you were a tease. What I’d come to expect from women. But I see now I was wrong. You’re different. You’re someone I respect. Which is why I’ve tried not to come on too strong.”

She sucked in a deep breath, and then slowly released it. “Thanks. Nice of you to say.”

“But?”

She scrambled for another reason beside the real one. “I...I had a bad ending to a relationship in Florida and–”

“I know.”

“You know?”

“I kind of pried it out of Celia.”

“Then you must understand I’m not ready to—”

“No need to explain. I only wanted to let you know how I felt.”

She looked away. As long as Moon Dancing was in her life, she had no room for Jack. She sought for a way to discourage further confessions from him.

He rose. “I don’t want to keep you from your shower.”

Megan managed to smile. “Thanks for stopping by.”

He swooped his hat from the floor and tipped it on in one fluid motion. “I’ll see you later on.”

After he shut the door she sighed, waiting until she heard his footsteps retreat down the stairs. Then she scrambled from bed, ignoring the hint of dizziness as she searched for clothes. She needed to see Shadow. To reassure him all was well.

CHAPTER 35

Simone disappeared.

She still couldn't fathom why the young woman would leave, apparently without first saying goodbye to anyone. Two days had passed since Mrs. Danvers found a farewell note in her empty bedroom. Still no word.

When Megan stepped through the kitchen door, the unease in the room hit her like the pungent odor of overcooked meat. Everyone had already assembled for dinner, proving that she was late. Some of the men looked up, nodding in her direction.

"Shadow settled for the night?" Daniel made small talk.

"Yes." She slipped into a chair, noting that not everyone was there. "Where's Jack?"

"Had to return to town. He'll be back later."

She nodded. The sheriff's office had already questioned several of them. Perhaps it was Jack's turn? When she glanced around, she noted how some of the men lacked their usual appetite. Conversation was subdued, humor and banter nonexistent. The absence of Mrs. Danvers completed the strangeness of the meal.

After a couple bites, she pushed her plate away. *I could have been kinder. I could have tried harder to befriend Simone.* Guilt crushed any lingering appetite.

When the sheriff had questioned her, he'd showed her the farewell note. Words like "Daniel betrayed me" and "I hate ranch life" had leaped off the page. The sheriff asked if Megan could explain the young woman's hostility. And why Simone had taken only some of her clothing but none of the things her mother had purchased for school. She had no reply.

It didn't feel right. Why had she run away when she had planned to move soon?

Megan spent the next hour cleaning up after the meal. Some of the men assisted, lightening the load, their desire to pitch in painfully sweet. *They must really care for Mrs. Danvers.* While she chatted with them, she kept her eye on the clock. Tonight was a full moon. Tonight, Moon Dancing would be waiting. She touched his bracelet that she constantly wore.

The kitchen was empty and Megan alone finishing up when the housekeeper entered the room. She looked around in surprise. "Dinner is done?"

"Yes." She hung up two dishtowels to dry. "Everyone was tired, so..." Megan gestured uselessly to the empty room.

"Understandable." The woman pulled her lower lip between her teeth. Her eyes glittered, two bright pink spots rising on pale cheeks.

She smoothed the towel one more time. "How are you doing, Mrs. Danvers?"

"Not very well." The housekeeper spoke in a shaky whisper.

Megan waited. What could she say that would

comfort her?

The woman tied an apron about her waist, the action almost mechanical. "Simone was always so headstrong."

"Don't you believe she ran away?"

Mrs. Danvers' head snapped in her direction. "I do not." She took an impossibly deep breath. "Simone flirted. And she loved having beaux who would do her bidding. But she would not have run off with someone I had never met."

Megan drew closer. "Is that what the sheriff's office is saying?"

"Yes. There is a rumor that a young woman whose description matches my daughter's was seen riding in a white truck, heading toward Cheyenne. The sheriff seems convinced it was Simone."

"Then he's not conducting a search for her?"

"No. She is not considered a missing person. And since she is twenty-two..." Mrs. Danvers crumpled onto a chair as though at the end of her strength.

Megan watched helplessly as the woman dabbed her eyes with her apron.

"It is not like her to leave without saying goodbye. I know something is not right." The housekeeper fumbled for a handkerchief which she pressed to her mouth.

"So she didn't write that note?"

"It is her handwriting. But I did not realize she was so angry." The older woman's eyes flickered. "She used to consider herself Daniel's favorite. But I thought that changed many years ago. I did not know she was so upset by your arrival."

Megan pulled up a chair. "Do you think it's possible that Simone had a steady boyfriend? One that you didn't know about? And they quarreled?"

"She always had a boyfriend. At least two or three."

"But what if there was someone very special in her life? Someone whose rejection hurt her so badly she couldn't recover?"

Mrs. Danvers gazed steadily at her. "What are you saying?"

"I heard her once or twice with someone. It sounded pretty serious." She withheld Jack's name.

The housekeeper's lips parted. "But...she was going to Denver. To school. If they were that serious, she would never have agreed."

"I'm not saying..." Megan sighed. "Sorry for bringing it up."

Mrs. Danvers laid a hand on her arm. "Perhaps my daughter thought he was going with her to Colorado."

She nodded slowly.

"Who was it? Who did you hear with Simone?"

Megan chewed her lip. "I can't say for certain."

"But you must have some idea."

"I really don't know. I saw someone. And heard..." She ducked her head, wishing now she'd said nothing.

"Late at night?" Mrs. Danvers finally asked.

"I'm not saying there was anything immoral going on," she hastily added. "And it was dark. They might have just been meeting on the back porch and..." Falling silent, she stared down at her clenched hands.

The woman sighed deeply. "You do not have to cover up for my daughter, Megan."

"I didn't want you to think that I was accusing her of–of anything."

The housekeeper patted her arm. "I have known of Simone's weakness. Perhaps it had something to do with an absent father. Daniel tried, I must grant him that. All my talking in the world would not change her search for love."

"I think I know how she felt." Megan studied the pattern of the floor tiles.

"You miss your father."

"Yes. But more than that. I can't condemn Simone because, well, because I think I understand her motivation." When the woman didn't answer, she added, "Remember Garrick? I really thought he was the man I wanted to spend the rest of my life with. Right up to a crisis in my life."

"What happened?"

"I got laid off. Money got tight. Garrick pushed me hard to move in with him. When I refused, he got ugly." Megan paused, the memories so stark that the incident felt like it had happened only the day before.

"Oh, Megan." Mrs. Danvers reached for her hand.

"It was a hard way to find out the truth about him. But up till then, I'd ignored all the warning signs." How could she have missed all of Garrick's blatant attempts to control her? He used a difficult situation to try and force her to go against her principles.

"My way or the highway," was how Mrs. Danvers had said it. That statement could be considered the flagship of his personality. And behavior toward Megan.

She took a deep breath, and then straightened. "I'm sorry. I meant to comfort you, but instead I'm telling you my woes."

"I am glad you did."

When Megan tried to pull her hand away, the woman hung on for one moment longer. "Tell me, did you learn anything from the experience?"

She thought for a moment. "Yes."

"Like what?"

"I guess the biggest is I'm glad I stuck to my convictions. Even when circumstances got difficult."

"Hard to live by sometimes."

Megan nodded.

They were silent for a few minutes before Mrs. Danvers rose. "It is getting late."

She leaped up as well, glancing at the clock. Eight forty-two. Megan gulped. Was Moon Dancing already waiting?

"I will see you in the morning." The housekeeper hugged her. "Thank you for sharing your heart with me."

"Thanks for listening."

The woman touched her cheek before walking away.

Megan waited until the woman was gone before moving toward the back door. As she paused on the threshold, she allowed her eyes to adjust to the gloom. A vehicle's headlights grazed the bunkhouse. Instinctively, she backed away.

Jack.

He pulled his truck up to the house, stopping by the kitchen door and cutting off her escape. She returned to the kitchen, and then headed down the hallway as she listened to his heavy step moving up the wooden porch. Why was he coming inside?

She scooted toward the stairs, then became aware that her uncle was still awake and in his study. Obviously, he was waiting for the foreman. Megan edged up to the second floor, out of sight.

Jack tapped at the study's pocket door.

"Come in," Daniel's voice called.

He disappeared inside.

"Shut the door, Jack. I don't want our conversation to disturb anyone."

He slid it closed, but imperfectly. Megan slipped off her shoes. Taking care, she crept down the stairs. Just a few more feet and she could get away undetected.

She'd taken three steps down the hallway when she heard Jack. "The sheriff has a lead on who Simone ran off with. It's an Indian who's been hanging around the area the last several weeks. I've even seen him around here."

Megan froze.

"Anyone been able to track them down?" her uncle asked.

"Not yet. But the sheriff is following that lead about a white truck."

As she listened, she barely breathed.

"So who is this man?"

"Not sure. No one knows his name, only a general description. Jed Harper, now a deputy, is checking into who this guy is. The suspicious thing about him is that he's only been seen at night."

They had to be talking about Moon Dancing! Though the white truck they mentioned didn't fit, everything else did. Were they going to pin Simone's disappearance on him?

"What about foul play?" Daniel's voice cracked.

"They aren't ruling that out yet. But, now that they have a description, they'll pursue him."

Her uncle said nothing for a minute. “I’ll be glad when she’s found.”

Silence reigned for several moments while Megan stood in the hallway. She was prepared for a quick getaway if Jack should suddenly come out of the study. A creaking chair told her that though he was shifting in his seat, he wasn’t preparing to depart.

Daniel spoke. “Did you see that repairman about Megan’s saddle?”

“Yes. I’ll pick it up tomorrow.”

“And he was convinced the saddle stitching was faulty?”

“Absolutely.” Jack cleared his throat. “I’m sorry I was a little hasty the day of the accident. I didn’t mean to worry you.”

“We were all a little panic-stricken that day.”

“Especially me,” the foreman said in a low voice.

“You care for her that much...”

The chair creaked again. “Maybe more than you want to hear.”

Daniel was silent a moment. “Truth be told, I wouldn’t mind Megan and you forming a serious attachment. I look forward to the day when you make an announcement about you two.”

She squelched her gasp. *I’ve heard enough.*

After she tiptoed down the hallway and into the kitchen, she put her shoes back on. Pausing at the door, she listened for a few more moments before slipping out. She’d just stepped outside when a hand closed around her mouth.

CHAPTER 36

“Do not be afraid,” said a familiar voice.

She squirmed out of Moon Dancing’s hold and turned to face him. “You scared me.”

In the bright moonlight, she could see his smile. “I did not want you to scream.”

Megan glanced around. “We have to get away from here. Jack’s in the house and may leave at any time.”

“Then come.” He took her hand.

They traversed the porch toward the pasture beyond the bunkhouse. The dogs came bounding toward them, making Megan catch her breath. How would they react to Moon Dancing? She needn’t have worried. Whimpering for attention, they ran to him. He let them nose his palm for a moment, and then he spoke. “Go.” With amazing obedience, they ran back toward the yard. He again grasped her fingers.

"Where are we heading?" She panted as she strove to keep up.

"You will see."

They reached the fence. Moon Dancing whistled, the sound low but distinct. A horse whinnied. A few minutes later, a huge gelding trotted up.

"How did you do that?" Megan asked.

He smiled. "I know horses."

And dogs. "You must have been working with him."

"I have used him before." He shut the gate behind them, and then swung onto the horse with little effort.

"And where do you think you're going?" She rested her hand on the gelding's shoulder.

"To a special place. With you."

"I can't. We need a bridle at least. How are you going to–?"

"You ask too many questions." He leaned down, hand extended.

She glanced around, debating the wisdom of taking the horse. Of going with him to who-knew-where.

"Megan." His soft, but urged tone lassoed her spirit and gently tamed her fear. He flicked his outstretched fingers toward her again.

Exactly like my dream.

Heart in her throat, she grasped his warm hand. He kicked the horse forward. At the same time he pulled upward, swinging her onto the horse behind him. She grabbed Moon Dancing's waist, fighting for balance. The gelding moved swiftly into a canter, his size easily carrying the both of them.

Megan merely hung on, awed by the ease with which he maneuvered the horse, using his legs to indicate the direction they were to go. At first she was nervous about riding bareback and without a bridle, but Moon Dancing seemed to have no such qualms. After a while, she began to enjoy herself. A sense of unreality wrapped around her mind as the horse's powerful muscles rippled under her.

Then she became more aware of the man to whom she clung.

He wore jeans and a T-shirt, but his feet were bare. In a way, he felt foreign to her yet in another, so very familiar. His silky hair brushed her face, smelling of wild grasses and spring rain. The horse slowed as they began to climb a hill. Using his feet and legs, Moon Dancing urged their mount on. She leaned forward, the gelding grunting as he strained to maintain the quick pace. On and on they went, cutting back and forth when the hill became too steep. The bright light of the moon guided their way, shadowing the rocks, boulders and shrubs that dotted the landscape. Finally, they reached the crest, but still didn't stop.

He kicked the gelding to a trot, his body adjusting to the horse's movements while she tried to relax into the new gait. Finally they slowed to a walk. Megan was able to sit a little straighter as she looked around.

Nothing could be seen but mountains, sky and stars. She gaped at the scenery which looked as though sprinkled with shimmering moon dust. "This is beautiful."

Again, they climbed, Moon Dancing intent on some destination. Finally, he stopped.

"Come." He swung his leg over the horse's head and slid off. He helped her down, his grip lingering at her waist. Taking her hand, he pulled her to the top of a huge boulder. The surface was flat and smooth, worn by rain and wind. She stared out across the panorama. Why had he brought her here? Below, the horse began to graze.

She slowly turned to Moon Dancing.

He was gazing at her, arms relaxed, feet spread. For many moments, neither of them spoke. The breeze lifted his hair, swirling across his face. Preternatural light sculpted his features, making his eyes spark. Megan felt as though time came to a standstill, her life focused on this one man at this one moment.

She expected him to come to her when she found herself stepping toward him. Without considering her actions, she touched his shoulders, running her hands across his chest as she'd done a hundred times with Shadow. Eyes softening with love, Moon Dancing sighed. She tangled her fingers in his hair, that feeling of familiarity pounding through her.

When his head bent toward her, she raised her face to meet his lips. He pulled her roughly against himself, his kiss engulfing her. She shuddered, emotions exploding.

"Say you will be mine. Right now." Moon Dancing murmured against her ear.

Be his...? What did he mean exactly? Megan stiffened. Did he want her to give herself physically to him?

"Say it, Megan of Fire." His voice grew urgent. When she again didn't answer, he lifted his head to gaze into her face.

"I...I can't."

His expression hardened, the muscles of his arm tightening. "I thought you wanted this. My touch. My kiss."

"I do. It's just that..." Biting her lip, she sought for how to explain her ambivalence.

His mouth flattened. "You are saying this is not right...unless we are bound?"

She nodded slowly. So much more needed to be said. But where to start?

He released her, and then stepped back. "But are you willing to bind yourself to me? Even though the curse may not be broken?"

Megan held her breath, afraid to voice her thoughts. "You mean, marry you?"

"Not in the way your people marry. I can give you only promises. Right here. Right now." He lifted his hands. "In the custom of my people. We will kneel and make a vow."

"A vow?"

"Yes." He fixed his gaze on her. "Is that not good enough?"

"We'll get married someday. I promise. Isn't that good enough?" Garrick's words slammed into her mind.

She pressed her hands to her cheeks. Everything in her screamed to give in to Moon Dancing. To agree to his wishes.

To give in to what I want.

She couldn't.

Megan shook her head. "I'm sorry. I can't." At the look of pain on his face, she hurried to explain. "Call me old-fashioned, but I can't give myself to you...unless we are legally man and wife." She looked away, unable to bear his disappointment. It buffeted against her, making his sorrow almost unbearable.

Finally, he spoke, voice low. "A promise is not enough?"

Why can't it be? Isn't marriage a mere convention?

She knew the answer without having to think. If promises were enough, she could have moved in with Garrick with no qualms. But somewhere along the line, she'd come to believe that marriage was more than just words. It was a binding covenant. For life.

When she raised her gaze to Moon Dancing, she straightened her shoulders. And hardened her resolve. The dawning expression on his face proved he understood she'd come to a decision.

He'll be angry. I know it. Or he would try to convince her otherwise. Just like Garrick.

Moon Dancing gently grasped her hand. "I am willing, Megan of Fire. I am willing to wait for you. For as long as needed. Until we find a way."

Her heart leaped with hope. A vortex of light and color burst around her. She gasped, staring upward as the moon seemed to shatter into a trillion pieces. The sparkling pinpricks showered down for mere seconds. Then it was over.

Megan looked at him. Had Moon Dancing seen the light show?

"Will you at least promise yourself to me?" He laced his fingers through hers. "Pledge that you will one day become wholly mine?"

Her heart was so full, she could barely speak. "Yes."

"I say it again...the curse may not be broken. You may be committing yourself to a half-man, half-beast. Until you die."

She inhaled deeply, so very aware of the solemnity of this moment.

“I can promise you nothing. Nothing but moments of joy between weeks of sorrow. As you grow older with the years, I will age only days.”

Megan swallowed convulsively.

“Are you willing to share in the curse that has hounded me for nearly two hundred winters?”

The universe seemed to screech to a halt, waiting for her reply. Heart pounding, she considered the monumental decision before her.

To promise herself to Moon Dancing might break the curse. But what if it didn’t?

Life stretched out before her. Could she forsake all others and be true only to him? And if they found a way to be married, would she be content in the moments they shared? As he’d said, moments of joy between weeks of sorrow.

Megan raised her eyes to his. This man, whom she’d grown to love so passionately, waited without speaking, giving her time to choose.

“Yes.” She rested her hand on his cheek. “Yes, I am willing.”

CHAPTER 37

On the light-splashed rock, they knelt together. Moon Dancing chanted in his language, arms lifted toward the sky. The breeze calmed, held back by some invisible curtain, secluding them in the eye of the night. Sound ceased except for his voice, rising and falling in hypnotic cadence. Then he lowered his arms, his singsong recitative sending chills down Megan's back. Finally, he turned to her.

He grasped her fingers and untied the bracelet he'd given her. With it, he bound both their wrists together. "I promise myself to you, Megan of Fire. To you alone, I will be faithful. With God as my witness. For as long as we both live."

He looked at her expectantly.

Heart full, she repeated his vow. "I promise myself

to you, Moon Dancing. To you alone, I will be faithful. With God as my witness. For as long as we both live."

His face pointed upward, raising their bound arms together to the sky as he chanted. Megan stared at him, overcome by his beauty. And by what she vowed.

He stopped, his voice echoing into the night, then back again. "It is finished."

Still bound to her, he rose, pulling her upward with him. He clasped her to his chest, holding her gently. His touch contained an element of sacredness, the raw desire of his earlier embrace missing.

A gust of wind buffeted them. He threw back his head and cried out in joy, the primeval sound rending the fading night. His call sent a thrill through her. Then he swung her around until she laughed.

He carefully undid the bracelet, and then tied it again to her wrist. "This is a symbol of our pledge."

Megan caressed the beads. "I will always treasure it."

For many moments, they merely held each other, gazing into one another's eyes.

Finally, Moon Dancing looked toward the sky. "The night flies. We must return."

She sighed, recognizing the truth of what he'd said.

He clambered down from the rock, whistling for the gelding. After helping her mount, he swung himself up behind her. With his arms about her, she felt cherished. Protected. When they reached the bottom of the hill, he didn't urge the gelding into a trot, but kept the pace slow.

What strange emotions whirled through her. She did not know this man, yet she knew him better than anyone else. She'd spent nearly every day with him, loving him in a way that she'd not understood until she'd accepted the truth that he wasn't a beast, but a man. He'd been her companion and friend, sharing a quiet, but deeper relationship than she'd thought possible. What she'd not been able to learn in his companionship had been completed by what he'd written in his journal. And when she'd gotten to know his thoughts and his soul, she'd grown to know him more quickly than if she'd spent months talking with him.

She caressed his arm. "Tell me...how did you get your name?"

He made a sound of amusement. "On the night of my birth the moon was full. My mother carried me to my father, still wet from her womb. I was his first born. When he held me up to the sky in thanks, he saw the moon dancing across the mountains in joy."

She leaned her head back against his shoulder. "And how did this curse come to be?"

He was silent for a long time. "I brought it upon myself." He expelled his breath as though the confession pained. "I was what you would call a prince among my people. Yet I grew arrogant. Selfish. Countless winters ago I was given a wife, bounty for our tribe's exploits. Yet I did not treat her well. Her father was a great medicine man. He warned me of my pride."

So, he had once been married. Countless winters ago? "What happened?"

"She and I were on a long journey. The day came for her to give birth. She cried out for me, because of her love. I favored my horse above her. She died, taking the life of my son with her. I have no offspring."

"How sad."

"Do not mourn for me. What happened, I brought upon myself."

"But you've changed."

"Too late to save her. And my son." His arm tightened. "Now I have only you. If I spend the rest of my days in a half life, I will be content knowing that you became mine. For this moment, I can rejoice."

By the time they reached the stables, the night had faded. Pale moonlight rippled through one dusty window.

"Will you stay with me, Megan of Fire? Morning comes soon."

"I will stay as long as you like."

After he made a place for them in the straw, he lay down. Megan curled up beside him. His heartbeat thrummed under her cheek as she rested her head on his chest. "You speak so eloquently. Yet you are from a different age, a different world."

"I have been around the white man many winters. I have learned of his ways, his talk. I have seen much. And know much. Yet, until you came, I was empty."

She sighed. *I as well.*

"You cannot know the bitterness of my life. To think as a man, yet live as an animal. Watching endless births and deaths, yet to be forever apart from both man and beast. Even my own people would not recognize or accept me for who I am. Or was. Only one other, who used to live here, helped me. One I would gladly call brother."

She lifted her head. "Trapper?"

Moon Dancing nodded. "He left me clothes. And food. Many times."

"I'm glad." She smoothed her hand across his chest. "And I'm glad that you gave up taking revenge on those who tried to harm you."

"Revenge?"

"By stealing mares. When you were a rogue stallion." When he frowned, she asked, "Didn't you run off with them?"

He moved his head back and forth in denial. "What do I want with mares? I am human. I have no affinity to them. No desire for them."

"Then where have they gone?"

Moon Dancing again shook his head. "Since I did not care, I never paid attention. But I have seen other things on this land."

"Like what?"

"Men who always look over their shoulders. Secret meetings. Deep holes in the ground."

"A mine?" She raised herself further. "On our property?"

"Yes. If you wish, I will take you to one."

"All right."

Moon Dancing's hand gripped hers. "Say nothing about this, until you can see it with your own eyes. Many moons ago I discovered it. The place may be gone now."

They were quiet for several moments. Then Megan said, "I went to visit the man who painted your portrait. Jay Rush."

"I remember him."

"He passed away, but I met his daughter. She told me that he had taken you into his home during a hard winter."

"He showed me kindness. The first white man to do so."

"His daughter was very gracious."

Moon Dancing moved restlessly, as though wanting to say more. "One time, I asked Jay-Rush why. Why he offered me shelter. Why he gave me his possessions."

Megan propped her head on one hand. "What did he say?"

"He told me of his God who loved me. Because this God gave, Jay-Rush gave." Moon Dancing's face grew solemn as he stared into the darkness of the stables. "He said God gave His most precious gift. His Son's life."

Moon Dancing said nothing for a long time.

A God who gives. Many times she'd heard of God when her aunt dragged her to church. But in the years she'd lived on her own, Megan hadn't thought much of Him. All the men she'd ever known were takers, not givers. Wasn't God the same? Hadn't He taken her parents away when she was nine?

She remained silent, not wishing to intrude upon Moon Dancing's thoughts. After a while, she again rested her head on his chest. Arm tightening about her, he pulled a blanket over both of them, and then resettled.

But Moon Dancing was not yet done speaking. "Because of him, of Jay-Rush, of what he did for me, of all he gave, I believe in this God now too."

Gray dawn crept into the stables, stealing her warmth. Megan awoke, shivering.

"Moon Dancing?" She groped for the blanket.

She could barely see his dark shape in the corner of the stall, crouched in a fetal position. He had cast aside his clothing sometime before she'd awakened. They lay in a heap beside her.

He twisted, then grew, stretching upwards, an unearthly groan straining from contorted vocal cords as they elongated.

She stared, horrified by what she saw, powerless to stop the process.

His form straightened, and then he shook a misshapen head. Hair sprang along the neck...one too long to be human. Where there'd once been hands and feet were now hardened hooves.

Tears streamed down her cheeks as the stallion staggered to his feet, head hanging low.

"Moon Dancing." She rose and embraced his neck. "I am yours. Forever. Whatever may happen."

Megan had never heard an animal groan as he did, the sound shuddering through her soul. Caressing him, she couldn't hold back the tears that soaked his coat. Now she wished she'd not slept, wasting the precious time they'd had together.

I wish the curse had been broken...

She was so engrossed in her sorrow that she didn't hear at first why he weakly raised his head. Whirling, she swiped the tears from her cheeks.

The door opened. Sunshine spilled into the stables.

CHAPTER 38

“Megan!” Jack’s voice sounded as surprised as she was dismayed.

When he stepped toward her, she saw Moon Dancing’s clothes still crumpled on the straw. She edged in front of them.

“What are you doing here?” He glanced around the stables.

“I uh, I guess I fell asleep in here last night.”

“Someone with you?”

She managed a tremulous smile. “Just Shadow.”

His gaze took in all of her. “Looks like you had a restless night.” He suddenly stepped forward and snatched straw out of her hair. Then he glanced at the stallion. “What’s up with him? Usually he doesn’t let me within ten feet.”

Megan wanted to move toward her horse, but didn't want Jack to see the telltale clothes behind her. Resisting the urge to explain, she folded her arms.

The stallion seemed disoriented, as though the transformation had taken something out of him. His eyes were glazed, appearing drugged.

Sunshine suddenly burst through the window, spotlighting the dancing motes of dust in the air. And the clothes. She chewed her lip while her mind remained stubbornly blank, providing no excuse to send Jack away.

His eyes narrowed. "You sure you were alone last night?"

"Um..." A lie stuck in her throat. She indicated Shadow. "Ask him." Though lame, the challenge was true. *Please just go away.*

Suspicion dawning, his face grew pale. Megan said nothing. He said nothing. Finally, a man's voice outside the stable distracted him.

"Guess I'd better help Blade."

"Okay," she said a little breathlessly.

He glanced pointedly at the straw behind her, then turned on his heel and left.

Megan avoided him the rest of the day, not because she felt guilty, but because she couldn't explain. Was any of it true? But the memory of Moon Dance's chanting over her banished all doubts. Several times a day, she found herself fingering his bracelet.

Her uncle cornered her after lunch. "Celia said you'd not been in your bed all night." A worried frown pinched his face.

She felt herself flushing. "It's true. I fell asleep in the stables. I hope you weren't worried."

"Of course I worried."

"I'm such a nuisance to you. I'm sorry." She kissed his cheek, allowing her hand to linger on his shoulder.

He looked up at her, a strange smile playing on his lips. "What's going on, Meggie? You're all soft-eyed and…"

Lacking words to describe her emotional state, she turned her face away.

"I hope this means you're happy."

She smiled at him. "I am. Very."

Megan took Shadow on a short jaunt in the afternoon, riding bareback without bridle or halter.

"I can't go far today." She patted his neck. "We'll go to the mine early tomorrow when we have more time."

Of course he understood, returning to the ranch when it grew late.

She took her time grooming him, and then let him out into the pasture. He ran back and forth along the fence line, showing off as he galloped, mane and tail flying. Megan sat on the porch, watching. He was beautiful, yet she wished with her whole heart that he stayed human. However a half-existence–no, it was less than that–was better than nothing.

Someday soon, she would have to consider how to move her belongings from Florida. She never planned on going back. Not while her heart was here.

"He's quite a horse," Blade said.

She jumped, sitting up straighter.

"Sorry. Didn't mean to sneak up on you like that." He touched the brim of his hat.

"It's okay. I was daydreaming."

"An acceptable occupation." He smiled comfortably, putting his foot on the bench's edge. "You've done a remarkable job with the stallion. Got any secrets you wanna share?"

Megan ducked her head so that he wouldn't see her smile. The only secret she had was Shadow wasn't what he seemed.

Blade tilted his head lower to catch her expression. "I guess that means you aren't going to."

"I have nothing to tell." She spread her hands. "You're right when you say he's quite a horse. He wanted to be tamed. That's the only secret I can think of."

"Well, I had to try." He gazed into the distance.

She said nothing, sensing that he wanted to talk more.

"Mind if I smoke?" He pulled out a pack and held it expectantly.

"Go for it."

He took his time retrieving a cigarette and lighting the tip. After a couple puffs, he again gazed at her. "Tell me if it's none of my business, but I was wondering what's going on between you and Jack."

"Did he send you to pick my brain?"

"No. I'm only asking as a friend to you both. Though I've only known you a short time, I feel like you're kind of a sister to me. And Jack, well, I've known him forever."

Megan smiled at his word choice. Forever. She felt like that with Moon Dancing. He was part of her soul. And would always be.

But after pondering that idea longer, she realized how appropriate that term would become for her. If the curse couldn't be broken, her life would feel endless. She'd grow old, die, and then be a distant memory to him.

Blade drew closer. "What's wrong?"

She shook her head. "Oh, daydreaming again."

"You care that much for him?"

Megan blinked, and then realized he was talking about Jack, not Moon Dancing. "Jack's a...a friend. Someone I can count on."

"But?"

She shrugged.

He stared into the distance, pulling on his cigarette. "There's someone else, isn't there?"

Her breath caught at the certainty in his tone. Jack must've talked to him about the incident in the stables. That's how he knew.

Blade studied her. "You look worried. Like I'll squeal or something." When she said nothing, he added, "Not hard to figure out. You're all dreamy-eyed. And it's not my friend you're looking at."

She looked away, mortified he'd weaseled that much out of her. Her silence had said more than if she had opened her big mouth.

He plopped down on the seat next to her. "You don't have to be ashamed of caring for someone else. That's the breaks of the game. Jack's done that to a dozen girls. About time it happened to him. Good for the soul."

Megan turned to him. "You really think so?"

"Don't sound like much of a friend, do I? But..." He blew out a stream of smoke. "I've always been the guy left behind while he dances off into the sunset with a girl. And I usually get stuck with the tab."

She smiled at his forlorn tone.

"So who is this guy?"

Megan glanced down at her hands clenched in her lap.

"Oh, sorry. It's all new and wonderful, right? You're blushing up a storm."

"Yipes." She put her hands on her cheeks to cool them.

"Hey, don't worry." He crushed his cigarette with his boot. "I won't pry any more, but I need to ask you something. You can tell me to buzz off or..." He stopped, waiting. "Or you can treat me like a friend. Someone who cares."

"All right."

Blade folded his hands, leaning his elbows on his knees as though the words were difficult to find. "Say this other guy suddenly takes a hike. Would there be any chance then? I know it's probably impossible to imagine at the moment, but...what if? Jack's still my friend. He once saved my life. And even though I've secretly resented him getting all the girls, I feel for him now. It's hard to love without hope of return." He rubbed his palms together, and then sat up.

She sighed, uncertain how to answer. Moon Dancing no longer there? Not possible. He would roam the earth longer than she. But Megan felt for the man beside her, a true friend who was putting himself out to find a way to give hope to another.

"I've always liked Jack, even when I was furious with him. Which was more than a few times."

Blade grinned.

"And I have to be honest and say once upon a time I seriously considered his interest in me." She picked at a hangnail.

"That a yes, then?"

She worried her hangnail, unable to look up and answer affirmatively. No, she couldn't even consider Jack. There was only one man in her life. Now and forever.

But Blade was waiting for an answer. She felt her shoulders rise noncommittally.

"I appreciate your honesty." He rose. "Guess it's time for me to get back to work." He took a couple steps, and then turned. "You won't tell Jack about our conversation, will you? He'd hamstring me."

"I won't."

With a tilt of his hat, Blade left. He strode across the yard.

Megan remained on the front porch for a little while longer, then headed inside, full of turmoil as she thought again of the curse. There had to be a way to break it. If only she could discover how.

She did some research online, but couldn't find anything specific about Moon Dancing or his situation. Frustration growing, she continued to worry her hangnail.

For more than an hour she read, combing through whatever legends she could find. A benefit of her search was she learned so much about the Native American people. How they lived, how they thought, what they valued. One thing of interest was the four virtues of the Sioux: fortitude, wisdom, generosity and above all, bravery. Megan sat back in her chair, exasperation ebbing.

Moon Dancing shows these virtues in abundance. All the time.

As she shut the computer down the cuticle that she'd chewed snagged on her jeans. What she needed was clippers to take care of it once and for all. She flung open her bedroom door and went into the bathroom.

On the way out, she stopped. The suitcase under her bed had been moved, zipper undone. Heart hammering, Megan pulled the luggage out. She opened the lid and searched the inside. Again, she looked, her breath coming in short gasps.

Moon Dancing's journal was gone.

CHAPTER 39

Ear-shattering thunder made Megan bolt upright in bed with a shriek. A few minutes later, another rumble shook the house. She clutched the covers, limbs trembling. The storm sounded right above her.

Who took the journal? She'd asked herself that question a hundred times already. An unknown someone had stolen her most precious possession. The diary contained Moon Dancing's essence, now lost.

When it had been taken was equally a mystery. She spent little time in her room. Hired hands and visitors came and went constantly. Doors were always unlocked. But why would someone steal the journal? Why not the money? Or knife?

To be on the safe side, she'd moved his other things, scattering them throughout her possessions.

But even then, she didn't feel secure. No one had seen her read the journal, yet someone had boldly and meticulously searched her room.

A chill crept down her back at the thought.

They were watching her.

Who? The question kept her awake until the morning hours when she crept away to the stables.

"We can't go today." Megan kept her voice low as she tangled her fingers in Shadow's mane. She leaned her forehead against his neck, wishing that Moon Dancing could put his arms around her. "My uncle would have a fit if I rode out in this rain."

The storm beat down on the roof, pounding its fury. What was wrong with her? Her roiling emotions had to be from more than the loss of the journal. Perhaps the day weighed down on her, filling her with anxiety. A gray, oppressive curtain hung in the air.

"Do you know that I once dreamed of being a horse? When I'd first started coming to you in the middle of the night. I dreamed I ran alongside of you. You raced a little ahead of me, as though to encourage me to gallop all out. I still remember that vividly."

She stopped to gaze into his eyes.

"You must be freed from the curse. We must live a life together as man and woman. I need you..." She stopped, sighing as tears threatened to overtake her. For the first time, in many years, she prayed.

God...if there's a way...

Shadow nickered encouragingly.

"I have to go. I promised Mrs. Danvers I'd help with lunch."

Megan stopped at the open door of the barn. Torrential rain hammered the yard, churning the dirt into clay. She'd be soaked and mud-caked by the time she reached the kitchen. How had Moon Dancing survived similar deluges? How would it be to endure years of storms, rain and snow?

An urge to run away welled inside. She'd take

Shadow and go. Go somewhere to get away from the vague fears that had begun to haunt her in earnest. She'd been so caught up in her love that she'd ignored the unease that permeated the ranch. But last night at dinner and this morning at breakfast, brooding disquiet strangled the atmosphere.

She splashed through the yard, slipping before reaching the kitchen. Mrs. Danvers already had started lunch. As the men entered for the meal, she found herself studying each of them, wondering who might have taken the journal. Later, after cleanup she headed upstairs to rest, a headache beginning to pound. The housekeeper went to town with Daniel, leaving Megan free to nap.

Later a shrill ringing woke her. She staggered up, rubbing her eyes as she answered the phone in the hallway.

"Megan? This is Sam Farrell."

"Oh, hello." She cleared her throat, trying to dislodge the cobwebs.

"Did I catch you at a bad time?"

"No, it's okay. What's up? My uncle isn't here and neither–"

"I just saw him a few minutes ago. Here in town. Can you speak freely?"

Megan hunched her shoulders, wondering at the implied secrecy. "Yes."

"Listen, I talked to your uncle and he insists that your accident was the result of faulty stitching. Is that true?"

"That's what they're saying."

"Who's saying?"

"My uncle. Jack."

The silence on the other end of the line seemed to go on and on.

"Megan, what do you believe?"

"I don't know. I remember riding one minute, then waking up on the couch the next."

"So you don't recall what happened?"

"No."

Again silence. Finally, Sam said, "What would you

say if I told you your accident wasn't caused by faulty stitching?"

The chill she'd felt earlier came back with a vengeance. "I don't know."

"I glanced at your saddle. I swear it was not a stitching problem. Now I'll admit, I didn't get a great look, but I remember Jack's initial reaction. At the time, he didn't seem to think that it was faulty either."

"But I heard him and Uncle Daniel." Megan realized that she confessed to eavesdropping. "Jack insisted that was the cause."

"Afterwards, I'm sure. But I don't understand why."

She passed a hand over her forehead. "Maybe he told my uncle what he wanted to hear."

"Possibly. I just don't know anymore."

"I heard about my uncle's accident. Do you know any details?"

"Yes, but it's nothing like yours, if that's what you're implying."

"Oh." But Megan had wondered. "But I heard you and my uncle talking. The day of my accident. What was all that about?"

The vet was silent a moment.

Did the call drop? "Sam?"

"Daniel was trying to green-break a mare. The horse went over backwards, landing on him..."

"I know about that. You two were talking about a different incident."

The vet made a sound of indecision. "He didn't want me to mention it. Ever."

"Why?" Megan pressed the receiver harder to her head. "Please tell me."

Still the woman hesitated. "A couple years ago, your uncle was working in the corral. When he had greater mobility. A lead snapped and his back was re-injured. That's why he's had to hire a caregiver."

"And you think that his and my accidents are related?"

"It sure seems like...well, I just don't know any more." Sam sighed noisily. "I can't do anything if no one will support me. Clearly, for whatever reason, Jack has changed his story and your uncle has bought it."

Why would the foreman hide the truth? A possibility assailed her. Had he been threatened by the person who'd done it?

Megan backed against the wall, suddenly aware of the dark, empty house. All the men were out working or in the bunkhouse. The thunderstorm would mask any sounds.

"Megan?" Sam asked. "You there?"

"Yes. I'm here."

"I don't want to alarm you more than I have already, but you know how I feel about what's been going on around this area lately. You need to be careful. All right?"

"Okay. I will."

"And keep your eyes open for anything weird."

"Like what?"

"I don't know. Maybe you and I can get together and compare notes."

"Yeah. Sure." She inched toward her room.

"Well, I have to go. I'm already late for an appointment."

"Thanks for calling, Sam. I'll let you know if I discover anything."

She hung up before Megan could say goodbye. The line went dead.

Before she pulled the earpiece away, she heard the audible click of another phone in the house being replaced.

CHAPTER 40

The morning dawned clear, and a little cool, a perfect day for Moon Dancing to show her the mine. As quietly as possible, Megan dressed and gathered her things, including his knife. After packing food into a saddlebag, she was ready. She left a note for her uncle and Mrs. Danvers, and then crept out of the house.

Shadow seemed eager to go. Before saddling him, Megan checked the tack meticulously. She didn't want any injuries while she was in the middle of nowhere.

To keep down the noise of her escapade, she kept him at a walk. As soon as they were far enough away from the ranch, she let him have his head. A trotting gate wasn't quick enough for him. The stallion moved fluidly into a canter. Megan settled into the movement, sensing she had a long ride ahead.

Shadow turned the way she and Jack had gone the day of her tour. The ground was still damp, steam rising as the sun edged higher into the sky. Droplets clung to the pinyon pine, spraying them both when they brushed up against the foliage. Rabbits suddenly sprang away when they got too close. As she rode, she grabbed a sandwich out of the saddlebags and washed it down with canteen water. During a small break, Megan took a couple of bites of an apple before handing him the rest.

They left the flatlands, heading into the foothills. Going was slower now with Shadow picking his way carefully over the rocks. The sun beat down, making her glad for the hat that deflected some of the heat. They reached the top of a hill, traveling along the crest like the night of her and Moon Dancing's pledge.

Shadow suddenly shied, making her grab the saddle horn. When he stopped, she leaned forward.

"What is it?" She kept her voice low.

His ears flicked back and forth, nostrils flaring. For many minutes, they remained still while he tested the air for sounds and scents. Then Shadow pressed onward. Again he stopped, this time ears and head pointed in the direction they traveled.

Megan passed a hand over his neck, feeling his trembling flesh. Again, he moved on, cautiously, quietly. The saddle creaked softly while the bridle jingled. Dislodged rocks rolled and bumped down the slope, like mountain bikers jostling each other in a race.

They climbed another hill, winding in and out of gullies and washes. The higher they went, the tenser Megan grew. Something wasn't right. Shadow knew it. She felt it. When he stopped a third time, she leaned forward. "What's wrong? If there's danger, we should turn back. I'll get the sheriff."

He snorted, his negative answer enough.

"Then let's go on. I don't know what worries you, but if we don't go back, we go on."

They reached another crest, Shadow pausing at the top. The breeze pushed against her back. Megan glanced around, feeling exposed. Then she saw a hole in the side of one hill.

"That the mine?" She pointed.

He tossed his head.

She snapped a few pictures with her phone. "I need a better look."

From her position, she could see where the dirt had been pushed out onto the hillside. They drew closer, losing sight of the hole as they skirted boulders and hills. Finally, they climbed the steep incline and Shadow paused at the top.

As Megan dismounted, she skidded on the loose pebbles. She climbed the rest of the way up, and then crouched at the top to peer around.

No one was in sight.

The mouth of the hole looked old, as though the mine hadn't been worked in a long time. She saw no equipment. Tin cans, soda bottles, faded cardboard, crumpled cigarette packages, and half-burned wood lay scattered on the ground. She ducked as she peered inside, the hole darkening to nothingness.

"Whoever did this didn't dig very far," she said. "I wonder what they got."

Behind her Shadow blew out his breath.

"Hold a minute. I see something." Intent on the shiny item on the cave floor, Megan leaned in. Then she wrinkled her nose. "Something smells nasty in here. Like rotting food."

The dank, still air grew heavier as she crawled inside even further. She turned sideways to allow in some light.

"Looks like a necklace."

She picked up the lacy chain. The odor grew stronger. Her stomach roiled.

When her eyes adjusted, she saw that the cave sloped sharply in the back. She got on her knees and leaned forward to look below in the yawning blackness. A coldness crept down her neck as she stared. Imagination made her think she saw something move. The stench grew overwhelming. In the shifting grayness, she swore she saw an outline.

"Probably a den of sna–"

Megan screamed, falling away from the hole. Then she crabbed backwards out of the cave.

"Let's go. Let's go!" She yanked herself onto the saddle. "Hurry."

Shadow slipped down the hill, scrambling to keep both of them from pitching forward. She pushed him hard, beyond thinking, consumed by fear.

There was someone in the cave. A dead someone.

After an eternity of questioning, the sheriff believed her about the body, especially when she pulled out the necklace she'd found and showed him the mine photos. She led him to the place, quivering in horror. Then they sent her away. Only later did she discover the identity of the corpse. Simone.

Late that night, Megan sat in the living room with her uncle, unable to stop shaking. She had no thought of going to bed. Daniel seemed frozen, staring at the floor. Mrs. Danvers was with the sheriff.

Hours crawled by until they heard the housekeeper return with Jack. Both entered the room, shoulders hunched and faces tight.

As soon as she saw Mrs. Danvers, she rose and hugged her. The poor woman seemed completely unaware of anything one moment, then the next hung onto Megan and began to wail. A long time passed before she could let go. The four of them stayed in the living room, talking quietly until the grayness of dawn shaded the windows.

Daniel cleared his throat. "Give the men a day off, Jack. No one should work."

"But there's still chores to be done."

Her uncle looked baffled as though uncertain how to handle the glitch in his plans.

"Don't worry," the foreman said. "I'll take care of everything."

Daniel looked at her with red-rimmed eyes. "Meggie, would you help as well?"

"Sure." Anything would be better than the ugly images that swam through her mind.

She followed Jack outside.

"Let me hit the bunkhouse first. Be right back." He strode away.

The foreman was gone only a short time before indicating with a nod that they were going to the stables first. Work passed in a blur. She walked through the motions of helping feed the horses, cattle, chickens. In the pungent warmth of the coop, she found herself sagging against the wall as the horror washed over her again.

Jack wrapped his arms around her, his silent sympathy soothing when she couldn't cry. Tremors consumed her, but no tears. Forehead pressed against his chest, Megan knew she should withdraw but she was unable to leave his comfort.

How she wished for Moon Dancing. She wanted his arms about her.

When she felt Jack's hand in her hair, she jerked back.

"I'm sorry." She folded her arms. "You've been so nice. And helpful."

"It's okay." His voice was soft as he reached to brush a stray curl off her forehead. "I was expecting you to rain all over my shirt, but you didn't."

"Sorry." She cleared her throat as it tightened. "You've been...I wanted to let you know I appreciate your friendship."

He leaned against the wall, chickens picking at the floor around his feet as he planted his hands in his pockets. "But it goes no further than that, does it?"

She ducked her head.

He sighed. "Well, this about does it. Unless you want to help milk the cows."

"I'm not qualified."

"I could teach you. It's really quite peaceful once you get the hang of it."

"Not today. Not now." She backed towards the door. "If you don't mind, I'm going to head to bed."

"Abandoning me?"

"I'm sorry. I really am." She bolted out of the coop.

She wanted to go to Shadow, but figured Jack would think she'd lied to him. Assuming Mrs. Danvers was sleeping, she quietly opened the kitchen door. Megan slipped off her boots, then left them by the back door.

She'd just reached the bottom stair when she heard low voices. Apparently her uncle and the housekeeper were still in the living room. Megan tiptoed up a few steps, but stopped when she heard her uncle say, "You really want me to send her back to Florida?"

"Not there necessarily," said the quiet voice of Mrs. Danvers. "Somewhere else."

Megan couldn't move, paralyzed by their conversation. Send her away? No. She couldn't go. Not while Moon Dancing and she were–

"What do you know, Celia? What aren't you telling me?"

Material rustled as though the woman fidgeted. Then she sighed. "I know nothing certain. Call it woman's intuition."

Her uncle was quiet a moment. "I need to think about this."

"Do not wait long, Daniel." Soft footsteps moved closer to the door. They paused. "You must send her away. After the funeral..."

"Celia..." His voice held an element of tenderness she'd not heard before.

Megan crept up the stairs. When she reached her room, she quietly shut her door and locked it.

Mrs. Danvers wanted to send her away. To protect her? From what or whom? Obviously she sensed the danger, whatever it was, wasn't yet over.

What did the woman fear that she wasn't admitting to Daniel?

CHAPTER 41

"I'm glad a lot of people showed up." Megan stood beside her friend on the front porch. A train of people came and went during the funeral lunch after Simone's memorial service.

A sad grin flitted over Sam's face. "Nice that so many folks want to give their condolences to Daniel and Celia. I'm sorry I couldn't make it earlier. How was the service?"

"The preacher did a nice job." Megan chewed on her lower lip, feeling like a hypocrite.

Nice. Everything was nice. *Right.* Attendance had been sparse, cut short by the lack of much to say. Simone's body had already been cremated and arrangements made to ship the ashes to France, her birthplace.

"Sorry about your loss." An elderly gentleman, hair slicked down, solemnly shook Megan's hand.

"Thanks so much for coming." She squeezed the hand of his portly wife, and then watched them shuffle down the stairs.

"I hear the sheriff's department has a hot lead." Sam spoke when they were again alone.

"Really?" She didn't want to admit she'd overheard Jack telling her uncle that Moon Dancing was their number one suspect.

"Yes. Some Native American. This incident has really stirred up the community."

This murder had been too close to home. That's what the paper had called it. Not a fall and accidental death, but murder. Megan shivered.

"Walk with me for a second." Sam took her arm and steered her away from the front door. "I want to know your theory about why Simone was killed."

"I don't really have one anymore."

"What was it to begin with?"

Megan shrugged, unwilling to communicate the ominous thoughts that rumbled in her mind.

"Then let me propose something." Sam pressed her lips together before leaning closer. "Simone knew about the mine. Someone has been helping themselves and she'd been in on it."

"Helping themselves to what?"

"Silver."

Megan raised her brows. "How do you know that?"

Her friend made a face. "Let's just say I have my sources."

"So you think she knew about it?"

"No doubt." Sam's mouth settled into grim lines. "Either they got tired of sharing or Simone got to be too big of a nuisance to keep around."

"They?" She sucked in a breath at the idea of more people involved.

"Stands to reason there're others." Sam brushed back her bangs. "It's difficult to get rid of silver ore on your own."

Megan pondered the implications. "You don't think

Simone just stumbled onto the mine?"

"That far out in the middle of nowhere?" The vet shook her head. "I'm betting she knew all about it. They lured her there and..." She left the sentence unfinished.

After a moment, Megan said, "If there were a 'they,' Simone had to have been close to one of them."

"Someone with connections?" Sam rubbed her lower lip. "Any ideas who her partner was?"

Megan shifted her weight. "No." She'd totally dismissed the suspicion of Jack being her lover. Not only had his attitude toward her been incorrect, but also he'd not been at the right places at the right times. The night of Simone's disappearance, he'd been in the house, playing checkers with her uncle until very late.

Though he masked his grief, Jack was as broken up about her death as everyone else. Megan could see it in his ashen face and weary shoulders.

"I wonder if there are any more mines," Sam speculated.

She straightened. "There could be more?"

"Sure. This is a huge ranch, lots of hills. A silver vein could run for a while, look like it played out, but reappear somewhere else."

"I guess I'll have to take some more jaunts."

The vet grasped her arm. "You be careful, Megan. If thieving and murder mean nothing to these people, another death won't either. You see something suspicious, don't investigate on your own."

"I won't."

"I don't trust that gleam in your eye."

"I'll be careful," Megan assured her again. "This is my place, too. No one should be allowed to steal from us."

When Sam's eyes narrowed, she realized she'd said too much. It wasn't common knowledge that the ranch belonged to her and Daniel. The woman let the comment pass, though.

"Maybe you should go with me," Megan suggested.

"I'd definitely feel better about that. There's only

my work to consider." Sam stared off into the distance.

"You saying no?"

"Absolutely not. This is important. I'll make time."

"All right." Megan debated. "What's your schedule like the day after tomorrow?"

"Open. You up for early?"

"Sure. Seven?"

"I'll be here with my horse."

"Okay." She smiled, glad to have someone with her on her rides. Especially while she hunted for more mines.

Sam glanced around. "You'd better get back to the well-wishers. I've kept you long enough. And this may sound morbid, but I'm hungry."

They headed back inside. Megan stood in line at the table though she didn't really feel like eating. Without thinking, she piled fried chicken, coleslaw, potato salad, and baked beans onto her plate.

If there was another mine, a newer one, then someone was still stealing from her uncle. And from her. If she and Sam could discover another one, the authorities might be able to find some clues that would lead to Simone's killer. That and stop the illegal operation.

She stared out the window, gradually becoming aware of Sam standing out by the corral. Was that the sheriff she was talking to? Their heads came together as though discussing something of importance. Shadow stood nearby, ears pricked forward. Listening?

I thought Sam said she was hungry...

"You're a thousand miles away." Jack interrupted her musings.

Megan straightened.

"You gonna eat all that?" He indicated the food.

"No. My hands needed something to do."

He cradled a glass of punch. "How are you doing?"

She sucked in a breath. "Okay."

He tilted his head. "Y'sure?"

His sympathetic tone made tears seep into her eyes. "Maybe a little shaken. Still."

"I can imagine. Not every day you solve a mystery."

"Solve–?"

"Yeah. Don't you believe you did?"

She held her tongue, afraid to say too much. Everyone believed that Moon Dancing was the culprit. Which was impossible. She couldn't prove otherwise though, without telling all. The sheriff and his deputies had grilled her about one point...how had she known the mine's location? Megan had repeated several times that it'd been a coincidence. Everyone knew she rode around the countryside. She'd stumbled onto the hole and investigated.

"I suppose," Jack said, running his finger down the side of the wet glass, "that the mystery won't completely be solved until the murderer is brought to justice."

"I think all of us would like that."

He met her gaze. "I'd like nothing better than to personally get my hands on..." He paused, clenching his teeth.

Megan touched his arm. "I'm sorry. Let's change the subject."

He nodded, but didn't speak.

The silence went on and on, but what could she say? She looked around the room at those who stayed to chat. The clock indicated that the lunch officially ended in ten minutes, but no one appeared ready to leave. She acknowledged a few people she knew by name when they looked her way. Then she noticed that the sheriff had entered the room with his new deputy at his heels. As taciturn as ever, Jed Harper looked painfully rigid in his spotless uniform. He was taking his job seriously.

"Things'll get back to normal by tomorrow." Jack broke into her thoughts. "Then life will go on."

"That'd be good." Megan turned to face him again. "I think the men would like to get back to work."

"And we're behind." He nodded. "If you'll excuse me, I think I'll say hello to the sheriff."

Megan watched him a moment, then gazed out the window. She'd like life to get back to normal. In a few days was a new moon. With the current suspicions and hostility toward Moon Dancing, she needed to plan where they could safely meet. She didn't want him to run into Jack who sounded like he wouldn't hesitate to pummel him half to death.

Though she had no doubt Moon Dancing could take care of himself, she wanted to avoid a confrontation between the two men. Especially now that Jack was friendly with the sheriff's department. And, in particular, Jed Harper.

Across the room, the two men leaned together, discussing something of importance.

She and Moon Dancing had to be careful.

CHAPTER 42

Sam showed up right on time, pulling a horse trailer. Ready with a prepared lunch, Megan went out to meet her friend in the yard.

"My uncle fussed about my riding off." She stifled her yawn. "Until I mentioned you were going with me. I think he feels a little better now."

"Glad to be of service." The vet patted the rifle scabbard secured to her horse's saddle. "Daniel knows I pack when I ride."

They headed in a new direction from any Megan had taken before. Sam said she had an idea to try out. While they rode, they chatted about their lives. Her friend asked many questions, shaking her head over the very different childhood than what she'd experienced.

"Was it hard growing up without parents, Megan?"

"I suppose. Perhaps more for me than a child who'd never known theirs. But how can you compare loss?"

"Do you remember them?"

"Very well. I'm sure I put them on a pedestal. You know, the perfect people. No doubt they had their faults which probably would have driven me crazy."

"So your aunt and uncle weren't very supportive?"

"Perhaps they were. Of course, I didn't appreciate them as a teen."

"A rebellious teen?"

"Very, but not externally. I obeyed and was the perfect student, but inside I seethed. My aunt is my uncle's wife's sister. No blood relation. So I figured they didn't have the right to dictate my life. The day after I finished high school, I moved out."

"And were totally happy from then on." Sam's mouth pulled to one side.

"Right." Megan laughed. "I bounced from job to job before I decided to go to college. Of course, my uncle helped. After I graduated, I worked for a couple different banks, did some free-lance consulting, and then came here. End of story."

"I don't believe that either. What made you pull up roots? I thought city folks couldn't stand the quiet of the country."

Megan thought through what she wanted to say. Not just for Sam's ears, but Moon Dancing. This was a chance to tell him her life, filtered through her conversation with the vet. "Since I worked as a consultant and was my own boss, I put in a ton of hours to finish a major project. I'd promised my uncle for years I'd come to visit." She shooed a fly away from her face before continuing. "The finished job and the end of a bad relationship decided the timing."

Sam nodded knowingly. "After my fifteen-year marriage finally crumbled I went to school to get my degree. My step-brother told me how beautiful the area was here, so I moved down when I could."

"Your step-brother? Have I met him?"

"Not sure." Sam looked away. "Speaking of beautiful, what'd'ya think of that scenery? I sometimes wish I'd become an artist to capture nature on canvas."

She looked to where her friend was pointing. A lone tree clawed the sky. The jagged brown looked like an upside-down bolt of lightning. Behind it stood the mountains, blue, imposing, swallowing up the horizon.

They stopped later for lunch. When they were done eating, they skirted hills and explored valleys, but found no other mining operation. Though Megan was disappointed that they'd discover nothing, she still enjoyed herself. Sam was an exceptional equestrienne. Come fall, she promised to take Megan on a hunting trip.

Only one incident marred their trip. Sam unexpectedly stopped and glanced around.

Megan reined in Shadow. "What's the matter?"

"I swear..." Her friend didn't finish her sentence. She frowned, standing up in her stirrups and scanning the landscape. "Wish I'da brought my binoculars."

"To look at what?"

Sam's mouth tightened. "This is the third time I've gotten the feeling someone's following us. I thought I saw something just a minute ago, but..." She shook herself as though to chase away the thought.

Megan scanned the horizon but saw no one. They rode on.

By the time they headed for home, she was tired but happy. A thought began to percolate in her mind which she waited for the right time to bring up. When the ranch came in sight, Megan realized that the right time had never come.

"Sam, could you hold for a moment?" She licked her lower lip, trying to find a way to voice her request.

"What is it?" The woman shifted in her saddle.

"I wanted to let you know that I enjoyed today."

"Then let's do it again."

"Great." She ran her fingers along Shadow's mane, thinking of him. "How about in a few days?"

Sam's brows rose. "All right. Got a particular one

in mind?"

"Thursday?"

"Fine by me." She shifted in her saddle as though to urge her horse forward.

"One more thing. I was wondering if I could meet you somewhere. Like halfway between here and town?"

She frowned. "That would mean an awful earlier start for both of us."

"I know. But that would save you from getting up much earlier than me."

Her eyes narrowed. "All right. If you want."

Megan's heart hammered as she imagined she'd created the perfect excuse to get away from the ranch so that she could meet Moon Dancing. "Let's say about seven then."

"Halfway between here and town?"

"Yes." She chewed her lip, in a quandary about what else to say.

"Seven." Sam nodded. "It's a done deal."

"Wait." Megan reached toward her friend. "One other thing. I've got something to do the evening before, but I don't want my uncle to worry."

This time, Sam backed her horse until she was right beside her. "What is it Megan? What are you up to?"

"Nothing dangerous. But I need to get away from the ranch in the afternoon. The day before."

"Where are you going to spend the night?"

"Out." She glanced away. "Please don't ask any more questions. I promise I'll explain someday. I know it's a huge favor, but could you support my story that I'm going to be at your place that night?" When she didn't answer, Megan looked up.

"You know, you've gotten to be almost a daughter to me," Sam said quietly. "But I don't have the privilege of dictating your life."

"Never mind. I'm sorry I asked. Just forget the whole thing."

"No. I want to help. But I'm a little nervous about what you're planning."

"It's nothing immoral or illegal. I swear. I just need

to take care of something. Personal."

Sam pursed her lips, and then glanced away, studying the sky, then the ranch in the distance. Finally, she sighed. "All right. You arrange it with Daniel. I hope he doesn't ask me." She looked Megan squarely in the eye. "Because I won't lie to him."

She nodded. "Thanks. I'll face the music if it comes."

"Oh, it'll come, Honey. You can be sure of that."

"I'm not going to lie to my uncle. Just... not tell him the whole truth."

Sam shook her head, but she said nothing. The gesture still made Megan uncomfortable. One day, she vowed, she'd tell Daniel. Just not now. Not so soon after the Simone incident. When the hue and cry died down in the next few weeks, she could meet Moon Dancing at the ranch as usual.

"I'll call you the day before to make certain everything's still set. All right?"

"Okie-dokie." Sam booted her horse toward the awaiting trailer.

Megan followed, her stomach still in knots. This was the only way to see Moon Dancing. Somewhere safe.

As she thought of him, her heart throbbed in anticipation.

CHAPTER 43

Her plan went off without a hitch. Megan called her friend to make certain everything was still a go, and then bid her uncle goodbye in the afternoon. He gave her a moment of nervousness when he asked if Jack could accompany her on the long ride. She resisted his suggestion and left shortly afterward.

Checking over her shoulder a few times, she made certain she wasn't being followed. Megan stayed on the road so that if anyone saw her, they'd support the story that she was heading to town. But that would only work until she turned off onto the dirt road.

"I'll tell my uncle I took a little siesta. If he finds out." The lies, though, were beginning to stack up. She hated the sneaking around. But now she understood Moon Dancing's comment about the torture of the weeks in between seeing him. How right he was.

She reached the grove early. Light filtered through the trees, throwing dancing shadows on the ground. The first thing she did was strip the tack from Shadow. He shook out his mane and snorted.

"Are you anxious too?" She leaned against his chest.

While she waited for nightfall, she busied herself getting the furs from the cave and shaking them out. Then she collected firewood. The recent rains had left the wood damp, making her uncertain about how successful fire building would be. Then she found Moon Dancing's buckskins and laid them out for him. The wad of bills bulged in one pocket. She took the money and buried it with the metal box that was still in the side of the hill.

As twilight deepened, she ate. Then she tried to build a fire. Her best effort defeated her. Apparently being born and bred in Wyoming didn't guarantee innate talent. The wood smoked and hissed, resisting the pitiful flames that licked cautiously at the branches before fizzling out.

Sighing, Megan gave up. She looked at Shadow. "I'll leave campfires up to you."

The night grew black, the absence of the moon dampening everything. Even the stars shimmered weakly in the heavens. She sighed again, waiting, peering into the night.

Shadow's low moan alerted her that the process had begun. He stood stiff-legged, head bowed, body trembling. Megan could barely see him in the darkness. Slowly, he folded his legs under him and collapsed. Awed at the transformation, she watched as he morphed from beast to man. The black shape shrank, gradually paling into flesh color. His back twisted, until she could no longer see his face. A pitiful groan finished the process until she blinked and saw that he was fully human, helpless as he lay in a fetal position, curled away from her.

After she grabbed a blanket and wrapped it around him, she helped him sit up. Moon Dancing released a painful sigh as his head lolled back onto her shoulder. Wishing she knew how else to help, she cradled him. Eyes closed, he breathed heavily as though at the end of his strength.

"I'm here. Don't be afraid." She stroked his hair from his face.

For many minutes, he seemed oblivious to his surroundings. Then his eyes flickered open.

"We're in the grove." Megan kept her voice low. "We're alone."

He shuddered and pulled the blanket around himself more tightly.

"I tried to make a fire, but I'm completely inadequate. Are you cold? I have hot coffee in a thermos."

He said nothing, still weak as he slouched against her. After a few minutes, he was able to sit upright, though he still appeared groggy. He shook his head as though to rid himself of the lingering effects.

"I'll get that coffee."

Megan fumbled in the dark for the thermos, glad that she'd taken advantage of the daylight hours to arrange everything. Steam rose as she poured the liquid into the cap. Then she held the black brew for Moon Dancing to drink. He grasped the cup and her hands as she steered it to his lips. After several tentative sips, he sighed, growing more alert.

"Better?" She smoothed the blanket over his shoulder where it had slipped.

"This is like the first time we met. When you held water to my lips." His dark eyes met hers, two spots of reflected light in their depths.

She smiled softly. "I do it again, gladly."

He blew out a breath. "I hate the weakness that comes over me."

"It'll pass." She again stroked his hair, loving the silky feel of it.

He touched her face, tracing the curve of her cheek, then chin. "I wish for your caress every moment of every day. When I am with you, as a beast, frustration consumes me because I cannot touch you as I want."

"And I, you." Emotion stung her eyes.

He stretched his arms, the blanket falling away from his shoulders. She studied his powerful chest, all corded muscle and sinew.

"Do you like what you see, Megan of Fire?"

She nodded, heat creeping up her neck.

He pulled the blanket closer. "Someday, I will be completely yours."

They sat together on the furs, staring into a bonfire, Moon Dancing dressed in his buckskins. Megan sighed, the sound mingled with sorrow as she thought of the night ending when she would again be alone. Morning would bring proof that their love was not enough to break the curse.

She vowed to be content. For now, to be with him was enough.

"Are you sorry you promised yourself to me?" His quiet question cut through the night.

"No. Never." She leaned her head on his shoulder as she watched the dancing flames. "Of course, I wish for you to be freed, but the moments we have are precious."

"These times, though few, are better than nothing?"

"Absolutely. Have no doubts about that." She caught the gleam of his smile. "I wanted to tell you...I did some research. About my heritage. Because I wondered about your legend."

"What did you discover?"

"I am a descendent of the Sioux as well...Western Dakota."

His eyes narrowed.

"I wondered *why me*. Why you thought I could break the curse."

"And...?"

"One of my ancestors was called 'Scares At His Shadow.' I thought perhaps..." Megan stopped speaking at the sudden intensity on his face. "What is it?"

"I know of him. A great warrior." His mouth moved for a moment, and then his eyes fixed on her. "He was a descendent of the medicine man I told you about."

A thrill ran through her.

Moon Dancing turned to face her as he grasped her arms. "Tell me...has anything strange happened since we first met?"

She wanted to joke that everything had been strange, but from the burning in his eyes she knew this was not a joking matter. "For one thing, I swear I could hear your voice in my head sometimes. But you knew that already."

"Anything strange in the sky? Or with the moon?"

Megan shrugged. "I thought...a couple times it looked funny."

"How?"

"One time it had a ring around it. Full of colors. Another time, it seemed...muted."

His face fell. "I thought perhaps..."

"I did see a meteor shower. At least twice."

His dark gaze again locked onto her. "Meteor?"

"Like falling stars. Millions of them. But I figured I imagined it since the shower was always over in a couple seconds."

"When did this happen?"

She thought back. "The last time was during the full moon. Just before we knelt on the rock."

His grip tightened. "And before that?"

Megan chewed her lip. "After you gave me your bracelet. Come to think of it, I was surprised you didn't see the stars."

His face turned away, brow tight. "I *did* see. But thought..." He didn't say anything for a moment. "Strength, sound judgment, an open hand of giving, fearlessness."

"Are you talking about the four virtues?"

His eyebrows rose. "You know of these?"

"I read about them. The words were different, but the meaning the same: fortitude, wisdom, generosity and bravery." Megan again waited while he pondered what she'd told him.

"Tell me, did you see the shattered stars the first night we met?" His quiet question cut through the night.

She nodded slowly. "Yes, just before Jack Crawford showed up. I was standing in the moonlight..." For some reason, expectation clutched at her, silencing her.

Moon Dancing's eyes darkened. "Three visions, four virtues."

Her heart felt as though it was about to stop. "Are you saying there is only one virtue left to fulfill?"

His expression again grew tight. But instead of answering, he rose abruptly and strode to the fire. Puzzled, Megan remained seated. A cold tremor ran through her.

"What is it, Moon Dancing?" When he didn't answer, she went to him.

"You are in danger." He wouldn't look at her.

She touched his arm. "How?"

He shook his head, eyes still fixed on the flames. "You must go away."

"And leave you? No."

"I will find you. But you must go from here." He finally gazed at her. "I hear things. Whispered voices. Plans."

Megan slowly shook her head. "I can't leave you. Not if we are so close to breaking–"

"Your safety is more important."

She combed her fingers through her hair, wincing when she snagged a tangle. "What if I rent a house, say in Cheyenne or Evanston. Would that work?"

"Tell no one where you are going."

"Not even my uncle?"

Moon Dancing's face hardened. "He is too trusting. He speaks with an open heart to the enemy."

"Who?"

"I will not yet say. I must find a way to expose them."

Them?

Despite her nearness to the fire, she shivered. He took her hand, splaying her fingers to look at the palm. "This is the hand that may someday cradle a child. *My* child. My inheritance. I must know you are safe though I cannot protect you myself." He leaned over and kissed her palm. "Swear to me, you will do everything to save yourself." When she didn't answer quickly enough, he squeezed. Hard. "Swear."

She gasped, a little fearful of his fierceness. "I swear."

Moon Dancing's grip relaxed. "You will go tomorrow. Understand? No time must be wasted."

"All right."

He leaned forward to kiss her. His lips were soft, tender, while his fingers stroked her jaw. When she pulled away, she saw the wetness of his eyes.

"I love you, Moon Dancing." Her own tears threatened to overwhelm. "Don't ever stop believing that."

He nodded, turning again to stare into the fire. His mouth worked, then his jaw clenched. "Now I understand the agony of love. The pain is here." He thumped his chest. "Like a thrusting spear."

The flames scorched the sky, crackling and hissing. Suppressed words etched his face. Finally, he looked at her.

"The curse is fulfilled." He suddenly turned and shook his fist at the night. "I die of love, Night Hawk. Is that not what you wished?"

Expecting something to happen, Megan held her breath.

Crickets chirped undisturbed. The river rustled, unhindered as it leaped rocks and battered the banks. The fire popped and spit, the light stretching toward the heavens. But the one called Night Hawk remained silent.

CHAPTER 44

Smoke from the fire stung Megan awake. Coughing, she sat up. Moon Dancing was gone. Across the gray-lit grove, she saw Shadow, still prostrate, the transformation complete.

Rushing footsteps made her twist around, but not quickly enough. Someone grabbed her hair and yanked her upright. She cried out, clawing at the vicious hold. As she staggered to her feet, she came face to face with Kit Gerard.

"Where is he?" He jerked. "Where'd he go?"

Whimpering from the pain, she clutched his wrist. Megan tried to wriggle from his grasp, but abruptly froze when he jammed the tip of a rifle under her chin.

"I'm not asking again. Where's the Injun who was here last night?"

"He...he's gone." Fear quavered through her voice.

"How? There ain't no way out of here 'cept down river." He indicated the water with a jerk of his head.

"I don't know. I just woke up."

Gerard's eyes hardened. "Don't matter. He won't get far." He shoved her. Megan's foot caught on the blanket and she tripped, landing heavily.

Another man approached, one she'd seen before. At Simone's funeral?

"He's gone." Gerard stomped toward his companion. "Head out and see if you can cut him off. I'll take her upstream in case he went that way." He turned to her. "Put on your boots."

Hands shaking Megan hurried to obey. She dared not look at the stallion, afraid that Gerard would see her worry. Shadow was still dazed and weak.

The former trainer dragged her up by the arm. "You lead the way."

They plowed upriver, dodging the overhanging branches.

"What do you want?" she finally asked him.

"For you to keep your mouth shut."

"You can't treat me this way. I'll report–"

"I said shut up." He jabbed her in the back with the rifle.

Megan walked on, taking her time, trying to understand what was happening. What did they want?

"You're part of the gang that has been illegally mining on my uncle's ranch."

"Don't you mean your ranch?"

She sucked in a breath, aghast that he knew. How'd he hear it? From Sam? She was the only other person Megan had told. Then she realized she and her friend had talked by the living room windows. Anyone could have overheard them.

"What do you want with me?"

"Now I don't rightly know at this point. I'd like nothing better than to put a bullet in your head, but not everyone agrees. Especially the boss."

When Megan faltered, he again shoved her.

"Hurry it up. I don't want to comb the country all

day."

They trudged further, but as Gerard had already guessed, the climbing got too treacherous. Finally, he stopped. "He couldn't've come this way."

Megan turned. *This might be my only chance.* Her life was probably forfeit. Gerard would kill her, and then shoot Shadow.

"Go back." He moved for her to pass.

She limped toward him, bending a little and putting her hand on her thigh as though it pained.

"What's the matter?"

"My leg–"

"Get a move on." He threatened with the rifle.

Deliberately, she slipped as she headed back down, ramming him. He clawed at air, the rifle clattering below while she scrambled away. She scrabbled sideways down the hill, not wasting time by looking back. Rocks scraped her hands. Branches whipped her face.

Behind her, Gerard swore. "Stop. I'm warning you..."

Splashing through the river, Megan ran on blindly. She fell. The current carried her downstream a little ways before a rock halted her. She fought to rise. As she thrashed her way out of the water, she twisted her knee. Lungs burned as she ducked under trees and scrambled along the mushy bank. She shrieked when wood chips stung her face, a loud *craack* sounding almost simultaneously. On she ran, pushing harder.

Where was the grove? It had to be close. Again, another sharp crack. Megan didn't have time to react the third time she heard a shot. Burning pain seared across her head. She heard herself screaming as she pitched forward. The sand sucked her down as she fell on her knees. Blood splattered onto her shirt.

Shadow thundered toward her, eyes blazing. She struggled upward, trying to grab his mane. Swiveling his body, he shielded her from Gerard. Boots full of water, she staggered in the soft sand. Shadow was too tall for her to climb onto his back. Her hands were slick, wet with blood. They slid on the silky strands.

No time...

"Hold it right there," Gerard said in a deadly voice.

She peered over Shadow's back. The man's rifle pointed at her. A deep gash marked one of his cheeks and mud covered his clothing. But it was the barrel of the gun that convinced her to do what he said.

"Get away from the horse."

Trembling, she tried to obey, but Shadow kept thrusting himself between her and the man. She couldn't get around him. Blood stung one eye and the wound in her head began to throb in earnest.

"I said get away," Gerard rasped.

"I can't."

"Move toward the fire. *Now.*"

She backed up, Shadow moving with her, his body in front of her. "Please don't do this," she said in a low voice to him. "Move away from me. Please."

"Shut up. I didn't say talk." The man strode forward. "You've been more trouble than you're worth."

"Let me tie up my horse. He's skittish." Then in a low voice, she said, "Moon Dancing, please allow me. I don't think he'll kill me. He's waiting for someone."

She grabbed the bridle and tried to get it on him while the man moved closer. He stayed warily at a distance while Shadow resisted, tossing his head to prevent her from putting the bit in his mouth.

"What's taking so long?" Gerard demanded.

"He's nervous. Just give me a minute." Megan doggedly tried to bridle Shadow who pawed the ground, resisting her.

A crack of a rifle in the distance drew Gerard's attention away. He lowered his gun, moving toward the sound. The next minute, Shadow knocked her backwards. It took only one terrible second to realize what he was going to do.

"No!"

The stallion rushed the man. Gerard wheeled and fired. Too late. His shot went wild. The horse knocked him down. The man rolled, then fired again.

Shadow screamed, Megan's shriek of anguish mingling with his. Horrified, she watched him reel away from the prostrate man. *Boom*. Another shot.

"No. *No*!" She ran toward him.

Blood gushing from his chest, Shadow collapsed slowly.

She grabbed his head. He let out a pitiful groan as his knees buckled.

"Shadow–" She couldn't catch her breath. "Moon Dancing–no!"

Already his eyes were rolling back into his head. She pressed her palms to the wound, trying to staunch the bleeding.

"You can't die! You proved yourself brave. You have to live..."

His warm blood soaked the ground, sand licking up his life. A long death rattle escaped the twitching body.

"Good." Gerard's voice rasped behind her. "I never did like that horse. But now..."

She saw the blur of the rifle. A brilliant light slashed across her vision before pain spun her into blackness.

"Megan." A soft voice called to her. "Megan."

She blinked and stared. Jack's face shimmered into focus.

She closed her eyes, relieved. It had only been a nightmare. Moon Dancing wasn't dead.

I must have hurt myself. They were trying to rouse her. Her sluggish mind couldn't put the events together. Did she fall off Shadow? Something about the faulty stitching on her cinch strap. Did that just happen?

When she opened her eyes again, she realized she lay under a tree. Sam was bending over her.

"Where am I?" The words croaked from her throat.

"Don't try to talk, Honey. You have a nasty bump on your head."

"What happened?" She felt the stickiness on her hands and resisted the monstrous truth. The sickening tang of metal burned her nostrils.

"There's been a shoot-out between the sheriff and Kit Gerard. You're okay, though. Jack rescued you."

"My horse." Megan tried to sit up, head pounding. "Where's Moon–Shadow? Where is he?" Horror gripped her. She couldn't stave the rising panic. "Sam, you've got to save him. He's wounded." Her voice rose to a shrill. "There's still time. Hurry!"

The vet's eyes crinkled with grief. "I'm sorry. There was nothing I could do. I'm so sorry."

"You mean–are you–?" Megan couldn't finish the sentence. "No. It can't be..."

"I'm so sorry, Honey. I checked your horse myself." Sam paused to take a deep shuddering breath. "Shadow's dead."

CHAPTER 45

"I recommend you take her away from here. As soon as possible." The doctor's quiet voice contained an element of urgency as he spoke to her uncle.

Megan pretended to sleep, the pill he'd given her still clutched in her hand under the blankets.

Go away! Leave me alone.

She had shrieked that many times in the last week. But no one listened. No one would let her mourn.

No one understands.

"I've given her a sleeping aid," the doctor went on. "She'll rest tonight."

His footsteps and Daniel's low voice faded. Megan listened a few moments before cautiously opening one eye. Her door remained partly ajar, but no one was in sight. She slipped from bed and quietly turned the knob until it latched.

Finally, some privacy. Irresolute, she stood in the center of her bedroom. What she wanted to do was go to the stables. Go to...

Shadow. Her heart cried for him the thousandth time.

"Shadow?" She whispered the name aloud, straining to hear him with all her soul. Nothing. No answering call in her mind.

He's gone. Forever.

She closed her eyes, still unable to comprehend reality. He would not be waiting. Or running in the pasture. Through the haze of lingering sedation and pain medications, the horrible truth pressed upon her. She touched her head. Someone had removed the stitches from the gunshot wound. Yes, that had happened. She hadn't imaged the injury or the blow to her head. She thought through the events that had followed the shootout in the ravine. Ten days, or was it eleven now?

They treat me like I've lost my mind.

"Shadow was more than a horse." She spoke quietly, reminding herself of truth.

No one understood. Megan had nothing left but a saddle and bridle.

"No. I also have Moon Dancing's things." All except his diary.

Longing for them washed over her. If she could but hold them and look at them...they would comfort her. Megan retrieved the suitcase from under her bed, but stared at the empty space inside.

"I remember. I moved them." She had put the small painting in a drawer, the money in the closet, the knife...no, that must still be in the stables. She had taken it with her the day she discovered the mine.

A search of her dresser drawers revealed nothing. Again, she rifled through the neatly folded clothing. Still nothing. She yanked on the drawers to dump the contents, but she couldn't dislodge them. Instead, she flung handfuls of clothing onto the floor. Breathing hard, she stared. With an effort, she calmed herself.

Maybe I didn't put anything there.

She rushed to the closet and ransacked boxes. When she didn't find any of Moon Dancing's possessions, she started pulling items off shelves.

"They have to be here somewhere!" Rising panic made her voice quaver.

She hurried into the bathroom and flung things. A glass shattered on the tile. A bottle of ibuprofen opened, pills bouncing and then rolling across the floor. Hair conditioner flipped off the edge of the tub and landed, lid popping open and liquid glopping out.

"Where are they?"

Megan ignored the bite of pain in her foot as she rushed back into her bedroom and dove into the clothing on the floor.

They have to be here. One thing. Some*thing.*

On hands and knees she again rummaged through the pile of material. Then she realized that Moon Dancing's bracelet was missing from her wrist.

"No! Who took it?"

Pressing her hands to her head, she sat back on her heels and rocked. It was on her wrist...yesterday. She distinctly remembered that. Didn't she? But where...?

"Megan!" Her uncle's voice sliced through the sound of her ragged breathing. He sat at the doorway, face white, hand on the knob. His gaze shot about the room.

"They're gone." She blurted out the only thing she could say to make him understand. "I've looked everywhere. Someone's taken them."

He said nothing, mouth agape, brow wrinkled.

"My bracelet..." She started to cry. "I have to find it."

Megan rose and pushed past him.

"Stop. Wait!"

Heedless of his cry, she dashed down the stairs. At the bottom, she slipped on the tile floor and fell. She glanced down, wondering where the blood had come from. Aware of footsteps pounding in her direction, she rose and slipped again.

Her foot. She'd cut her foot. Bright red smeared the shiny floor, making it slippery.

"Jack, help! Stop her." Daniel's voice called from the top of the stairs.

Through the front door she sprinted. *The car. I have to get to the car.*

Megan fumbled with the door handle, and then leaped in, hands scrabbling across the seats. A spot of color on the floor made her catch her breath. She grabbed the bracelet just as someone pulled on her leg. Clutching it to her chest with both hands, she allowed Jack to haul her from the back of the car.

"I found it." She heard herself sobbing. "I found it."

"Megan..." Jack's voice was ragged. Without another word, he lifted and carried her back to the house.

She was aware of her uncle meeting them in the foyer, of Mrs. Danvers holding his hand, of Jack clutching her tightly. Nothing mattered.

I have Moon Dancing's bracelet. Crying in relief, she pressed her face to Jack's chest.

"Tomorrow." Daniel's voice grated. "Tomorrow, Jack. Take her away from here. I don't care where. Just go."

"Yessir."

Megan began to laugh, the consolation of finding his bracelet overpowering the momentary panic. The beads dug into her palm as she clenched them. She calmed herself with the truth. *I'm not crazy. He really existed. I have his bracelet.*

Her eyes rose to the portrait in her uncle's living room. From the painting, Moon Dancing seemed to smile at her.

Everything was going to be okay.

Megan stared at the pink sky, vaguely puzzled that the sun had risen every morning and set every evening without her being conscious of it. *Four weeks.* Four weeks had passed since the shootout. Was it possible that she was still alive? That she had survived this long and terrible nightmare?

Fifteen days of traveling within the state, ending in Cheyenne, had helped restore her peace of mind. Although she once questioned why they couldn't stay put in one place. Jack had assured her that seeing the whole state would be beneficial.

She gripped the railing as she deeply breathed the hot August air.

He came out onto the balcony that their two hotel rooms shared. After glancing around, he rested his hand on hers. "You okay?"

"Yeah." She managed a small smile. "And ready to go home."

He tilted his head to look at her. "Y'sure?"

"I have to face reality someday." She spoke more bravely than she felt. *Am I ready to return to the ranch? To all the memories?*

His fingers moved, gently caressing her skin. Megan took in a slow breath, forcing herself not to jerk away from his touch. One of many in the last week. Would he bring up marriage again? He'd asked her a couple nights ago. Though she had no reason to refuse him, she wasn't ready to say yes. He had appeared to squelch his disappointment, but she noticed more and more his look of yearning.

A sound below the veranda made him pull his hand away. He leaned over the railing, posture rigid, brow furrowed.

She, too, looked. "What's the matter?"

He straightened, the forced smile unable to disguise the worry in his eyes. "Nothing."

A hotel employee was throwing something into the garbage bin. A door below slammed.

She studied Jack. "Do you still think someone's following us?"

Her companion shrugged elaborately. "Nah." He put his arm around her. "I'll protect you in either case."

She managed a small smile. "I know."

Again, Megan allowed his embrace. The second in two days. She sought to relax the tension in her shoulders. In the weeks they'd been traveling, Jack had been nothing but respectful. She'd appreciated the fact that he'd held himself back from getting too physical, doing nothing more than occasionally holding her hand or putting a casual arm about her.

Truthfully, she'd been comforted in his arms when she'd found herself unexpectedly crying. He'd merely held her until she'd calmed. Never had he asked the reason for her tears. But she knew that he'd guessed she mourned for more than her horse. Though the horror of the shootout had faded, she still grieved.

Jack's arm tightened. "You still think about him?"

Megan took a quick breath. Could he read her mind? Did he know she dwelled on Moon Dancing?

"Of course I miss my horse." She pressed her lips together, fingering the beaded bracelet that she constantly wore.

Jack looked ready to say something more, but clamped his mouth shut. Whatever he suspected, she would not confirm. Moon Dancing's memory was sacred. Hers alone.

She met his gaze. "I'm ready to go forward in life. And put everything behind me."

His expression relaxed while a small grin tugged at one corner of his mouth. "You saying you want to forget my dramatic rescue?"

Megan touched the scar at her temple, a reminder of how close death had come. "No, I won't ever forget that."

"Good. It'd be real tacky of me to remind you."

This time she smiled.

"Let's pack. We'll head out tomorrow."

CHAPTER 46

When they reached the ranch the next evening, her uncle and Mrs. Danvers greeted them with humbling cheer. Megan's throat grew tight.

"It's good to be home." She gripped her uncle's hand, holding it longer than necessary.

"Good to have you back, Meggie." Daniel studied her face.

"Hungry? We waited dinner for you." The housekeeper indicated the brightly lit hallway to the kitchen.

"Sounds great to me." The foreman tossed his hat onto a chair and headed toward the kitchen.

They settled at the table where place settings awaited. Jack held Megan's chair, his attentiveness making her cheeks grow warm as her uncle's eyes narrowed.

"I hope he treated you right," Daniel said.

"I was the perfect gentleman." He reached for his napkin. "Ask Megan."

She ducked her head as she remembered the kiss he'd try to steal at her hotel door the night before. Not ready for that, Megan had turned her head aside. He'd frowned, but hadn't tried anything else.

"Daniel, tell them the good news." Mrs. Danvers placed a bowl of rice on the table.

"Celia and I are getting married in one week."

"Not that." The housekeeper blushed as she smoothed her apron.

It's about time. "How wonderful!" Megan smiled at them both. "I always knew you two belonged together."

"Celia thought so too, only my mule-headed stubbornness kept me from agreeing."

"For years," Mrs. Danvers added.

"Congrats, boss." Then Jack glanced at Megan and smiled. "Someday we hope to have good news as well."

She caught her breath at his bold announcement.

Daniel slapped his shoulder. "That couldn't please me more."

"How soon?" Mrs. Danvers smiled softly at Megan.

"We–we haven't yet–I hadn't..." She stammered to a halt.

Jack had the grace to look sheepish. "Sorry, I kind of jumped the gun. Megan hasn't said yes." He paused. "Yet."

She stared down at the clenched napkin in her lap. *How could he...?*

Daniel cleared his throat. "Ah, I understand. Well, give it time."

Fixing her gaze on her uncle, Megan determined to steer the conversation elsewhere. She'd deal with Jack later. "What's the other news you mentioned?"

"Kit Gerard's gang has been arrested. All but the ringleader. The sheriff traced activity as far as Wendover, but unfortunately lost the trail after that."

"You need not worry." Mrs. Danvers sat beside her. "Four thousand dollars have been recovered from Mr.

Gerard's bank account. Not much. But the group has been routed. They will not come back."

"I hope not." Megan shuddered.

"You've got me to protect you now." Jack put his arm around her. "I'll take care of you."

She tried not to stiffen, still miffed about his premature "announcement." Perhaps sensing her mood, his hand dropped away.

"Have no fear, Meggie." Daniel nodded. "Jack'll watch out for you. With him by your side, you have nothing to worry about."

By my side? She bit her lip, resisting the urge to correct the misconception that any day they would announce their engagement.

Jack leaned forward. "So, nothing new on the gang leaders?"

Megan perked up. "Leaders? More than one?"

"Nothing that I've heard." Daniel didn't look up as he busily sawed at his roast beef.

She stared at Jack. Perhaps his friendship with Jed Harper gave him inside information.

"A slip of the tongue." He shrugged. "Pass the salt, Celia?"

Jack dove into his meal, but she got the feeling that he was holding something back. To protect her? Since her arrival back home, the unsettled feeling in the pit of her stomach seemed to grow. And it had to do with more than the empty corral and stables. Shadow was missing. A huge hole gaped in the middle of her life.

But now, knowing the ringleader, or rather leaders, hadn't been apprehended? She wasn't sure she'd sleep well. Malevolence still lurked somewhere nearby. Megan could feel it.

Tired from the long day, she headed down the hall. She hoped she had endured the last giggly bridal shower she'd have to go to. Who knew that mature women could act so silly? Mrs. Danvers had tolerated the ribbing with her unflappable good nature, but Megan grew annoyed at the adolescent humor. Not all of it had been aimed at the housekeeper. She, too, had been the brunt of veiled insinuations. About her and Jack?

Had he leaked the gossip? She was tempted to tell him to back off...or else.

In two days, her uncle's wedding would be over. Then life could get back to normal.

Whatever normal is.

As she climbed the stairs, she leafed through the mail Mrs. Danvers had given her, pausing over an envelope with no return address. Megan didn't recognize the handwriting. The stationary was plain, the scrawl definitely masculine. She'd just torn the flap and taken the letter out when she heard her uncle.

"Meggie, that you? Would you stop in here a moment?"

"Coming." She headed down the hall, mail still clutched in her hand.

Daniel smiled. "I wanted to say good night before you retired."

"I'm going to sleep very well tonight."

"You partied to death?"

"Almost. I gotta warn you, you'll need an extra shed to hold all the wedding gifts."

"I'm sure Celia will manage." He chuckled. "But all this gift-giving has put me in the same mood. Do you mind getting one?"

Megan frowned. "The groom isn't supposed to give gifts."

Daniel waved a negligent hand. "Look at it as a pre-wedding gift." He held out an envelope.

Pre-wedding? She didn't dare ask if he meant his own marriage or was hinting at her future one.

Megan cheeks grew hot as she opened the envelope. The document announced she was the proud owner of Daniel's newest filly. "Oh. You didn't have to do this." Eyes stinging, she hugged her uncle with one arm.

"I know she'll never replace the horse you lost...but maybe you'll grieve less." His voice grew husky.

"Thank you." She held on a moment longer.

"That's all I wanted. You look beat."

"I feel it too. Good night." She kissed his cheek, and then straightened.

The wrinkled cover of a book on his nightstand caught her eye. Her heart pounded as she stared.

"What's wrong? Megan?" Her uncle touched her hand.

"Where did...?" She swallowed and pointed. "Where did you get that?"

"What?" Daniel turned in his chair. "The book?"

She nodded.

"Found it recently at an antique store. While you were away. Why?" When she didn't answer, he wheeled himself so that he could peer into her face. "What's the matter? You've gone white."

"I–I've seen it before."

"You can see it again if you like." He retrieved the book.

Megan felt as though her heart stopped as she smoothed her hand over the cover. This really was Moon Dancing's journal, the one that had disappeared from her room. It was a miracle that his diary had come back into her life. Except for his beaded bracelet, she had nothing else of his. Everything else was missing. Were they all a figment of her imagination?

But the book. She had it again.

"Sure you're okay?" Her uncle gently touched her arm.

"Yes." Megan clutched the journal to her chest. The mail that had been under her arm fluttered to the floor.

Daniel grabbed his tongs to retrieve the letters.

"Let me." She hurried to pick them up. After she straightened, she struggled to find the right words. "How far...how much have you read?" She had trouble speaking.

"Just got started. The writing in the first half is intriguing. I thought about consulting an expert."

She couldn't take a normal breath. "Would you mind if I borrowed it? To read while I'm in bed?"

"I thought you were tired."

"This will help me sleep." She smiled tremulously, afraid he would say no.

"Take it." A frown still wrinkled his brow.

"Thanks. Good night." She took her mail and left.

When she reached her room, she locked the door and then tossed her mail onto the bed. Then she sat, holding the book and running her fingers over the cover. She closed her eyes, dreaming of him.

Kicking off her shoes, she prepared to lean back and read the familiar and beloved words. But the letter that she'd opened and not yet read, sat on the top of the mail. The lined paper, torn from a notebook, lay open, the words visible.

Megan picked it up and read the unsigned message. Then reread it.

"Get away from Jack Crawford. Your life is in danger."

CHAPTER 47

Megan didn't sleep well that night. Not only did the ominous letter make her toss and turn, but nightmares awakened her several times. She kept reliving the death of Moon Dancing. His blood not only soaked her hands, but also drenched her shirt and jeans. She awoke, sobbing.

What was going on? She'd thought she'd come a long way in recovering from the trauma. During her travels, she'd not once had a nightmare. Why should they plague her now?

She got up and reexamined the warning letter. The handwriting was scrabbled, as though the person was in a hurry. Why? Because of guilt? Fear? Or was this a prank?

The envelope and paper were plain, and a little

smudged. The postmark indicated that the letter had been mailed locally. Still, she had no idea who might send her a warning. What did they know about Jack that she didn't?

Then there was Moon Dancing's book, not intact as she'd first thought. The last recorded pages, the ones with her name on them, had been torn out. Someone wanted the references to her obliterated.

Whatever the reason, the vandalism made her unease grow.

"I'll be there, bright and early tomorrow," Sam reassured Megan on the phone later that morning. "We'll make Celia the most beautiful bride in all of Wyoming."

"Thanks, Sam."

The conversation was winding down and her friend was about to hang up.

"One more thing," Megan said.

"What did you forget?"

"Nothing. I was just wondering..." She paused, trying to figure out a way to word her request without alarming her friend. "I never asked you what you saw the day of the shooting. Would you mind if we talked about it now?"

"We've been discussing a wedding and you want to talk about death?"

"I'm sorry. I need to close those chapters in my life. But I can't as long as I have unanswered questions."

"All right." Her friend took an audible breath, pausing as though gathering her thoughts. "If you remember, we'd agreed to meet halfway between the ranch and town that day. At seven. I got to the halfway point earlier than expected. Rather than stand around, I rode on, even though I told myself I didn't know which direction you'd be coming from."

"Go on," Megan encouraged when she stopped.

"I heard a rifle shot from somewhere in the foothills. I couldn't tell exactly where it came from, but

I saw Jack riding down the road toward me, hell-bent-for-leather. Whatever the reason, I was going to find out too.

"I must've been no more'n ten minutes behind him. He was heading for Gypsy Gulch. I heard other shots, which scared me to no end. By this time, I figured they had something to do with you. And you were in danger."

"You were right."

"Boy was I ever. I had my cell phone. And I called the sheriff. Apparently, Jed Harper had been suspicious of Kit Gerard and had been following him, so he was already on the scene. There was a shootout between Gerard and Harper. In the middle of the deal, Jack showed up and protected you."

"Did you see any of this?"

"No. My horse stepped into a hole. 'Bout broke both our necks. By the time I got there, the shooting was done."

Megan absorbed the information. "How did Jack know where to find me?"

"The sheriff asked the same thing. Apparently, Jack'd been suspicious of Kit Gerard too. He and Jed had been working on the case together. Everyone is still patting Jed on the back for his bravery. Kind of wiped out the bad reputation from the past."

"Which is what, exactly?"

"He had some trouble with the law down in Cheyenne. He and two buddies."

Two? Megan chewed her lip. Hadn't Jack said that only Jed had been involved in a crime? Assuming this was the same incident he'd been talking about.

"Did I answer all your questions, Megan?"

"I think so. If I remember something else, can I call you?"

"I got my cell if I'm not in my office."

After Megan hung up, she sat thinking. What nagged at her? Perhaps it had something to do with the story Jack had told about Jed Harper. He'd claimed his friend had implicated him in a crime in which he wasn't involved.

One way to find out.

She waited until her uncle and Mrs. Danvers left to do some last minute errands. Since Megan had volunteered to serve the men lunch, the couple said they wouldn't be back until late afternoon. Then she went into the library and did some research. Although she couldn't find much online, she did locate the name of the detective who'd handled the investigation. She jotted down his name and number.

The house was quiet, but to make sure she remained undisturbed, she checked several windows. Out Daniel's study, she saw Jack standing by the pasture, talking to Blade. Their heads were together as they discussed something that made Blade throw back his head and laugh.

Huh. They are about the same height and built. And they shared the same broadness of shoulders. She'd never noticed that before.

Feeling the pressure of time, Megan dialed the number.

Forty minutes later, she reread the information she'd recorded on a piece of paper.

Jackson Crawford, Edward Neals–Blade?–and Jedediah Harper had been arrested for armed robbery of a convenience store. The two were seventeen and Jed eighteen years of age. A couple people had been shot, but had recovered. All three teens had gotten off on technicalities. None had served jail time.

Jack lied to me. He'd said that only Harper had been involved. That he'd implicated Jack in the crime.

Megan stared at her notes, seeing nothing, wondering why he would hide the truth. Of course at the time, they had only been casually discussing the incident. But still...

Unable to dismiss her unease any longer, she rose and paced. He had lied to her. The event had happened a long time ago. Why gloss over something this important? Especially if he wanted to pursue a relationship with her? She couldn't help but wonder what else he might have lied about. What else he might be hiding.

Two people had been shot. Had he pulled the trigger? Her discomfort grew the longer she considered the implications.

When the men came in for lunch, she waited until they were nearly through before telling Jack she needed to talk to him afterwards. Eyes alight, he nodded.

"What's up?" His face was wreathed in smiles as he met her in Daniel's office.

Megan stepped behind her uncle's desk, keeping her distance.

"This looks serious." The laughter lines eased from his cheeks.

"I'm, well..." She pressed her fingers to the desk's surface. *Get it said!* "I want you to stop spreading rumors about us getting married. I know you have, so don't deny it."

"What?" The word snapped out. His smile instantly disappeared.

"You heard me."

His head tilted. "I thought we had an understanding."

"Then obviously what we understand are two different things."

"You've practically said yes. And you've been leading me on. For months."

"Leading...? No, I'm afraid that's your imagination. I've treated you as a friend. You've pushed further."

"Friend?" His fingers twitched at his side. He calmed himself with an effort. "The way you've hugged me recently was more'n a little friendly."

Her face grew hot. No use defending herself. He'd only twist her words. "That won't happen again." While they'd traveled, she'd let down her guard. Jack had somehow sensed that. And had taken advantage.

His eyes narrowed. "What do you mean?"

Megan bit her lip, wishing now she'd waited until her uncle could be present. Though the conversation would've been uncomfortable, having him there would have been wiser. She would squelch all rumors. Once and for all.

"I asked you a question." Jack stepped closer.

"I don't want you trying to kiss me again. Or hold my hand. Or even touch me until we've talked out a few things first."

"Like what?"

She took a deep breath. This had to be said. She might as well stop dodging the issue. "I called Cheyenne this morning. I found out that you, Jed and Blade were all involved in that armed robbery. You should have gone to jail, but didn't."

"You've been getting nosy."

"You told me only Jed was involved. Why'd you lie?"

His jaw jutted.

She took a deep breath. "This is precisely why I can't be involved with you. Marriage must be based on trust. And honesty. I value those."

Still Jack said nothing.

Why not? Why no defense? Or explanation? Something!

Megan raised her chin. Obviously the conversation was over. And so was any future relationship with him.

She moved from behind the desk and walked toward the door. He hadn't moved. But when she stepped beside him, he finally spoke. "I'm not gonna let you screw this up."

"What?"

He turned, eyes cold. "I've worked a long time to put this deal together. I'm not gonna let you go off and do something stupid."

"Deal? This isn't a business takeover."

"Call it what you want. But we are getting married."

She shook her head at his persistent illogic. "Jack. Get it through your head. I'm not in love with you. I never will be."

"Love? So you're in love with someone else. Who is

it?”

She bit her lip, regretting she’d said anything.

“I asked you who it is.” He spoke through clenched teeth.

“That is none of your business.”

When she stepped toward the door, he grabbed her arm.

“Let go of me.”

“Not until you give me a name.”

She tried to shake off his hold, but his fingers tightened. “You’re hurting me.”

“Can’t be Gossner. I know it’s not Blade, though I sometimes wondered. Then it has to be one of the hired hands. Which one? Hayford? Charlie? Or maybe the half-breed?”

Megan twisted in his grip, eyes burning. “Let me go.”

“Not until you give me a name.”

“So you can do what?”

Jack’s mouth settled in hard lines. “Teach him he shouldn’t touch what doesn’t belong to him.”

“I am *not* your property.” She wrenched out of his hold and backed away. Fear shuddered through her. *What has gotten into him?* Megan stared at the foreman, feeling like she was seeing the real man for the first time.

His face tightened, eyes dark. Brooding.

“Just because you saved my life doesn’t mean you own me,” she said in a low voice. “Please leave.”

Jack glared at her as though he’d not heard her.

The study door suddenly slid open. Megan started. Blade came in and methodically shut it behind him.

The cold look on his face made her gulp.

CHAPTER 48

He then smiled, but the gesture was far from his usual charming expression. Blade looked at his friend. “Well...I’d say you handled that about as good as a dog handles a skunk.”

“Shut up.” Jack clenched his hands.

“She’s gotten under your skin, my man.” He leaned against the door. “I’d be flattered, Megan, if I were you. Jack actually loves you. Even though you went sorta crazy there for a bit.”

She backed away another step. Why shouldn’t the man who wanted to marry her love her? Blade was treating this like it was unusual.

“She still doesn’t get it, Jack.”

“She will. Eventually.” Tone flat, he stared at her.

Blade plopped into a chair and leaned his foot

against the desk, rocking back. “You have no choice, Megan. You gotta marry Jack. This deal’s too big.”

She tried to swallow the dryness in her throat. “What...what deal?”

“The deal we have with our San Francisco partners. We think the hills around here are packed with silver. Y’know, Silver Springs? Not a whole lot, but enough to keep us happy for a while. Probably gold too. We’ve not been able to survey a large area. Makes people suspicious. But...that’ll change soon.”

Realization hit her. “You dug the mines.”

“Not personally. Jack and I were too busy. He was trying to hook up with you while I...” He shrugged and smiled. “I was busy with my little French coquette.”

Simone. He was Simone’s lover. And killer.

“You...and Simone?”

“I couldn’t have her hurting you. Well, not after I found out about your vested interest in the ranch.” Blade rocked back. “You’re right, Jacko. Megan’s smart.”

He looked at her, eyes narrowing, then back at his friend. “Think it’s wise to blab so much?”

“I’m only letting her know we’re serious about this marriage thing.”

She clenched her hands. “If you think I’ll marry Jack now–”

“I have no doubt.” Blade took out his Bowie knife and sharpening stone and began to run the edge over it.

Megan’s heart banged against her chest. “Killing me won’t accomplish–”

“Kill you? Wouldn’t dream of it.” He smiled pleasantly. “If we’d wanted that, you’d have died months ago. No, no. Besides, your death would upset my friend. And he not only likes the gleam of silver, but his hands are itching to get a hold of your trust fund. And, well, you too.”

She ran her tongue over parched lips. How much did they know about her money? About the ranch?

“You get to stay alive,” Blade went on in a smooth voice. “That’s why Kit and Simone are no longer part of the group. Neither of them wanted to follow directions. Pranks on your horse were one thing, but when Simone started messing with your tack..." He shrugged, and then fixed his gaze on her. "You, Megan, are valuable. However...not everyone around you is."

The room shrank, squeezing down on her.

"That bathtub upstairs is right slippery," he went on calmly. "Randy's told me how Daniel's nearly fallen a couple times. Anything can happen." Blade eyed her. "Still not convinced? Give me a minute." He pulled out his cell phone and pushed a number. After a moment, he spoke into the phone. "Yeah it's me. You see them? Just a sec. I'm putting you on speaker. Say that again." He held up the phone.

A voice spoke. "I said I got a fix on O'Connor and Danvers in town. Just say the word and I'll take 'em out."

Horrified, Megan closed her eyes. *They'll kill them if I don't cooperate.* And Sam too? When would it stop?

"Hang tight." Blade snapped the cell shut. "That show you we're serious?"

I'll do anything they want.

"Looks like she's ready to listen, Jack." He spoke cheerfully. "What do you think?"

The foreman glared at his friend.

"We've got it all arranged. Clear riding ahead," Blade continued. "Tomorrow, you stand at the altar and–"

"Tomorrow?"

"Yeah. We thought a double wedding would be sweet. While you were in Cheyenne, Jack got the marriage license and everything. Even a pretty dress."

She recoiled from them. "Impossible. I didn't sign any–"

"Wasn't hard to hire someone who kind of looked like you. O'course, Jack's sweet-talking helped. And was easy to borrow your driver's license. Since we're part of Daniel's wedding, we already have tuxedoes. Everything's all set."

She shot Jack a look, now recalling the mysterious

errand he'd run in Cheyenne without her.

Blade went on. "Make sure you say, 'I do' with a smile because I get to be the best man. That's me. Always hanging around, hearing stuff, noticing things when people think they're being so sly. Good ol' Blade, friendly, harmless. Folks tell me all sorts of stuff all the time. Simone was a gold mine–pun intended. And there's Abe telling me about some of his clothes disappearing one night. And thinking he saw this Indian slipping through the window. You didn't know about that, Jack, did you?" Blade grinned at Megan.

"Was it Trapper?" He clenched his hands.

"Now, don't get all worked up. Was this other fellow. Some sort of chieftain, or so he called himself. Wrote some pretty things about Megan. I tossed the pages, Jack. Knowing how much they'd bother you. He really liked her hair. And other things, of course, but I–"

"Shut up." Jack kicked the chair, making it thump as it righted itself.

A scowl on his face, Blade rose, his huge knife still in hand. "You really need to watch your temper, my friend. It'll get you into trouble someday." The two men squared off.

Would they fight each other? From the anger etching their faces, Megan hoped so.

Blade was the first to speak, his gaze never leaving his friend as he slowly sheathed his knife. "Explain to your bride that I'll be up close and personal tomorrow. And to make sure everything goes off without a hitch, my sniper buddy will be in the church loft."

Jack shot her a glance. "There won't be any problems."

"Better not be. You're in this up to your neck, my friend. Like me." He turned, nodding in Megan's direction. "You behave yourself."

Blade strode out of the room.

For many moments, she stared at Jack, mouth dry.

Please, let this be a nightmare. Please let me wake up.

No matter how many times she closed and opened her eyes, he still stood before her, a brooding expression on his face.

He finally spoke. "I never intended for you to know."

She had no reply.

"I still love you."

Megan turned away.

"Blade means what he says. Your uncle would be dead before you could say a word. You heard the guy he has following them. One phone call and..."

She hugged herself, rubbing her arms where Jack's fingers had bruised.

"You shouldn't have pushed me," he said in a hard tone. "If you'da kept your mouth shut, everything would've worked out."

"I would have found out eventually. You can't hide your real self forever."

"I haven't. You've always seen me for who I am. In that way, I've been honest."

She made a sound of disgust. "Honest? You've stolen from my uncle, though he trusts you like a son. It's not just the silver, is it Jack? Did you have anything to do with those missing mares? You wanted my uncle to fail...so you could do what? Miraculously save the ranch? Like you did me? Only now I'm betting that wasn't as daring as I've been told. You suddenly showing up at the right place at the right time."

He mouth tightened. "I did save your life. Kit was going to put a bullet through your head."

"So you murdered him."

"No."

"But it was in cold blood, wasn't it? To make the story work and get everyone off your back. The Kit Gerard gang, arrested or dead. No one looks anymore for the other culprits. And when mining operations start on the Double O, no one questions it."

A ghost of a smile touched Jack's lips. "You're one smart girl, Megan. I've always loved that about you. But don't let intelligence get in the way of common sense. Tomorrow, we're getting married. You're not going to say a word to anyone. Ever."

CHAPTER 49

Keep smiling. Look into his face. Act happy.

Megan reminded herself of countless other things she must do to pull off the charade. The music was over. She and Jack were positioned at the altar next to Daniel and Mrs. Danvers. Nearby stood Blade. All the men were resplendent in black tuxedos, cut western style. Her gown was frothy white lace, the skirt full. She wore a white hat, bedecked with tiny silk roses thanks to the resourcefulness of Sam and the housekeeper.

All a sham. All meaningless. All designed to trap her in a marriage that would benefit thieves and murderers.

Blade's frown warned her to put her fake happy face back on. She hiked up her smile. From the corner of her eye, she could see her uncle's caregiver. In the front pew, Randy watched them all with narrowed eyes.

"Dearly beloved." Speaking in fatherly tones, the preacher glanced at a slim red book. He was the same man who'd conducted Simone's funeral.

How appropriate.

"We are gathered here today to celebrate the joining of these men and women..."

I can't do this.

"...in holy matrimony..."

I must. Or people will die.

"...insofar as they have agreed..."

Sam's dress rustled as she dabbed her eyes.

I feel faint.

The preacher went on while Megan fought to keep her frozen smile in place. How had she managed to fool everyone last night? During the teary-eyed embrace of Mrs. Danvers when Jack had announced they'd decided to get married. And did Daniel mind a double wedding? She'd watched the shoulder-slapping and boisterous congratulations of the men. Her uncle had cheerfully agreed.

Jack had chosen the best time to make the announcement, during dinner when all the men were present. To keep everyone distracted, Blade had rolled out a keg. So much noise and revelry had consumed the night that no one had noticed her reticence. Despite the half-glass of beer Jack had pressed into her hands and insisted that she drink.

"Would you please face each other?"

Megan abruptly came back to the ceremony as the foreman quietly cleared his throat.

She turned. Doing double duty as matron of honor, Sam took the bouquets of both brides.

"Take each other's hands please."

Jack grabbed her fingers, his hot ones proving how cold hers were.

Don't think about him. Don't think...

As she raised her eyes, she could see her uncle beaming into his bride's face. Jack squeezed her hands, bringing her attention back to him.

The preacher nodded, signaling the next aspect of the wedding. Megan moved to the decorated table behind him. Three candles waited, two lit, the squat middle one untouched. She pulled the left taper out of the socket, then bent to light the middle one the same time Jack did. Her hand shook so much she could hardly light hers. He steadied her wrist.

To her right, her uncle and Mrs. Danvers were lighting their own candle.

A woman began to sing, her cultivated voice filling the space as a recorded accompaniment came over the speakers. Megan took her place in front of the preacher again, fighting to fix a smile into place. Jack took her hands. Beyond him, she could see one of the chapel's beautiful stained glass windows. Stables and a baby in a manger.

She squeezed her eyes shut.

If you can hear me, God, now would be a good time to do something. Moon Dancing said You are a God who gives...please provide a way for me out of this hell.

The song ended, several people sighing in pleasure. Sam sniffed in happiness.

The minister again consulted his book. "After one little technicality will come the best part." His grin widened. "Then we'll be done."

He glanced up as the church door opened and closed. Then he again studied the pages.

"Daniel and Celia have consented to join their lives, after having lived many years apart. However, it must be asked that if there is any reason why these two should not marry, let them speak."

No one objected.

The preacher now turned her direction.

"Jack and Megan have consented to join their lives, after having lived many years apart."

She stared stonily into Jack's face. Her heart hammered against her throat.

"However, it must be asked that if there is any reason why these two should not marry, let them speak." He paused for only a second before adding,

"And now, they will all say their vows which–"

"There is a problem," said a loud voice from the back of the church.

Jack's face snapped in that direction, his grip crushing her fingers.

Megan stared. The sheriff moved forward, his height and bulk filling the aisle. The audience turned to gaze at him.

He planted himself squarely in the middle of the church. "There's a problem with this wedding taking place."

Feeling dizzy, she closed her eyes. Was she was hallucinating? What problem could there be? Had the sheriff found out about his crooked deputy? Jed Harper must have spilled something about Jack, then.

She glanced to the loft in the back of the church. Where was the man Blade said would be up there? A small movement in the shadows behind the pews proved he lurked, ready to fulfill Blade's threat. As long as he endangered her uncle and Mrs. Danvers, she would refuse to say anything.

"Chad," the minister said in surprise. "What's going on?"

"I'm afraid Megan Gillespie cannot marry this man."

"Why not?"

Everyone seemed to hold their breath, including Megan.

"She already has a husband."

The chapel grew so quiet that she could hear a bird chirp outside. A child wailed, his cry cut off by a sharp hush from his mother.

"That's impossible." Jack turned his full fury on the sheriff.

The minister's face broke out with perspiration. "What did you say?"

"She already has a husband." A man moved from behind the sheriff. "Me."

I know that voice!

Her panting breath filled her hearing as her gaze sought him…he who was so familiar, so beloved.

Dressed in jeans and a fringe shirt, he stepped forward. His long, black hair was bound, dark eyes unescapable.

"Moon Danc–" Megan's knees buckled. The pain of Jack's relentless grip kept her standing.

"I don't know who you are, but you have no right to make that claim." The foreman grabbed her arm and jerked her upright.

Her uncle wheeled forward, then swiveled his chair so that he could look at both Megan and Moon Dancing.

"She's never been married," Daniel said. "If this is some horrible prank, then–"

"I am her husband." His gaze fixed on Megan. "Ask her."

All eyes turned to her. She opened her mouth, but no words came out. She stared at her uncle who sat between them.

If I say anything, he'll die. And Mrs. Danvers and...

"Is this true? Megan!" Daniel slapped the arm of his wheelchair. "Is what this man says true?"

Jack pinched her arm cruelly.

She imagined blood all over her uncle. And Mrs. Danvers. Blood all over Moon Dancing.

No. Not again. She couldn't live through that. Not if she could prevent their deaths.

"I–I–c-can't..." She stopped. "You don't unders–"

"Deny it." Jack's whisper rasped in her ear. "Deny it, or else."

Megan cried out as he squeezed her bruised arm.

"Do it!"

Moon Dancing bolted forward, so swiftly that she didn't see him move. One minute he stood beside the sheriff, the next he was halfway up the steps.

Jack shoved her aside as he sprang. A woman shrieked. Megan tripped over her dress and fell against Sam. A pedestal and basket of flowers toppled onto Mrs. Danvers, knocking her down. The minister leaped out of the way, his book flipping into the air.

Blade reached into his pocket. Screaming, Megan fought to scramble to her feet. The sheriff unholstered his gun as Blade pulled one out of his jacket. She leaped toward Daniel who leaned out of his chair, reaching for the still prostrate Mrs. Danvers. Throwing herself on her uncle, Megan knocked him to the floor. A loud crack resounded in the chapel. Then another. Several people shrieked. She heard rushing footsteps. Children crying. Underneath her, Daniel's eyes were closed.

"No," she cried. "No!"

"Megan." Mrs. Danvers was on her hands and knees, pulling his arm. "Help me."

Sam crawled next to them. Together, they tugged Daniel under a pew, until they were shielded from the pandemonium around them. When Megan peered up, the vet yanked her down. She caught a glimpse of Moon Dancing and Jack fighting. The sheriff struggled with Blade, another man running to help. Another shot boomed, shattering the wood of a pew.

Mrs. Danvers shrieked. Her cry matched Megan's and Sam's.

The man in the loft. He's trying to kill us all.

Nothing more sounded for a few moments, then another shot reverberated. This time, plaster fell in a shower on their heads. All around them people cowered under pews. Children cried and a baby screamed while a woman sobbed. A man suddenly yelled, a sickening thud abruptly cutting off the sound.

Silence reigned, except for the muffled whimpering of the people still in the chapel.

"It's all right folks," boomed the voice of the sheriff. "Everything's under control."

"Megan." An insistent voice spoke nearby.

She cautiously raised her head.

"Do not be afraid." Moon Dancing held out his hand to her.

She touched his fingers, still unable to believe he was really there. Really alive. He pulled her up and the next moment, she was in his arms. He hugged her tightly.

"I thought you'd died." She buried her face against his neck.

"I did. But that's why I live now. Because I gave my life for you."

The fourth virtue. Bravery. She half-sighed, half-sobbed. "The curse is over? Really and truly?"

"Forever." He cradled her face between his hands, knuckles raw, cheek bruised.

She carefully touched a swelling lump above one eye. Then Megan looked behind him. Blade was unconscious, an ugly knot on his forehead. Jack was handcuffed, face down on the floor. Randy was nowhere to be seen.

"You all right?" Ben Gossner came rushing up the aisle, holding a rifle. Whose side was he on? She shrank away while Moon Dancing slid his arm around her protectively.

"Oh, this isn't mine. Belongs to that guy over there." Ben indicated the man who lay sprawled on the floor below the loft. "Trapper got him."

"Thank..." She gulped the dryness in her mouth and tried again. "Thank you."

"Sure glad you didn't marry that jerk." Ben's huge grin made his split lip bleed. "In spite of my letter."

"You sent that warning?"

He shrugged. "Somebody had to tell you about him."

"Get off me. I'm all right." Daniel pulled himself out from under the pew, and then sat up. "Would somebody tell me what's going on?"

The sheriff approached their group. "This man, Moon Dancing, has been working with me for the past month to solve the remainder of the mysteries around your ranch. Because of his and Trapper's invaluable assistance, we have enough evidence to prove that Blade Neals and Jack Crawford are the two ring leaders in the illegal mine operation on the Double O."

She stared at Moon Dancing, her heart almost too full.

"With his help, Daniel, we've located other mines. Recently worked."

"What about Jed Harper?" Megan asked. "And my uncle's caregiver?"

The sheriff's eyebrows went up. "You know about them?"

"Only what they told me."

"What else can you tell me?"

"Blade threatened to kill Uncle Daniel and Mrs. Danvers if I said anything." She shuddered.

Moon Dancing's grip tightened around her waist.

"That all sounds very interesting." The annoyance in Daniel's voice rippled through the room. "But I don't care about it at the moment. I want to know who this man is." He pointed at Moon Dancing.

Megan smiled at her uncle, a strained, still tremulous gesture. "He's...my fiancé."

"Husband, by Sioux laws," Moon Dancing corrected. "But the white man's laws, sort of."

"What do you mean, sort of?" Daniel growled. "Is she your wife or not?"

He took her hands. "If she will have me, I will be her husband. Forever."

"I will." Her words barely came out above a whisper. "I made a promise and I mean to keep it."

"But you will need a license." Mrs. Danvers spoke in her usual, practical way. "And that takes time. But I do not think Daniel and I..." She looked at her bridegroom.

"That's right." Reality crashed down on Megan. "We can't get a license without a birth certificate. And we can't get that because..." She left the obvious reason unspoken.

"Not a problem." The sheriff stepped closer. "Let me take care of that. Been working on a solution already."

"Seems to me we have a wedding to finish." Sam now spoke. "You all got me into this fancy dress and I'm not going to waste the effort. Besides, I can tell Celia and Daniel don't want to wait."

The housekeeper's blush made her look ten years younger. As she gazed at Daniel, he reached for her hand.

"I'll go round up the folks," Ben volunteered in a happy voice.

The sheriff nodded. "Let me clear out the trash,

then we can get started." He shouted directions, quickly restoring order to the chapel. People began to move cautiously into the pews. The sheriff's men cleared the building of Jack and the others.

Moon Dancing leaned closer. "I have confidence in this lawman. It will not be too many days until we are wed."

Words failed Megan, especially as he again slipped his arm about her and held her close. She still had trouble believing he was really there. That he had saved her from Jack and Blade.

"I am sorry I could not let you know I was alive. We could not risk Crawford finding out." Moon Dancing kept his voice low. "We had to let him believe he was safe. That way, he walked into our trap. But I was never far from you. Either I, or Trapper, were always close."

"Always?" Understanding dawned. "Was it you that followed us as we traveled?"

He smiled. "Yes. But the one you call Blade also had someone watching. We had to be careful."

"Megan." Sam beckoned her. "You're the bridesmaid. And your fiancé is the best man. Get over here, you two."

She looked around at the still-chaotic chapel. Not only was Moon Dancing a sight with his bruised cheek, but she had to be as well. Her dress was torn, arm throbbing from where Jack had squeezed so hard. Her hair felt askew, hat missing.

The others there didn't look much better. She saw various stages of injuries, proof that there'd been a brawl. Megan started to giggle.

Reseated in his wheelchair, her uncle growled. "What's so funny?"

"This whole scene. No doubt, this is a real western wedding."

"Then let's get this show on the road." Daniel shooed the minister toward the front, following behind. "Start over. From the beginning."

They took their positions, Megan unable to look at anyone but the man she loved. Across the space, Moon

Dancing had eyes for no one but for her.

The ceremony flew by.

"I now pronounce you, man and wife." The minister pulled out a handkerchief to mop his brow.

Light burst into the chapel through the stained glass windows. Megan sucked in a long slow breath at the glorious sight. Thankfulness filled her to bursting.

"You may now kiss your bride."

As her uncle reached for his wife, Megan gasped when Moon Dancing strode across the space and gathered her into his arms. He kissed her long and hard.

Ben whooped.

She chuckled, wanting to tell Moon Dancing that the minister didn't mean him. But that no longer mattered. Especially when he kissed her again.

"Someday soon," he whispered in her ear, "you will be completely mine."

"I already am." Megan hugged his neck. The glory of it still seemed difficult to grasp.

"And now," Daniel's voice interrupted, "I have a question."

They turned to face him.

Her uncle pointed at Moon Dancing. "I want to know why he looks like the portrait in my house. How is that possible?"

Smiling, she shrugged. Before she could fabricate an answer though, Moon Dancing had one ready. "Megan called to me from her dreams. Because of her, I live."

Daniel frowned.

"It is true." The warrior met his gaze steadily, but his expression eloquently forbade any more questions.

Megan slipped her hand into his. "And because of him, I now am alive too. And home. For good."

EPILOGUE

"I don't know how he does it." Daniel looked up at Megan. "He's tamed them all in a matter of hours. Not even Kit Gerard met with that kind of success."

She smiled as she watched her husband stride confidently in the midst of a dozen horses. "It's a gift."

Her uncle nodded. "I believe it."

Inside the main corral, Moon Dancing approached a horse. Minutes before, the mare had fled from him, but now with his full attention on her, she calmed. Had he said anything? Megan strained to hear. Nothing. Yet, with the horse's ears pricked forward, she seemed to be listening.

In mere moments, he approached the mare and was now nose to nose with her.

"He did it again. Huh." Daniel's brow wrinkled in amazement. Then he tapped the armrest of his wheelchair. "Well, all this work has made me hungry. You coming up to the house for lunch?"

"I'll wait for my husband. Looks like he and Trapper are almost done."

"Okay. I'll tell your Aunt Celia to save you some food."

Megan grinned, still liking the sound of Mrs. Danvers' new name. "That'd be great."

After her uncle departed, she rested her arm on the fence, and then leaned her chin on it. Never did she tire of observing her husband's skill. Though she imagined she knew the reason, she still couldn't help but be enthralled with how he understood horses. And how he seemed to communicate with them on a different level.

He glanced over at her, and then grinned. After the once-skittish horse nuzzled him, he wandered toward Megan. "What are you smiling at?"

She shrugged. "You. I love watching you tame them."

Moon Dancing turned again to the mare, then looked back at her. "She wanted to be. I merely show her how." He stepped closer and touched her hand. "Come away with me."

"Now? Where?"

"You will see." He smiled, clearly taking pleasure in his secret.

In the three months since they'd married, Megan had learned the delight of letting him surprise her. "I should get gloves. And maybe heavier coat if—"

"I will keep you warm."

The look in his eyes already warmed her. He laced his fingers through hers.

Hand in hand, they traversed the perimeter of the corral. Didn't they do this one moonlit night not so long ago? The similarity struck her more forcefully when Moon Dancing whistled and a familiar gelding trotted toward them.

After helping her mount, he swung up behind her. It wasn't long until the gelding moved from a trot to a loping canter. Arms about her, Moon Dancing's body shielded her from the cold breeze at their backs. With the season rushing toward winter, they wouldn't have many more days before snow covered the land.

Recognizing their path, she smiled. Indeed he was taking her to the flat rock where they had once made their vows. The gelding slowed as he climbed the steep path. Finally they arrived.

Moon Dancing helped her dismount, then handed her up to the surface of the rock.

Enjoying the chilling air and the brightly lit view, she inhaled deeply. When she turned, her husband was watching her, an intense look on his face. As soon as she noticed, his expression relaxed.

"What is it?" Megan went to him.

He looked away, then back, taking a moment to answer. "Do you have something of importance to tell me?"

She sucked in a quick breath. How could he have possibly guessed? Because she was still uncertain of her pregnancy, she had not planned to say anything to him yet. Not until she'd gotten confirmation.

His dark gaze bore into her.

She didn't want to give him false news, but couldn't hide what she'd already begun to suspect. "How did you...?" A rush of emotions made her throat tighten.

"I see a change. Here." He rested his hand on her abdomen. "And here." He caressed her cheek. "Megan...do you carry my child?"

Did he want this baby? His stern tone and frowning brow filled her with trepidation.

She couldn't stop her eyes from flooding with tears. "Perhaps. I think so, but I'm not a hundred percent sure."

"I am. And you know as well."

Slowly, she nodded. What would he do now that he knew?

He released a pent-up breath. Then he slowly sank to his knees.

Trembling, she could say nothing. Finally, she managed to whisper, "Don't you want this baby?" She swallowed. "I know it's so soon since..."

Still kneeling, he looked up. "Yes. I want this child.

More than anything."

Tears of relief spilled onto her cheeks. "I'm glad. I was afraid..." She couldn't give voice to her worry.

Moon Dancing's response still puzzled.

She knelt before him. "What is wrong, my love?"

"Nothing." His tightening jaw and averted gaze told her to wait. When he finally raised his eyes, she saw in wonder that his lashes were wet.

Without speaking, she rested her palm on his cheek. Touching his smooth, warm skin allayed all her fears. She spoke softly. "Don't be afraid. Tell me."

"When I first knew..." He paused, staring into the distance. Many moments passed before he continued. "I was thinking of the God who gives. Once, I had everything, but valued nothing. Then I had nothing, and I learned to be grateful for the smallest of things." Moon Dancing again fixed his gaze on her. "And today, I have the most precious gifts a man could desire. A wife whom I love and who loves me." His jaw flexed. "And now... a child."

She smiled through her tears.

He took her hands. "Shouldn't we thank this God who gives so much?"

Megan slowly nodded.

His dark eyes glittered. "Then join me. Let us together praise our great God."

As Moon Dancing raised their hands to the sky, he chanted in Sioux. Megan closed her eyes, the sound reverberating throughout her being. Though she could not understand the words, her spirit soared.

Without a doubt, she knew Moon Dancing spoke the truth. God indeed had given so much for which they should be grateful. To Him be all the glory and honor and praise.

Author's Note

Although the characters in this story are purely fictional, one name is based on a historical figure: Scares At His Shadow, my ancestor. I trust this great warrior would not mind my using his name.

Anna welcomes your letters. You may contact her at www.annazogg.com or write to her at P.O. Box 1642, West Jordan, Utah 84084.

20641432R00189

Made in the USA
Charleston, SC
18 July 2013